Be Your Somebody

Natalie Knolls

Contents

Content Warning

This book may contain content that may be sensitive to some readers. While the characters and story are fictional, the struggles they deal with are very real. As an author and therapist, your mental health is important so please take care of yourself first.

These topics include:

Mention of sexual and physical childhood abuse including child trafficking (no graphic details)

Mention of Child trafficking

Substance abuse

Some gun violence

Mental health

Repressed memories

On page PTSD flashback (no graphic details)

Explicit open-door sex scenes

Some vulgar language

Overdose

Stalking/harassment/blackmail (not by either MC)

If you or someone you know struggles with any of these issues, please reach out for help. You are not alone.

Dedication

This is for those who feel broken beyond repair. You aren't.

Chapter 1

Goodbye is never easy

Avery

Goodbye is never easy

Late Fall 2022

THE BLACK CURSOR ON my computer screen mocks me with its constant blinking. The document is blank, but my mind is not. Goodbye is a short, simple word with the ability to inflict heart-wrenching pain. A two-syllable word that has the power to shatter someone's soul into a million pieces.

That's how I feel right now. Everything was good until it wasn't. Promises broken, trust demolished all within a matter of seconds. Cas said this time would be different. He said he changed—he even had the damn proof to show me. Plus, he was different. He was goofy, kind, and thoughtful. I waited years for him to come back, only to be robbed again by his vices. Everything feels up in the air. Uncertainty about our friendship threatens to hold me captive. But I know better. History repeats itself, but they never said I had to be along for the ride. So I made a choice...I just don't know with one hundred percent certainty that it's the right one. The only way to know is by ripping off the Band-Aid. My heart's contents begin to spill onto the page, the delete button being abused the most. No more dancing around Cas and his struggles with addiction. It's not even a dance I enjoy, despite my knowing it all too well.

Lying on my desk is a white envelope with his name scrawled across it. Tears cloud my vision as I place the printed letter inside, but it isn't until it's sealed that I lose it. My body collapses to the ground and I wonder if this is how it ends for me. Death from a broken heart. My lungs can't seem to get enough air despite how desperately I gulp for oxygen. My heart never reaches its resting place, no matter how much I remind myself this is for the best.

The off-white envelope now weighs heavy with sorrow. Memories of our friendship cover every inch of my childhood bedroom and it's suffocating. They say if you love someone, let them go. If they were truly yours to begin with, they'll come back. The question I ask myself, though, is do I want him back? My heart has already withstood so much when it comes to Cas. I know if we repeat this cycle for a third time, I won't survive. I'm exhausted both physically and emotionally. So for now, it's time to let him go. I truly believe that for Cas to thrive in this lifetime, we need to go our separate ways. I refuse to enable him further. I once believed that if you loved someone fierce enough, loved someone hard enough, it would help them change. Given my history with Cas, that has proven to be false. I can't force someone to change if they don't want to. But what I can do is put myself first. By putting myself first, I'm showing him how he should be treating me. Maybe we can be friends again someday, but for now, I just can't. Something tells me Cas has to hit his rock bottom for the necessary changes to be made permanent.

My phone rings incessantly, but I have zero motivation to answer it. Silence fills the room for about three seconds before the ringing begins again. My intuition has me on my feet and picking up the phone to see

Evelyn, Cas' grandma, calling me. My heart plummets to my feet, instinct telling me my whole world is about to crash.

"Hello?" I answer, right before she utters the seven most gut-wrenching words I've ever heard.

Chapter 2

Cassidy

It was only just a dream

What the hell? Where am I? What happened to me? My eyes widen with panic as I adjust to my surroundings. Wait a second. I look around at the sage-colored walls decorated with random posters of various musicians from Pink to Panic! At The Disco. A dresser-vanity made of oak covered with various beauty items stands before me. On the wall closest to the door is a walk-in closet cut from the same material as the dresser. My eyes fall to the queen-size bed covered in a forest green comforter, buried beneath an alarming amount of throw pillows that complement the wall perfectly. Across the room is a bay window overlooking my grandparents' yard and the lake where the neighborhood kids play. I'm in Avery's childhood bedroom. But how did I get here?

I scrub my hand down my face, but the scene doesn't change. I run my fingers through my hair, racking my brain while questions flood my system like those severe weather alerts. The last thing I remember is feeling cold and alone.

My body shivers and my teeth chatter. Thoughts of crawling under the covers of Avery's bed to defrost the iceberg that has formed around my body has never felt more enticing. Instead, I focus on the sounds around me. The birds chirping. The cars rushing by. The faint sounds of children laughing while they play. It makes me crave the boy I once was. The boy who, with the help of his grandparents, finally escaped from the big bad wolf.

The faint sound of a siren makes my stomach churn and my brows scrunch with confusion at such a visceral response. Where did that come from? It's as if my brain and body are trying to communicate, but are speaking two different languages.

"Cas? Honey, are you hungry?" Avery asks, her voice floating up from downstairs. Hearing her speak sounds like drinking hot cocoa on a cold evening. I grin and rush downstairs like a kid on Christmas morning, eager to tear through their presents.

There she is, my beautiful Avery, with her hair piled atop her head in a messy bun. She wears a lavender pajama set and her feet are bare. She's humming quietly to herself, but just loud enough for me to hear the smooth melody of Can't Help Falling in Love by Elvis Presley. My girl is a talented musician, but I wish she saw herself through my eyes. If she could do that, there would be no room for doubt in her head. She's beautiful, kind, and the most incredible person I know.

Acting on instinct, I walk toward Avery, wrapping her in my arms and reveling in her touch. I bury my face in the crook of her neck, allowing the warmth of her body and sweet scent to ground me. She startles for a second, caught off guard, before melting into me. What's happening right now has to be real. It would be cruel if it weren't.

"I love it when you sing."

Even though I can't see her, I know she's scrunching up her face in disgust. I spin her around so that she's facing me. She lets out a surprised gasp and her eyes widen when she looks at my face.

"Avery. When you sing, your soul transports to another world. When you sing, you and the music become one."

My words come out breathless only because I feel so passionately about this. Tears glisten in her eyes, so I gather her against my chest and allow her to feel. She wraps her arms around me and we hold each other in comfortable silence.

"Thank you," she whispers.

I pull back just enough so that I can see her face. "For what?"

"For saying that. For being here. Most importantly, for being you, Cas." Her words are love arrows to the heart. My lips graze her forehead before I remove myself from her arms as the sudden urge to dance with her takes hold of my mind. I glance around the kitchen, searching for my phone, only to come up empty.

"Are you looking for this?" she asks while holding my phone in her hands. I grab it and, without hesitation, find the song she was humming earlier. I put it on the highest volume before grabbing her hand and pulling her towards me.

She lets out a sultry laugh, throwing her head back, giving me perfect access to her throat. My thoughts turn from innocent to dirty in seconds, but she's facing me again before I can act on them. As we sway to the music, I can't help thinking I could get used to this.

I love having her this close to me, feeling her heartbeat fall into rhythm with mine. At this moment, the outside world ceases to exist. It's just Avery and me in the kitchen, swaying to the soothing sounds of Elvis.

She tilts her head up towards me and opens her mouth, but instead of words coming out, all I hear is a siren. I shake my head and try to focus on what she is trying to say, but the sound of the siren intensifies. Suddenly, everything is fuzzy and the scene before me disintegrates like sugar in hot coffee.

This new scene is hectic and fuck, it's bright. Can someone turn down the goddamn lights?

"He's back!" someone shouts. He's back? Who's back? Who are they talking about? And do they have to talk so loud? My head feels like it's about to split in half.

I try to move, but I'm trapped. The same person who shouted moments ago is pushing my head down and telling me to relax. They may tell me to relax, but it makes me panic even more. What the fuck is happening?

"Stop moving or you'll make it worse. Just try to rest. We'll be at the hospital soon," another person says.

Wait—hospital? What do they mean by the hospital? Why am I going there?

"Avery? What happened to Avery? Where is she?" I croak out. Panic floods my system as thoughts of us dancing in the kitchen infiltrates my brain.

"I'm sorry, sir. I don't know who that is," the first man says.

"Where is Avery? How did you find me? Why did you take me away from her?" I'm becoming progressively more frantic with each question.

Why won't they answer me? What do they mean they don't know Avery? I was just with her, damn it. Are these people stupid?

"Sir, you weren't with anyone. We found you in an alley alone." His tone is worried. Wait, they found me alone in an alley? So, if what these people are saying is true, did all that happen with Avery? I try to hold onto the memory with her, but then I start to question if it was a memory or—

Of course it was a fucking dream. Knowing everything was nothing but a fantasy means Avery and I aren't together. Hell, we aren't even friends. Chaos surrounds me. People are shouting random numbers that make no sense to me. My body shakes and bumps periodically as I feel the pressure of multiple hands holding me down. My body may be still, but my mind is still racing with thoughts of Avery. Then I hear that sound again—the one Avery made in my dream—and it has me panicking. The second my heart rate increases, I hear this irritating noise. It started out rhythmic, but quickly picked up speed before letting out one long shriek. My eyes roll back into my head, but not before the feeling of three consecutive jolts hit me in the chest as blackness swallows me whole.

I attempt to hold onto the slowly fading memory of Avery, wanting more than anything to drown in her emerald-green eyes and get lost in her beauty. But of course, I don't get what I want. Instead, I see an image of me curled under a metal fire escape next to a dumpster that reeks of dirty diapers and expired food.

My body shakes so violently you would think someone was tasing me. Everything is in fast-forward mode, making what I see difficult to comprehend. My vision is hazy around the edges. One moment, I see something pierce my skin, and then next, I collapse to the ground. My heart beats at an alarming rate and my body starts to convulse. Wait, am I being electrocuted?

"His heart rate is getting too high," a man shouts at someone. "Cassidy, can you hear me? Cassidy? Damn it, we're gonna lose him. Fuck, we need to hurry."

It's hard to focus on anything except my body rebelling against me, but I can still hear the faint sound of the siren. Is that a horn? Fuck, that sound is annoying and does nothing to stop this weird sensation radiating through me.

After what feels like a lifetime, I feel the cold air whipping against my face. I don't remember it being this windy. Before I can even process what's happening, the weather suddenly changes to warm.

What the fuck is going on? Am I hallucinating? Can someone even hallucinate the weather?

"Tell me what's going on," a man says. But wait, this isn't the same man as before. The voice is deeper and raspier in tone. What in the ever-loving fuck is going on? And why isn't someone trying to put a stop to the fucking madness that's happening inside my body?

"Drug-induced seizure. The patient's heart rate is all over the place. We found him in an alley—" There's that word again. I wish they would stop bringing it up.

I'm just desperate for this feeling to stop. If it stops, I can go to Avery and be the man I was in the dream. I will do whatever it takes to be that person for her. But instead, my eyes begin to flutter rapidly. I hear the faint sounds of more shouting and a long, steady beep before everything fades to black for the second time.

My mind transports me to a new scene. A graveyard. What the fuck? Why am I in a cemetery? Who died? My stomach bottoms out, thinking of the people who could be buried here. Avery? My grandparents? My feet have a mind of their own as they pull me toward a random tombstone.

As I stand in front of the grave marker, I can't help but think this isn't right. I rub my eyes and the salt from my palms stings, but nothing changes when I remove my hands. The name I see is no one else's but my own. I move closer, afraid to touch it. It reads:

Cassidy Michael Andrews

Born April 5th, 1998—?

Wait, why is there a question mark next to it? What does that mean? I'm in that Charles Dickens story, wanting to plead with whoever will listen that I'll change. I promise I'll change my ways, that I'll be better. But no one is there, so I make a vow to myself. I will be the man Avery always somehow saw in me. This thought dances around in my head before I jolt back into the four walls of an unfamiliar room. Panic bubbles in my throat as I take in my surroundings and realize where I am: in a hospital room, cold and alone.

Chapter 3

Cassidy

The Aftermath

FUCK, THESE LIGHTS ARE like staring directly into the sun. The room begins to spin and pain radiates behind my eyelids, forcing me to close my eyes. Minutes pass and the pressure behind my eyelids lessens, so I decide to test the waters by opening them again. When the pain doesn't come, I open them all the way. Fuck. Nope. Abort mission. My eyes snap shut with the quickness of a shutter release on a digital camera. I sure as hell hope I won't have to keep them shut forever.

I attempt to move into a sitting position, but I'm tangled amongst various chords. The only option I have is to shift to my side to prevent hurting myself further. I clumsily move to my side, but nausea punches me in the stomach. I have about five seconds to do something before I end up vomiting all over myself.

I blindly search for something to use and my fingers find what I *hope* is a bucket. The sound of my retching echoes throughout the room so loudly you'd think I was in a cave. The nausea fades, but my body decides to introduce its friend, dizziness. My brain is stuck on a Tilt-a-Whirl that increases its speed with each rotation.

"You're going to feel like this for a while. It's totally normal," a woman says. I open my eyes to slits to get a good view of her. She is pretty and her curly black hair that's in a ponytail is doing everything in its power to escape its captor. She's slim and tall, dressed in Pepto Bismol colored scrubs. I scan her face and notice warm hazel eyes and a smile that is patient, yet stern. Her face is completely bare with a tiny mole above her lip.

"Fuck. What's your name? I mean, I could look at your nametag, but that would require opening my eyes all the way, and that didn't go so well last time." My laugh quickly turns into a coughing fit, causing her to bring me the bucket. My head is under construction and my mouth feels like sandpaper. This has to be the worst hangover I've ever experienced.

I can't keep doing this shit. It's too much. This time will be different. It *has* to be different. If I want to fix things with Avery, I can't teeter the line between sober and stoned. If I keep fucking up like this, I can kiss any chance I have at a life with Avery goodbye. So yes, this completely sucks balls, but I'd take this sick feeling any day over losing her forever.

That word—*sick*—triggers what now seems like a Pavlovian response as my body dispels even more crap from my stomach. I'm surprised I'm still getting this sick. I don't have anything left in my stomach. This fucking sucks.

"Cassidy, you need to take it easy. To answer your earlier question, my name is Poppy. I'm what they call a substance abuse nurse so I know a thing of two about withdrawal symptoms. Have you overdosed before?" she asks. I shake my head and she continues. "Well, it's going to be like this for at least the next three days. You'll experience all sorts of symptoms eerily similar to the flu. I'll continue checking on you and try to make you as comfortable as I can."

"Thank you," I croak, my throat raw from the stomach acid. "I'm sorry you have to clean my puke. That's a real shitty job."

She looks at me and just laughs. "Oh, honey, I've been doing this for nine years. I've seen it all. You just rest now and I'll send the doctor in shortly. If you need anything, please let me know. I'll be back to check in on you later in the afternoon," she says before walking out the door.

I close my eyes and focus on breathing through the dizziness and nausea. Shouldn't they have something to ease the intensity? Even if they do, they probably won't give an addict anything. I mean, why would they? Giving an addict pain pills is as helpful as giving a sex addict a porn subscription.

As soon as the doctor enters the room, my first instinct is to flee because holy fuck, he's intimidating. I mean, this man appears to be in his fifties and is built like a massive linebacker. His face is covered with frown lines, trophies of his older age, and his hair is the perfect mix of salt and pepper. Is it too late to request a new doctor? The nurse was so sweet and friendly, but it seems like the man before me would rather eat nails than deal with my ass. You know what happens when you assume, though.

"Hey, Cassidy. How are we feeling today?" The doctor's soft-spoken voice takes me by surprise. I half expected him to growl at me. I've received so many nasty looks from people as if I'm the dirt beneath their shoes. Everyone always has shit to say about those with addiction issues, but they never ask themselves why someone would use it in the first place. He must sense my thoughts because he laughs loudly, jolting my body as if lightning struck me. "I bet you thought I would be a jerk, didn't you?" he asks.

I nod my head as he continues. "Yeah, I get that all the time. My wife always yells at me to fix my face, but what can you do? Anyway, the nurse told me you got sick a couple of times. Are you experiencing any headaches, dizziness, or body shakes?" he asks.

I haven't paid much attention to how the rest of my body feels, probably because I've been getting sick every five seconds. Is someone throwing bricks against my skull? Because fuck, it hurts.

"Can I answer D, all of the above? I also get hot really quickly. It's like one second, I feel like I'm in an ice bath, and then the next, I'm sweating balls," I say.

He nods his head before speaking. "These are all normal, but won't last forever. Are you experiencing any heightened anxiety?"

Anxiety? That word tastes sour in my mouth. I don't like to talk—let alone express—my feelings. By the time I went to live with my grandparents, I'd already learned how to lie and hide everything below the surface. Oh, they tried their hardest to get me to open up, but I've only been able to do that with one person: Avery.

Summer before Cas & Avery's first year of high school

Dad was back at his bullshit again. They tried to hide it from me, but didn't realize how loud they got when they were mad. I had to leave before I said or did something I'd regret. I reached for my new phone and texted someone I knew would be there.

> **Me: Dick?**

> **Avery: ...dick?**

Dick? What is she—*oh shit*! I looked down at my phone. My face grew hot and my palms were sticky with sweat. I wish there were a way to delete that message from our brains. Being so wrapped up in my inner turmoil, I didn't realize what was happening in my body. My stomach felt jumbly and my heart picked up speed. What was happening to me? Was this how I would die? Death by autocorrect? I shook my head at those thoughts and forced myself to respond to her message.

> **Me: Dock! I meant dock.**

> **Avery: Everything okay?**

The word *dock* had been our codeword for when we needed to talk. A part of me wanted to say forget it. The more people you let in, the more you set yourself up for disappointment. The thought of sharing a part of me with her didn't scare me as much as I thought it would. *Shit.* I've been so in my head that I had left her on read for five minutes.

Me: Kind of. I'll meet you down there.

Avery: I'll be there.

I'll be there. That small, but powerful text had the ability to take away my anxiety. Avery has always had that effect on me ever since I moved in with my maternal grandparents. Avery was the light to my dark side and everything I could've ever asked for in a best friend.

I ran down the stairs, and the minute I opened the backdoor, I saw her. The sun was beginning to set fire to the lake, and there she was. Her hands were on her hips, head tilted toward the sun as her wavy-red hair billowed around her. She must have sensed my presence because she turned in my direction with the most breathtaking smile. My steps faltered and I could hear the thunderous sound of my heart ramming against my chest. She's so beautiful. I can't help but think about that feeling I experienced earlier today. What was the word for it? *Crush.* I couldn't have a crush on my best friend—that would fuck everything up.

"Cas? Why are you staring at me like that? Is there something on my face?" Her smile was replaced with a frown as she frantically wiped her face.

"Huh? I mean–I–uh. No, you don't have anything on your face. Your face is fine. I mean, it's more than fine...I mean, uh—" I stammered.

"Cas, what's wrong? You're acting all funny." Concern danced beneath her green eyes as she searched my face for an answer.

"My dad." Two words, but by the look on her face, she knew.

"I hate that man. I'm sorry, Cas. I know he's such a tough topic to talk about." She reached out to touch my arm. The brush of her fingertips sent electricity throughout my body, jolting me.

"I—did I shock you?" Avery asked while she jerked her hand back.

Yes. " No, I um. I'm not sure what happened." My eyes turned downward as my feet shuffled a rock back and forth.

Avery blinked a few times before she nodded. I knew she didn't believe me, but she let it go. "Well, I'm sorry, Cas. It just breaks my heart that he has this effect on you." Her voice croaked on the last word, so I brought her into my arms and noticed how right it felt. I've hugged her plenty of times, but this time, however, felt different. It felt like the start of two lives intertwining to create something beautiful.

Present Day, Late Fall of 2022

Thinking about Avery makes me feel claustrophobic. My heart is beating way too fast. Is this how I die? Oh fuck, is this a heart attack? I find myself in a panic loop. The more my heart races, the faster the beeping from the machine goes which in turn makes me panic even more.

"Cassidy, I need you to focus on your breathing. Can you do that?" the doctor asks, yet I can't seem to control my breathing. He reaches into one of the many cabinets and pulls out a brown paper bag. "Here. Take this and put it over your mouth. Just focus on taking nice, slow, deep breaths into the bag," he instructs.

I follow his instructions and focus on the rise and fall of my chest. My frantic breathing begins to regulate and my heart is no longer threatening to leap out of my chest. I attempt to return the bag to him, but he shakes his head.

"Keep it. You seem to have elevated levels of anxiety, which can happen during withdrawal."

"Anxiety? I don't have anxiety. I'm not crazy." My voice sounds like I swallowed a squeaky toy with how high-pitched it is.

"Having anxiety doesn't make you crazy, Cas. It makes you human. Everyone has some level of anxiety because it keeps us safe. When you obsess about things you can't control, it borders on unhealthy. Lots of professionals, myself included, have anxiety." I open my mouth, but the words refuse to come. I'm not sure what I wanted to say, anyway, so I let the doctor continue.

"Now," he continues, " I want to discuss your options for when you get discharged."

"My options?" I ask.

"Yes. You should probably seek some treatment. I have a folder of resources with some of the top rehab facilities in the area. I highly recommend you consider them," the doctor says, his tone suddenly switching from soft to serious.

"What if I want to do treatment at home? On my own?"

"That's an option. Honestly, though, I don't think doing this type of recovery at home is in your best interest. You're extremely vulnerable in the beginning stages of sobriety and should have addiction specialists to help you recover. Just look these over in the next few days when you feel better. I'll be by to check on you sometime later today or tomorrow. Until then, call any of the nurses assigned to you and they can help you." He says this with a smile before turning to leave the room.

He starts to open the door, but pauses and turns to look at me. "I'm happy you pulled through. You have a good soul, kid. I can see it in your eyes. Take care of yourself, Cassidy." He finally walks out the door.

I spend what feels like hours contemplating my next move. I could do all this recovery shit on my own or I could ask for help. One option has my skin crawling with anxious hives, while the other has me thinking about that graveyard scene. To get my life back, I'll have to put my pride aside and go to rehab. All this thinking gives me a headache. When I place the folder on the table next to my bedside, a white letter falls to the floor with a soft thud. I bend down and my body makes the same noise as someone who stomps on bubble wrap. As soon as I have the letter in my hands, time stands still and the air whooshes out of my lungs. My name decorates the front of the envelope in a penmanship I'm all too familiar with.

Chapter 4

Avery

Emotional whiplash

Mid Winter, 2023

I AWAKE WITH A smile as I cling to the dream of Cas and I swaying together in the kitchen. I clutch onto dream Cas like a lifeline. The real Cas. The happy, sober Cas. But the dream disintegrates. Reality slaps me in the face with the force of a polar vortex wind. It's been three months since he overdosed. And every time I think about his journey with sobriety, I get whiplash.

The word *sobriety* sets off a chain reaction in my brain. Visions of Cas and I flicker across my mind like a movie trailer. I watch as Cas tries to reenter my life during my sophomore year of college. I watch tears cascade down my face while I repeatedly push at his chest. I watch as Cas hands me his sobriety chip while disbelief and shock play across my face. And the cruelest memory of all: watching us rekindle our friendship only for it to be demolished by his personal demons.

Who wouldn't get goddamn whiplash from that clusterfuck? Addiction is complicated, but I can still be upset and hurt.

The familiar sound of a doorbell startles me out of my thoughts, the muscles on my face contort with confusion. My heart beats like a drum solo inside my chest, loud and chaotic. I almost fall out of the bed with how quickly I remove myself from beneath the covers. I grab my robe that hangs off my bedroom door and slowly make my way downstairs.

I open the door, and to my surprise, Evelyn and Michael Andrews, Cas' grandparents, look at me with matching, hopeful expressions. Evelyn's once-long hair is now a chin-length bob of sleek, gray hair. She's a petite woman with the most transparent blue-green eyes I've ever seen, and today, she's in jeans and a canary yellow sweater. Evelyn has a spit-fire attitude and isn't afraid to call you out. She is also one of the most loving and compassionate women I've ever met.

Michael is the spitting image of Cas—all dark hair, now gray with age, and the same piercing, wolfish-gray eyes. He's the silent broody type when you first meet him, but after a while, he is the sweetest man you'll ever meet. Evelyn and Michael are the prime examples of that grumpy sunshine trope Brianna is always swooning over.

As I stare into their weathered faces, I notice their smiles don't reach their eyes. The last time I saw this look was the day Cas overdosed. I still hear the words Evelyn said to me playing on repeat in my head. *"Cas overdosed and he's in the hospital."* That phone call changed my life. I had previously contemplated if giving him the letter would do more harm than good. But hearing his grandmother's distraught tone through the phone was my last straw. I knew I had to let him go.

Over the years, I've repaired my relationship with setting boundaries. I always caved when it came to Cas. He was my best friend and I was desperate to keep him. Desperate to be by his side. But in doing so, I lost myself. I missed the Avery who was fun and bubbly. It wasn't just Cas who got lost beneath the rubble, I did, too. So yeah, I wrote the letter for the both of us, but I was the priority here. Me and my mental and emotional health were the priority. Then, seeing Evelyn hunched over in a chair, shaking with silent tears filled me with rage. It's one thing to put me through his antics, but doing this to his grandparents? Seeing the look of pure devastation on their faces was the push I needed to let him go.

The sound of a throat clearing brings me out of my journey down memory lane. "Hi, Avery." Evelyn's voice is cheery, but she doesn't know how to act around me. Not now. I wanted to give them space after Cas overdosed. If I'm being honest, I was doing everything possible to avoid them.

"Cas, is he? Is he okay? Did something happen?" My words come out frantic and rushed.

She shakes her head at me and relief spreads like wildfire throughout my body. "No, dear, he's fine. He's been in rehab for the last three months. He gets discharged tomorrow. It was his idea to go, believe it or not." She laughs, coming out a tad shaky.

"That's, um, that's great. I'm glad Cas is doing well." I look down at my feet, unable to meet her gaze.

"I'm sorry we haven't been by to see you. We needed time after we saw your letter," Michael adds. I glance up at Michael and his face is unreadable.

Remorse slams into me like an offensive tackle. This was the one thing I wanted to avoid, but I knew I wouldn't be able to for long. It didn't stop me from hoping, though.

"I-I'm sorry. I didn't want you to read that letter or see you after I gave it to Cas. I couldn't stand to see you hurt or disappointed in me. I just couldn't go through it all again."

"Honey, look at me," Evelyn says. I hesitate, so she lifts my chin with her hand. "We could *never* be disappointed in you. At first we didn't understand ending your friendship the way you did. But after attending a few support groups for family members of addicts, we realized why you did it. He hurt you so many times. You had to put yourself first. We totally understand your reasoning." I don't deserve her gentle tone.

"We still love you, Avery, and we always will," Michael chimes in.

I burst into tears as the weight I've been carrying these last three months rises to the surface. Before I realize what's happening, I'm wrapped in a group hug while my body shakes like an earthquake. Being away from Evelyn and Michael for all this time has been challenging. I didn't realize how much I missed them.

"Oh, honey, don't cry. Everything will fall into place. I firmly believe that." Evelyn says while stroking my hair.

"I just, it's been so hard to let him go. I miss him every single day." My words come out broken as my body surrenders to my uncontrollable sobbing.

"I know you do, honey. Cas misses you, too but he's not the reason for our visit. Right now, we're here for you. We wanted to see how you were doing. I can't imagine how these last three months have been for you." Her words are soft, which makes me feel comforted, yet ashamed.

"I just don't understand how the both of you can stand here and be concerned about me. He's your grandson and I'm just Avery, your next-door neighbor." I sniffle.

"Avery, honey, I think we should go inside and talk. If we keep talking on your porch, I'm afraid we'll all freeze to death," Michael says. I nod my head, reluctantly pull out of their embrace, and step back for them to enter.

"Do you guys want any coffee or tea?" I ask as they take off their many layers.

"No, thank you, dear. I'm okay. Michael?" Evelyn turns to her husband, who shakes his head in response.

We make our way to my couch. I don't have much time to make myself comfortable before Evelyn turns to me with a fierce look in her eye.

"Avery," Evelyn grabs onto my hand, giving it a gentle squeeze before continuing. "You aren't just our neighbor. Yes, Cas is our grandson, but you are part of our family. He hurt you. Your feelings are valid, and Michael and I hurt for both of you. We just want what's best for the both of you. The two of you need time to heal, and who knows, maybe down the road, you can fix what's been broken. Maybe you won't. Regardless of the outcome, Michael and I love you very much."

I've lost so much in my life already. I couldn't stand the possibility of losing Evelyn and Michael. I look up into both of their smiling faces and break out into a watery smile.

"Thank you. I didn't know how much I needed to hear those words until now. I love you both so much. I'm still so frustrated with Cas, but I do miss him...every day. He's everything to me. I'm not sure if we could ever be friends again, but just know he'll always be a part of me. Personal feelings aside, I *am* happy he finally got help."

Evelyn goes to speak, but Michael places his hand over hers to silence her. "Avery, we love you right back. I'm so proud of you for sticking to your principles. It shows how strong you are, and that's something I admire about you. We just wanted to stop in to check on you and also apologize again for our silence. We won't keep you any longer. We need to prepare for Cas's homecoming."

They both lean in to kiss me on the cheek before embracing me in a group hug before leaving.

As soon as I shut the door, I race over to the mantel above the fireplace where my parents rest peacefully in the ceramic urn. It's painted a beautiful off-white, with lavender lilies decorated throughout in delicate strokes. While they aren't here physically, I can still feel them.

My mother was a vibrant woman, always humming some tune while dancing throughout the house. I remember hours spent in the kitchen, blasting music and baking cookies. It was normally just the two of us, but when Cas moved in next door, he eventually joined us. More often than not, the majority of the cookie dough magically ended up everywhere but in the bowl.

While my mom was the life of the party, my dad was more laid back. I may take after my mom in regard to the random singing, but as far as my personality goes, I'm my father's daughter. At first, he appears quiet. It's when he becomes comfortable around someone that the goofball comes out. That's me. I remember always feeling like an oddball because I could never just go and talk to someone without overanalyzing everything in my head. When I was diagnosed with anxiety at fourteen, everything about me made sense. It's why I had more of a difficult time making friends, except Cas. It's like my soul had been searching for his, because the second I laid eyes on him, the anxious thoughts were silenced. When I told Cas about the anxiety, he went into overdrive, asking me what I needed and how he could help me. He used to be so compassionate, so understanding. But when I tried to confront him about his own anxiety, his tune changed real quick. That's a wound I don't think will ever heal.

The only way to get over that is with Cas owning up to his wrongs. And given everything that's happened recently, I don't see that happening. That's probably why this whole ordeal with him hit me so hard.

I reach out and touch the cold ceramic urn in an attempt to be close to them. "Oh, Mom and Dad, what do I do? Did I make the right decision with Cas?" I know I won't get a response, but I ask regardless. When I'm met with the expected silence, I do the next best thing and call my bestie, Brianna. My parents' struggled for years to conceive me. When they finally had me, that was it for them. I used to ask for a sibling every day when I was around six-years-old. Eventually, it got to a point that my parents had to sit me down and explain why that wasn't in the cards for them. I was devastated. I've learned through therapy that it plays into why I have a hard time letting my guard down with people. It's probably why I all but tackled Cas to the ground, telling him we would be friends. Something inside me needed whatever was inside him.

So Brianna is the closest thing I have to a sister. We have been thick as thieves ever since sophomore year of college when we literally ran into each other in the hallway. We were both on our way to class, but never made it because we laughed so hard. Bri's loud, eccentric personality compliments my quiet, timid nature. She's the sister I always wanted, but never thought I'd have, let alone deserved.

The phone rings twice before I hear Bri's peppy voice. "Hey, girl, what's up?"

"Bri, I need a distraction. Let's do something."

"Ya know I'm all for distractions, but why do we need one?"

"Cas—" Was all I was able to get out before Bri cuts me off.

"Got it. I'm on my way. I'll pick up cookie dough ice cream, your favorite sparkling water, and some crazy face masks. Give me fifteen minutes," Bri says before hanging up.

True to her promise, Bri barges in fifteen minutes later, arms full of reusable grocery bags. I go to help her unload everything so I can give her a proper hug. The second my arms wrap around her body, all the tension drains from mine and I let out a breath I didn't realize I was holding.

"Thank you for coming." My voice cracks.

"Of course, Aves. I got you, always." She squeezes me for a few seconds before letting go.

Bri sets up everything on the coffee table in the living room while I search for two spoons for our ice cream. When I reenter the living room, Bri is cuddling under a fuzzy blanket with a panda sheet mask on her face. I scramble toward the couch and crawl under the blanket alongside Bri.

"Here, put this on before we eat our ice cream." In Bri's hand is a crazy, sloth-looking sheet mask and I can't help but chuckle. She would pick the sloth for me. We have been doing silly sheet masks since our college days. It makes my heart all warm and fuzzy. I apply the gooey, cold mask to my face before turning toward my best friend to make a silly face. Well, an even sillier face because I'm already wearing a sloth-face mask.

"Do you want to talk about it or do you need a moment to process it?" Bri asks.

"Nope, I'm good. But, I think I just need to vent it out." Bri nods in understanding before I share everything that happened this morning. She reaches over to squeeze my hand, not letting go until I do. She's always been good at silent comfort. Besides Cas, Bri is the only other person who I felt an instant connection with.

I don't think I took much of a breath while sharing everything, because I felt out of breath when I finished speaking.

"So yeah, that's been my morning. You know me, overthinking is my specialty. I just feel like I—" Bri's palm on my knee has me stopping mid-sentence.

"Avery, that was a lot that happened this morning. Give yourself some time to let it marinate before you add any more ingredients to the pot. Remember what you learned in therapy. Use those challenging skills, girl. And if you can't, then I got you. So take whatever you were about to say and reword it inside your head. Because I know for damn sure you are not about to be mean to my best friend."

I lock that suggestion away for later, knowing full well she's right. Instead, I focus on laughing, reminiscing on our college days, and taking silly photos for my Instagram. While there's nothing I want more than to have the life we had in my dream, I know I can't throw away the work I've done on myself over the years.

Chapter 5

Cassidy

Journey to healing

REHAB ROUNDHOUSE KICKED MY ass. We had to adhere to a strict schedule of group and individual therapies where we would discuss why we were there and how to avoid returning. My least favorite part of therapy was talking about my feelings, seeing as how historically that was always met with a fist to the face. It was always *'you have nothing to cry about'* or *'I'll give you a reason to cry',* followed by the smacking sound of a fist meeting flesh.

My body always braced for the blow that never came. Still, I spent a lot of time fighting and challenging the therapist. What would sharing my feelings do? No matter how much I challenged my group leaders, they'd always push back. Listening to others share their stories gave me the courage I needed. Each time I talked during group therapy, my chest became less tight. For the first time, I felt free.

I'm gathering everything into my suitcase when I hear a knock on my door. "Come in."

I am interrupted mid-packing to see my therapist, Jason, standing in the doorway. He stands a few inches shorter than me with wavy blonde hair and blue eyes. He's wearing his usual uniform: a knee-length cardigan over a white t-shirt and dark-wash jeans. He might look friendly on the outside, but he's a no-bullshit guy underneath it all. We didn't click at the beginning of our sessions, with me challenging his authority more often than not. As time went on, I began to lower my defenses and identified that he wasn't *actually* a threat. Slowly, I stopped challenging his every move and began to understand and appreciate his methods. Honestly, he gave me the kick in the ass I deserved.

"It's discharge day. You've come a long way in the three months since you've been here. How are we feeling?" he asks.

"I feel good, a lot stronger than before. I feel like I've learned a lot about myself. Plus, I miss sleeping in my own bed. And it's all thanks to some hard-ass counselor who liked putting me in my place. I feel like I finally have a good head on my shoulders."

"I remember a bullheaded know-it-all who tried to manipulate me into seeing things his way. It's been an absolute pleasure to watch you let go of your stubbornness and began to accept other people's perspectives. That's not an easy feat." I find myself laughing at that, but my smile immediately falls when I see the look on his face.

"What?" My body tenses and it feels like a million pine needles are poking me.

"How are you feeling about seeing Avery again?" he asks.

I wince. "Honestly? I'm nervous as hell to see her. I understand why she wants space, I hurt her too much," I let out a frustrated sigh while racking my fingers through my hair.

"I sense a but coming." Damn Jason for being so astute.

"But I'm still so pissed she ended our friendship in the form of a letter instead of having an actual conversation," I all but growl at Jason. I could have kept this all in my head and overanalyzed every detail, but it feels counterproductive to what rehab has taught me. Look at me, learning shit from therapy. A chance a glance at Jason and see his lips pursed, wearing a now familiar challenging expression across his face. And I have a feeling I won't like what he's about to say.

"Just tell me," I sigh.

"I'm going to need you to be honest with yourself here. If she told you in person, would you have let her go?" he asks.

"I...fuck, you're right. I probably would have done anything and every-thing to bargain with Avery. Knowing me, I'd have filled her head with false hope and broken promises."

"I'm glad you're using some of that self-reflection we learned. I'm going to need you to hold onto that when it comes time to seeing her again. You are in charge of your emotions, not Avery. And if you want to fix that friendship like we talked about, you need to keep your emotions in check. If you find yourself getting too heated, pause for a moment before anger forces you to say something you'll later regret.

"That being said, that's not the reason for this visit. I think it would be beneficial for you to continue therapy when you leave. You still have an unhealthy view when it comes to your anxiety, and I think you need more than three months to work on it. We've also only scratched the surface of why you chose to use drugs, and as much as I want to help you, it's beyond my scope of practice. Here are a couple of referrals for you to use, if you want. It's imperative to deal with the traumas we face in life and I think therapy will continue to be helpful," he says.

"I'm not sure I want to continue therapy. As much as it helped me, I'm a little burned out." I take the resources from his outstretched hand and mutter my thanks.

He nods and glances down at his watch. "Well, it was a pleasure working with you, Cas. I mean this in the nicest way possible. I don't want to see you back here again. Take care of yourself," he says.

I shake my head while laughing. "Thank you for everything you've done for me. I appreciate it." Gratefulness swims behind my expression as appreciation for everything he's done for moats my voice. He just nods his head and walks out the door.

I race against the clock to pack the rest of my stuff before heading downstairs to wait for my grandparents to arrive. I sign myself out at the front desk and collect the remainder of my personal belongings taken from me upon entry. They took our electronics away, wanting us to focus on our recovery. Holding it in my hand now, I realize how much of a blessing it was not having it.

I make my way outside, planning to sit and wait, but then I see my grandparents' black Honda CR-V pull up. The car jolts to a stop and I find myself crushed between them in the tightest bear hug, only seconds after they exited their vehicle.

"Hello to you, too." My words come out breathless as they hug the life out of me. "I missed you, too, but y'all are about to cut off my air supply." When I step back, I see the tears swimming behind my gram's eyes. Seeing her cry is a shock to my system. She's tough as nails and it breaks my heart all the more when she cries.

"We've missed you so much. We're so glad you're coming home," Gram chokes out.

"You look good, kid," Gramps says.

"I feel like I'm finally in a healthy place. My mind is a lot clearer than it was three months ago. Now, can you help me load all this stuff? I want to go home and sleep in my bed."

"Of course, of course. Let's go, " Gram practically shouts as she and my grandfather throw my stuff in the trunk. I can't shake the feeling they want to tell me something but aren't sure how to broach the subject. You could cut the tension in the car with a knife. I've had one thing, well, *one person*, on my mind since that dream.

I've asked my grandparents about Avery too many times. They probably think I'm pathetic. I *felt* ridiculous, but I needed to know she was okay. I open my mouth to ask them about her, but no words come out. As we drive home, I realize we'll finally be in the same vicinity again. That thought both relaxes and terrifies me. I take a deep breath, finally getting the courage to ask about her, but my grandmother beats me to it.

"We went to see Avery the other day," she says.

"Oh? H-how is she doing?" My words stammer out of my mouth, only to be met with silence. This heavy, unsettling feeling nestles in the pit of my stomach and bile feels thick in the back of my throat.

"What's wrong? Is she okay? Is she hurt?" I demand.

"She's hurting, Cas. We went over to talk to her, see how she was doing. She's still struggling with everything. I know you want her back in your life, but it might be more difficult than you thought." Defeat wraps my body in barbed-wire chains, threatening to poke holes in the small sliver of hope I have.

"Oh," was all I could say. What else did I expect? Did I think she'd forgive me just like before? I mean, during rehab, I held onto a string of hope that we'd work through this. My grandmother's words are the scissors that cut that string in half.

My gram reaches out to hold my hand, offering her support. "Cas, you have to give her time. Things haven't been easy for either of you. I truly believe everything will work out how they're supposed to. Don't give up on her. But most importantly, don't give up on yourself. We just got you back. We can't lose you again."

Rationally, I know she makes sense, but I'm so disheartened by everything that I question things. A part of me wishes I would have died in that hospital because the pain of losing Avery forever is too much to bear. Speaking of losing Avery, her letter echoes in my head. It's a letter I've read so many times I could probably recite it word for word.

My Dearest Cas,

It pains me to write this more than you will ever know. I truly value our friendship. You mean the world to me. You are so kind, funny, loving, and energetic. You have so much life in you that I don't think you realize all you have to offer. We have been through so many ups and downs in our lives, and you will always be a part of the best memories of my life. You will also be part of some of my worst memories. Seeing you hurting yourself in high school was brutal. It was like I lost my best friend. You were no longer the same person I met all those years ago. You were cold, distant, and irritable. I didn't know how to handle you. You cut me out of your life and it crushed me. Then you got clean and I finally had you back. I was so happy to have my best friend again. It was one of the best feelings ever. Then your father came back into your life, and you started shutting yourself off to me and the world. You became the man I couldn't bear to be around again. I can't do it anymore, Cas. I just can't. I hope you heal and find your worth, but I can't be around to watch the destruction without it tearing me into a million pieces. I can't keep putting you before myself, not anymore. It's with this letter that

I have to let you go. I never thought I would have to do this, but I need to. I haven't been myself since you relapsed and I need to find me again. I just can't do that when constantly worrying about whether you are alive or dead. I can't fix myself when I'm continually trying to fix you. So this letter is my goodbye to you. You will always be in my heart, but I just can't. Maybe we can be in each other's lives again one day. I hope we can. If that time comes and you are ready, come and find me. I can't promise to welcome you back with open arms. I can't promise that our friendship will ever be the same. If you do come back, you need to show me that you've changed for the better. Don't change just to get me back. That won't work and I don't want that weight on me. Change for you first and let the rest fall into place after that. You are worthy of a long life, Cas, and I hope one day you see that. Your words will only take you so far. Your actions speak louder. I'll always cheer you on from the sidelines, but I'm letting you go for now. Please take care of yourself.
-Avery

My gram had to pry it out of my cold, shaky hands when I first read it. I'm surprised it didn't end up ripping in half. It wasn't healthy for me to read it as often as I have, but it was the only thing I had left of Avery.

My mind drifts back toward the dream. Despite everything that's happened over the last three months, I can still feel how we moved together in a choreographed dance like a phantom pain. Traces of her lavender-vanilla scented skin still lingers in my nose. The ghost of her touch whispers like the wind against my skin and I yearn for the comfort only she can provide me. The sound of her melodic laughter fading to black is a haunting reminder that she isn't here. That she wants nothing to do with me. And why would she? I'm not who she wants. I'm not who she needs.

The soft click of the car door shutting startles me from my internal dialogue.

Home.

I'm finally back home.

So why am I not more excited? My eyes glance over toward the house next door, knowing full well it's the reason for my melancholy demeanor.

That her absence is the reason for this void in the pit of my stomach. I know I need to move, get out of the now freezing car, but I'm stuck. My eyes are glued onto Avery's house, with hope swirling in my heart. Hope that she'll come sprinting toward me like she did when she was eight, and leap into my arms. Five minutes go by, then ten, but nothing happens. Her silence feels like a baseball bat to the windshield, shattering my fragile hope like glass beneath my feet. I rub at the ever-growing ache within my chest and force myself out of the car and head toward the house.

The hairs on the back of my neck standing up is my first clue that something doesn't feel right. My entire body feels itchy. It's like someone is watching me. *Cas, you're just being paranoid.* I turn around, scanning the street, only to find nothing. Even though I can't see anyone watching me, my heart rate doesn't return to a healthy pulse. I quicken my pace, practically running towards the front door. The second I hear the lock click, my back hits the door and I work on calming my racing heart.

My mind is a chaotic mess and a full-blown debate is happening in my brain. One voice tells me to keep fighting. The other says to give up. How can I see Avery every day and not have my heart crushed into a million pieces? Is it worth all of the heartache? Is she worth all of the suffering? I scratch that last question from my mind because I know the answer already. Avery is—and will always be—worth it. I just need to make her believe that this time is different.

I need to see her and have this long overdue conversation, but I'm in a losing game with exhaustion. I crawl into bed, hoping a nap will help me feel re-energized so I can talk to her. I close my eyes, intending to sleep for thirty minutes, but when I wake up, it's the following day, feeling emotionally drained.

Chapter 6

Cassidy

In a long-term relationship with loneliness

TODAY I'M TALKING TO Avery about the letter. My body thrums with nervous energy, my arms and legs tingle as if ants are crawling all over my body.

My eyes fall to where it sits on my dresser and my heart feels like a stampede of horses. Despite its emotional heaviness, I reach for the envelope and head downstairs. The sweet scent of chocolate chip pancakes assaults my nose and my mouth begins to water. My grandmother tries to get me to eat, but my stomach is too queasy with anxiety. She glances down at my hand, and when her eyes land on my face, she gives me an encouraging smile and practically pushes me out the door.

I fill my lungs with the crisp January air, focusing on the rise and fall of my chest. The wind tousles my hair, forcing me to brush the stray tendrils away from my face continually. I'm halfway down my driveway when I notice Avery talking and laughing with Bri on her porch. She's truly captivating.

Sadness is a bowling ball barreling toward me, looking to knock down its pins. Seeing Avery's face light up has emotion weighing heavy in my throat. I sprint back to my house before she notices me. As much as it hurts, it might be best to keep my distance for now.

My gram looks at me with confusion at my sudden reappearance. "That was either the quickest conversation known to man, or you didn't talk to her." Her words are the arrow and my heart is the target. They hit me exactly where it hurts the most.

"I- I couldn't do it. When I saw her outside, smiling and laughing I just couldn't. I don't want to be the reason for her unhappiness."

"Oh honey, I'm sorry. That must have been hard for you to see her. But you two have gone through so much together. I don't see you not being in each other's lives. Please don't give up." My throat threatens to constrict, so I just nod my head.

My mind is a hamster running at full speed on its wheel and my body feels as if it's on fire. In desperate need for air, I sprint past my grandmother and out the backdoor. It's a typical winter day in the suburbs of Chicago. The sun may be shining, but damn, the wind has a bite. My feet lead me past the dock between mine and Avery's house. A smile spreads across my face when I remember all the ridiculous names for jumps we would make up before entering the water. I don't let myself linger on those memories for too long, not wanting to break my heart even further.

Loneliness and I have been in a long-term relationship for years. It likes to control my life, often making me feel isolated, even when surrounded by people who love me. I have Frank to thank for that. Life with him was never easy, with him choosing to get high rather than parent me. If Frank had his way, he would have kept pounding into me. My grandparents eventually intervened, freeing me from the shackles that tied me to my father. Despite their unconditional love and affection, I still had invisible ankle weights of emotional pain weighing me down. Pain that I continuously ignored, which in turn led me down the same path as my father.

I shake the mental cobwebs in my brain and focus on the nature-made ice rink before me. Despite looking solid enough to skate on, that is not the case. Especially when accidentally falling through the ice at twelve-years-old. My body shivers just thinking about it, but it's still a positive memory because Avery and I drank our weight in hot chocolate that day.

The sound of the snow crunching beneath my feet echoes around me. Nature's music comes from the birds chirping and trees dancing in the breeze. As I stand, I force myself to deal with my feelings. If running from your feelings was an Olympic sport, I'd take home the gold year after year. People were a distraction, a perfect way to tune out the feedback in my head.

Using drugs freed me from my mental prison. Now that I'm sober, the years of avoidance are coming back to bite me in the ass. The thoughts I used to run from are now as loud as banshees in my mind.

I have done some fucked up shit, and most of it revolves around the one person I never wanted to hurt. Avery was the one person I could always connect with. She was able to break down a good chunk of my walls, but I never let her all the way in. If she saw the real me, she'd abandon me like everyone else seemed to.

Seeing her today reminds me of the familiar sense of safety. It took about two seconds for my inner demons to ruin it by reminding me how reckless I was with her. Watching her smile felt like a punch to the gut. I desperately want to be the reason for her happiness. Damn it, I need to talk to her. I'm scared she'll laugh at me or slam the door in my face. But I need to try, at least. I go back home with a renewed sense of determination to get Avery back into my life.

Early Spring, 2023

It's been months since my failed attempt at talking to Avery. My nerves are a knotted ball of yarn in my stomach, but it's now or never. I get dressed as quickly as possible, holding onto the sliver of confidence that I'm clinging to. I look at the letter that's been sitting on my dresser for months after my first attempt to talk to Avery. My hand hesitates briefly before grabbing it and heading out the door toward my fate.

With each step, my mind and body are tangled Christmas lights. It's not until I'm standing on her front lawn that I notice my body is vibrating. I take a moment to compose myself by appreciating her house. Avery's place reminds me of something straight out of a storybook, whereas my grandparents' house is the typical suburban house. Leading up to her front porch is a cobblestone walkway colored with shades of gray and tan, with perfectly trimmed hedges lining the outside. Cream-colored paneling covers the exterior with a shingle-style roof in the color musket brown.

A string of fairy lights decorates along its edges and a large double door in the middle of the house is the same color as the roof. Like most houses on the block, Avery's is open with an expansive front yard. The only significant difference is her front porch juts out farther than other houses on the block, giving her a more expansive view of the neighbors. The entire house feels as if it's been transported right out of a fairytale, but what catches my eye is the gorgeous matte black fountain. It has a thousand pennies from all the years of throwing them in and making wishes.

Here goes nothing. The sound of the creaking gate zaps my system like a fly caught in an electric swatter. My breath comes out in quick, shaky puffs of air as I approach her front door. My knocking matches the frantic beating of my heart. It takes a moment for her to open it, but I'm completely taken aback by what I see when she does.

Avery has always been gorgeous, even as a teenager. Her auburn hair cascades in soft waves past her breasts, resting just above her waist. The emerald green of her eyes cast their spell upon anyone who glances her way. She'd make the perfect Merida if they made it into a live-action movie. Her cream-colored skin looks baby-soft, and all across her cheeks and nose sits a smattering of gold-dusted freckles. She glows like a goddess beneath the sunlight, causing an electrical current to zip down my spine. Her lips are all full and pouty, and I want to grab her to see if they taste as sweet as they look. Her once slim, girlish figure is now curvy in all the right places. My fingers twitch with the impulse to trace my hands over her body, but I barely resist.

I can't help but smile because she's genuinely breathtaking and always has been. My gaze returns to her face and my smile drops, unable to figure out what she's feeling. All I know is that she doesn't seem all that happy to see me.

My throat feels like I inhaled sand dust. "Hey, freckles." Avery's eyes flash momentarily with anger before she slams the door in my face.

Chapter 7

Avery

He can't be serious

Early Spring, 2023

WHEN I OPEN THE door, the last thing I expect to see is Cas standing on the other side. It's been months since he's been home. I take a minute to assess the man before me and instantly frown. He looks good. He *always* looks good.

The tall, lanky boy in high school is now all man with a broad chest and the sexiest forearms I have ever seen. His eyes are still piercing as ever, reminding me of a wolf, all gray and intense. His jawline is so sharp it could cut glass. My fingers yearn to touch him, but I restrain myself. Fuck, he's sexy. The last time I saw him, his skin was gray and sunken, but now it's healthy and glowing. Cas has naturally tan skin and it looks like he's stepped out of a tanning bed. My eyes land on his lips and my mouth waters, thinking about what they'd taste like. Then he opens his mouth.

"Hey, freckles."

Freckles? How dare Cas use my childhood nickname. I'm so pissed off, the only thing I could think to do was slam the door in his face. How *dare* he call me that? What gives him the right to use that name? I stand against the door, praying he'll go away.

"I know you're leaning against the door right now, Aves. I'm not leaving until we talk," Cas says, irritation coating his voice. Of course, *he's* frustrated. The nerve of this man to be frustrated with *me* after all he has put me through. I grab my jacket, open the door, and slam it behind me.

"You don't get to use my nickname anymore, Cas. We aren't friends anymore." My voice shakes angrily.

"Since when? I know I fucked up but—" he responds.

"You did fuck up. You fucked up when you chose drugs over me, for like, the millionth time. You fucked up when you had me in a constant state of anxiety thinking you wouldn't wake up one morning because you took too much. You fucked up when you shut me out of your life again. So yea Cas, you fucked up. And I'm done playing second fiddle to your addictions." I shout. Goddamn my therapist will be proud of me.

Anger and hurt flicker like flames behind his eyes. I should have considered his feelings, but then again, he never cared about mine. I feel myself begin to over analyze everything I'm saying in my head, but I reel it back and repeat the mantras my therapist taught me. *I'm deserving of love. I am allowed to put myself first. I am a strong, independent woman. I am not selfish in prioritizing my own needs.*

"I-I'm sorry, Avery. I never meant to hu—"

"*Never meant to?* Then why hurt me repeatedly if you never meant to? It's like you never stopped to think how your actions would affect me. You were more obsessed with being high to give a damn about me." My voice cracks at the last word. I know the last part wasn't fair, but I am too angry to care.

"You know that's not true. I've always cared, Aves. I still fucking do. How can you just stand there and not know how much you mean to me? I'm better now. So excuse me for being upset when you're standing there throwing my past in my face. That's a low blow, even for you," he scoffs. My hands curl into fists at my sides.

"Don't tell me it's a low blow. Yes, you may have gotten help and I'm so happy for you. But don't you don't get to stand there and come at me. You have no clue how hard it was to watch you destroy your life. I'm still picking up the pieces you demolished with your carelessness. And you want me to just forgive and forget? Unbelievable. You're seriously unbelievable." I start heading back into the house, but he grabs my arm and stops me.

"You wrote me a goddamn letter, Avery. Are we not gonna mention the fact you took my heart and smashed it to pieces? Forgive me if I'm upset that you decided to end years of friendship with a goddamn piece of paper. I have every right to be pissed off. I can't put words in your mouth, but you can put them in mine? Real nice, Ave!" He shouts.

I yank my arm out of his grip and spin around so fast I'm surprised I didn't get whiplash. I push at his chest a couple of times while yelling at him. "How *dare* insult me right now. You hurt me, Cas. I couldn't take the pain of being second best anymore. Drugs were always your priority, and you threw me to the side like I was trash." Hot, angry tears cascade down my face and my body shakes with emotion.

"I never tossed you aside. You're my best friend, Aves. Well, at least I *thought* you were. Now, I'm not so sure. Avery, can we just start over?"

I let out a slow, shaky breath. Years of therapy have taught me not to say anything in the heat of the moment. I said some hurtful things in retaliation, so I need to step back to maintain my peace.

"I don't think we can, Cas."

"But I—," Cas stops midsentence when I place my hand in front of his face.

"I think you should leave now. We're talking in circles, and I don't want to keep fighting with you. We are grown-ass adults, not teenagers. Yet here we are, fighting like we did in high school. Please, just go home."

"I'm not leaving until we fix this. I'm sorry—" Cas pleads.

"*Sorry?* Cas, do yourself a favor and look up that word in the dictionary. If you were actually sorry, we wouldn't be having this conversation. I deserve to be treated with respect and love and right now you aren't understanding where I'm coming from. If you really want to fix things then you need to leave before you hurt me any further."

"Avery. We can't just throw away our friendship. Can we just forget—" he pleads again.

"No, Cas, we can't. Until you understand where I'm coming from, I don't see a future in being friends. Just go," I reply.

"Avery, you don't—" He abruptly stops as Bri places a hand on his shoulder.

"I believe she asked you to leave, Cas," Brianna says. The sound of her voice has him jumping back in shock.

"This doesn't concern you, Bri. It's between Avery and I," he responds.

"Avery is my best friend, so that makes her my business. I know you care about her, Cas, but she asked you to leave. You think you mean well, but you both need to cool off. Listen, I'm happy you got the help you needed, and I'm proud of you, but she needs some space right now," she replies in a firm tone.

He looks back at me for something I'm unsure I can give him. His words sting and my tears cascade down my face more freely. Devastation replaces his anger and that look cuts deep into my core. I don't like seeing him so hurt, but I can be sad for him and heartbroken for what he put me through. As he walks away, his body hunches. His footsteps are rushed as if he's trying to run away from the pain of our conversation. Hell, even I want to run away from the pain, as well.

"Let's go inside, Avery. It's cold outside, and I think we need some hot cocoa and a good cry," Bri says while wrapping her arms around my body. Fuck, my heart hurts and I wonder to myself if it will it always be like this.

Chapter 8

Avery

UNO is a dangerous game

I CLUTCH AT MY heart, hoping to keep it from shattering in a million pieces. This hurts too much. I glance at Bri who's standing next to me with a soft, comforting expression on her face. She's always been that for me. When life gets tough or I fall into an anxious spiral, there's Bri, ready to tackle anything I throw at her.

I glance at my best friend and take a moment to admire her. Bri is a tall, curvaceous woman with long, wavy, chestnut brown hair and the most beautiful amber eyes set in a permanent smolder. She's a walking sexual fantasy for men; and they buzz around her like they're bees and she's their queen.

Bri accepts me for who I am, but she also challenges me to step outside my comfort zone. In Brianna's world, there's no room for second guessing. She just goes for it, something I envy. Yet, since our first meeting sophomore year of college, I have started to blossom. Going out for trivia nights once a month with my coworkers. Karaoke nights have also made a triumphant return which is something I missed doing dearly. Hell, I've even attempted to date. *Attempt* being the keyword. I have my standards, and no one ever seems to measure up. It's either that, or the date goes so poorly that I practically crawl out the bathroom window of the restaurant. The last disaster date I wasn't feeling particularly myself—the anxiety monster was winning hard that day and he had the audacity to ask if it was my time of the month. Needless to say, I bolted out of there like an Olympic track star. If I hadn't met Bri, I wouldn't be doing any of these things.

Other than Cas, she's the only person who knows me. At one point in time, the three of us were inseparable. We spent lots of nights together playing games and laughing until we cried. As Bri and I walk into the house, I notice UNO cards sitting on the table from a game night I hosted with some work friends and I laugh.

"What are you laughing at? I only caught the tail end of that conversation and it didn't feel that lighthearted."

I smile while pointing to the UNO cards. "I'm just thinking about all those game nights we used to have. If I remember correctly, you both teamed up against me, making me draw like eight cards every other hand."

Bri looks at me with false innocence while placing a hand to her chest. "*Us* do that? Why, we'd never. How dare you accuse me of such a thing." That statement would have been believable if not for the giant smirk on her face.

My sophomore year of college felt like the year of Murphy's Law. I was struggling to finish my classes due to my anxiety being at an all-time high. Then I got the call that my parents passed away in a car accident. And days later, Cas comes strutting across campus looking for me and it was just all too much. I was having daily panic attacks. Trying to cope with my parents' death while repairing my friendship with Cas was a lot.

While it was a lot to handle, I was thankful for Cas and Bri. They were my lifelines and game nights became my sanctuary. Without them, I'm not sure If I'd be the person I am today.

I wrap my arms around my best friend, allowing her comfort and love to seep through me. "Thank you," I mutter.

"Always." Bri's response, while simple, is powerful and just what I needed. Bri points to the couch and then motions toward the kitchen with her head. She doesn't say anything, but I know she wants me to crawl under the covers and get comfy.

I'm sitting on the couch when Bri brings over two mugs of hot cocoa. I whisper my thanks as she cuddles with me under the fleece blanket. We sit in comfortable silence, and I'm eternally grateful, because I'm not ready to talk yet.

After a while, Bri puts her empty cup down and turns to face me. "So, are you ready to talk?"

I nod my head and turn to face her. "I-I wasn't expecting to see him so soon, you know? He caught me off guard. It got heated and we said some things. Some I stand by, but some I regret. I know he cares for me and wants me in his life. I *want* to be in his life, but..."

"But?" she prompts.

"But I'm not ready yet. You remember what it was like when Cas was sober. How we hung out all the time, laughing and playing games. You also saw what his relapse did to me. Cas is a living, breathing version of that Katy Perry song, pulling me in with his promises only to turn around and go back on his word. The day he overdosed, I wrote him a letter letting him go. It tore my heart out to write it, but it needed to happen. If both you and my therapist taught me anything, it's the importance of putting myself first. So, that's what I did."

"Ahh, that makes sense. That's why he was acting that way today. It doesn't give him a right to treat you that way, but it all fits."

"No, it doesn't give him the right. He was hurt and angry. While I understand that, it seemed he wasn't seeing things from my perspective. Cas can sometimes get tunnel vision, only focused on one thing. He just wanted to go back to before and I can't do that." My throat is so thick with emotion that I'm surprised I could even speak.

She nods. "I get this is difficult for you, but I am also proud of you for standing your ground. You and Cas have always had an intense connection. I can't imagine how difficult it is to hold him off, especially when he finally got the help he needed."

"Ugh, it was so hard. There were moments that I thought about saying *fuck it* and letting Cas back in. But I know better than that. Still, he looked good, though," I say.

"Girl, that man *always* looks good. I want to lick him from head to toe while also wanting to punch him in the face," she says. My laugh comes out shaky. This woman knows how to cheer me up. I lean over, press a friendly peck on her cheek, and wrap my arms around her.

"Thank you," I say softly.

"Girl, you've already thanked me already. What are you thanking me for now?" she asks.

"For being you. For always being my support system, my bullshit detector, my comedian, and most importantly, my best friend. For encouraging me to step outside of myself and let the true Avery shine. I'm glad you bumped into me in the hallway all those years ago." I turn to smirk at her, knowing I'm poking the bear.

"Excuse me, but *you* bumped into *me*. How many times are we going to have this debate?" She laughs. "All jokes aside, you are the best person I know. Right now, things are all over the place, and it seems like you and Cas are heading in separate ways, but I have a strong feeling you'll find your way back to each other," she says.

"Yeah, maybe."

Exhaustion takes over my body, so I rest my head on her lap. When I woke in the morning, Bri had gone off to work and left me a note that said she loved me and would text me later. It causes me to break into my first authentic smile since my interaction with Cas.

I push all Cas related thoughts begging to take over my mind aside as I get ready for the animal shelter. I was never allowed to have a pet growing up due to my parents' allergies, so volunteering at the shelter in high school was the only way I could safely satisfy that urge. I knew one of my purposes in life was to work with animals. In college, I wanted to major in veterinary medicine until I realized I would have to put animals down. That realization had me so distraught I didn't leave my dorm for three days. Bri dragged me out of my dorm room and called me her little Eeyore the entire evening. The next day, I changed my major to animal science and never looked back. It just felt right. It felt like me.

I'm now the adoptions counselor and it's everything I've ever dreamed career wise. I have the best coworkers in the world. I technically don't have to work. With my inheritance and my parents' life insurance, I have enough to live comfortably. I enjoy watching my furry friends find their forever homes. It also satisfies the urge to adopt one of my own, but unjustified guilt overcomes me every time. It feels like I would be betraying my parents somehow by bringing a cat into the house. It makes no sense, but it's a feeling I can't shake.

As soon as I step into The Furry Hearts Sanctuary, I beeline for the cat jungle gym in search of my favorite feline friend. The room is painted in a soft wisteria color with little wall decals in the shape of paw prints scattered throughout. Running along the wall are cat scratchers and ledges mounted for our more adventurous cats. Every corner has a cat tree of different shapes and sizes. There, perched on top of the avocado-themed cat tree, is the gray cutie with green eyes I've grown attached to. I walk over to her and she all but leaps into my arms, purring and marking her scent against my neck. The thought of her getting adopted has me feeling melancholy. If only I could pull the trigger and just adopt her....maybe someday. I let out a soft sigh before putting her down and getting a head start on my morning tasks.

Chapter 9

Cassidy

The emotional floodgate

MY BRAIN IS ALL sorts of twisted right now. The plan was to go over there, smooth things over, and Avery would forgive me like she used to. Is it fair of me to assume she'd forgive and forget so quickly? No. But fuck if I still can't be pissed off. I mean, she flat-out refused to be my friend. Okay, she didn't refuse *exactly*, but she didn't jump at the opportunity, either. I pace around my room, wavering between being pissed at her and understanding where she's coming from. So why was this time any different? Fuck, my mind is a complete clusterfuck.

A knock on my bedroom door jolts me out of my thoughts. "Yeah?" I demand. My voice shakes with anger and frustration, making it come out harsher than intended. The door opens to my gram standing on the other side, looking at me like I broke her favorite vase. Shit.

"Excuse me? Who do you think you're talking to?" she fires back.

"Sorry, I'm just in a mood and didn't mean to take it out on you," I reply.

"Cassidy! You can be angry all you want, but you will *not* take it out on me. I did nothing to cause this foul mood you've been in since you got home. You will not sit there and disrespect me, you hear?" All I can do is nod my head in response.

"Good. Now, here's what we are going to do. You and I will make hot caramel apple cider, put on our comfiest clothes, and sit on the couch to talk. Something tells me your brain is going full speed and you need someone to help you slow it down."

I simply nod, knowing there's no sense in arguing with her. While picking out my favorite pair of sweats and band t-shirt, I mentally prepare myself for an emotionally exhausting conversation. Sharing my feelings with her shouldn't be this intimidating. If I'm able to spill my guts to total strangers in rehab, I can do so with my damn grandmother. I remind myself that I'm no longer the kid who people used as a scapegoat for anything that went wrong. People can think I'm a troublemaker all they want, but my gram knows me probably better than I know myself.

Growing up being known as the addict's kid, no one took me seriously. I was labeled a troublemaker before I could ever prove them wrong. Whenever something bad happened, I was the first one questioned about it, and there was no point in proving my innocence.

My nerves shake like branches on a tree in the middle of a storm. *Deep breaths, Cas* My heart races at the speed of light, but I still force myself to go downstairs. Look at me, doing things that make me uncomfortable. Will I like it? Probably not. Will it make me feel better? Probably.

I enter my living room to see Gram has set up a cozy little atmosphere. The lights in the living room are dim, with the only light coming from the candles that are always lit and the lamps on both sides of the couch. Today's scent is Christmas tree farm, bathing the room in an evergreen, pine, and spruce scent. It's as if I've been transported into a scene in a Hallmark movie where the main characters search for the perfect Christmas tree. Knowing my gram, she probably has all of those movies recorded so she can watch them at her leisure. Gram sits on our teal couch that has one too many fluffy decor pillows. While she's focused on organizing the ciders on the serving tray, I'm standing in the entryway, feet superglued to the floor.

Gram smiles softly and without glancing up, acknowledges my presence. "Are you going to keep standing there? Or are you going to sit down next to me?"

I make my way to her at a sloth's pace, my flight reaction ready to activate at the drop of a hat. Immediately after sitting down, Gram pulls me into a side hug and just rocks me back and forth like you would a newborn baby. I haven't had this type of affection in ages. While I was using, no one could get through to me. No amount of hugs, loving words, or tenderness could break through my stubborn exterior. I've missed this. I've missed it so much that I don't realize I'm balling until my gram whispers her reassurances that everything will be okay and to let it all out. I'm a shaking mess within her arms, but I have lost the will to care.

I let out years, decades of locked up emotions onto my gram's shoulder, and the more I cry, the lighter I feel. My body begins to relax, and despite the raging headache that's brewing behind my eyes, I'm ready to talk. Before I can stop myself, I'm spilling everything that happened. She listens, letting me talk without interruption as I recount everything that happened. My anger and frustrations from earlier slam into me like a freight train.

Gram lets out a soft humming sound, but I wasn't expecting what she said next. "Remember when you and Avery first met?" She strokes my hair as I let out a watery chuckle to our first meeting.

"Yeah, she was a firecracker, even then." I laugh. I had moved in with my maternal grandparents' house when I was eight, after various attempts to get me out of the hellhole I was living in. Living in the house with my dad was a complete nightmare. I was told he wasn't always the asshole he is today. Him and my mom were high school sweethearts and had gotten married right out of high school. They ended up getting pregnant after about their third or fourth try. Everything went smoothly with the pregnancy, but my birth is a different story. I guess she ended up hemorrhaging enough that she passed away shortly after having me. My dad never got over her death, often blaming me for killing her.

The final straw was when my dad took me to a drug deal that went south, and instead of coming back for me, he fled, leaving me in the car. I don't know how I knew to get out of the car and run, but instincts took over and I fled. The cops found me walking alongside one of the busiest roads and took me into the station and called my grandparents.

I was a very shy, reserved eight-year-old, but that didn't stop Avery from marching over to me and demanding we would be friends. I believe her words were, "Hi, I'm Avery. You and I are friends now," before grabbing my hand and dragging me over to the dock behind our houses.

I smile at that memory. "Yeah, she didn't give me much of a choice when it came to being her friend. She was my first real friend." It's one thing to have that thought in my head, it's another to verbalize it out loud. I messed up. And I'm not just talking about what just happened. My eyes burn and my vision blurs as more tears threaten to spill.

My gram squeezes me one, two, three times before turning our bodies to face each other. Her hands cup my face as she gets ready to tell me some hard truths.

"You had a rough day yesterday," she says. The comfort from her words feels like drinking hot tea when you're sick. "You and Avery are hurting and have a right to your feelings. You both said things in the heat of the moment, but—" I find myself sitting at the highest point of a roller coaster, waiting for the inevitably steep drop. She noticed the sudden change in my body language because she squeezed my shoulder, offering reassurance before continuing.

"But it seems like you weren't viewing things from her perspective. Your anger and hurt shoved your empathy aside, and you weren't able to understand her pain. Maybe you needed time to process that letter and the feelings it brought up in you," she says.

A laugh escapes my mouth all too quickly. Gram gives me the same look she used to give me when she caught me doing something I wasn't supposed to growing up. The look has the opposite effect on me now, and I laugh even louder. "You sound like my therapist. He said something along those same lines when I was getting ready to leave rehab. I expected her to forgive me right away like she always did."

"Do you think that's fair of you to assume that? Maybe you wanted things to go *your* way, and when they didn't, you threw a fit." Her sharp tone causes me to wince.

If you can count on Gram to be anything, it's honest. Her words swirl around my mind as I try to understand things from Avery's perspective.

Rehab taught me a lot about addict behavior and how we crave the instant gratification of the high. It was the perfect escape from the monsters hiding in my closet. I found myself deep in the throes of the addiction cycle. Manipulation was my weapon of choice and it caused me to burn many bridges—especially the friendship bridge I had with Avery.

Panic threatens to put me in a chokehold, so I begin to pace around the room. I think about the dream life I had with Avery and the promise I made to myself. Shit, I just broke that promise.

You're a no-good, stupid child and no one will ever love you. You're just a fuck up like me. I stop mid-pace when I hear a voice I haven't heard in a while. He has no space in my head. As much as I want to cave into those hurtful thoughts, I won't. I allow myself to wallow in my self-pity, giving negativity its moment in the spotlight before kindly telling it to fuck off. I'll never grow if I keep listening to the negative voices in my head.

Am I disappointed in myself for going back on the promise I made? Yes. But I have to allow myself a sliver of grace, knowing I can't be perfect out of the gate. So the best I can do is own my shit.

"Gram, I messed up. I told myself that I wasn't going to hurt people intentionally. The second I got home, I broke that promise. She has every right to be upset with me. She has every right to never *speak* to me again." The last words come out behind a sob. Well, the dam has officially broken again.

My gram brings me into her arms, letting me soak her shirt with my tears...again.

"You two have way too much history to have it all thrown away now. So you said some things and didn't hear what Avery was saying. What are you going to do about it now?" she asks.

"I-I don't know. Maybe I just have to live with what I did. Maybe I'll have to be without the most important person in my life," I whisper.

"I don't buy that for one second. You need to own up to what you did and then fix it. It won't be easy, but you'll find a way if Avery is as important to you as you say she is. First, take a few days to let her calm down and work through her stuff while working on yours. You love Avery, don't you?"

"Of course I do. Avery's my best—" She shakes her head, cutting me off.

"That's not the type of love I mean," she responds with a knowing look.

My gram is wise, but my feelings for Avery were my best-kept secret. I guess Avery is the only person who doesn't know my true feelings. I look at my gram and nod my head in confirmation.

"Then you'll have to show her how much she means to you. You took advantage of her kindness. She's afraid you'll do it again. The question to ask yourself is, are you willing to be patient with her? Most importantly, are you willing to be patient with yourself?" she asks.

I let her words sink in for a minute. Am I patient enough to do this when all I know how to do is be impulsive and demanding? Can I give Avery what she wants, hell, what she deserves? I'm not sure of the answers to those questions, but there's one thing I'm sure of.

"She's worth it. Avery is worthy of having the best version of me. And I'm going to try my hardest to give her everything she deserves," I say.

My grandmother smiles and nods her head. "That's what I thought." She kisses my forehead before leaving me alone with my thoughts. I have no idea how to win her back, but I'll do everything in my power to show her that this time, I'm serious. I will be the man she always thought I could be.

Chapter 10

Avery

Cas thing? What Cas thing?

Mid Spring, 2023

IT'S BEEN WEEKS SINCE our argument and Cas' radio silence speaks volumes. After an emergency session with my therapist, my conflicting feelings disappeared. Thank goodness for therapy, it's been a lifesaver. I've been going to Olivia on and off since I was fourteen. She knows my whole life story. She calls me out when I need it, but does it in a gentle way as she knows how sensitive I can be. I still stand firm in what I said to him.

I worked too damn hard to put my own needs first, only to crack the moment Cas uses my childhood nickname.

My body tingles with a familiar sensation that hasn't happened in years. I could go into my bedroom closet, grab my journal, and write, but it holds too many painful memories. And to be honest, I'm not ready to revisit the feelings that the journal will bring up. I used to love writing, but that part of me died long ago.

My feet must have a mind of their own because I find myself in my childhood bedroom. I made the move to my parents' old room as a way to remain closer to them, but also as an escape. Reminders of Cas fill every inch of the room and my eyes sting with sadness. One wall has a timeline of photos throughout various stages of our lives. One picture in particular catches my eye, causing me to linger.

We were fourteen. It was the day I won second place in a songwriting competition. I was so angry at him for submitting the song on my behalf. Granted, I wasn't outraged, but I was more anxious. What if they laughed at me? What if they thought it was stupid? I know how people view Taylor Swift, so what if they think I'm like the Wish version of her?

My fingertips dance across the cold glass of the photo of us; my heart aches for the girl who was so obviously in love with her best friend. I glance closer at the image and what I notice takes my breath away. I'm smiling at the camera with my arm around Cas, but his attention is on me. He looks proud, but there's another emotion I can't place. My hand drops to my stomach in a poor attempt to keep the butterflies at bay. He's everywhere in this room. These memories sit heavy on my chest, and I need to leave before second-guessing every decision I've made since Cas' return. The door closes with a soft click, locking away those painful memories. They're too much to deal with right now.

Today, I wanted nothing more than to run into Cas' arms. To forget all the bullshit he put me through. Then he gave me that cocky smile on his face as he used my childhood nickname, and it had me boiling with anger. I couldn't let him off the hook. I *always* let him off the hook. Cas is good at many things, and being charming is one of them. I was in a constant state of disappointment every time I put his needs before my own. It was so easy to believe him when he said things were different. But when my therapist informed me about addict behavior, my entire perspective shifted.

So, as much as I wanted to let him back in when I saw him on my doorstep, I didn't. He has to show me he's changed and working on himself. From what I witnessed the other day, he still has work to do. Despite his attitude during our conversation, when I looked into his eyes, I saw clarity. Yeah, I'm pissed at him, but I couldn't help but feel joy that he finally got help.

The sound of the door opening pulls me from my thoughts and I see Bri walk in, followed by her brother, Max. Those two have been inseparable since they were little, practically doing everything together. I first met Max the summer after my second year of college. He drew me in with his dimpled smile, wavy, brown hair, and eyes like honey. He's a year and half older than Bri and I, so naturally, my crush was instantaneous. Bri has always encouraged me to be bold, be brave. Well, I don't think she meant for me to do that with her brother. Our only intimate moment happened when Bri was at work. We were sitting next to each other one minute, and the next, I straddled his lap as we made out.

We were still going at it when Bri came home and caught us, and instead of getting mad, she laughed and said she called it from a mile away. Nothing ever really went anywhere with Max, but Bri brings it up any chance she gets. To this day, I don't regret it. It made me feel powerful to take control sexually. Something I haven't been able to do since.

I look at Bri's face and know what she's about to say before she even says it. "You remember Max, don't you, Avery? You should know him well, seeing as you had each other's tongues down your throats." She snickers.

"Yes, of course, I remember, but thank you oh so much for the reminder," I say to her before turning to her brother. "Hi, Max. It's good to see you." I hug him, and in true Max fashion, he lifts me off the ground and spins me around.

"Hey, hot stuff," Max says, eliciting a very high-pitched squeal laugh from me. When he places me back on my feet, he takes a moment to assess me from head to toe before smirking. "Looking good, Ave. Wanna recreate that moment? We can send Bri away to give us some privacy," he says, wiggling his eyebrows.

I roll my eyes before I push playfully at his shoulders. "You can't handle me, Max." I laugh. "What are y'all doing here?"

Bri holds up a giant takeout bag. "I thought the three of us could have dinner and plan on how you're going to handle this whole Cas thing," she says.

"What Cas thing? Wait, who's Cas?" Max asks.

Bri answers before I even open my mouth. "He's Avery's best friend, who she's totally into."

"I'm not into Cas, Brianna!" I shout.

"Yeah, okay, *suuuure,*" she says to me before returning her attention to her brother. "He's *totally* into her, too. They got into this big argument and it got pretty heated." Bri goes on to summarize everything that happened before I can stop her. Once Bri has set her mind on something, she won't stop until she gets it.

It shouldn't surprise me that Bri is as intuitive as she is. The girl has a sixth sense for this shit. The one thing she's wrong about is that Cas feels the same. If he did, why would he have said all those things to me?

The sound of Bri clearing her throat brings me out of my head. I see both of them staring at me, waiting for an answer.

"What?" I ask.

"Did you hear anything we just said?" Bri asks.

"No, sorry, I was uh-I was in my head," I admit.

"We asked you if you plan on talking to Cas anytime soon?"

"I'm not sure. I want to work on our friendship again, but a part of me is still hurt by what Cas did and said to me—not only recently, but all those years ago. My friendship and feelings don't feel too important to him." I shrug.

Bri and Max share a look before bringing their attention back to me with matching shocked faces.

"You're kidding me, right?" Max asks. "From what I just heard from Bri, the man is infatuated with you. He wouldn't have gotten so angry if he didn't have feelings for you. My buddy, Asher's brother, struggled with addiction. He told me just how awful it was to witness. They only *just* started talking to each other a couple of years ago." I notice Bri wince at the sound of his name, causing a smirk to spread across my face.

"Still have the hots for Asher, Bri?" I'm hoping to shift the focus toward her for a minute.

Bri shoots me a murderous glare before speaking through gritted teeth. "I do *not* have the hots for him. Don't try to change the subject.

We're talking about your relationship with Cas and how you two need to hook up already because it's so obvious," she says. Despite her dislike for Asher, I know there's something there. Whenever they're in the same room, the chemistry is so intense people can get secondhand horniness.

"Bri, you don't know wha—" was all I managed to get out before being interrupted by a knock on the door. I wasn't expecting anyone today, so I'm confused as to who it could be. I start to get up, but Max places a hand on my shoulder, keeping me in place.

"I got this. You two keep talking about how you wanna hook up with your best friend and Bri wants to fuck mine," he says, throwing a wink toward his sister. She growls and flips him off before he walks away.

I am arguing with her about not liking Cas in that way when I hear the sound of two male voices. Bri and I tiptoe towards the door, ready to intervene if necessary.

"Who the fuck are you?" says the man on the other side of the door. I don't have to guess who it is. I *know* that deep voice. Cas.

Shit.

"Who are *you*?" I hear Max reply.

"Where's Avery? I need to talk to her," Cas responds.

"Yeah, I'm not letting you in until you answer my question," Max responds. Cool, calm, and collected, that's Max for you.

Bri and I exchange a worried expression. Cas sounds like a man suddenly cut off in traffic. I need to go over there before anything happens.

"Oh wait, you're Cas, aren't you? I'm Max. Nice to meet you," I hear him say. Max reaches out his hand toward Cas. I can't see him, but I can just imagine his goofy, lopsided grin. Cas looks down at his hand, then up towards his face with murder dancing beneath his eyes.

"Get your fucking hand out of my face," Cas demands.

Yeah, now's probably a good time to intervene. I walk towards the door, clearing my throat before placing a hand on Max's shoulder. "I got it from here, thanks," I say.

Max searches my face for any sign that I might need his help. I shake my head, silently communicating that I got this. Max nods his head and places a quick kiss on my cheek before walking off. I focus on Cas, who tracked the gesture and looks like I punched him in the gut. We stand in the most awkward game of chicken I've ever played with neither of us willing to make the first move.

"What are you doing here?" I ask, but it's like talking to a brick wall. Cas looks as if he's completely dissociated. I don't think he even heard my question. I open my mouth to repeat the question and notice Cas jolting out of whatever trance he is in. He turns and walks away, but not before I see a flash of hurt cross his handsome face. I watch him leave, confused as hell at this whole exchange. With my back against the door, I stare at Bri in shock.

"What just happened?" Bri asks.

"I have no fucking clue," I respond.

"Huh, weird." Bri shrugs before collecting the empty wrappers and tossing them in the trash. She's pulling on her sweater when she turns to face with a determined expression. "Hey, I found this ad on Facebook the other day and thought of you. I immediately clicked the link and printed out the flier. This has your name written all over it, Ave."

Bri is great at many things, but subtlety isn't one of them. Case in point, the smile on her face tells me she didn't stumble across whatever she's holding accidentally. My eyes scan the top line: *Songwriting contest: winner gets to sign on with a record label.* All the blood drains from my face and I sway from the sudden dizziness. My throat threatens to close in on itself and my entire body feels like I'm wearing the world's itchiest sweater. I can't do this. I just can't. I'm not a songwriter anymore. But how do I tell my best friend that I've lost my ability to write? Every time I take a pen to paper, my mind is blank.

"Wow, Bri, uh, thanks for bringing me this. I'll think about entering." My voice wavers a little, ultimately giving up my calm facade. I hope she doesn't notice, but of course, Bri, being perceptive, picks up on it.

"Hey, what's going on? I thought you'd be jumping for joy, but you look like I told you that you have to give a speech in your underwear. You okay?" she asks.

"Oh yeah, I'm fine. It just, well, it caught me off guard, is all." I slow down my words, hoping to convince her I'm calm when I'm anything but. She studies me for a moment with a frown on her face. She doesn't believe me, but she's letting it go. I let out an internal sigh of relief.

Hours after Bri and Max leave, I hyperfocus on what happened with Cas. He demanded to see me, but the second I came to the door, he walked away, disassociated. I'm fighting a losing battle with exhaustion, so I head upstairs.

The sound of crinkling paper as I open my bedroom door reminds me of another thing I'm obsessing over. I let out a mournful sigh before opening the door with my other hand. I put the competition flier face down on my dresser and cover it with books so I can forget it exists. I knew it would be another sleepless night as I lay in bed. I feel like I'm at the part in a scary movie where ominous music alerts the audience that something terrible is about to happen. I'm unsure what or when it'll happen, but I know I won't like it. A deep sigh escapes my mouth before I turn off my bedside lamp and hope the sleep gods grant me a peaceful rest.

Chapter 11

Cassidy

Wannabe Ken Doll

WHAT THE FUCK JUST happened? I went over to apologize, and when the door opened, there was a random man. Who was that guy, and why the fuck was he in Avery's house? I have no right to be this pissed off, but I am. I thought we could talk and start to make everything okay again. I didn't know she'd be dating some wannabe Ken doll. Just thinking about that man makes my blood hot with rage. He doesn't deserve Avery. No one does.

My gram knows something is up when I enter the house and slam the door. I feel the heat of her glare burning into my back, but I just continue walking away.

"I know I'm not supposed to do that. I'm sorry. I don't need a lecture from you right now," I say without turning around, stomping up the stairs towards my room where I slam yet another door. I'm pacing my bedroom floor like a cheetah chasing after its prey. What does Avery even *see* in that dude? The guy is a total bro. Anyone with eyes can see that. Avery needs to be with someone who gets her and sees her for all she is. Someone who makes her laugh. Who will hold her when she cries. Someone like—someone like me.

I have loved Avery since I was a teenager. I just never said anything because I didn't want to ruin the best friendship I've ever had. I settled on only being her friend because having her in that capacity is better than no Avery at all. I always wonder what would have happened if I dared to go for more with her, but fear always won. I almost went for it during a Fourth of July block party one year, but I chickened out at the last minute.

Fourth of July Block Party. Age fourteen

Our neighborhood had been throwing a Fourth of July block party for as long as I could remember. There were so many different activities to choose from. A dunk tank sits in the center of the blocked-off street, and a few spots down, children laugh as they get their faces painted. Towards the end of our neighborhood, there is a makeshift dance floor where couples are swaying under fairy lights. Avery and I were currently getting our faces painted and decided it would be fun to choose the other's design. For her, I chose a cat because the girl was *obsessed* with them. For me, well, she decided to be funny and chose a unicorn. So while she walked around with something that fit her personality, I had to walk around with a damn unicorn and watch as people pointed and laughed at me, including Avery.

My gaze flitted between the dance floor and the girl next to me, trying to gain the courage to ask her to dance. Why was this so fucking hard? Embarrassment and self-consciousness had held me back from going for it. She'd probably laugh at me or think it meant more than it did. But would that be so bad?

Avery looped her arm through mine and rested her head against my shoulder as we walked, causing familiar sparks to flow. Being this close to her felt nice, but of course, being me, I ruined it by being awkward.

"Wanna dance?" I shouted at her, which caused her to startle. Well, that was smooth—way to go, Cas.

"Huh?" she asked, her face scrunched in question.

"I mean, I-uh. I was wondering if you, you know, wanted to dance? Like with me?" I stammered out. A blush crept across her face. Great, I just embarrassed her—cool move, dude. I wracked my brain, trying to find a way out of this, but her response caught me off guard.

"I, oh, um, yes, sure." She looked down at her feet, avoiding my gaze. I removed her arm from mine to take her hand. I noticed that my palms were sweaty a tad too late and hoped she didn't get grossed out by it. We slowly made our way to the dance floor and just stood there. She was probably waiting for me to make the first move, but I was terrified.

"Cas? You okay?" she asked. I could play it off cool or I could be honest. I chose the latter.

"I, uh, I've never actually danced like this." I gestured toward the other couples, swaying to the music. She let out a soft chuckle, which caused my focus to land on her.

"I haven't either, but it doesn't look that hard. I guess we just copy everyone else?" She bit her bottom lip. My eyes flickered to her lips and I couldn't help but wonder what it would be like to kiss her.

"Cas?"

"What? Oh, uh, yeah, right. Copy what they do." I took a moment to glance at the people. Getting into a position should be a dance in itself. I placed my hand in hers while she put her other one on my shoulder. I put my hand here—wait, are the men holding their partners by their waists? Am I supposed to do that? I cleared my throat before placing a hand on the middle of her back. We were miles apart as we danced alongside the other people. It wasn't until some random person approached us and pushed us closer together.

"Get close to her, man. You don't need to save room for Jesus," some random man said.

The second he pushed us together, our gazes locked and it took us both a moment to realize the rain had started to fall. I couldn't care less because I had Avery in my arms, and it felt good. The dance floor became less crowded as the rain continued to fall, but I was content where I was. I thought back to Avery biting her lip and the urge to kiss her returned.

I removed my hand from her back and reached up to tuck a few strands of hair that were stuck to her face from the rain behind her ear. My hand remained cradled against her now color-streaked face from the rain washing off the paint as I searched her eyes for a sign. Before I could lean in, I chickened out and jumped away from her. Confusion and what looked like hurt crossed her face, but I excused myself before I made an ass out of myself.

Present day, Mid Spring of 2023

I need a distraction, so I grab my keys and head downstairs instead of focusing on what happened. Gram is still working in the kitchen and tries to stop me.

"And where do you think you're going?" she asks.

"I need to get out for a while." My voice comes out clipped, but I leave before I can hear her protest. Right now, I just need to escape. I don't want to sit and deal with my feelings. I get in my car with no direction in mind and head out.

I wasn't sure of my destination until the local bar came into focus. Damn it, I shouldn't be here. This place holds so many bad memories. All the times my grandparents came to pick up my wasted ass is just as embarrassing as getting a boner while giving a speech in the middle of class.

The word *mistake* flashes in my mind like an applause sign. I'm newly sober, but my legs move before my brain has time to process what's happening. Before I know it, I'm inside the bar, swearing to myself for being here. *I'm not here to drink. I'm just here to distract myself from my thoughts.* I repeat that mantra in my head. My mouth salivates from the idea of alcohol touching my lips. I mean, if Avery isn't going to be in my life, what's the point in staying sober? *No.* I didn't get sober for her. I did it for me first, then for her.

Fuck. My body feels like someone put superglue on my shoes when I see who's working. Asher Larsen. Damn it, I'm not in the mood for judgment. He's kicked me out too often for causing fights and doing things I shouldn't do. I'm still standing in the doorway when he finally glances my way. The smile Asher was wearing turned into a grimace. Well, it's now or never, I guess. I'm still stuck in place when someone forcefully nudges me out of the doorway, forcing me to make my way toward the bar.

The bar has mostly stayed the same. The walls are a dark cherry covered in signs and posters of various shapes, sizes, and colors. The bar top itself is mahogany with wooden stools to match. It's not a particularly busy night, but I notice a few regulars who all eye me cautiously. My chest tightens and my hands fist at my sides with anger. I can't blame them for thinking I'm up to no good. I did a lot of damage back then, but it still hurts that people view me this way still.

Asher finishes up with his customer and hesitantly makes his way over to me. He starts to pour me a whiskey neat, my previous drink of choice.

"No thanks, man. Can I get water instead?" I ask.

Asher shoots me a skeptical look. "Water? Why?"

"I'm not drinking anymore, man. No alcohol, no drugs, just want a distraction. Now pour me some goddamn water," I demand.

Asher scans my face trying to figure out if I'm fucking with him. I guess the look on my face must convince him that I'm serious because he switches the whiskey for water.

"Well damn, good for you. Let's hope it sticks," Asher says.

"I plan on sticking to it. I...I don't ever want to be in the hospital again. Overdosing sucks ass." Just saying the word *overdose* has goosebumps forming on my skin. A brief glimpse of me lying cold and alone in the dark alley flashes in my mind.

"I bet. My brother had his issues with addiction. I saw all sorts of things no one should ever see. He's sober now and can talk to you if you need extra support," he offers.

"Wow, uh, thanks. I might take you up on that." My voice shakes with emotion. I wasn't expecting that type of response, honestly.

"So you said you needed a distraction tonight. What's up?" he asks.

Getting someone else's perspective on this situation would be nice. The only male friends in my past had substance issues like myself. Once I figured my shit out, they bolted. I don't know how to do the whole *friend* thing, well, except for Avery, but I managed to fuck even that up.

"When I got home from treatment, I went to see Avery to fix our friendship. I—"

"Avery Douglas?" he interrupts.

"Yeah, how do you know her?" My voice comes out accusatory.

"Woah, man, chill. I don't know her in the way *you're* implying. She's just friends with my buddy's sister. I haven't seen that woman in forever, though. She, uh, still friends with Brianna?" he asks, his tone wavering a bit.

"Uh, yeah. Bri looked like she wanted to punch me in the dick the last time I saw her." I can't help but chuckle at myself.

"Sounds like my bear—I mean, uh, *Bri.* " *His bear?* Asher's face is crimson. I'm guessing he didn't mean to let that nickname slip. Interesting.

Asher clears his throat before asking, "So what did you do to cause Bri to go American Ninja Warrior on your ass?"

"Well, Avery and I fought, said some nasty things to each other."

"Hmm," was his only response. The silence between us became uncomfortable, so I forced myself to continue.

"Earlier today, I went over to apologize, but a man opened her door, catching me off guard. I was angry and demanded to see Avery, but this dude wasn't budging. Eventually, Avery took over, but this asshole looked at me before kissing her cheek and going back into the kitchen. I walked off before she could confirm what I already knew," I say.

"Which was?" he prompts.

"That she was dating someone. This Max dude looked like a wannabe Ken doll. It was awful," I say, resting my head in my hands.

"Wait! Hold up, Max?" he asks.

"Yeah, why? You know him or something?" He looks at me for a minute before busting out laughing.

"The fuck? Why are you laughing at me?" I demand.

"Because-because," he stammers while laughing. "That's Bri's brother you're talking about," he says, his laughter growing louder, pulling questioning stares from people throughout the bar. I offer them a tight-lipped smile before turning my attention back to Asher.

"And that's funny because?" I ask.

"Trust me, they aren't dating. Avery's like a sister to him," he says while laughing and wiping tears from his eyes.

"Yeah, right. I saw how the man looked at Avery," I said, but the tension eased out of my stomach like a balloon slowly deflating. Asher is a straightforward dude, so he wouldn't lie about this, would he?

"Seriously, man, nothing's happening. Max is the *least* threatening guy ever, so you have no reason to be jealous of him. I can't wait to tell him you think he looks like a Ken doll wannabe."

"Ugh, please don't," I groan. "Wait, I never said I was jealous."

"You didn't have to. It's written all over your face. You got it bad," Asher says, his tone matter-of-fact.

He excuses himself to return to serving other patrons, leaving me with my thoughts. I need to learn to get all the information before assuming. Regret hits me in the head with the same intensity as walking into a glass door.

Asher calling me out on being jealous has my guard up. Was I that transparent? I sure hope not, because if Asher could pick up on my feelings, Avery could, too. She can't know how I feel. The possibility of her not returning those feelings would feel equivalent to shredding my soul to pieces. She wouldn't have written that goodbye letter if she had feelings for me, too.

Shit. Now, all I can think about are the emotions the letter evoked. Shame is a boulder inside my chest, refusing to budge. I missed many moments in Avery's life because I cared more about myself. My insides twist together and my face feels hot. This is why I don't do feelings, it's too damn uncomfortable.

I should go home and sleep it off or call one of the referrals for therapists. But my need for a distraction still needs to be fulfilled as I sit here sober inside a bar. I tell myself to leave before I do something I'll regret. Even though I just had water, I placed a ten-dollar bill on the bar and said my goodbyes. As I collected my things, Asher handed me a piece of paper with his and his brother's numbers. It says I can contact either of them anytime. I thank him and make my way outside.

That's when I see a curvy woman with long, blonde hair that rests just above her ass. She's dressed in a short, red dress so tight her breasts are practically spilling out of the top. She has legs for days, amplified by her ankle-breaking, black heels. Her skin is tan and looks like silk. My gaze travels slowly toward her face where I see piercing blue eyes underneath long eyelashes. Her head cocks to the side, and her bee-stung lips curve into a sultry smile that's inviting and dangerous. She's *exactly* what I need right now.

"Hey, I'm Giselle," she says in a smoky tone.

My gut shouts at me to get in my car and drive away. Everything about Giselle screams bad news, but I need something or someone to distract me from these feelings. "Cas. Listen, I'm going to be honest. I'm in a bad mood and need a good distraction. I'm not sure if you have a boyfriend or anything. But, if not, do you want to go for a ride? I don't want any relationship. I'm just interested in one night. If you're cool with all that, I'm this way," I say, jerking a thumb toward my car.

She pulls on her bottom lip while she thinks about my offer. Avery's face comes to the forefront of my mind, but I push her away. This is a complete dick move, some would say toxic, but I just want to forget everything right now. Something tells me Giselle is the *perfect* solution to my problems. She checks me out again before returning her hunger-filled eyes to meet mine.

She saunters up to me and leans into my ear. "It's your lucky night. I'm looking for a good time and I *don't* do boyfriends," she whispers before scraping her teeth on my earlobe, causing my dick to twitch. We barely made it into the car before she whispered everything she wanted to do to me. My tires squeal with how quickly I pull out of the parking lot.

We made it to my house in record time and I noticed my grandparents' car was missing from the driveway. I thank my lucky stars. We make our way up the stairs as we pull each other's clothes off, exploring each other with quick intensity. Giselle is proving to be exactly the distraction I need.

I had no idea what trouble she was about to cause. Had I known, I would never have gone through with it.

Chapter 12

Avery

Breakfast and a show

I SLEPT LIKE ABSOLUTE garbage and I'm starting my day in a foul mood. My fight with Cas feels like one of those annoyingly catchy TikTok songs that gets stuck in your head. I lay in bed feeling dumbfounded, attempting to piece everything together.

My stomach grumbles, interrupting my internal crime-mapping of the emotions displayed on Cas' face and the meaning behind them. The shock of the cold floor startles me and jumpstarts my energy. I quickly find my favorite pair of pink slippers that have since lost their fuzziness due to how ancient they are. I haven't had the heart to throw them out as they were my mom's. Wearing these old, dull, slightly rough slippers keeps me connected to her. Despite their age, they are still intact and haven't fallen apart. My arms stretch above my head and I hear the slight pops of my body, waking up due to being stiff from sleep. I need some coffee. Maybe it'll have the answers to my many questions.

The sweet, savory smell of hazelnut consumes my kitchen. As I breathe in the nutty aroma, my mouth begins to anticipate the joy of a fresh cup of coffee.

Something about the silence of an early morning just does something for me. I love listening to the birds chirp their morning hello while the trees dance softly in the wind. Memories of my dad and I sitting on our porch come to the forefront of my mind, leaving me feeling heartsick. Dad's cup consisted of black, sludge-like coffee, whereas my mug had marshmallows with a splash of hot cocoa. We spent hours sitting and watching the birds flutter between trees while discussing our day. Tears prick behind my eyes and a sad smile stretches across my face. Those were—and will always be—some of my favorite moments with my dad.

My moment of peace is rudely interrupted by the sharp, shrill sound of my phone ringing from the table where I tossed it moments earlier. There's only one person who would call so early. I let out a sigh and hit the answer button without glancing to see who it was. "Hi, Bri," I say, putting the phone on speaker and placing it on the counter while preparing my breakfast.

"Someone's up early. Have some sexy dreams about a certain next-door neighbor?" she teases.

"More like tossing and turning, trying to figure out what happened yesterday. Our fight was like days ago, Bri. My head is spinning and I'm so confused."

"Maybe it has nothing to do with you?" she asks.

"Who else would it be about, though? He saw my face for two seconds before stomping off. Did Max maybe say something to him to get him all upset?"

"Ugh, classic miscommunication trope. Figures. Max didn't say any-thing to me about it. He stayed over last night, so let me get him and you can ask him," she responds.

"Miscommunication what? Wait, No, you do—" I start to say, but she already calls for him. The sound of muffled voices fills the background before I hear Max's voice through the phone.

"Hey, hot stuff! Something going on with your man?" he asks.

Bri and Max are insufferable by themselves, but when they are together, their insufferability only amplifies. "You *know* he's not mine!" I shout.

"Sure, sure, but you want him to be. What did Mr. Boytoy do?" he asks.

"Did you say anything to him before I came to the door? When you left, Cas looked at me with a wounded expression before storming off." I crossed my fingers and hoped he had the answer to Cas's strange behavior.

"Nope, not really," he replies, then recounts his entire exchange with Cas. Any hope for answers popped like a knife to an air mattress. Ugh, this puts me back at square one. Whatever crawled up his ass yesterday puts us back in the same cycle we've been in for years.

"Ave, are you still there?" Bri asks, jolting me out of my thoughts.

"Yeah, I'm still here," I replied.

Bri chuckles. "You didn't hear what I said. I asked if you could talk to him about it. You two circle each other like a hawk stalking its prey. I don't know what's so complicated about all of this. When you talk to him, you'll get your answers. Boom! Problem solved. Then y'all can finally hook up and end this *will they or won't they* game," she says.

"I'm *not* having sex with Cas, Bri. But I guess I could ask him about what happened yesterday. I mean, how else am I going to find out? This man is so locked up emotionally that I have to force it out of him sometimes."

"Good, now go do it before you chicken out. I demand to know what happens. Oh, gotta go. Be bold, Avery. Max says bye, too, by the way. Oh wait, one more thing," she says.

"Yeah?" I ask.

"Have you looked into that songwriting competition? I think you could win, Ave. You have such a gift with words; the world needs to know." Shit. I'm naive to think she would have forgotten the contest.

"Um, not yet, but I promise to look at it soon." I'm glad she isn't standing in front of me because my expression most likely screams *liar*.

"Okay, good. It's such a fantastic opportunity for you. Okay, gotta go. Love you, bye," she says before hanging up.

"Love you, too, Bri," I say into the phone while shaking my head. My stomach grumbles for the second time this morning, alerting me that I have yet to eat. I don't have the patience to make an elaborate meal. So, it looks like it's a Greek yogurt and a bagel type of breakfast today. As soon as everything is ready and plated, I grab my coffee and head outside. I place my breakfast on the small, matte-black, round table between matching Adirondack chairs with yellow cushions. I take a moment to inhale the crisp spring air, enjoying the serenity it brings before having to get ready for work. It's still early morning, so the atmosphere is chilly and the dewdrops shimmer like diamonds across the grass in my front yard. I close my eyes and focus on birds chirping and cars driving on the main roads.

My eyes are still closed and I'm enjoying my uninterrupted bliss when a high-pitched giggle startles me. I decide to ignore it, knowing it's probably one of the neighbors, and focus on the taste of coffee hitting my tongue. Then it happens again, but this time, I hear someone grunt. What the fuck? I think before opening my eyes to investigate what's going on.

I look over to the house on my right, seeing nothing. My body freezes as realization washes over me. The sound is coming from Cas' house. I find myself unable to resist the urge to look over, and that's when I see Cas with some random girl. My stomach feels like I have eaten something that has expired. My throat thickens with emotion, seeing Cas with his hands on her ass and her legs wrapping around his waist. I can't see her face, but I know the type: long, blonde hair with curves for days under a tight red dress. I've time-traveled back to high school when he would hook up with girls similar to the one who's tongue-fucking his throat. Now, I get a front seat to a porno I never wanted to watch.

"Get a room!" I shout in their direction. I didn't sign up for breakfast and a show. Their lips part and Cas looks in my direction, annoyed at the interruption. I can barely resist rolling my eyes when the blonde shoots a glare my way. Of course, she's beautiful. She's a man's walking wet dream.

"Fuck off and mind your business!" she shouts.

"Hey, back off of her, okay?" Cas replies to her before forcefully removing her legs from around his waist and dropping her to the ground. She looks at him with a pouty, disappointed expression.

"It's my business when you're going at it in front of the house. I'm trying to eat my breakfast and want to keep it in my stomach. Thank you very much," I say, returning to my food.

When I thought this was all done, she struts toward my house. Oh, *hell no*. I do *not* want this bitch anywhere near my house. I stalk toward her, trying to keep her from stepping onto my property.

"Giselle, stop. Seriously, leave her alone," Cas demands, trying to reach for her arm to pull her back, but he isn't fast enough.

"No! This bitch thinks she can talk to me this way, so I'm going to give her a piece of my mind," she says. Her eyes shoot daggers into mine. She sneers at me before continuing. "Don't come at me with this all high and mighty shit. It's not my fault you can't land a man like that, so don't come at me with your petty, jealous bullshit," she scoffs.

"Jealous? Honey, there's nothing to be jealous about. I just don't want to see you two pawing at each other while I'm eating breakfast," I say and turn around to make my way back to my house, already over this conversation and mentally thinking of ways to play human bowling with Cas and my car.

"*Someone's* bitter they aren't getting laid. Aw, but it's not your fault you were born looking so...plain. You look like the type of girl to complain to Mom and Dad. Privileged little bitch," she says.

I wince before turning around to face her again, tears stinging my eyes. My parents' death can be a touchy subject for me, but something tells me Giselle won't care. She takes one look at my state and starts laughing. My face feels like I've spent too much time in the sun and embarrassment floods my body.

"Tears? God, how pathetic. Go on now. Run along to Mom and Dad. They'll tell you how fucking *special* you are. You'll never be able to please a man like I can, honey. Girls like you could never do what I do. When men want to be fucked properly, that's when they come to me." She smirks.

I shoot a brief look toward Cas before walking away. Of all people, Cas knows how much their death has taken its toll on me. Hell, he fucking knew them.

It took two steps before I heard Cas going off. "That was uncalled for. You have *no idea* how special that woman is. She's a far better person than you'll ever be. It's time for you to go. Now!" he yells. Well, at least he got one thing right this morning. I am special, but he sure as hell isn't treating me like I am.

"*Her*? I mean, look at her. You seriously think a girl like her will do all the things we did last night?" Giselle's tone screams TBS: toxic bitch syndrome.

"Get the fuck out of here. Oh, and lose my fucking number." Those are the last words he says to her before he starts calling my name.

Chapter 13

Avery

We can't keep doing this

I FEEL AS IF my anxious thoughts are a rip current, threatening to pull me under and take me away. Why does Cas do this? More importantly, why does he do this to *me*? Cas continues calling after me, but I can't deal with him now. I slammed the door behind me the second I entered my house, my breakfast and coffee quickly forgotten. My body collapses onto the floor and the dam holding back my tears breaks. I hear him knocking and shouting my name, but it hardly registers with how hard I'm crying. How could he just hook up with someone like her? It's like high school all over again. I remember him strutting around with girls like Giselle all the time and it completely gutted me, knowing I would never be the girl he wanted.

After a few moments, the knocking stops and the silence of Cas's absence is deafening. *Did he leave?* A part of me is relieved he left, but I can't shake the disappointment that he didn't stay and fight for me more. The sound of a soft sigh from the other side of the door startles me.

"Avery, I'm sorry. Giselle was out of line. Can you open the door? Please?" His voice sounds rough, like he smokes a pack of cigarettes a day.

So, we're having this conversation. My knees pop with how quickly I stand up to open the door and with enough force to knock Cas backwards.

I'm pushing into his chest, pushing him back further. "Seriously, Cas, her? God, it's like you haven't changed at all. Doing the same old shit that you did in high school. You probably won't stay sober long, either." Heartbreak pours out of me with each quivering word I spew. I'm so wrapped up in my pain that I don't realize the words that left my mouth before it's too late. I don't mean it. I'm drawing in my sadness that my emotional brain told my rational brain to take a hike. His whole-body flinches from the impact of my words; his eyes are a storm cloud of agony. Guilt rises like bile in my throat. "Cas, I didn't—" but he ends up cutting me off.

"I deserve that. I'm sorry, I won't bother you again," Cas says before walking away.

With a heavy sigh, I walk inside and close the door, unable to watch a dejected Cas walk away from me. Fuck, I shouldn't have said what I said. Using someone's insecurities against them is one thing, but using someone's illness against them? That's a new type of low. It makes me feel no different than Giselle, if I'm being honest. As much as I want to open the door and run after him, I don't. Emotional exhaustion takes my body hostage and my back feels superglued to my front door.

I knew back then I made the right choice by choosing me. It's so easy to fall down the rabbit hole that is my friendship with Cas. My hand clutches my broken heart as I reminisce about the years I went without Cas by my side.

Years without my best friend or battling conflicting feelings of anger, sadness, and loneliness. Years of stolen glances and yearning for the boy

I once knew or wondering if I had done the right thing. Despite the things he had done and said to me, I never hated him. I just couldn't get myself to do that. Deep down, he was still that eight-year-old boy who held my hand when I cried or made-up silly jokes to make me laugh. What hurt the most wasn't him using but mourning the boy who once was.

My feet feel like lead. Walking upstairs requires double the effort with how emotionally exhausted I am. I curl into the safety and comfort of my bedding, and the second my head hits the pillow, I'm out like a light.

It's been one week since Cas practically dry-humped that bitch right in front of me. Flashbacks of all the girls he would fuck around with in high school play in my brain on a loop. The green monster inside my chest threatens to come out, but I don't want to admit I feel jealous. Admitting that means I still have feelings for him. Ugh, who are you fooling? You still love the man. You never stopped. I let out a long, frustrated sigh. Fuck men, and fuck feelings. They suck!

Cas has been stopping by daily to attempt a civil, adult conversation, but I still don't think he fully understands. I'm in the middle of getting ready for work when the sound of a knock startles me. I know who it is before I even open the door. I could ignore the knocks, but knowing Cas, they will become more consistent.

I open the door, ready to speak, but he beats me to it.

"Just hear me out. If after everything I've said you still don't want to talk to me, then I'll leave you alone." Desperation pours out of his voice.

I let out a soft sigh before stepping out onto the porch. "Okay, but I don't have long until I leave for work."

"I'll take it. I've made a lot of mistakes in my life, but hurting you is by far the worst one. I went to the bar last week, and I—"

"You went to the *bar*?" My voice is slightly louder than I intended, causing Cas to flinch.

"I needed a distraction. I swear I didn't drink or anything. My mind has been a fucked-up mess since our fight and I needed to get out of my head. So, I went to Aces and sat with Asher while he worked. I was so upset about our fight and then seeing you with Max, I just snaped. After I word-vomited to Asher he called my ass out for being Jealous of Max."

"Jealous of Max? Cas, nothing is going on with Max and I." I can't help the laugh that bubbles out of my throat.

"I know that now. He told me there was no reason for me to feel intimidated by him. There's no excuse for hooking up with Giselle. I kept seeing him plant a kiss on your cheek and I reverted back to what I always do. Even after knowing nothing was going on between the two of you I got jealous of your friendship. And then memories of what used to be started playing on repeat in my mind. I was jealous that he gets to be a part of your life and I'm stuck watching from the sidelines. And I know I don't deserve to feel jealous because I messed up, but I do."

"Cas, we can't keep doing this. *I* can't keep doing this. This whole toxic cycle we've been in since high school needs to stop. Do you even remember how it was in high school? When you were too busy getting high to come to my choir concerts? Remember when I had that solo, a solo I worked my ass off for, by the way, and you promised to be there in the front row?"

"I-I—" Cas stammers.

"I also remember our fight in the freshman hallway where I was begging and pleading with you to get help, but you brushed me off like I was a measly, little crumb. Do you remember those cruel words you said to me that day?" I ask. A look of recognition glitters in Cas' eyes, but I'm too heated to stop.

"You said, and I quote, *'God, when did you get so clingy? We aren't fucking so you don't get to be like this'.*"

"Well, did you forget the part where you compared me to my father? You know how I feel about him, and you still said that shit to me." Cas responds. Those words still haunt me to this day. His father has always been a sensitive topic for him, but I didn't care. I regretted it the moment I said it, but the damage was done. Just like the damage was done when I told him he won't stay sober.

"You're right. I shouldn't have compared you to him. I was so hurt and frustrated and said some shitty things. Things I immediately regretted. Speaking of saying shitty things, I need to apologize for what I said last week. I—" I begin to speak, but he interrupts me.

"Avery, you don't have to apologize. I deserve—" but now I'm the one interrupting him.

"Let me just get this out. It takes a lot for someone to seek help and I threw that in your face. In that moment, I was that fifteen-year-old me was afraid of history repeating itself. Watching you with Giselle, well it sucked. Regardless, I shouldn't have hurt your feelings to protect my own and for that, I'm sorry." I swallow back my pride while reassuring fifteen-year-old me that everything is okay. That I have her back.

"I'm sorry too. I've been a mess since that letter..." Cas pauses a moment, giving me the perfect opportunity to talk about the elephant in the room.

"Writing that letter destroyed me. I couldn't keep getting my hopes up only to have you stomp all over them. I want—no, I *need* to know I matter to you, Cas," I say.

"You *do* matter to me, Avery. More than you'll ever know," he replies.

"If I'm that important to you, then why hurt me?" My voice comes out raspy.

"I'm scared. I'm afraid you'll think I'm just a no-good junkie, just like my dad. My default mode, courtesy of my father, is self-destruction. I self-sabotage before someone can have the chance to hurt me. Something my therapist called me out on, actually. Deep down, I didn't feel that someone like was ever worthy of your friendship or kindness." His words are a knife, hitting me directly in my heart.

"Cas," I whisper. How can he seriously think like that? He's the most important person in my life; all I want is to know and see all of him. It makes me both sad and angry that he can stand there and talk about himself like that.

"With all that floating around in my mind plus the letter, it threw me over the edge. So, I found a distraction and took her home. No one feels more disgusted with me than I do, especially after the things she said to you. She's wrong, by the way," he says.

"Wrong?"

"You're worthy of someone who will love you completely. Whoever that guy ends up being, he'll be the luckiest man alive because he'll get to call you his," he says.

Both of us have tears in our eyes and matching heartbroken expressions. My arms itch to wrap around Cas and give him the comfort he needs, but I still have things to say. He starts to speak, but I put my hand out to stop him.

"Listen. While I'm happy you're finally being real with me, your words won't cut it anymore. If you want to be in my life again you need to do something about it. The warranty on those words has expired. You want our friendship back?"

"More than anything!" he responds.

"Then prove it to me! Show me this time is truly different." As I close the door, his hand on my arm stops me. I look up at him with questioning eyes.

"I will prove to you, Aves. I'm going to make sure you see just how much I want you," he says before walking away.

With a nod, I close the door, my head spinning with all the words we exchanged. A part of me is hopeful Cas will stick to his promise, but the doubt screams in my ear through a megaphone.

As I set them in the sink, his words hit me:

"I'm going to make sure you see just how much I want you."

Those words cause my heart to beat in a frantic and desperate rhythm in my chest and a pulsing sensation in my core.

Chapter 14

Cassidy

Sobriety isn't a one size fits all approach

It's been weeks since my last conversation with Avery and I've made zero progress in devising a game plan. My brain feels like scrambled eggs, trying to figure out how to convince her that I both need and want her. I pace my bedroom floor, gripping my hair in frustration. Coming up with a game plan shouldn't be so damn difficult. How am I supposed to show her how I feel? I stop mid-pace when a flash of white catches my eye. I stand frozen, thinking back to Avery's letter. This piece of paper, however, is significantly smaller. Now that my heart isn't threatening to leap outside my chest, I walk toward it and see a familiar name etched in black ink: Asher. I grab my phone and type out a quick text.

> **Me: Asher, it's Cas. You told me to reach out whenever I needed help. I wanted to know if that offer still stands.**

> **Asher: Hey, that's cool. Would you be willing to come hang out at the bar?**

> **Me: Yeah, that's fine. When?**

> **Asher: Are you free now? It's dead here, so we should be good.**

> **Me: Sounds good. I'll be there soon, thanks.**

I grab my keys and head downstairs. My grandparents are sitting next to each other on the couch. My grandpa is fiddling with his camera while my grandma is reading one of her many romance novels. They both look up with matching happy expressions when I enter the room.

"Hey. I wanted to let y'all know I'm heading out to Aces. I need to get someone's opinion on what to do with the whole Avery situation. Not that she's a situation. I mean, uh—" I stammer.

Gram places her bookmark in her novel before placing it on the table and patting the empty spot next to her. "I understand what you mean, Cas. I'm glad you're being proactive about everything. A year or so ago, you would have sulked and gone on some self-destructive bender. I'm so proud of you, both of us are." Gram squeezes my hand and my grandpa just grunts his agreement, refusing to look up from what he's doing.

"I, uh, thanks. That means a lot. I just wanted you both to know that I'm heading there for a reason and not to, ya know, drink and stuff. I've not only destroyed Avery's trust, I obliterated yours. I'm working on changing all of that. I don't think I ever said I was sorry for all that I put you through. I know how y'all feel about my father..." I pause and take a breath, those words coming out through clenched teeth. "I never wanted to be like him, yet I ended up being exactly like the bastard. You never deserved that. You never deserved a grandson like me who destroys everything he touches. But I'm going to promise you that I will continually work on myself. You both took me in when you didn't need to. You saved my life, and I repaid that by falling victim to my own demons. Not anymore. I'm going to really make sure things are different this time around." The last few words waver with guilt and disappointment at all the mistakes I've made.

I expect my gram to speak, but it's my grandpa that decides to chime in.

"We never, not once, regretted the decision to take you under our care. We love you very much, even the parts of you that you deem unlovable. While our trust in you is fragile, it isn't completely severed. You have so much in you. I saw it when you were eight and I see it now. I remember that spark you had when you came to work for me at my photography studio. You were finding yourself again, and it was a sight to see. I have no doubt you'll find yourself again." My grandpa isn't known for being the most emotional talker, but when he does, his words hit the intended target every time.

"Have you thought about going back to NA and AA? I know back then, it was helpful for you. Maybe it's worth giving it another try?" Gram asks.

I think back to when I got sober the first time. I didn't have a crew of doctors and nurses helping me out. I was doing it all on my own. And while I enjoyed the meetings, I didn't always feel connected to the content they discussed. Maybe it was because deep down I wasn't truly ready to get sober. Or maybe it was because of the constant judgment I felt from my peers and sponsors. I'm not sure, maybe with enough introspection I can figure it out, but I'm not sure I'm ready to dig that deep just yet.

"I don't think that avenue is for me. Getting, and remaining, sober isn't a one-size-fits-all approach. Some benefit greatly from attending those meetings. I don't think they were for me. Rehab helped me with a generalized understanding of substance abuse issues. My therapist there gave me a solid arsenal of coping skills that I feel are working for me right now. If I need extra help, I promise I will take it. I don't want to end up in the hospital again. Anyway, I just wanted you both to hear it from me on why I'm headed to the bar and not from a neighborhood local who still has their opinions about me."

"Thank you for letting us know. We love you, and stay safe. We are a text or call away. Have fun," my gram says. Worry lingers in the air like a virus with the only cure being complete and full transparency. I'm going to be proving myself for quite some time. I peck both of my grandparents on the cheek before heading out the door. It's about ten minutes from my house to Aces, but I make it in eight. Wow, he wasn't kidding when he said it was dead as I looked around at an empty parking lot. The second I walk into Aces, I spot him immediately. He's pouring a drink for someone, but glances my way, giving me a nod to take a seat. After a few minutes, he walks to me with a large glass of water.

"What's up?" he asks.

"So, the last time I was here, I hooked up with a girl I met outside. I took her back to my place, and well, things happened. The next morning, things went to complete shit. Avery lives next door to me, and Giselle and I—" I say, but the look in his eyes stops me.

"You hooked up with Giselle? Damn, dude, do you *have* a death wish?" He shakes his head.

"I know that *now*. Anyway, Giselle practically jumped me in the front yard when I was walking her out and—"

"Avery saw, didn't she?"

With a quick nod, I continue. "She sure did. Giselle went crazy on her and said some awful things. I told her to leave before chasing after Avery to apologize for everything. Avery ended up saying some things that I can't get out of my head. I know you said your brother had some addiction issues, so I'm wondering if you could help me."

"Sure. Lay it on me," Asher says. That's when I tell him about our conversation and how Avery is tired of me making promises, only to fall back into my old ways. Asher nods his head and lets me speak. It's refreshing to have someone just sit and listen without making assumptions or pretending they know what's best. After I finish talking, he silently stands there with a contemplative look. I grow more antsy, the silence ticking like a clock in my brain. I open my mouth to speak, but he beats me to it.

"You know that's some toxic shit, right? You hooked up with Giselle right after you knew Max and Avery weren't a thing. If I were her, I wouldn't give you the time of day. You're lucky you were able to talk to her. Like, deal with your shit, man. And how you did it wasn't the smartest way to go about it," he says.

I lay my head in my hands, aggressively rubbing my face. "Yeah, I'm aware. Look, she wrote me this letter that tore me apart. I'll admit I fell back into my old addict habit of being selfish. I'm not saying it's right. I don't want to do that anymore; I already messed up. I need to be better."

"So with my brother, he would go in these patterns of making all these promises to be a better person and stop drinking and get sober. He would be good for a while before slipping back into old habits. It became very frustrating watching him repeat the cycle, and eventually, I learned to stop believing him when he said he would change. Honestly, I didn't trust him until his two-year sober anniversary. Sounds to me like Avery needs to learn to trust you again, and you need to show her," he says.

I'm ready to argue, but Asher holds his hand up to stop me. "Don't come at me with the *'but I have proven to her she can trust me'* bullshit because I assure you, you haven't. I don't know everything about your relationship with Avery, but I know what it's like to watch someone in your life struggle with addiction. She just wants to know this time is different. Actions speak louder than words. Can you honestly look me in the eye and say that what you do and say are the same?" he asks.

I pause, giving myself a minute to think about it. Then it all comes flooding back to me. All the times I would go to her saying that I was finally getting sober and wanted to be her friend again, only to relapse days later. I missed all the crucial events because getting high was more important. All the time, I made drugs a priority over anyone else in my life. Including Avery.

"Shit," I say.

"That's what I thought. Before you spiral into self-doubt, that's how the addicted brain works. You know that more than anyone. Avery needs to know she's a priority in your life, and I think she's all talked out. The question to ask yourself is, what will you do about it? More importantly, is she important enough to you *to* do something about it?" he asks.

"Of course she is. She's the most important person to me in my life," I reply.

"Then you have to work your ass off, man." He shrugs.

"How do I even begin to do that? I keep trying to come up with ideas, but my mind draws a blank."

He pauses, and his face looks like he's solving a complex equation. He's quiet for a few minutes before speaking. "Emphasize to Avery how important she is to you. Find a way to remind her of the good times while showing her the friendship you *can* have. She needs to feel secure with you instead of questioning everything. Find a way to give her that sense of security back, and you'll have your friendship back, as well," he says.

"How do I remind her of the friendship we used to have? That sounds impossible," I express.

He shrugs before speaking. "Can't tell you that, man. That's something you have to do on your own."

"Thanks." I sip my water and focus on the coldness sliding down my throat.

"Ya know, you're working on repairing your relationship with Avery, which is great, but what about you?" Asher asks.

My face wrinkles like a bulldog with how hard I'm frowning. "Me? What about me?"

"I mean exactly that. People who struggle with substance abuse can replace one addiction with another. I don't think it'll be a good idea to become addicted to her. You need to have your own identity, man. So, who is Cas?"

"I..." I pause. *Who am I?* I've only known the broken and the bruised. But what more is there to me? "I mean, well, I'm an addict. I guess that's who I am."

Asher shakes his head before putting down a glass he was cleaning. He leans his elbows on the bar and looks at me. "Nah. That isn't who you are. It's a part of you, but not all of you. What do you like to do? What makes you feel good? Me, I love reading. Nothing greater than getting out of our shitty world for a while. Stuff like that is what I'm asking."

I've been an addict for so long that it takes me a moment to think about my passions. I close my eyes and try to free myself of every thought that comes into my head. I see a ten-year-old Cas holding a camera and sitting and listening to his grandfather teach him all the technical jargon. I think about how having that camera in my hands made me smile.

My eyes flutter open and I see Asher patiently waiting. "Photography. I love to take photos. When I got sober years ago, I worked in my grandfather's studio. I would assist him with lighting, prop staging, and setting up and removing his equipment. I loved doing it. Shit, I can't remember the last time I thought about picking up my camera."

"Maybe it's time to do that again. Finding the balance between your passions and reconnecting with Avery, while challenging, might be necessary."

"Damn, how do you know all this shit?" I chuckle.

Asher shrugs. "I've gone to therapy with my brother a time or two."

We spend the rest of our evening just talking and hanging out in between customers. When I'm not talking to Asher, I'm avoiding all the eyes drilling holes into my back. I won't give them the time of day, they don't deserve it. I can't recall when I ever had an actual, genuine male friendship. There's something about Asher that puts me at ease. Despite my past and our history together, he doesn't seem to see me as broken or defective. Maybe it's time I start seeing myself differently.

Chapter 15

Cassidy

The best friend bootcamp

MY CONVERSATION WITH ASHER has been playing in my head for weeks, but my brain is still an empty canvas. What does he mean by *'remind her of our friendship'*? I needed to prove myself to her through my actions, but I could only think to talk to her. I scrub my face aggressively, irritated that I can't figure it out. I thought about contacting Asher again to get more guidance, but he's right. I need to figure this shit out on my own.

Feeling suffocated by the walls of my bedroom, I make my way downstairs in desperate need of some air. One of the many pros of rehab is learning to find healthy outlets for our feelings. I found that going for a walk or run mixed with some strength training has saved my mental health. Sure, I may have some abs from it, but that wasn't the end goal. I just want to feel better, and I feel incredible after a workout.

I glance over toward Avery's house and wonder if she thinks I've given up on her. I haven't talked to her since our last conversation. She made her demands, and I can't go to her now without a plan. She was so hurt the last time I saw her. I keep praying she hasn't given up hope. I let myself take one more glance at her house before I continue.

Something about walking along the water is soothing. My mind is eerily quiet and my body is calm. The dock comes into my line of sight and I pause a moment, allowing happy memories to fill my mind. Instead of continuing down the path, I make my way over to sit down. I stare out at the water and remember all the times Avery and I would sit in this spot whenever we needed a break from life. I laugh as my mind revisits the jumps we would do and the ridiculous names we would come up with while in mid-air.

Other memories are like a blizzard in my brain. I remember Avery and I sneaking out of the house to stargaze, pushing each other on the swings, playing games at the park, having movie marathons, and baking cookies. No matter what we did together, I was always happy. We both were.

Remind her of the friendship you used to have.

The lightbulb in my head goes off. I reach into my pocket for my phone to text Asher before I lose my train of thought.

> **Me: I've figured out what I want to do to win Avery back. Are you busy?**

> **Asher: I'm at work and my buddy is coming to hang out, but you're welcome to hang out with us.**

> **Me: Be there in thirty.**

I like hanging out at Aces. Who knew I could hang out in a bar and not get shit-faced? My friendship with Asher has also been a pleasant surprise. Having someone else in my corner who will be supportive, but also call me out on my bullshit, is something I've needed.

Twenty-five minutes later, I'm sitting at one of Ace's bar stools, hanging out with Asher while he makes drinks for the other patrons. I'm drinking my water and minding my business when someone sits on the stool next to me. Whoever it is must be Asher's friend. I glance up and come face-to-face with the man that was at Avery's house. *Fuck.*

"Oh, hey, Cas. Didn't know you'd be here today," Max says as he claps me on the back. How is he so chill with me when I was a complete ass to him?

"Yeah. Hey, listen. I'm sorry for being such a dick to you that day at Avery's house." I put a smile on my face, hoping he won't cuss me out.

"I'd be jealous, too, if someone was after my girl." Max's face breaks out into a lopsided grin so contagious you can't help but smile back.

"Thanks, man. Wait, she's not my girl..." is all I manage to say.

"She is," Asher and Max respond, simultaneously. Asher walks over to us with a drink in his hand for Max.

"She's not. We're just friends. Well, trying to be, I guess." I look at them as they glance at each other before bursting into laughter.

"So, this plan is solely for rekindling your friendship and nothing more? I call bullshit," Asher huffs.

Max looks between the two of us, looking like a lost puppy. "Wait, what am I missing?"

Asher turns toward Max to fill him in while I groan into my glass. "Cas wants to repair his relationship with Avery. He says it's just to be friends with her again, but after his little jealousy stint when he saw you at Avery's, I think it's more than that." Asher and Max look at me with knowing grins on their faces.

Bastards.

"Wait, you were jealous of *me*? You didn't think Avery and I—" Max starts to ask the question, but my grimace stops him. Then, within seconds, Max is wheezing because of how hard he's laughing.

"Me and—me and Avery? Dude, no. We kissed once a long time ago, but yeah, that's—oh God, that's fucking funny."

"Wow, gee, thanks," I grumble. But it's hard to stay irritated. Max is a golden retriever, a child in an adult body.

"Okay, okay. So what plan do you have?" Max genuinely asks. I tell them about my walk and how I thought about everything Avery and I used to do together. Asher takes out a pad of paper and writes down each activity.

1. Play at the playground

2. Hang out by the dock

3. Stargaze *make sure to include her favorite snacks*

4. Bake cookies together

Asher rips out the paper and hands it over to me. Thinking of these things in my head is one thing, but seeing them on paper makes them feel real. Despite the air conditioning, my body feels hot and my heart rate accelerates. I expected only to feel panic at this plan, but there was excitement, as well. I look up from the paper, knowing this might just work, but still, I need some reassurance. I'm nervous that she'll think my idea is stupid.

"What do you guys think? You think it'll work?" I ask, my voice wavering with uncertainty.

"It feels like you took my advice seriously, so I'm cool with it," Asher responds.

"Knowing Avery, I think that'll work. It's like a best friend bootcamp." Max shrugs. I whip my head in his direction.

"Best friend bootcamp? That's genius. Thanks, man. And to be clear, it's just to rekindle my friendship. Besides, I doubt she'd want me in that way."

"That is the dumbest thing I've ever heard," Max deadpans. "Avery's into you."

"It's true. I mean, Giselle hooked up with you, so clearly, you aren't hideous. That woman is picky," Asher chimes in.

"He hooked up with Giselle?" Max is shocked, but there is a quick flash of something before it disappears. Asher just nods his head with a smirk on his face. He totally saw that look on Max's face, too. "That was stupid as hell, dude. I hope you plan to stay away from her. Okay, now let's get back to this list. When you get to the part about baking cookies, get messy. Rub some cookie dough on her face and neck. Hell, have a food fight. Now *that* sounds hot as fuck. Then you'll have an excuse to lick it off of her, and if things progress from there, well, you're welcome." Max is so much like his sister, Bri. It's scary.

"Yeah, let me do just that. Avery will *definitely* let me lick the cookie dough off her body." I laugh at the ridiculousness of it all.

"Trust me, she'll love it," Max says.

I glance at Asher with a *can you believe this guy* face, but he's nodding in agreement with Max. "Sorry, dude, but I agree. From what you've told me, I think she'll let you lick it off of her."

The rest of the evening fills with laughter, and Max and Asher plotting how to move me out of the friend zone with Avery. Making friends as an adult is hard. Almost everyone you come in contact with already has their set friends, like Max and Asher. Yet, they want to take me in and include me. All of my friendships in the past, besides Avery, have been surrounded by drugs and lies. Am I going all in with the two people in front of me? No, but I am trying to allow myself to have these types of friendships.

As I walk out of the bar and towards my car, I see a shadow pass out of my peripheral vision, causing me to feel like a deer in headlights. My breathing becomes heavy as I prepare for whoever is there to approach me. But nothing happens, making me think that I imagined the shadow. I don't let out the breath I've been holding until I pull away from the bar parking lot.

I head home, thinking about the friendship I'm creating with Max and Asher. It feels incredible to be myself around them and have them accept me without hesitation. They know of my past issues and still want to be around me. While productive, this day has been emotionally draining and I'm exhausted.

I start to get ready for bed, but then I remember my conversation with Asher about my interests. I glance at my closet, knowing my camera is likely collecting dust. Before I lose motivation, I move toward the box in the closet, and as I pull it out, an album falls to the floor. I pick up the black, leather-bound book and move toward my bed, placing my camera on the nightstand. I haven't seen this thing in ages. I flip through the book and see a plethora of pictures.

Some are photos of my grandparents dancing in the kitchen. Others are landscapes and sunsets. But the ones that stick out the most are of the person I'm trying to win back. There's one in particular that stands out to me the most. It's at our spot on the dock; the sky is a mix of reds, yellows, and pinks blended seamlessly. Avery is sitting at the edge of the dock wearing a yellow sundress with daisies on it, her hair in a loose ponytail. Curly tendrils escape her hairband to frame her face. She looks to be aggressively writing in one of her many journals, her tongue peeking out in concentration. I run my fingers over the photo. She looks radiant. Looking at this still image of Avery, I notice inspiration bubbling within me. I want to capture every moment with her. I want to stare at these photos years down the road and be able to remember everything.

Max's words about Avery being into me replay in my mind as I lay in bed. Would trying to be more with Avery would be such a terrible idea? Does she want to be more than friends as severely as I do? I push those thoughts aside, knowing that self-doubt isn't too far behind and I'm too tired to think. I crawl into bed and prepare for the inevitable nightmares.

Chapter 16

Avery

Radio silence speaks volumes

Early Summer of 2023

MY ANXIOUS MIND HOLDS my sanity hostage as more time passes from my last conversation with Cas. He couldn't have changed his mind, could he? Yet, his radio silence speaks volumes. My mind is an aggressive game of tug-of-war between wanting to stand my ground or cave and go to him.

Bri picks up on my sour mood and brings up my least favorite nickname, her little Eeyore. She tries to invite me out multiple times, but I always decline. After the fourth time of declining Bri's invite, she shows up at my door in a tight black dress that stops mid-thigh and six-inch heels. With her wavy chestnut hair down, she's a complete knockout—she always is.

"Bitch, we're going out. No excuses. Now, get your Eeyore ass upstairs and change out of those clothes." When Bri has her mind set on something, there's no changing it. I let out a frustrated growl as I headed upstairs with a smug Bri trailing behind me. She spends no time going through my closet and tossing out a pair of high-waisted jean shorts and a white crop top. Not wanting to attract attention, I apply the minimum amount of makeup: tinted moisturizer, lip gloss, and a coat of mascara. As soon as my sandals are on my feet, she's dragging me out of the door.

Our town has few bars, so we end up at Aces, despite Bri's pleas to go elsewhere.

"Hey, you're forcing me out tonight. So what if your boo happens to be here." I smirk.

"I am not opposed to murder, Ave. I've watched enough *Law and Order* to know how to hide a body." Her smirk has me rolling my eyes and I let out an unladylike snort. The bar is busy, but we find a spot off in the corner. I give Bri my drink order as I save our spots. Two people are working behind the bar tonight. One is Asher, but the other is someone I haven't met. From afar, he's total eye candy. With gauges in both his ears and arms covered in tattoos, all the women in the bar seem to be eye-fucking him. He's not buff, but he's not super skinny, either. The second he notices Bri, a sinister smile plays across his face, blinding me with the sexiest dimples I've ever seen. He walks over to her, but not before I catch him smirking at Asher.

Meanwhile, at the opposite end of the bar, Asher is shooting daggers at the man. Oh, poor Asher. He wants Bri, but she's not giving him the time of day.

A laugh escapes my lips right as I see someone head toward me out of the corner of my eye. I'm preparing myself to turn down anyone who hits on me, so I take a defensive stance. When they come into full view, my face turns into a scowl. *Giselle.* The last person I wanted to see when I was trying to rid myself of thoughts of Cas.

"Well, look who it is," she purrs.

"Giselle," I murmur while looking back at the bar. She follows my gaze and lets out the most villainous laugh I've ever heard. She condescendingly pats my hand before opening her stupid mouth.

"Honey, if you can't get a man like Cas, what makes you think you can get someone like him?" Her words ooze liquid venom. I want to snarl at her, but I refrain, knowing that's what she wants.

As if that statement wasn't enough, she leaned in and whispered, "It was my name Cas screamed. I know how to make him come. I don't think I can say the same for you. Maybe I should visit your friend Cas. Go for a repeat performance." She smirks.

Before I can say anything, Giselle is falling backward. "Got a problem?" Bri asks.

Giselle turns toward Bri and looks down her nose at her. "It's none of your business, *Brianna*. I was telling your *friend* here to stay away from what's mine." Giselle all but snarls Brianna's name. Giselle is an azalea—pretty on the outside and deadly on the inside. She gives off bitch pheromones. Giselle's gaze glides up and down Brianna's body like she's scoping out her competition.

"Oh, Giselle, it's been a while. I can see you're still a bitch who likes to cause drama for the fun of it. If you think any of the guys you hook up with actually want you, you're fooling yourself. They see you as a fuck and dump. No man will ever actively choose you," Bri snarls. I'm momentarily stunned by Giselle's sharp intake of breath and the brief look of what appears to be hurt. The guilt I feel—despite Giselle being an awful person—is brief when she decides to open her mouth. The curse of empathy, we even feel bad for the assholes.

"Funny, that's not what Asher said the other day. Pity someone with your, well, *curves,* can't land a man. I mean, some men are into plus-sized women, so I'm sure you *could* find one." Giselle's smile rivals Maleficent's, while Bri's scowl could cause anyone to burst into flames. Giselle dramatically flips her glossy, blonde tresses while wiggling her fingers before shoulder checking Bri on her way out.

Bri snarls at her back before turning to me. "Hey, Ave, are you okay? You know she's just being a bitch, right?"

Giselle's bitchiness killed our happy vibes, so we paid our tab and exited the bar. We head back towards Bri's car in complete silence. I'm so in my head about the conversation with Giselle that Bri has to slap my arm to get my attention.

"Huh?" I ask.

"I asked if you were okay. You know Giselle was doing that on purpose, right? She's a real snake." Bri's concern warms my heart. God, I love this girl.

"Yeah, I guess—Giselle's on a power trip or something. I'm not sure why she's so mean to me. Before tonight, I've only interacted with her outside of Cas' house."

"It's because she's jealous. She hates her own damn life, so she goes and destroys other people. She's the type of girl who peaked in high school. Trust me, I went to school with her. I was even friends with the bitch. She's fucking awful."

"You went to school with her? Wait, you were friends with her?" My face shows my shock and my voice comes off incredulous. *How did I not know this?*

"Ugh, unfortunately. I don't know how I was ever friends with her. Giselle was always a nasty bitch. I tried to forget about her the second I left high school. She hasn't left her petty bullshit behind. Seriously, Ave, Giselle isn't someone to stress about. You have to focus on you and Cas, and what's happening there. What *is* going on between you two?"

I relay our conversation while she listens. I tell her about my demands and the regrets I'm battling with. I tell her about Cas' radio silence and my fears that he's changed his mind.

"I don't think he's changed his mind, Ave. He's probably trying to figure out how to make it clear he's trying. Girl, that boy would do anything for you. You verbalized your expectations, and I'm proud of you. As much as you want to go back to him and say screw it, don't. Hold your ground and let him come to you. If you're tired of going in circles with him, you need to stick to this. Trust yourself because you know what you're doing," she says.

I nod in agreement and put her words aside to mull over later.

"Omg, wait. How are you feeling about what Giselle said? I don't believe Asher hooked up with Giselle. He's way too into you to do something that stupid," I say, watching as a kaleidoscope of emotions plays across her face. Bri can deny it all she wants, but deep down, there's something there with Asher. But, of course, Bri being Bri, she just shrugs it off.

"Asher can hook up with whoever he wants. I could give two shits about what that man does and who he does it with." Bri's voice sounds sure, but her body language screams otherwise. Her shoulders curl into themselves, and you can feel a hint of defeat and disappointment radiating off her body. I let it drop for now, knowing there's a time and place for pushing Bri.

We ended up at another bar down the road from Aces and had a blast. Unlike Aces, this bar has karaoke, a personal fave of mine. So, while Bri flirts with every man in the bar, I'm on stage giving the performance of my life. Bri often asks me why I can sing karaoke without a problem, but when it comes to my own music, I freeze. And every time I tell her that my songs are a representation of what I'm feeling and going through. Sharing those with the world is equivalent to someone being able to read my every waking thought. Plus, I'm not bearing myself to the world when I sing *Ironic* by Alanis Morissette.

At some point in the evening, someone puts out a tip jar and I end up making a hundred and fifty dollars. I plan to take that money and donate to my local rehabilitation center for addictions, something I've been doing for years. I normally donate a good chunk of my paycheck to different organizations each month, but for obvious reasons, substance abuse issues are near and dear to my heart.

I think about Cas and everything that went down. A huge part of me wants to forgive everything. But if I want things to change with Cas, I need to put myself first.

Chapter 17

Avery

Best friend bootcamp item one: play at the playground.

NINE WEEKS. IT'S BEEN nine weeks and I'm still waiting on Cas. *Men.* You set boundaries with them and they get butt hurt. My feet move around the kitchen in a frustrated blur when a knock interrupts me mid-stride. I make the short walk from the kitchen to the front door. When I open it, Cas is on the other side.

His hair is an unkempt mess like he's been running his fingers through it. One wavy tendril rests against his forehead and my fingers ache to touch it. He's dressed in a navy shirt, black jeans, and his favorite black Converse. My gaze travels upwards and notice he has an adorably nervous smile on his face. Cas taking his time has been fueling my anxiety. Maybe he didn't forgive me for all the hurtful things I said to him. Maybe the damage is done and there's no coming back from it. My mind keeps spiraling, but then Cas' words snap me out of it.

"I know. I took my time. I'm sorry. I've wanted to come so many times in the last month—"

"But?" I interrupt. My anxiety sits heavy in my throat as I wait for his response.

"I took what you said seriously. I spent a lot of time coming up with a plan to show you that this time is different. That I'm different. My trash can is an avalanche of one bad idea after another. Everything had to be perfect because you deserve to know how much you mean to me," he says.

Damn it, my heart is swooning. Why does Cas have to be so charming and considerate?

I let out a long sigh before speaking. "I'm sorry. I jumped to conclusions. You gotta admit, two months is a long time to wait for someone. I thought you...I thought you changed your mind..."

"I would never change my mind, but I get why you thought that. I promise I didn't mean to take so long. I went to Asher for advice on how to get you back. Well, after he chewed my ass out for my toxic behavior. Remind me not to get on his bad side." Cas laughs while rubbing the back of his neck—a tell that he's nervous.

"Asher Larson?" I ask, completely stunned.

"Yeah. He said you knew him," Cas responds.

"Oh I do. I just didn't realize you guys were friends."

"It surprised me too. The amount of times he kicked my ass out of his bar, I thought he'd always hate me. He's a good dude. He told me I fucked up with you one too many times. He told me to get my head out of my ass and remind you of what our friendship used to look like."

"Smart man. So, why are you here?"

"Got any plans right now?"

"No, I—" was all I got out before he dragged me to his car. "Wait, where are we going? Am I even dressed okay? What's going on?" My questions are coming out in rapid succession.

"You're *always* dressed okay. We're going to the park like we used to," he says matter-of-factly.

"The park? Wait, why?" I ask, dumbfounded.

"All part of my plan to fix our friendship," he repeats as if I should know what that means. I notice a piece of paper in Cas' other hand. My attempt to read what it says fails because he quickly tucks the piece of paper into the pocket of his jeans. My frustration only lasts a second when I see the giant grin on his face. There's this sense of determination in how he looks at me, with his hands on his hips and his face looking confident. I haven't seen Cas look like this since we were kids.

We stand in a semi-awkward silence, mostly on my end, until he chuckles before opening the passenger side door, waiting for me to get in. I do and watch as he rounds the outside of the vehicle, getting in himself. He's still wearing that goofy grin, and my heart melts like a snowman against the summer sun.

We're all buckled in when Cas moves closer to me and my mouth goes bone dry. I can feel my pulse in my throat. "What are you—" I ask before he shifts his body, grabbing something from the back. He puts it in my lap and I just sit there, ogling him. It isn't until he clears his throat that I look down. His camera?

"Wow. I haven't seen this in ages. Wh-why are you giving it to me?"

"Not giving it to you, Aves. I need you to hold onto it until we get to the park. I don't want it shifting around in the back seat." This is the second time he's used this nickname, but it doesn't make me as angry as when he first used it.

I can't help but feel conflicted about everything as we make our way to our destination. I'm desperate to believe things are different this time. That this time he'll remain sober. I've waited forever and a day for the old Cas to come back. I pine for the compassionate, kind, and loving boy who meant everything to me. But him taking his time coming to me gave all the ammo my anxiety needed to go off the rails. My heart threatens to leap out of my chest and fall at his feet, declaring my love for him. I want nothing more than to beg for him to not fall back into his old patterns, but now isn't the time. Instead, I choose to look out the window. I must have been lost in my thoughts because the sound of a throat clearing has me jolting out of my seat.

"A penny for your thoughts?" he asks.

I have two choices here: aim for total transparency or keep it all locked away.

"I'm just thinking about random stuff." I chicken out, not wanting to spoil this moment. I sneak another glance over his way and he seems nervous. His fingers rapidly tap out a beat on the steering wheel. It feels like he's purposefully avoiding my gaze.

"A penny for your thoughts, Cas?" I repeated his question back to him. I don't expect him to be honest, so his vulnerability takes me by surprise.

"I'm nervous that I'll fuck this whole plan up. I don't want to disappoint you," Cas replies.

"Oh," is all I manage to say. *Oh? That's all you can think of saying, Avery?*

Cas glances over my way. His body slumps and his eyes hint at disappointment, but it's gone as quickly as it came. Guilt threatens to slice through me like a sword, but when I open my mouth, no words come out. Cas begins talking before I can attempt to try again. "You don't want to do this, do you? Damn it. I knew this list was a stupid idea. I'll turn the car around and we can—" I stop him by gently squeezing his forearm, ignoring the jolts of electricity that flow through my veins in response.

"No, I love it! I'm impressed and touched that you'd go through all this trouble for someone like me."

"Avery. I would do whatever it takes for you. It's not because it's someone like you. It's because it's *you*," he admits. I blink back the tears that threaten to fall. I remove my hand from his arm and cradle it against my chest.

While the car may be silent, my mind is anything but. When Cas asked me what I was thinking, I wimped out. I wasn't expecting him to be so open with me. I bite my lip as I contemplate my next move. I should tell him something.

"Bri thinks I should enter a songwriting competition," I blurt out. Well, shit. That's not what I meant by sharing something honest. You went from zero to one-eighty with that tidbit. I peek out the window. I try to gauge if I could tuck and roll safely without injuring myself, but we aren't going slow enough for that. So, being the masochist that I am, I look at Cas to get a read on his thoughts. Cas's silence is deafening while my anxiety shouts through a megaphone. He doesn't say anything the rest of the drive. I shift in my seat to stare numbingly out the windshield, my hands folded neatly into my lap.

We pull up to the park and Cas practically leaps out of the car. My freeze response has kicked in. It isn't until Cas knocks on the passenger side window that I realize I'm under the safety of the seatbelt. I let out a soft sigh before unbuckling my seatbelt and opening the car door. I place the camera on the vehicle's floor, and the second my feet touch the ground, his arms wrap around my waist like a boa constrictor. He's spinning me in circles, sending jolts of shock and electricity to buzz throughout my body.

"I'm so proud of you! Please tell me you're entering because people need to hear your voice." His giddiness is contagious, and I can't help but throw my head back and laugh.

"Cas put me down. I don't think you want me puking all over you." My voice is a mix of laughter and shouting. Can someone laugh-shout? Well, I just did. He eventually stops spinning me, and his hands move from my waist to my shoulders.

"I'm serious. I want you to think about this. Think of the lives you'll change with your voice. Before you say you aren't good enough, just promise me you'll do it," Cas begs.

Cas hits me with a pleading expression. He could ask me anything at this moment and I'd say yes. He has this effect on me. Despite our ups and downs, I want to do everything to make him happy. Insecurity usually threatens to play its mind control games with me, but with Cas, they're silent. I need to trust my abilities, but having Cas believe in me makes it easier. With him by my side, I can be the fearless woman he claims to see.

Cas reaches out to tuck a piece of hair behind my ear before leaning in. His hot breath against my ear causes a tingling between my legs, making me press my thighs together.

I'm not sure what I thought he planned on saying, but it wasn't this. "Wanna race?" he asks. But before I can answer, he takes off running.

"Cheater!" I shout at his retreating back before running after him. The sound of his laugh has me momentarily stunned. Damn, I didn't realize how much I had missed hearing his laugh until now.

When Cas shouts at me to move my ass, I realize I'm supposed to be chasing after him. Cas is already halfway to the swings. I take off after him, quickly closing in on the distance between us. Without giving it much thought, I jump on Cas' back, causing us to come crashing down. It feels like we're recreating the scene where Simba jumps onto Nala after they reunite.

We roll around in the grass, but instead of it being soft, it's dry, almost hay-like. From an outsider's perspective, we probably look like animals rolling around in a barn. I find myself hovering above him, with his hands gripping my waist. My attempt at escaping from his clutch fails. Within seconds he reverses our positions with the swiftness of a pro wrestler, knocking the breath out of me. Thank God no one else is here as we lie on top of each other in the park. The desire in Cas' eyes makes my blood heat, and my body pulses like the bass in a car. His hand reaches out toward my face and my body stiffens.

Um, what is he doing? Is he going to kiss me? Holy shit, it's going to happen. Does my breath smell bad? It's not like I can check without giving myself away. My eyes flutter closed and my lips part automatically. This is the moment I've been waiting for. *Remain calm, Avery.* It's not like you're a terrible kisser. Wait, what if he thinks you're a lousy kisser? Ugh, the embarrassment alone will be devastating. Instead of cupping my face, his fingers briefly brush my hair before pulling back, taking the excitement with him and leaving disappointment in its wake.

My eyes snap open in time to catch him licking his lips as he stares at mine. I hold my breath, waiting for Cas to make his move. The moment disappears as quickly as it comes, and discontentment weighs heavy in my chest.

Cas clears his throat before showing me a leaf. "You, uh, had this in your hair." His voice comes out rough and gravelly. He cages my head between his forearms, locking us in a sexually charged version of the try not to blink game. If I moved just the slightest bit, our noses would touch. I could make a move.

I'm giving myself a mini pep talk internally while Cas stares at me with a heat so intense it threatens to give me third-degree burns. I momentarily lose my breath as his eyes drop toward my mouth for the second time. I just want to grab his face and pull him toward me, but that seems aggressive. Our bodies are so close that I can feel the sledgehammer pulse beating inside his chest. His eyes meet mine and I jut my chin out, giving him the green light to rip the cord of tension and put his mouth on mine. Just as I think he's about to grant my wish, his entire body tenses. Cas' heart rate spikes dangerously, thrumming in his neck, and his eyes flit past our intertwined bodies while searching for something or maybe someone. I squirm beneath him, hoping to glimpse what he's looking at.

Cas's attention snaps back to me and his expression goes from intense to playful in less than two seconds. He's jumping off of me, taking the warmth with him.

"Stay right there!" he yells before returning to his car. I'm just lying on the ground wearing a dumb look. I try to get up, but Cas shouts to stay still as he runs back toward me with his camera in hand. All I hear are the sounds of my heart thudding and quick shutters. I love watching Cas' eyes shine with passion as he takes photos. With all the different angles and him moving this way and that, it's easy to get lost. He clicks the camera again, and his face changes when he looks at the photo. Cas' throat bobs and his eyes darken slightly. Before my brain can compute the look he gave, Cas slings the camera around his neck, yanks me to my feet, and moves us toward the swings.

I'm still in my head, attempting to decipher the look he gave me when Cas pushes me toward one of the swings. Cas is a jungle gym kind of guy, so the fact that he wants to put my favorite before his own has my heart soaring with happiness. That's one thing Cas excelled at when we were kids, going above and beyond to make me happy.

Snapshots of Cas and I playing at the park during our childhood flutter around in my mind. No matter how often I asked him why we didn't do what he wanted first, he'd shrug it off like it wasn't a big deal. After about the fifth time I asked, he caved and said he loved how my face lit up whenever I was on the swings.

Being a full-grown adult sitting in the swing hits differently. The seat is snug and uncomfortable as it hugs my hips. I don't remember the rubberized tire tread of the swing being this cold. The silver chains holding the swing in place are more difficult to grasp onto and one wrong move of your fingers and you'll get pinched. The smell of freshly laid mulch causes my nose to scrunch in distaste. I don't remember it smelling this badly. It's not the same as when I was a child, but I don't care. I close my eyes and just let go.

"I almost forgot how much I loved feeling like I was flying." I pump my legs faster and faster, going as high as I can while listening to the creaking sound of the chains. I open my eyes to see if I'm going higher than him, but he must have stopped swinging a while ago. He's sitting there with the same expression he had earlier.

"Why are you staring at me like that? Come on, start swinging with me," I say.

He shakes his head, reaches for his camera, and snaps one, this time only taking one photo. He momentarily stares at the electronic viewfinder on his camera before his gaze meets mine. His expression holds something I'm not used to seeing from him: lust mixed with what seems like awe.

Cas clears his throat before speaking, "I love watching you swing. You're face lights up and you...you look beautiful and carefree. I missed that." The emotion in his voice causes butterflies to swirl in my stomach. I forgot how *affectionate* he can be sometimes, and his words threatened to pull me into his orbit.

Thanks to his little confession, I am no longer swinging as high as I was. He jumps out of his swing to stand behind mine to grip my chains. Even if I didn't see him move with my eyes, my body would have felt his presence instantaneously. Goosebumps break out across my skin and my body hums with sexual tension. Then he started pushing, which only amplified my senses. It's like I'm in one of those sensory deprivation tanks. Every time his hands press against my back, tingles shoot throughout my body, leaving me wanting and breathless. He then rushes to the front of the swing to push me some more, but this time, his hands are near my hips. Heat begins to pool between my legs, and even though there's a slight breeze in the air, I feel hot.

"Oh my god. Remember when we used to run around to the other side before the swing beat us there? I loved doing that." He laughs, causing that flutter in my belly to increase.

I nod my head as words fail me. Of course, I remember. I just don't remember it ever being this intense. The tension in the air is a taut bowstring, and I can't help but wonder if he feels it, too. He's in front of me again, stopping my swing instead of pushing me, causing my body to slam into his. He places his hands atop mine. My eyes lock onto his face and his expression causes my entire body to shiver. He stares at my mouth and I bite my bottom lip in response. Cas's throat bobs and his chest heaves as my lips to part on their own accord. He's finally going to kiss me. I've wanted to do this since I was fourteen.

I clear my throat, breaking the tension, and he jumps back as if my body is a taser. I immediately miss the warmth of his hands on mine. I need to speak before something happens that we can't take back.

"Want to go to the jungle gym?" I say, wanting to extend our time here as much as possible. When he shakes his head no, disappointment washes over me.

"I think we should probably head home. I should get you home before the park closes and the cops come and kick us out," he says.

"Oh, okay, that makes sense." I can't bring myself to look into his eyes. I have this sudden urge to cry and don't want to do it in front of him, especially because there's no real reason for them.

Of course, he knows something's up. Cas waits for me to look at him, but I refuse. "Avery, please look at me." I shake my head. The tears that threatened to come are now pouring out of my eyes. "Avery," he tries again. When I look into his eyes, I expect him to say something, but he just brings me into his arms and holds me. He strokes my hair while whispering comforting words.

"God, I don't know why I'm crying. It's, well, we haven't done this in so long and it's bringing so many feelings. I-I don't want this to end," I say, tightening my grip.

"You don't want what to end? This moment or our friendship?" he asks.

"Both. I don't want you to go away again. I loved doing this with you today. It reminded me of how it felt to be carefree, like when I was a kid. I forgot about it until you reminded me. So, I guess I'm trying to say thank you for today."

Cas lets out a soft sigh. "Avery, I can't say I'm sorry enough times for what I put you through. I'm not going to be perfect at this, and I'm guaranteed to fuck up, but I'm willing to try. Seeing you smile does something to me. I'm not sure I can explain it yet. It's the best feeling in the world, making you happy. But it's getting dark and I don't want us to get in trouble."

"Okay," I respond. We stand there for a few more moments, neither wanting to let go. Then something that happened earlier comes into my head, and I'm asking the question before thinking it through. "Cas?" I ask.

"Hmm," he responds.

"What happened earlier? When we were, uh, on the ground. You were with me one minute, and you were somewhere else the next." I bite my lip and try to control my rapid breathing. I'm not sure why my body is reacting this way, but that moment spooked me a little.

"Oh, uh, nothing. I thought I saw something weird. It's nothing." His words say one thing, his body language says another. I know Cas isn't telling the truth, but I let it go for now.

We reluctantly pull out of our embrace and head towards the car. I look back at the swings and smile. New memories hold hands with the old ones in my head, and the person next to me is responsible for it all. Today reminds me of how we used to be and how we can be. I peek in his direction and notice him writing on that piece of paper from earlier with a massive grin before putting it back in his pocket. I can't remember the last time I've ever felt this content. I'm so content that I almost missed his reaction to something on his phone.

Chapter 18

Cassidy

It's time to talk to someone

Hɪ, ᴍʏ ɴᴀᴍᴇ ɪꜱ Cas and I'm a recovering addict. I remember that euphoric feeling of heroin hitting my system, sending dopamine pulsing throughout my body. That false sense of calm and happiness filled the tiny cracks in my system from my father's neglect. I lived off that imitation of happiness for years, never truly knowing what authentic joy felt like. Being sober, I'm experiencing things through a fresh lens. Making Avery smile yesterday, I felt the same euphoric feeling hit my system. After years of forcing myself to feel happiness, who knew I could feel it genuinely? I guess what they say is true. More often than not, people with substance issues often replace one addiction with another. If Avery and her radiant smiles are my addiction, then I'll keep doing what I can for my next hit. Because I know what withdrawal feels like, and one from her is something I don't think I'll come back from.

When I get home, my grandparents are in the kitchen. I try to contain my smile so they don't ask me any questions, but I fail miserably.

"Well, well, well. What's got you smiling like that?" my grandpa asks, lips upturned in a smirk. Before I can answer, my grandma decides to give her two cents.

"It's more like *who* has him smiling like that, and we both know who. So, you must have made up with Avery?" she questions.

Grandmothers honestly do know all. If I were participating in a try-not-to-smile challenge, I would be out within the first round. The more I try to school my face, the wider my smile becomes. My face says it all, but I want to share this moment with them.

"I took her to the park and we hung out there for a while." And before I can stop myself, I'm word-vomiting my plan to reconnect with Avery. I make sure to leave out that we almost kissed...*multiple times*. You don't want to discuss certain things with your grandparents, the almost kiss being one of them. I'm also not sure how to feel about it yet. My palms tingle with phantom heat from the feel of her hips. Every part of me wanted to kiss her at that moment, but I stopped myself. Avery might have looked like she would have welcomed my lips on hers, but she's not fully ready to trust me just yet. And kissing her would mess up my plan, no matter how much I ache for it.

After the conversation with my grandparents, I spent the remainder of my evening editing photos and putting them into a photo album. After placing them in their individual slots, my eyes honed in on one photo in particular. The sunset background perfectly complimented her fair complexion, her auburn hair contrasting perfectly against the gritty grass. She wore a shy smile and her eyes shone with raw vulnerability. She was just heart-stoppingly stunning.

On top of all that, I can't shake the thought of someone watching us from my mind. Of course, when I looked up, no one was there. Then, a text message from an unknown number and the back of my neck breaks out in goosebumps.

Unknown: You are nothing but a junkie. Just wait. Your time is coming.

This text could be from anyone. I have burned a lot of bridges in the past. But my gut tells me to keep an eye out. Something about this text feels familiar.

My grandma yells from downstairs that dinner is ready and my stomach responds with an aggressive, rumbling sound. Shit, when was the last time I ate? I head downstairs, prepared to devour whatever is in the fridge.

"Oh, Cas, your grandfather and I are leaving for a few days to stay with some friends. Try not to cause too much trouble now," my gram says while patting me on my cheek. She tosses me a knowing smirk before walking away. Before my struggles with addictions, they used to go on frequent weekend trips to their friend's house in Wisconsin. They were so concerned for my well-being that they stopped and it was a burden I carried for a while. After sitting them down one evening after dinner, I told them about said feelings and we ended up as a puddle of tears. It was very cathartic, so I'm glad they've taken it upon themselves to start these trips again.

I see that Gram made chicken parmesan for dinner—my favorite. I go to get a drink from the fridge and notice a single bottle of Heineken beer in a six-pack container. Before I came home, my grandparents got rid of all the alcohol from the house. Looks like they missed one. I grab it to throw it out, but when my hand grips the bottle, my mouth goes dry and everything goes dark. It's like I tripped into a black hole, tossed into another reality.

Goosebumps dust my entire body and a chill slithers down my spine. The room is dark except for the tiny window that lets in a small sliver of light. I walk toward it, hoping it will provide a clue as to where I am. I'm left feeling disappointed when it doesn't offer any insight. That sliver of the sunshine supplies no comfort within my body, just a strong sense of unease.

I desperately move around the room, looking for an exit, only to come up empty. It's as if I stumbled across a secret passageway, locked myself in this cold, dank room, and don't know how to get out.

During my frantic search, my breath comes out as a hiss when I stub my toe on a metal-like object. The pain continues to throb, but my curiosity outweighs the sting. My shaky hands feel for what I've run into and come across a soft, stiff-like object. When I push down on it, a loud creaking sound fills the room—a mattress. The material beneath my hand is cold, hard, and thin enough that I feel the springs poking into my skin. I snap my hand back as if the object in question pierced my skin. I hold my breath and listen for something or maybe someone. Time is at a complete standstill in the darkness and I'm unsure how long I've been standing there.

I'm about to sit down when I hear muffled voices above me. I strain my ears, trying to decipher what they're saying. The hair on the back of my neck stands on end. Something about them feels familiar. My stomach feels like I have drunk spoiled milk while hot lava swirls inside my body. My heart rate beats dangerously fast and my breathing becomes irregular. I don't know where I am or how I got here, but I need to get the hell out. My arms become tingly and I feel like I'm about to pass out.

Present day, Summer of 2023

A soft touch on my shoulder jolts me back into reality. My ears are ringing and I hear the faint sound of glass smashing somewhere in the distance. Panic is still bubbling in my throat. I frantically search for the source of the sound, only to notice I'm back in the safety of my kitchen. The feelings I experienced in that dark room still lingered. I let out a shaky breath and see my grandmother looking at me worriedly.

"Cas, what's the matter? You don't look so good." Her words shake with concern, her eyes wide with fear.

Bile rises in my throat. I bolt to the bathroom before I empty my stomach's contents on the kitchen floor. My world feels like I'm hanging upside down on the monkey bars. I can't catch my breath. I rush into the bathroom and start dry heaving in the toilet. After a while, I lie down, allowing the bathroom tiles' coolness to calm me down. My gram's concerned voice sounds muffled, as if my body is submerged underwater. My mouth opens and closes like a fish as I force words out, but I can only manage a whimper. I hear her retreating footsteps and push myself into a sitting position to check if the sickness has passed. I'm getting ready to push myself off the floor when I hear a knock.

"Cas, honey. I have ginger ale and crackers for you. Can I come in?" I nod my head before realizing she can't see me. I have zero energy to walk toward the door to let her in, so I slither over and twist the knob, swinging the door open. I take the ginger ale first, chugging it down. I'm grateful for the cold carbonation sliding down my throat. I take the crackers from her next and focus on bringing small bites to test my stomach. I eat the rest when I realize I won't be sick anymore.

"Cas, what happened? I came back downstairs and you were just staring into the fridge. I was coming over to yell at you for wasting electricity, but you were ice cold and clammy when I touched you. You jolted out of your skin the minute my hand landed on your shoulder, dropping whatever you were holding." I try to look at things from her perspective, but only remember that dark, cold room. How did I get there? More importantly, *why was* I there?

"Gram, I-I don't know what's going on." My head falls into my hands and I focus on trying to steady my heartbeat.

"That's it. Michael and I are staying home. We'll reschedule our trip."

I snap my head out of my hands. "No. You will not cancel your trip. You deserve it. I'll be fine, I promise," I say, hoping my lack of confidence doesn't give me away.

She stares at me for a minute to see if I'm being honest before letting out a sigh. "Okay, fine, but you need to promise me something. If you have anything like this happen when we're gone, you'll call either of us. I don't care what time it is. We'll come home." She can be so demanding at times, but I can't help but love her for it.

I stand on shaky legs and practically fall into her outstretched arms, needing to wrap myself in her warmth. "I promise. If it happens again, I'll call. Now, get out of here and go have some fun." I kiss her cheek and practically push her out the door. She hesitates and looks back at me, concern etched across her face. "Seriously, go. I'll be okay." She pauses for another moment before finally walking out the door.

My eyes are heavy with exhaustion from whatever the hell just happened. I don't remember much of anything that transpired in the last five minutes, but I somehow managed to crawl into bed. I was hoping for a nice, peaceful sleep, but my mind had an ulterior motive. My sleep is restless. My mind is like one of those flip books, with each page turned to show more details of the dark room.

I wake up in the middle of the night in a cold sweat from a vivid nightmare. I peek at the time on my phone through slanted eyes and see it's 2:00 a.m. My entire bedding is tossed haphazardly onto the floor, and when I bend down to pick them up, they're entirely damp. I do a quick smell check to see if I'd had an accident, but thankfully, they just reek of sweat. Sleep is out of the question for the rest of the night, so I grab all the sheets and blankets and bring them to the wash.

I'm not sure what's going on or why it's happening. It all feels so sudden. Why now? Every time I close my eyes, I transport back into that dark room with the soft murmurs of voices. I have no idea where I was or who they were, but something in my gut tells me it's not good.

I feel numb. My body has locked out all happy feelings and thrown away the key. Even my day with Avery doesn't bring me joy. I'm supposed to have plans with her later this week, but the desire to crawl under my blankets and hide is strong.

I have to wait for the blankets to finish washing, so I do what I can to distract myself. I head upstairs to deep clean my room. I'm engrossed in this unpleasant task when my hand grazes across a familiar, red folder. I flip through it and stumble upon the referrals page. My former therapist listed five mental health professionals in my area who specialize in trauma. *Trauma?* Why would he put those referrals in here? I don't have any trauma. I'm fine, everything's fine. It was just one bad dream. It's not going to happen again.

Little did I know that these nightmares would be happening for the next few weeks. Every time I close my eyes, wishing for sleep to take me, my nightmare demons come knocking instead, wanting to play. The scene mostly stays the same, except for a few new fun little features I didn't ask for. Despite how many times I've entered whatever alternate reality this is, I still can't find the damn door.

I pull back from everyone, not wanting to burden anyone with my problems. I have zero energy and have barely showered in the last few weeks. Avery has stopped by the house a few times, but my grandparents told her I'm not up for visitors right now and I'll call when ready. Shutting her out makes me feel guilty, but my depression has me in a chokehold. She probably thinks I don't care about her or that I'm brushing her off, and that thought alone makes the guilt intensify.

Another week goes by and things aren't getting any better. I notice my cravings for drugs and alcohol have increased. I hate feeling this way, but I hate myself more for wanting to fall back into old habits. My eyes flicker toward the red folder that sits on my dresser. It's time for things to change. I grab the folder and head downstairs. My grandparents are drinking coffee in the kitchen. When they notice me standing in the entryway to the kitchen, they give me matching questioning looks.

"I think I need to start talking to someone. My former therapist gave me this before my discharge and it has a list of therapists in there. I didn't think I would need one, but whatever's going on with me isn't improving." I let out a long breath and await their responses.

They glance at each other and my grandfather is the first to speak. "Okay," is all he says. My grandfather isn't a man of many words, but his "okay" is enough. I looked at the list and settled on someone named Dr. Z. I made the call and set up my first appointment before losing my courage. A sense of pride swells in my chest and I pray that this next step will provide the answers I seek. Now, it's time to face Avery. I've been avoiding her for weeks and need to go over and apologize again. I sigh and head to her place, hoping she won't slam the door in my face, no matter how much I might deserve it.

Chapter 19

Avery

Best friend bootcamp item two: go to the dock

I haven't seen Cas in a month. I've gone to his house only to have his grandparents tell me he isn't doing well. I don't understand his radio silence. Reflecting on our time at the park, I can't find any logical reason for his absence.

A knock on the door pulls me from my anxious stupor and déjà vu ripples down my spine. I knew who would be standing on the other side. Cas is dressed in a white tank top and colorful swim trunks with a towel draped over one shoulder, his camera bag on the other. His smile doesn't reach his eyes and intuition tells me something's wrong. I don't have much time to think about what's off about him before he starts speaking.

"I know. I fucked up again. This month has been really hard, but that doesn't excuse my behavior. I told you that this time was different and I pulled a disappearing act. I'm—" But I put my hand up to stop him from continuing.

"It's okay if you don't want me in your life, Cas. I can handle it." I look down, not wanting to meet his eyes. The sound of the towel hits the ground with a soft thud, and within a matter of seconds, his arms wrap around me enveloping me in the smell of fresh pine.

"No, Avery, just, no. This was all me. I haven't been myself this last month. My grandparents weren't lying when they said I wasn't doing well. I didn't know what was going on with me. I still don't. I couldn't bear bringing you into my drama. I've already done that to you enough in this lifetime. No one should have to see me like that. I didn't even want to see me like that."

I've really come into my own, but sometimes I need reassurance. The word reassurance and I are new friends. I always thought that needing a little extra comfort made me too needy. Looking at it from that viewpoint, though, really stunted my personal growth. One time in therapy, Olivia gave me some homework to start asking for reassurance from those I love. She said it would be easiest to do it with those I felt safe with. So, I began to practice with Bri as well as my boss, Tanya, and little by little I was able to do it. Granted, there's always room for improvement, but I'm proud of myself for how far I've come. With Cas, it might be awhile. Our friendship is still fragile and new, so I just need to let whatever happens happen and hope I can continue to improve on asking for what I need.

"Cas..." My voice comes out in a whisper. My fingers touch the crease between his brows, attempting to smooth out the worry.

Cas stares at me, looking like he wants to tell me something. The moment passes as quickly as it begins, and he's suddenly pulling out of the embrace with a smile back on his face. "Today isn't about my fucked-up life, though. Today ."

"Cas, listen to me. You can talk about it with me. You know I won't judge you. Whatever's holding you back from letting me in, I promise you I'll still be here," I say, unable to let it go.

"Avery, please just drop it. I don't want to talk about it now. Please?" I would have kept pleading for him to let me in, but something in his eyes told me it wasn't the time to push him.

"Okay, so will you tell me why you're dressed like that?" I wave my hand up and down at the ridiculousness of his outfit.

"We're going to the dock, freckles. Remember when we used to make silly names for jumps and had competitions for who could make the biggest splash?" His fake smile is replaced with a genuine one and I mirror his expression. My heart warms when I think about how special the dock is for me, for us. Whenever I fought with my parents or needed space, I would go to the water and sit with my feet dangling off the edge. Cas would often join me, and we would sit in comfortable silence.

"Oh, I remember how those crazy jumps all started. A certain *someone* pushed me in the water with all my clothes on before calling out a ridiculous name and jumping in after me," I say with a playful punch to his shoulder.

"I have no idea what you're talking about. I would *never* do something like that. You must have me confused with someone else. Are you planning on changing into your swimsuit, or do I have to drag you down there in what you're wearing?"

I roll my eyes because he would *totally* throw me over his shoulder and toss me into the water with what I have on. I run upstairs and search for the perfect outfit. Not that I care what he thinks. I'm *definitely* not hoping to get a reaction out of him. Still, I have no idea what to wear.

I pull out my phone to FaceTime Bri and pray she answers quickly. She picks up on the third ring.

"What's up?"

My words come out quick and frantic. "I need your help. Cas showed up and we're going swimming by the dock." Lucky for Bri, she's used to this by now.

"You need to look hot, got it. Okay, show me what we're working with." I choose to ignore her taunting because I'm pressed for time. I show her at least five suits before Bri shouts her approval at one in particular. In my hand is a black one-piece with a cris-cross pattern down the front exposing the middle of my stomach. There's also little to no material in the back to cover my ass. I put it on and then propped the phone up so she could get a glimpse.

"Of course this is the suit you choose. My ass is practically out, Brianna," I exclaim.

"Exactly. Now go and knock him dead, which won't be hard to do with that outfit," she says before hanging up. I go into my closet and pull out a white, oversized t-shirt to cover up before heading down.

"Alright, I'm ready." Cas grabs my hand and I bite my lip to stifle a gasp. Goosebumps cover my entire body and it takes effort not to shiver. This happens every time he touches me.

We make it to the dock and my heart flutters with memories of doing this as kids. Back then, we had the innocence of childhood and we could care less about each other's swimsuits. I refuse to let any doubt linger past a few seconds. I look good and I know it. Back in high school, I looked like a twig and I hated it. Since then, I've been blessed with subtle curves and I am owning it.

Cas has already taken off his shirt and shoes, and I can't help but ogle his body. My eyes play pinball with his six pack abs and I can feel my fingers tingle with the urge to leave possessive claw marks.

His golden skin glows beneath the sun's rays and I notice little beads of sweat forming, causing my mouth to crave something salty. His chest alone could make any girl weak in the knees. I've been wrapped up in those arms hundreds, if not thousands of times, but seeing them completely bare has me clenching my thighs together. I groan internally as I stare at his tattoos. Tattoos in general are sexy. But tattoos on Cas? My hormones don't stand a chance.

Cas has a full sleeve of random designs that probably tell some story, but my eyes are laser-focused on one tattoo in particular. On his right hand is a tattoo of a flower. Not just any flower though, is that...is that a lavender lily? How did I miss that? Is that tattoo new? My vision begins to blur as my mind tries to process why he would get my favorite flower tattooed on him. I rapidly blink away the tears and continue ogling this beautiful man. His body looks like it belongs on one of the covers of Bri's ever-growing collection of erotica novels. Just give the man an ax or a rope, and boom, you'll sell millions of copies.

My eyes travel further down his body towards the sexiest legs I've ever seen. Seriously, he could probably split a watermelon in half with those thighs. Then there are his calf muscles. Glorious, delicious, strong calf muscles send a fresh wave of lust throughout my body. Who knew legs could be so damn sexy?

How is it legal for someone to just look like *that?* I want to walk over to him, lick him from the delicious V of his hips to his neck, making tiny bites along the way. Shit! No. I can't think like that. This is Cas, he's my friend.

I hear him clear his throat. "My eyes are up here, Avery." My face and neck feel hot, and I know I'm as red as a tomato. *Take a deep breath in, then out,* I repeat to myself. My eyes meet his and he's staring at me, arms folded over his chest with a smirk.

"So, you going to change out of your shirt or are you planning to swim like that?" he taunts. I smirk, knowing that when I take off my shirt, his eyes will bug out of his head.

I turn around, knowing full well my ass is out for the world to see. The second I whip my shirt off I hear him groan behind me. I throw a smirk over my shoulder and see him staring at me with the same hungry look he had at the park, but slightly more intense. I turn around, smiling. I *know* that look is far from platonic.

Cas makes a slow sweep of my body, stopping at my chest, and he licks his lips.

"Hey, Cas, my eyes are up on my face, not my boobs," I say, giving him a taste of his own medicine.

"Huh?" He's clearly still distracted.

"Let's just get in the water, hotshot." I shake my head and walk past, fully intending to get in the water, but then an idea strikes. My eyes flick toward Cas to find him still distracted by my breasts. A distracted Cas is perfect for what I plan to do. I didn't hesitate before running full speed at him, but I guess he wasn't as distracted as I thought because he suddenly grabbed and tossed me in. *Asshole!*

"Nice try," he says as soon as I surface. Cas sets up his camera and I hear rapid shutter sounds. I have a scowl on my face from him throwing me in, but of course, he just laughs at me before jumping in himself. "Typewriter," he calls while still in the air, mimicking the motion.

I try to swim away to avoid the splash, but he's too quick. He grabs me by the ankles and pulls me back, and I end up slamming into his back. His hands circle my waist and a gasp escapes from my mouth. His breath was a cool breeze on a hot summer night. The kind that sends a shiver throughout your body, making you pull your jacket tighter. "You cold?" he asks. I shake my head and try to swim away. His hold tightens around me and I can feel his reaction to my body. I barely resist the urge to rub myself against him when he whispers in my ear, "You just had to wear that suit, didn't you?" When I turn my head back to face him, we are so close our noses are practically touching. I close my eyes and my lips part naturally, ready for him to make his move. But then he pulls his head back and spins me around so we are chest to chest. The sound of the camera disappears into the background, he must have done some sort of continuous shutter setting.

"You have no idea how much you affect me. I don't know what to do about it. Hell, I don't even know how to feel about it." If we were standing on land, this confession would have knocked me off of my feet. I'm not sure what to say right now. The air between us is so charged that it's hard to breathe. Finally, his grip on me loosens and I swim towards the dock to get some distance.

"Did I do something wrong?" He follows my lead and swims back to the dock.

"No. I just can't think while you're touching me." I grab my towel so I can lie down and process everything. Of course, he does the same thing and plops his towel next to mine. He turns the camera off before plopping down next to me, our hands only inches apart.

"God, you're beautiful," he says, completely taking my breath away. *Well, that was random.* My face turns shy and I try to hide behind my hands, but he grips my wrist before I can do anything.

"Seriously, you are. It's more than just your looks. It's every single thing about you. But what I love the most is your heart. It's so genuine and open. It's probably why you're so talented at songwriting. You can tap into your feelings and words just seem to pour out of you. It's something I both envy and admire about you. Which reminds me. Have you given any more consideration to the songwriting competition?"

I blink rapidly, trying to process everything he's said. Doubts fall down like rain in the middle of a thunderstorm. If he knew the real reason for my hesitation, our conversation would be very different.

"I uh-no, I haven't," I respond honestly.

"Why?" he asks, a scowl etched across his face.

"I'm not-I can't—I just can't. I don't think I can do it. I'm not very good at—" The look on his face stops me cold.

"Avery. I don't ever want to hear you say you aren't good enough. You understand?" I flinch at his words, surprised at how angry he got at such a small thing. I remain silent, causing him to repeat my name. "Avery, did you hear me?"

"Y-yes, I heard you. I won't say it anymore," I stutter.

"Good, now let me hear you shout My name's *Avery, and I am a damn fantastic writer.*"

"I don't—" I begin to say, but the fire in his eyes has me changing the direction of my words. "My name's Avery, and I am a damn fantastic writer," I whisper.

"Good, now louder and like you mean it!" he shouts.

"My name's Avery, and I am a damn fantastic writer!" I shout, causing both of us to laugh. God that felt good to say. We laugh until we can't breathe. Within a matter of seconds, the energy goes from playful to intense.

My gaze drops down to our hands. Cas' eyes follow mine and he extends his pinky out. His eyes meet mine and I know what he wants to ask, but I can tell he's afraid to vocalize it. I obliterate his indecision by intertwining my pinky with his. I tug on his pinky three times, to which he then tugs back three times. The pinky tug thing was something we did as kids when we needed to let the other know we were there. Doing this now as an adult only makes it that more special. The only difference is now, this small touch causes my whole body to ignite. We stay there, gazes locked and pinkies intertwined for the next hour or so. I remove my pinky from his only to run my fingers across the tattoo on his hand, causing his hand to flex. A frown forms across my face as I try to find the best way to ask about the meaning.

"Just ask, Avery." He laughs.

"Did you, um, why did you get this?" I can't seem to meet his gaze, the nerves in my stomach are the snow in a recently shaken snow globe.

"Avery, look at me." When I still haven't looked up, he tilts my chin with his hand. "You know why," he says.

"It's my favorite flower," I whisper.

"I know, and you're my favorite person."

I could get used to these intimate moments with Cas. I look away first and close my eyes, bathing in the sun's rays. I'm completely and utterly content, and it doesn't have anything to do with the sun or swimming.

"Hey, Ave?" Cas asks.

"Yeah?" I respond

"Being with you. Spending time with you again, it's everything to me. I know I have a long way to go to prove to you that things are different but thank you for at least giving me a chance. Especially when I know I don't deserve to take up more of your time."

"Cas. My Casanova, I just want you to see how worthwhile your life is. I want you to love and accept yourself because you're worth it. You always have been. I've known it since I was eight-years-old."

"Yeah, I remember you bulldozing your way over to me, practically knocking me down with a bone-crushing hug and claiming me as yours." Cas chuckles.

"Still one of the best decisions I've made, if I do say so myself. I tend to have good taste in friends." I blush knowing that the word 'friend' is a funny word for me. I've known for a little over a decade that Cas was it for me. No amount of dating or casual flings would ever fill the spot reserved for the man next to me.

"Let's go, freckles. It's starting to get chilly outside and I'd rather you not catch a cold," Cas says, interrupting my thoughts. Both of us are fully dry by now, so we place our clothes back on and make our way back to our houses. I assumed we would just walk side by side, talking, laughing, and reminiscing. But then Cas squats down in front of me, encouraging me to hop on his back, something we haven't done since we were kids. I let out a child-like giggle before hopping on, my legs wrapped around his waist, my arms hanging around his neck. Then Cas takes off in a sprint, jostling me this way and that. I love being around this playful, inhibited Cas, and I only hope I continue to see all the colors of his beautiful heart.

Chapter 20

Cassidy

Best friend bootcamp item three: stargazing

Mid Summer of 2023

RECONNECTING WITH AVERY HAS been everything. She's no longer this shy, little girl who would hide behind me. No, the woman before me has truly blossomed. Seeing her self-confidence shine is amazing to watch. I've done a lot to diminish her sparkle, but yet here she is, the brightest star in my universe. Everything about her is grounding for me; therapeutic, in a sense.

Speaking of therapy, it's been an integral part of my routine. An addition I'm eternally grateful for as the nightmares are now a daily occurrence. In the dreams, I'm in that same setting of the dark, dank room, but little sprinkles of details are added each night. The most recent addition to the dream is the face of a scared boy. He's no older than four, maybe five, sitting on the bed, his knees drawn to his chest attempting to shrink himself as much as possible. The more I push myself to remember, the more frustrated I become when I can't figure it out. I put a mental bookmark on those thoughts so I can focus on my current plan of action with Avery.

Most of the photos I took yesterday weren't usable except for one. We were chest to chest, our faces so close. You can feel the heat radiating off the still photo. So much so that I jerked off to that photo once or twice. Fuck, okay. Three times.

With two more items on my best friend boot camp list left, it feels like things are starting to go back to normal with Avery. That moment in the water, I slipped up by telling her how she affected me before pulling her up against me. I could swear there was a flash of hunger in her eyes, but I backed away before making a move and ruining everything. Still, I couldn't keep my eyes off her. She's always stunning. But underneath the sun's rays, she's even more breathtaking. Her skin glistens and her eyes shine. It is one thing to lay next to her, but having our pinkies interlocked robbed me of my oxygen. Who knew that such a small gesture would cause my pulse to jackhammer beneath my chest?

I'm still stuck in that memory when I hear my phone ping with incoming texts. Not again. Why the fuck does this keep happening to me?

> **Unknown: Ignore me all you want, but you can't escape me. Watch your back.**

Small black dots threaten to steal my vision, but I keep breathing through the panic. Why does this keep happening? And, more importantly, what the hell do they want from me?

I click out of the text conversation and focus on regulating my breathing. Tomorrow has to be perfect. I have already checked the weather; there is only a ten percent chance of rain, so we should be good. When we were little, Avery and I would wait for our parents to go to bed before sneaking out with a blanket and snacks to stargaze. One of the benefits of living in the suburbs is the view of the sky is typically clear of the lights and smog from the city. This all stopped when high school started, though, and my heart breaks for all those lost years. Those moments were always my favorite, which has me more nervous about recreating this memory than any of the other ones.

Shit, I need to head to the grocery store. I frantically grab my keys still revved up from the text I got and practically fall out my front door. Avery loves sweets, but she also is a sucker for salty. So I make my way down the aisles, grabbing double stuffed Oreos, flamin' hot Cheetos, watermelon Sour Patch Kids, and sour cream and onion Pringles. I also grab some sparkling water: blue raspberry for her and black cherry for me. As I prepare to head to the checkout, I run through the checklist in my head making sure all my bases are covered. Something colorful flashes in my peripherals and instincts are telling me to check it out. Alongside one of the aisles are some beaded bracelets. My fingers play with the beads as memories of giving her a similar one years ago play in my mind. One day when we were swimming, it broke off her wrist and fell into the water. We spent hours looking for it, but came up empty-handed. I'd never seen her so upset before and felt so guilty that I couldn't find it. I grab it without a second thought and make my way back towards the checkout. The bags of groceries are in my trunk, but I clutch onto the bracelet like a lifeline as I drive home with the biggest grin on my face.

I place everything I bought in the pantry and look around for something else to do. The more I keep busy, the less time I have to worry. Without my grandparents around, I have no one to take my mind off the text. I love being around my grandparents, but it's nice to have some alone time. I know they worry about me, especially when I wake up from my nightmares screaming. I try to keep everything bottled up so I'm not a burden to them. I do the same with Avery, although the more I'm around her, the more I want to let her in—but it scares me.

I need to get out of my head, so I go for a quick walk. The sun is beginning to tuck itself in for the evening setting the sky on fire. The nighttime August air is starting to cool down some, but I can still get away with a light zip-up hoodie. I fill my lungs with fresh, early evening air, allowing the crisp, earthy smell to wrap around me like a sweatshirt fresh out of the dryer. It's soothing, comforting, intoxicating. My mind is clear and my breathing is even. At this moment, I'm not a recovering addict or a fuck up. I'm just me...just Cas.

In desperate need of a nap, I start towards the direction of my house when something captures my attention. Avery sits outside with a book in one hand and a mug in the other. Every time I see her, my heart stops and my breath catches in my throat. You would think that my reaction wouldn't be as intense after years of being around her, but it happens every single time. Sensing my presence, she glances up from her book and smiles before putting her book down and lifting her hand to wave. I return the smile and wave easily, barely resisting the urge to run over and kiss her.

Her hair dances like flames underneath the setting sun. Her eyes are my night light, keeping me safe from the monsters that hide in the dark. Avery's always been that for me, my glowing light guiding me home and to safety. Avery is beauty personified. She has all of me and doesn't even know it. She returns to her book and I make my way inside so I can attempt a quick nap before tonight.

I'm nervous because I'm upping my game with the stargazing. I have everything ready for tonight. I don't want to give my plans away, but I want Avery to wear enough layers in case it gets too cold. I bring my phone out to pull up our text conversation and type what I want to say.

> **Me: Hey. Bring a sweatshirt or jacket in case you get cold. Meet me outside at 10 p.m. I think you'll like what I have planned.**

> **Avery: ...So you won't let me know what we're doing?**

> **Me: Nope, see you later.**

I chat with my grandparents for a few hours, catching up with them and seeing how their vacation is going. Despite talking to them for two hours, it still isn't time for my evening with Avery, so I do something that I dislike immensely: clean the house. Therapy this afternoon wiped me out emotionally, especially with how today's session went. My therapist challenged me left and right, calling out all my intrusive thoughts. Regardless of all of that, I was able to share some of my career and life goals with her—something I wouldn't have done even a year ago.

Sharing my personal goals with her while she sat there nonjudgmentally felt freeing. While I'm grateful my grandparents are helping me out financially so I can focus on my sobriety, I don't want to mooch off them forever. I want to be able to provide for my future self and family. Family. Avery. Those two words are forever synonymous in my heart. I wouldn't mind seeing a few mini-Avery's running around.

Being emotionally exhausted tends to put me out for the rest of the day, but cleaning and organizing everything in the house has me feeling oddly energized. Maybe it's a control thing? Or maybe it's the anticipation of getting to see Avery soon.

My phone is pinging every other second, alerting me that my group chat with Asher and Max is very active. They have been asking about the whole best friend bootcamp experiment since it started. I engage as much as I can while I continue to clean the house, and before I know it, it's almost time for the next boot camp item.

I head down to set everything up about fifteen minutes before Avery is due to arrive. This proves to work in my favor because my nervous energy that's swirling in my body makes it harder to not smush the snacks. Everything is in its place and as I walk back to my house, I glance at the time on my phone. Five more minutes to go and the nervous butterflies have only amplified.

Deep breaths, Cas. I repeat that mantra as I walk toward our meeting spot and freeze. Avery is standing there, nervously playing with her fingers. Today she's dressed in a white, cotton sundress resting just above the knees, white Keds, and a black sweater hanging over her arm. Her naturally wavy hair is down and her face is bare. If I thought she looked good in the sunlight, it was nothing compared to how she looked blanketed underneath the moon's glow.

While she's distracted, I take out my phone and snap a few photos. I normally prefer my camera, but because I was in a rush I forgot to bring it. She glances up and her smile lights up her entire face. I make my way over to her and reach out to give her a hug, but she looks down at my hands.

"What's that?" she asks, pointing to the box.

I had forgotten entirely about the bracelet the moment I saw her. My anxiety triples as my gaze shifts toward the box in my hand. I should have never bought the damn bracelet.

"It's nothing. It's stupid, really." I can't bring myself to look at her, afraid of what I'll see in her eyes.

"Is it for me?" Her voice comes out in a whisper and I nod, unable to speak. "Then it's definitely *not* stupid." She grabs the box from my limp hands and opens it. I hear her gasp, and then nothing. Complete silence. When I hear a sniffling noise, my head snaps up. The bracelet hangs limply in her hands and tears are pooling in her eyes.

"Shit. Don't worry I'll just take it back to the store. You won't have to see it anymore. I'm sorry for making you cry." I reach for the bracelet only to have her tighten her grip and shake her head.

"No, it's not that. I love it, Cas. It looks like the one you gave me when we were kids," she whimpers as tears continue to fall, but there's a soft smile on her face.

"Can you put it on me?" I nod. My hands are so shaky with nerves that it takes two tries for me to actually get the bracelet on her wrist. The rainbow beads are the perfect contrast against her peachy skin. My grip is still locked around her wrist, and like Rose from *Titanic*, I never want to let go. Bravery seems to be the theme for the day because I don't think twice about interlocking my fingers with hers and I'm rewarded with a full-on, ear to ear grin. All my anxiety whooshes out of me and I match her grin with one of my own. With her hand in mine, we walk toward the blanket and snacks. I hear her gasp before she lets go of my hand to run the rest of the way over to our setup. I miss the warmth of her hand in mine, but seeing the pure joy on her face makes up for the loss.

"You did all this for me?" She looks at the setting, completely awestruck, before turning to me.

I'd do anything for you, I think to myself. Avery beams up at me as she makes herself comfy on the blanket. I don't move to join her, content with watching her figure out which snack she wants to open first.

"Are you just going to stand there or are you going to sit down next to me?" Avery pats a spot next to her, hoping I will join her. I smile before closing the remaining distance between us to sit down beside her. My eyes flutter closed as I listen to the sounds of random snacks being opened while the crickets' songs fill my ears.

The sound of the blanket shifting and plastic ruffling has me snapping my eyes open. Avery has put aside the snacks and is now lying beside me. She reaches for my hand this time and I barely resist the impulse to bring our joined hands to my lips. My fingers play with her bracelet as we discuss our day and relive some of our favorite childhood memories. She tells me about almost getting bit in the ass by a feral cat at her job, and I can't help but chuckle. I remind her of the time a garter snake snuck into my grandparents' home. How she came barreling, tongs in hand, ready to take the snake back outside. And she graciously reminded me of the time a bird shit on my head while we were riding our bikes.

I think about my earlier conversation with my therapist and feel the urge to share it with Avery. Besides my grandparents, Avery is the only person who encourages me to push myself and chase after my dreams. I can either take the leap and share it with her, or allow my imposter syndrome to keep me as a prisoner. Okay, here goes everything.

"So, I've been thinking about my purpose in life lately. I'm glad I can spend this time focusing on my sobriety while my grandparents help me out, but I don't want to keep living that way," I say.

"I understand that. I get that way sometimes, too. I love working at the shelter, but I feel like there is more out there for me. I mean, I get to take care of all these animals and help find them forever home. But, it doesn't feel like enough sometimes. On the plus side, I get to hang out with all the kitties without feeling guilty," she replies.

"Guilty? Guilty about what?" I ask, but Avery quickly changes the conversation.

"The sky is just so pretty. I love gazing up at the stars." She no longer wants to talk about the cat, so I let it drop. I put this information into the folder marked *Avery* in my mind to access at a later time.

I go to speak, but I'm rudely interrupted when a drop hits my forehead. A few more drops fall down my face and I panic. It wasn't supposed to rain today. I begin to frantically collect everything before it gets wet. Avery helps me, and eventually, we make it up to my house with just enough time to spare before the downpour starts. I toss everything inside before walking back to meet Avery to take her home. The choice to be brave strikes again. I pull out my phone before losing the nerve. When I find the perfect song, I reach my hand toward her.

"What are you doing?" She looks down at my outstretched hand.

"Dancing with you in the rain." She hesitates only briefly before placing her hand in mine. We walk toward the grass and I spin her around twice before our bodies softly collide. One of my hands falls upon her lower back while the other is holding her hand. Our faces and bodies are pressed close together as we sway to the beginning notes of *Can't Help Falling in Love.*

Rain continues to pelt our bodies, but I'm so wrapped up in her I hardly notice. Avery snuggles into my chest as my chin rests atop her head. My thumb traces imaginary patterns across her knuckles, eliciting a soft moan that shoots through my body. The sound of Avery's unapologetic laughter as I spin her in and out is my new favorite song. She tosses her head back, lost in her bliss, providing the perfect opportunity to inhale her intoxicating scent. She gasps and her gaze snaps back to mine, our mouths mere inches apart. I let my eyes linger on her lips briefly before returning my attention to her eyes.

I place one hand against the base of her throat, feeling shivers ripple down Avery's spine. Our breathing quickens. In one swift move, I could kiss her. I shake off the thought, knowing how important it is to finish what I started before putting our hearts on the line. With great restraint, I pull back and try to ignore the flash of disappointment in her eyes. *Me too, Avery. Me too.* Within seconds, her frown is replaced with a superficial smile, and it kills me not to pull her in and kiss her. Instead, I grab her hand and walk her home. When we arrive at her house, I lean in and slowly push wet hair out of her face, committing every beautiful detail that is Avery to memory. Her eyes widen and her lips part, and I can't help but think this woman will be the death of me.

My forehead rests against hers and I feel my heart click into place. I'm completely lost in love with my best friend and I don't want to be found. My thumb strokes her cheek, the softness of her skin feels like bed sheets made of the highest quality silk. "Goodnight, Avery."

"Oh...Goodnight, Cas." Her voice comes out in a whisper. I give her hand a quick squeeze moving in the opposite direction toward my house. I glance over my shoulder to see her watching me, cradling her hands against her chest. It physically hurts to walk away without kissing her, but everything comes in time, and with Avery, the timing needs to be perfect. Because when I cross that line, there's no way I'll be able to go backward without destroying my heart.

Chapter 21

Avery

Best friend bootcamp final item: baking cookies

A SMILE HAS BECOME a permanent fixture on my face for the last twenty-four hours. I can't stop thinking about how magical last night was. The stargazing, the dancing in the rain, the fact he went out of his way to buy all my favorite snacks? Swoon! Plus, the song he chose had to be a coincidence, right? He couldn't have known about my dream with him. The most amazing part of the night lies upon my wrist. A lazy smile stretches across my face as my fingers lazily play with the beads. I remember how distraught I was when I lost the original one he gave me, so this feels extra special.

He came so close to kissing me last night. But instead of feeling blissfully happy, I'm left needy and confused. I *know* I wasn't the only one feeling the moment. At least, I don't think I was. Ugh, men. My mind is mentally pulling petals off a flower and chanting the *he wants me, he wants me not* mantra.

I'm itching to talk to Brianna about this, but I already know what she'll say: *Girl, just hurry up and make the first move already.* I roll my eyes at the thought because it's a very Bri thing to say.

I need to clear my head, so I get dressed and make my way outside to sit by the dock. My footsteps come to a halt when I see Cas already sitting there, dressed in his usual dark gray shirt and black jeans. As much as I want to be alone with my thoughts, I'm happy he's here.

"Hey, handsome," I say. His head snaps around towards me and my smile fades. His usual bright eyes are now vacant and dull. I rush over to him in a panic seeing the purple circles under his eyes and the ghostly pale of his face.

"Hey, what happened?" Cas looks up at me, all glassy-eyed with tears he's clearly holding back. As soon as my arms come around him, he completely loses it. His head is in his hands and his body violently shakes as he cries. I've never really seen him this upset before. If I listen closely, I can hear a small cracking sound inside my heart. We sat for what seemed like five minutes with me rubbing comforting circles against his back. His head is still in his hands, but his body has stopped shaking and his breathing has evened out.

"Cas." At the sound of my voice, his head comes out of his hands revealing a face that mirrors a wounded child. I place my hands on either side of his face, wiping his tears away with my thumbs. "Cas, talk to me."

"I just had a rough night. I didn't get any sleep." His head nestles in the space between my neck and collarbone.

"Oh Cas, I'm sorry. Do you want to talk about it?" He shakes his head in response and I can't help but feel a small zing of hurt. This isn't about me, though. There's a reason why he's not sharing this with me, and I just have to be patient. He needs to rest, but when I attempt to shift out of his hold, his grip tightens, locking me in place.

"Avery, please don't go. I want to tell you, I just, I don't know how to yet. And if I did tell you, it would come out as gibberish. I'm running on like three hours of sleep."

"I'm right here, Cas. I won't leave you, but I think you really need to get some sleep so," I stand up and see a look of hurt flash across his face. Cas struggles with trusting people to do what they say they're going to do. Cas is already starting to shut down, an automatic response from years of being let down. So when I reach my hand out toward him, his shoulders relax and Cas heaves a sigh of relief.

"Let's go," I say. Cas stares at my outstretched hand with a look of bewilderment.

"You need a nap. So, we're going to go to my house so you can sleep. That way, if you end up having another nightmare, I'll be right there to help you with whatever you need."

Cas eventually grabs my hand, and once he's up, he pulls me into his arms. "Thank you," he whispers. "Thank you for being here. I don't know what I did to deserve someone like you." When he clutches my hand, his heartbreaking words squeeze my heart.

Cas zombie walks toward the couch the second we're inside. I excuse myself to gather all the nap-time necessities. When I return, I'm greeted with an already passed out Cas with a scrunched up expression, almost as if he's bracing himself for the inevitable nightmare. I don't know what's going on. I just know that whatever it is has him feeling vulnerable and maybe scared? Despite how his face looks in his sleep, Cas' body takes up most of the couch. He looks lost, yet peaceful at the same time. I know the two contradict themselves, but it feels like the perfect descriptor for him at the moment. I tiptoe toward him, not wanting to rouse him, while I place a blanket on top of him. The second I place the pillow under Cas' head, though, his eyes snap open, startling me just enough to have me jump back.

"I'm sorry. I didn't mean to wake you, Cas. I was trying to give you a pillow to lay on."

"Can you—never mind." Cas' face begins to turn red and he looks away too quickly.

"Can I what?" I could hardly hear my voice behind the sound of my heartbeat in my ears. Maybe he wants me to leave him alone, or he doesn't want to be here with me in my house.

"Can you lie down with me?" His eyes look at me with the hope of a child. His question catches me off guard and I just stare at him dumbfounded. Hurt flashes across his face with my continued silence. He mistakes it for rejection because he quickly adds, "Unless you don't want to. It's okay. I'm sorry if I made you uncomfortable."

The edge of the couch makes a soft creaking noise as I sit down. I palm my hands on either side of Cas' cheeks, needing him to understand that what I'm about to say I truly mean it. "No, you didn't make me uncomfortable. You just surprised me. Of course, I'll lie down with you."

He scooches over to allow me to lie down first. Once I'm situated, Cas' head rests on my stomach, his hands hug my waist. I repeat the same circular pattern on his back as I did earlier, and within seconds, his breathing becomes steady. Even in sleep, Cas has a guarded expression on his face. Like there's something bubbling underneath the surface and it's causing him emotional pain. As I sit here rubbing his back, I can't help the tears that sting behind my eyes at the thought of him battling some tough demons. There's nothing I want more than to take them all away from him, but knowing I can't makes me feel useless. My eyes begin to feel heavy and my breathing becomes slower. I decided to rest my eyes for a few minutes.

I wake up and feel something heavy on my chest. Disoriented, I look up to see Cas wide awake and lying on top of me. Damn it! I wasn't supposed to fall asleep. I was supposed to be providing him safety in case he had another nightmare. I totally suck at this comforting thing.

"Well, good afternoon, sleepyhead," he says. I take a moment to look at his face. Gone are the bags under his eyes and his face is no longer ashen in color. Actually, he has the goofiest grin on his face, and it makes me smile knowing he's happy.

"I wasn't supposed to fall asleep with you. What kind of protector can't stay awake? Did you sleep okay? Any nightmares?" I ask.

"No, that was the best night's sleep I've had in ages. You're really warm and comfortable to cuddle with. I could get used to lying in your arms." He nuzzles my stomach and I let out a squeal.

"Stop, that tickles!" My voice comes out breathy.

"Oh, does it now?" The look he shoots me is pure mischief. Before I know what's happening, he's tickling me mercilessly. My laughter continues, eventually turning into snorts.

"Okay, okay, stop it. I can't breathe!" I scream. He stops abruptly, but his hands are spread out across my ribs. He's looking at me like I'm his favorite meal and he hasn't eaten in days. I clear my throat and shift out of his arms, needing space before I do something I'll regret.

"W-What time is it?" I ask, changing the subject.

"Time for our final adventure," he says, getting up and pulling me with him, practically dragging me towards the kitchen.

"Final adventure? What do you mean by final? Like after today, that's it, no more adventures?"

"What? No. I plan to go on a lifetime of adventures with you. It's all part of my plan." *Plan? He has a plan?*

Cas rubs a thumb between my brows, smoothing out the wrinkles that must have been there from a frown I wasn't aware of.

"All in time, Avery. All in time," Cas says with a smirk.

"Okay, captain vague. What do you mean 'all in time'?" My arms are crossed in front of me and I cock my hip to the side, causing Cas to laugh.

"Patience, freckles, patience." His words are choked out behind his laughter. Jackass.

"You ready?" His face breaks out into a playful grin.

"Ready? Ready for what, exactly? And what's with that sly grin of yours? I'm not sure how to feel about it," I say wearily. He slowly makes his way over to me with a devilish look on his face. I let out a noise that falls between a gasp and a laugh when he tosses me over his shoulder and moves toward the kitchen.

"To bake cookies," he says as he places me down on the counter, making my breath come out shaky.

"Uh, wait, what?" Clearly, words are a struggle today.

"Yes, cookies, like we used to do with your mom, remember?" he asks. I look at him. He is still somewhat sleepy, but incredibly sexy. God, why does he always have to look so damn sexy?

"Uh, yes. Cookies, right." My face feels flushed, and words prove to be a continued struggle for me. He shoots me a cocky grin, clearly knowing how much he's affecting me right now.

I swallow the emotion lodged in my throat at the memory. My heart feels both full and empty at the same time. Cas knows how important this specific memory is to me and the fact that he included this in whatever plan he has means a lot. I may miss my parents every day, but baking cookies with Cas makes me miss them a little less. Cas isn't filling the void they left, but he's helping patch the holes that loneliness has left on my heart.

Chapter 22

Avery

Always

THIS KITCHEN IS PURE chaos as we work in tandem to gather everything we need. Bowls and measuring cups of various shapes and sizes are scattered everywhere. All the ingredients we need to bake cookies cover the kitchen island. I think of how messy this will be, but I can't help to smirk at the fun we're about to have.

I clap my hands together, something I've been known to do right before stating a game plan. "Okay," I say, rubbing my hands together. "So, snickerdoodles for you and double chocolate chunk for me?"

My mind might not always be neat and tidy, but coming up with a game plan is something I thrive off of. The anxious part of me craves control. So when things inside my brain feel disorganized, I find ways to gain control in other areas.

"You know me so well," he says. I grab my wireless speaker and connect my phone to it, then hand it over to Cas, letting him select the playlist. We start baking as soon as the music starts playing.

At first, everything is going great. The two of us are working together as if we've been doing this for years. The air starts to become more charged when Cas reaches around me to grab something he needs, placing one of his hands on my hip. He could have easily asked me to grab it for him, but I got the sense that he wanted an excuse to touch me. *I'm* not going to complain. Things only become more intense when he wraps his hands around my waist while I mix the dough. His breath tickles my neck, causing tiny jolts of energy to surge through my body.

"If you keep distracting me like this, the dough isn't going to turn out right." I chuckle.

"Maybe I want to distract you," Cas whispers before sniffing my neck and letting out a groan.

"You smell good, like honeysuckle." He spins me around while I have a spoonful of cookie dough, causing me to accidentally smack him across the face, leaving a trail of gooey cookie on his cheek.

"I'm so sor—" was all I managed to get out before I burst out laughing.

He takes a step away from me, tilting his head to the side, his expression unreadable. "Oh, you think that's funny, do you?"

"Hey, you spun me around when you *knew* I had a spoonful of dough in my hand. This is on you." He steps toward me, looking at me like a starved man in search of his next meal, causing all the moisture from my mouth to evaporate. I'm not sure what he's planning to do, but I'm surprised when he dips his whole hand in the mixture.

"You know, if you wanted a taste, you could have used a spoon." Before I can react, he's looking at me with a wicked grin and I slowly start to back away from him.

"Don't. You. Da—" I'm cut off when his hand smears cookie dough all over my face and neck.

"You didn't!" I screech.

"Oh, I did! You really should be careful when baking, Avery. You've got some stuff all over your face and neck." His eyes are wild and his grin is mischievous.

"That's because you smeared it all over me. Now I need to go wipe it off." I start to move past him, but his hands are suddenly on my waist. Within seconds he's placing me on the marble countertop, putting me directly in his line of sight.

"Allow me," Cas says. It all happens so fast. One second he was sitting me down on the counter, and immediately after he's caging me between his arms. I can feel his breath on my neck, but I don't have time to think because he's licking my neck. Cas is licking my neck! A moan escapes my mouth without my brain's permission. His tongue moves slowly up my neck and to my cheek, licking the cookie dough off my face and leaving a trail of goosebumps behind.

"Mmmmmmm, you taste sweet," he moans, his face suddenly a hair's breadth away from mine. Surely he's going to kiss me, but he doesn't. He gazes down at my lips before backing away.

"You are a frustrating man, Cas," I blurt out.

"I am?" he asks.

"You keep saying all these things to me and almost kissing me, but never do anything about it." He pauses, and inside my head, I'm berating myself for being so bold. *He's not going to want to date you now, Avery. Way to go.*

His eyes grow more intense by the second. I want to snatch the words from his brain and throw them in the trash. Damn me and my teenage fantasies and hopes. I go to open my mouth, but he blurts out a question.

"You mean that?" he asks.

"Hmm? Mean what?" *Damn it's hot in here.*

"You really want me to do something about it?"

"Um, yes?" My voice raises as if asking a question. *Be bold and brave, Avery.* I clear my throat and try a different approach. "Do you want to do something about it?" Yeah. Turn it back onto him, see what he says.

His eyes scan my face and I see a look that hasn't been there since we first danced together. Cas looks at me like I'm one of the most important people in his life, like I'm the answer to his prayers.

My mind was so hyper-fixated on what his look means that I missed what he said.

"Ave?" Cas cups my face, his thumbs rubbing back and forth on my cheek. "Did you hear me?"

"I-no." I let out a breathy laugh.

"Yes, I want to do something about it."

Cas' words are seeping into my brain as slow as honey. He wants to try? That's what he's trying to say, right?

"I can hear your thoughts, freckles. Your brain has never thought very quietly. Yes, I want to try with you, if you'll let me."

If I let him? Okay play it cool, Avery. We don't need you acting all Buddy the Elf on him. I look into his eyes and fight to hold in the giddiness. My teeth are digging into my bottom lip to prevent a giant smile. *Chill out, Avery.* Cas chuckles before using one of his thumbs to rub against my bottom lip, rubbing until I free it from its prison. It's so tempting to take his thumb into my mouth and suck on it. I'm so stuck on this thought that my mouth forms a soft O and I glance at Cas from underneath my lashes.

Cas' throat bobs as his thumb rests on my bottom lip. I could do it. Just open my mouth a tad wider and do it. He makes the decision for us both by stepping out of my arms and clearing his throat.

"Avery?" The hoarseness of his voice sends heat straight to my core.

I swallow a few times before answering his question. "Yes." Short and to the point, and quite clearly the only thing I can manage to say.

"Okay. Cool. Yeah cool." Cas is rubbing the back of his neck while looking at his feet. Are we being bashful right now? Hmm, I think I might like this side of Cas. Who knew bashful could be so sexy. "You, I, um..." He clears his throat before continuing. "Let's finish these cookies and maybe we can watch a movie or something?"

We take separate spots in the kitchen. It's better this way. Safer this way. We don't need the fire department called on us because we set the house on fire from burnt cookies while we were occupied doing...other things. Once all the cookies are cooling off, we make our way to the front room to watch a movie. I move to sit down on the other side of the couch, but Cas has his hands on my hips, pulling me to him. I collapse onto his body and my face is so close to his. After a heated moment, Cas plants me right next to him and instinct has me cuddling into his side. His arm is wrapped around my waist, my head rests in the crook of his neck, breathing in his masculine scent.

It would be so easy to fall asleep, cuddling up next to him. I mean, we did it earlier. I decided to sneak a look at Cas, just wanting to stare at him for a moment. When I peek at him, he's already staring at me. Confusion invades my mind at the look on his face. The word *finally* comes to mind. It's as if Cas has been waiting for this moment all his life. I can't really explain why it feels this way. It just does.

"Why now?" I blurt out. The look on Cas' face becomes more intense. "Now?"

"Yeah, why are you interested in me like this now?"

"Baby, it's not just now. I've always wanted to do this."

Always. That word has warmth radiating throughout my body. *Always,* I repeat in my mind. Could we have been doing something like this all along? As soon as the question enters my mind, I know the answer. No, we couldn't have been. We both had to go our own way first before coming together.

Instead of responding to his comment, I snuggle in deeper. He presses a chaste kiss on top of my head. This isn't something new. He's kissed my head before, but given everything that's happened today, it feels like more.

The movie ends too soon, yet we still haven't moved from our spots on the couch. His fingertips run down the length of my arm and back up again. I let out a soft hum and my eyes flutter closed. I was content with taking a nap with Cas wrapped around me, but his words have me jumping out of his embrace.

"Avery, will you go on a date with me?"

There is a computer glitch in my brain and it takes me a moment to speak.

"Yes." Simple, yet powerful enough of a response.

"Perfect, I'll pick you up tomorrow at seven." He sends me a flirty smile and a wink before getting up to leave.

"Wait, what am I supposed to wear? Wait, don't you want to try the cookies?" He looks over his shoulder and smirks at me.

"I already got my taste of the cookies, and I liked it—*a lot*. As far as what to wear, you look sexy in anything you put on," Cas says. And with that, he walks out the door.

Holy shit. I'm going on a date with Cas. My neck still feels hot and tingly from where he licked it. I abandon the cookies and kitchen mess altogether and run upstairs to tear through my closet. Now that this is happening, I need to look my absolute best.

Chapter 23

Cassidy

Therapy is lifesaving

TODAY IS MY FIRST date with Avery. Instead of excitement filling my body, I feel disconnected. It's as if I'm watching my body from afar. Why does this have to happen today, of all days? My phone pings with a reminder to leave for my therapy session in twenty minutes. Maybe Dr. Z can help me figure out what the hell is going on during therapy today. I'm in a daze driving to therapy as my thoughts drift back to my first session.

First Therapy Session

I didn't want to be here. A therapist wasn't going to help me. I was too damaged. I wasn't sure what I was expecting as I walked into the building, but it wasn't this. The waiting room consisted of two overstuffed, chocolatey-brown chairs with a wooden coffee table in the same color directly in front. As soon as I sat down, the couch completely enveloped me, almost like it was trying to tell me I was safe. The walls were a soft white or cream color, I couldn't tell from the dim lighting. Soft meditation music drifted through the speakers, bathing me in a tranquility that helped regulate my breathing. The peacefulness of the space threatened to lull me to sleep, but the door opened and out walked a woman. She seemed to be in her mid-thirties with wavy brown hair and eyes so blue they were almost transparent. Her smile was warm and genuine. Before my brain could process what it was doing, I was on my feet.

"Hello, you must be Cassidy. My name is Dr. Z," she said, reaching out her hand. When my hand grasped hers, the remaining tension I had held in my body melted out of me.

"Hi," was all I managed to get out.

"If you're ready, you can follow me," she said. Dr. Z gave me the choice to enter the room or leave. I nodded my head and followed her into the room she'd gestured to. Her office had hunter-green walls with random quotes scattered across them and two velvety, dark brown chairs that looked soft and inviting. An oil diffuser sat in the corner and next to it a basket that I assumed held every oil imaginable.

The therapist must have caught me looking, because she spoke. "Feel free to get up and pick a scent or two. I have a booklet in the little drawer underneath if you want a specific scent combination." Her voice was as smooth as butter with undertones of patience and understanding.

I flipped through the booklet and noticed various combinations, from relaxation to sleep to memory enhancer and, finally, anxiety relief. After mixing the proper drops into the diffuser, I turned it on and allowed the smells to hit my senses. Who knew the combination of lavender, roman chamomile, and clove would be relaxing? I sat back down, ready to get this session over with.

"So, have you been to therapy before?" she asked.

"Yeah, during my treatment last year, but that was for my addiction issues. I've never really focused on my mental health before," I replied.

She nodded her head and continued. "That's great that you took the opportunity to heal. I know this can be intimidating. The fact that you showed up today is huge. Our first session will be mostly information gathering so I can help find the proper diagnosis and treatment plan for you."

"Diagnosis?" I panicked. "I thought I was just coming here to talk. Why do you need to diagnose me? People will think I'm crazy," I stammered while looking for my exit.

"Mental health is nothing to be ashamed about. It's more common than most like to believe it is. I have had my own battles with mental health," Dr. Z tried to reassure me, but it confused me instead.

"You have mental health battles? How is that possible? You're a therapist. You aren't supposed to have problems," I said, completely dumbfounded.

Dr. Z blinks a few times before softly chuckling. "Being a mental health professional doesn't mean I'm free from my own issues. I mean, who would want a therapist that's perfect?" she asked. I never thought about it that way. If my therapist were perfect with no problems, I probably wouldn't talk to them. *Not that I would talk to this therapist*, I thought. Coming to therapy was just a one-time deal then I'd be back to pretending my problems didn't exist.

"Okay, so today is more about me asking what feels like very intrusive questions. You don't have to disclose everything, only what you're comfortable with. I need as many answers as you can manage, but a little summary is fine if it's too much. So first, let's talk about how you are feeling right now and what brought you in to see me."

I sat there for an eternity as I pondered her questions. My first reaction was to lie, but that felt counterproductive. If I'm honest, though, that meant admitting there was a problem with me. Either option felt like a loss, but waking up in a cold sweat panicking was getting old. I took a deep breath in and swallowed my pride. Then I told her about not knowing how I felt. As I went into why I was there, she asked more invasive questions.

"That has to be such a scary feeling waking up in a panic. Can you tell me more about the symptoms you're experiencing?" she asked. But before I could answer, I was distracted by her pulling out a notepad.

"What are you doing with that notepad?" She must have heard the terror in my voice because she reassured me.

"This is just for me to take notes on what you tell me today so that I can remember what you told me later. I only take notes when I find it's important for me to remember something or when gathering key information. I then transfer all of my notes to a password-protected document right before shredding the physical copies. If you need reassurance, my shredder is in the corner over there." Dr. Z nodded her head in the direction and my eyes followed toward the small, black, box-like object.

"Does that ease some of your anxiety?" I nodded my head and continued to answer all her questions. It wasn't until we got on the topics of substance use and family that my heart began to race and my face felt too hot.

The room began to disintegrate before me. The sound of Dr. Z's voice slowly faded into the background before I was transported to that same scene I had in my grandparents' kitchen. I was unaware of how long I was in that alternate universe, but Dr. Z's calm, buttery voice pulled me back.

"Cassidy? Are you with me?" I blinked rapidly and found myself in the same four walls I had walked into earlier. "What are five things you see in this room?" I looked at her hesitantly, but obliged. I mentioned the green walls, diffuser, brown chairs, dark brown door, and a little clock next to the diffuser. She then has me tell her four things I can touch, three things I can hear, two things I can smell, and one thing I can taste. Before I realized what was happening, my heart rate slowed down and I was back in her office again.

"What you just experienced is a flashback," she stated and began to educate me on what they are and why they exist.

"Flashbacks? Are you telling me that was what I've been experiencing every morning?" She nodded at me, and her next words stopped me cold.

"Yes, I believe so. They are one of the many symptoms of PTSD."

"PTSD? But I'm not a war vet, so I'm not sure how I could have that," I said, completely baffled.

"PTSD comes from any significant traumatic experience. Flashbacks are a way of remembering that experience."

"But I don't remember anything that bad ever happening to me. In these 'flashbacks,' the place I'm in seemed familiar. I'm only able to catch quick glimpses, never the full picture before I wake up in a panic."

"That can happen, too. Our body stores our trauma and protects us until we're ready to deal with it. Oftentimes, we tend to block out difficult feelings due to their uncomfortability. What have you done to cope with intense feelings when they come?" she asked.

"I, well, I..." I hesitated. A part of me still felt shame at my upbringing, but fuck it. If I'm to get any better, I need to share it all. The good, the bad and the ugly. I took a deep breath before letting Dr. Z know about my abusive childhood with my father, Frank, and how it got so bad that my maternal grandparents stepped in and took me under their care. I'd shared it all, even the shit about me turning out like my father in regards to being an addict. I'm out of breath and exhausted from divulging everything to her. My hands fidgeted in my lap, my eyes remained downcast, afraid to look up. Her silence felt deafening, and even though it was brief, it felt like it went on for eternity.

"Okay, so it seems that substances were used as a distraction skill to avoid feelings. You're currently sober now?" I nodded and she continued. "Now that you have taken away your only coping skill, everything's emerging tenfold. I think if we continue to work together, this trauma that's been so stuffed down will resurface. We can then begin to understand what's been going on." She continued her questioning and I was drained by the end of the session.

"So that's our time for today. I think that weekly appointments might be helpful for you right now, does the same time next week work for you?" I took a couple of minutes to think about my answer. On the one hand, I wanted to just go to therapy just to say I did it and move on, but, on the other hand, something was telling me that Dr. Z was how I would get answers. Following in my father's footsteps was no longer desirable to me, so I nodded my head.

"Yes, that works for me. I'll see you next week." I'm unsure how I made it home, but I was out like a light the second my head hit the pillow.

Present day

Cas's therapy appointment

It's been a couple of months since that first session, and honestly, most times, I look forward to seeing Dr. Z. But today, I'm incredibly grateful. I need answers. We begin with our typical weekly check-in before she asks me what I want to focus on today. I explain the feelings I have been experiencing as she nods along empathetically, this time choosing not to take her notes.

"And today, I am supposed to feel happy and excited because, well, remember when I talked about Avery?" When she nods, I continue. "We're going on our first date later today."

"How exciting. I see why you're supposed to feel excited and happy. You've been waiting a while for Avery, haven't you?" I nod and she asks her next question. "It must be frustrating feeling so disconnected. Tell me, have you had any more flashbacks this past week?" I nod.

"Yes. And I'm not sure if the flashbacks are getting worse or better. They've been happening almost every day. And now, there's also a little boy who looks strangely familiar. He's scared and alone, and I don't know why, but I feel scared and alone, too. It is the most bizarre experience ever. Is this making any sense?" I ask her.

"Actually, yes, and it looks like there are some confused feelings, as well. I think that's a natural emotion, given what you seem to be dreaming about. I have a thought I would like to share, but it might be possibly triggering. Remember, at any point, if you need a break to collect yourself, all you have to do is ask. Are you okay if I share my thoughts?" I nod once, hoping to hide the terror over what she's about to say. Of course, she picked up on my feelings because she's that good.

"Before I continue, let's take a few of our four-six-five deep breaths. In for four, hold for six, and out for five. As you're doing that, let's say to ourselves *I am not my anxiety nor my trauma. Anxiety doesn't mean I'm broken, it means I'm a warrior.* I think five of these will be helpful, but if you need more, let me know."

My relationship with my anxiety has come a long way. Something I used to hate with every fiber of my being is now something I've learned to embrace. Some days are easier said than done and Avery is a huge reason for the shift in thinking. As someone who struggled with it her whole life, I realized the more I hate that part of myself, the more I hate that part of her. And hating any part of her doesn't sit well with me. So yeah, I have anxiety and PTSD. Some days are easier than others to accept that, but I'm a work in progress and my healing is a journey not a destination. Ever since the topic of anxiety came up in therapy, guilt has weighed heavy on my chest. I need to apologize to Avery for all the hurtful things I said. I need to own up to the things I made her believe with my cruel words. But every time I find the courage, my voice stops working and it feels like I'm on the verge of a panic attack. I know I'll have to have this conversation soon because if I want a future with her, I have to atone for the mistakes of my past.

We breathe together, and after the last four-six-five breaths, I feel calmer and let her know she can continue. "Okay, so with what you've shared so far, both verbally and with your journal, I'm wondering if, in this most recent flashback, the little boy you are seeing is actually you."

I sit with those words for a few minutes, on the verge of understanding.

"I mean, maybe? I feel like I'm so close to an answer, but find myself up against this brick wall that's keeping me from understanding what the hell is happening," I say, exasperated.

"You have accomplished so much already in a short time. Even though you feel frustrated right now, it's important to remind yourself to be patient and have some grace. Let's try shifting our approach for a second and see if maybe we can get that answer."

She asks me to write out the scene that has been like a broken record in my head for the last couple of weeks. She hands me a pen and paper and tells me to first write out the flashback and then to continue with whatever comes into my head.

I spend the next ten minutes writing what I remember. When I begin the free writing, I'm transported back to that scene.

I'm back in the dark, cold room with only a single twin bed with red sheets. That same boy is sitting there looking small, but this time I hear a familiar voice: my father's. This time I'm able to walk on the rickety stairs and that's when I see my father talking to two different men that seem familiar. One man was arguing with my dad about not having the money for the stash. I see a wicked grin pull across my dad's face that causes my body to freeze as bile threatens to rise in my throat. My dad makes a bargain that has my body going ice cold. My feet won't allow me to move. I desperately need to warn the little boy downstairs, to warn myself of the danger headed my way. The other two men have the same evil smirk on their faces as they move past my father and head downstairs. With each creek of the steps, my heart beats harder in my throat.

The sound of my therapist's gentle words pulls me out of the memory.

"You remembered something, didn't you?" Dr. Z asks.

With my nod, the words come pouring out of my mouth. I notice that my chest is getting tight and my breathing becomes more rapid. How could I have forgotten something that big? I stand up without warning, desperate to release this buzzing energy inside me. I pace the office while Dr. Z watches me walk the perimeter of her office, trying to shake off the panic. I can imagine how insane I look, and my go-to deflection is to play it off with a joke. "I know. I look like I just escaped the mental hospital or something." I laugh without humor.

"Want to know what I think?" she asks, causing me to stop mid-stride and nod my head for her to continue. "I think you remembered a very traumatic situation that you've blocked out for a long time. And you're feeling scared and panicked."

"But why am I just remembering everything *now*? Why wasn't I able to do or say something when it happened? I can't believe how stupid I am for just remembering all this now when it happened forever ago. Like, I just let them do that shit to me." Nausea threatens to take over my body and I begin to get lightheaded, so I sit down. My therapist must pick up on this because she starts guiding me through a deep breathing exercise while doing some more grounding.

"Cassidy, you are not stupid for remembering this now, nor are you stupid for not doing anything to save yourself then. I have some information that I want to give you that might help provide answers to your questions." She makes her way toward the floor-to-ceiling metal filing cabinet as my gaze focuses on the quote box atop the cabinet. I remember from my first session and had to fight the urge to roll my eyes back then, but now, I no longer want to do so. It reads, *"You must let yourself feel it before you can heal it."* It's scary how accurate it feels at the present moment. She turns around with the packet and catches me reading the sign.

"That's such a great saying. We, myself included, don't like to feel any intense emotions, so we often block them out or push them down. This leads me to this packet. I want you to read through it when you are ready and willing to accept and understand the information. There are reasons why you're only remembering what happened now and this packet might help relieve some of your guilt and frustration with yourself. Now, I know you said you remembered things. You are more than welcome to share what you know in this safe space, or you can tell me whenever you're ready." Her words are so comforting that the words escape from me before I can stop them.

"He said it'll be our little secret, and if you try to tell anyone, you *will* regret it," I say. I try to slow down my rapid breathing. I finally look into those calm, blue eyes and confirm her earlier thought. "I am that boy, and they sexually abused me."

Chapter 24

Avery

Nobody stands me up

EXCITEMENT SIZZLES IN MY body like bacon on a hot pan. This has been a fantasy for so long, and never in my wildest dreams did I think it would happen. I am finally going on a date with Cas. The thought alone makes my heart soar like an eagle taking flight. I'm sure my nonstop giddy dancing has nothing to do with the rapid thumping of my pulse.

With excitement, though, comes anxiety and all the possible worst-case scenarios. *What if he realizes I'm not what he wants? What if this doesn't work out and I lose my best friend again? What if he doesn't show?* Ugh, fucking anxiety.

These thoughts do nothing to calm my nerves. The inside of my head looks like a murder board with strings floating every which way. If my face doesn't give my feelings away, my room sure does. My closet looks like it had a temper tantrum all over my once spotless floor. Everything needs to be perfect tonight, and that includes my outfit. I'm still freaking out when Brianna walks into the room.

"Did your closet throw up?" she asks, staring at the mess at my feet.

"I, uh, can't figure out what to wear." I look at her hopefully. If anyone knows how to handle my chaos, it's Brianna. "Help me." She finally looks up at my face and bursts out laughing. "Rude," I say. "Here I thought my best friend would come and help me sort through this shit, but she comes in and laughs at my clear distress. Might have to put out an ad for a best friend."

Bri clutches her side as she slowly recollects herself before speaking. "Ha, like you can find anyone as amazing, talented, beautiful, and wonderful as me. Get real, Ave. I'm the best person to ever walk into your life and you know it. You gotta admit, though, this is funny as hell. Miss *always has her shit together* is a complete mess."

I roll my eyes, but end up laughing with her. "You know it's not nice to gloat, but you're right. My room is a complete mess. I'm a complete mess. Please help me, oh amazing, talented, beautiful, and wonderful best friend a girl can have." My pleading has a hint of sarcasm, but Bri doesn't miss a beat.

"Thank you for recognizing my awesomeness, even if it was said with sarcasm. Okay, let's take a look at what we have. We want Cas to toss you over his shoulder and have *you* for dinner instead." Bri winks at me. She fucking *winks at me.* The audacity of this woman. We spend what seems like hours finding the perfect outfit. Cas didn't give me any details about where we were going. Not having all of the information mildly irritates me. The last thing I want is to show up in a tight dress with heels I can barely walk in if we are just going to the local pizza joint.

We finally land on a tight, silky, lavender slip dress that stops mid-thigh and pair it with sky-high, white, peep-toe heels. We leave my hair down in waves, letting it rest over one shoulder. I put the final touches on before walking over to the mirror to give myself a once over. I twist my body every which way and I'm in complete amazement at my reflection. I can't remember the last time I felt this beautiful. I cup my face, careful not to ruin my makeup, which is stunning yet subtle. Bri has many talents, but makeup is definitely high on that list. There's a gold shimmer dusted across my eyelids, and atop that is the faintest hint of eyeliner. My eyelashes have always been naturally long, so I wear just a hint of mascara. My hands move down the curves of my body and I have to hold back happy tears. Bri would kill me if I ruined her work. The sound of Bri clearing her throat shakes me out of my moment.

"Ave, you look stunning. He won't be able to keep his hands off of you for long. I bet ten bucks you don't make it to the restaurant," she says. With that thought, my eyes widen with panic knowing we've never done anything physical. The possibility of kissing Cas has fear buzzing through my body like I'm drunk on tequila shots. The thought of actually *having sex with him*? I'll admit, Cas has starred in many of my solo fantasies, but actually being that vulnerable with him terrifies me.

Bri doesn't know about our lack of intimacy because I'm afraid of her response. She's always been more open with her sexuality, whereas I've always been more timid. But I've never been good at hiding my emotions from her because she immediately notices the shift in my demeanor.

She's speaking before I can collect myself. "What's going on here? I thought Cas being unable to keep his hands off you would make you blush and be all cute. Instead, your face is all scrunchy and weird." Damn it. Why is she so good at reading me?

"Um, well, we uh, we haven't *exactly...*"

"Shut up! You haven't? Like not even kissing?" My face must have said it all because she says, "You do like him, right? I mean, y'all practically eye fuck each other when the other isn't looking." She is completely gobsmacked.

"I do, I-I like him a lot. I mean, we've come close plenty of times, but neither of us ever follows through. It's not like we don't want to because we do. Well, at least, I think we do. I know *I* do."

"Well, how does he make you feel? And I'm not talking about emotions, but physically?"

"Bee." *Fuck, when did it get so hot in here?* It feels like I ate an entire bag of flamin' hot Cheetos.

"Aves." She juts out her hip and quirks an eyebrow, waiting for me to answer.

I let out a groan before relenting. If I don't, we'll be here for ages. "He makes me feel erotically charged all the time. When he looks at me, my throat fills with dust and I just want to climb him like a tree. Does that answer your question?" I sass back.

"So pretty much he makes you horny and you wanna fuck like bunnies. Got it."

"I didn't say—ugh, *yes* that's exactly it. I wanna lick his abs and have him fuck me into next year."

"Yes girl. Now, I believe my hot best friend has a date with her man tonight. I expect full details from start to finish—especially how many times you finish. If you know what I mean." She wags her eyebrows at me and I roll my eyes at her.

"Yeah, yeah, yeah, now get out of here. Cas should be here soon and I don't trust you to keep your mouth shut."

"I am deeply offended you would think—Yeah, you're probably right." Bri takes her time gathering her things. She's stalling, so I take the liberty of picking up her stuff and throwing it at her before shoving her out the door. Her laughter fills the halls and slowly fades away as she makes her way outside.

Cas will be here soon and my stomach is doing a full out gymnastics floor routine. I stop when I start to wobble around, remembering my death trap heels. The last thing I need is to go to the hospital with a broken ankle. As the time inches closer to seven, I can't help but feel that something's wrong. Which is weird because nothing happened today to elicit such a feeling. I try to free my mind of the thought, but it's stuck like superglue. This is supposed to be a happy day, not a day of overthinking. Telling my brain to stop the negative thoughts is like telling a toddler no. You tell a toddler no, and they just do it, despite you while giving you a wicked grin.

It's finally time, so I anxiously walk up to the door and peek out one of the large rectangular windows only to see an empty driveway. Cas is probably just running a few minutes behind. I try to shake off my concerns, telling myself there's nothing to worry about. Yet part of me remains unconvinced. My footsteps echo as I walk over to my navy L-shaped couch and try to wait patiently. With each passing minute, my mind and body grow more nervous as the worst-case scenarios from earlier play through my head like a broken record. It's now a quarter to eight. Worry and anger float around in my body, with anger taking the lead by a wide margin.

What the fuck. How can he just stand me up like this? He was the one who asked me out, not the other way around. If he didn't want to go out with me or changed his mind, why not have the fucking decency to tell me instead of making me wait here like a damn fool? My anger grows with each thought. I have two options: keep waiting around letting my feelings fester or march up to his door and demand an explanation.

My feet have me up off the couch and out the front door before I realize what's happening. I stomp my way over to his house and pound on his front door, ready to give him a piece of my mind. When he opens the door, the color completely drains from my face looking at his disheveled appearance. All my anger is replaced with fear.

Chapter 25

Avery

You are stained glass

CAS STANDS THERE, BUT it feels like he's lightyears away. My nerves from earlier reads a solid nine on the Richter scale.

"Cas, hey, what's wrong?" Terror has my voice all wobbly and I'm practically shouting at Cas. It doesn't matter, though, my words aren't breaking through his trance.

I try again, but this time reach for his hand, desperate to break through his deadpan expression. "Cas? You're starting to freak me out." My touch only causes him to flinch so hard that I stumble back. I would have fallen on my ass if he didn't reach out to grab me. Cas blinks rapidly, attempting to reacclimate himself to the present moment. When his eyes finally meet mine, he looks at me with a confused expression.

"Hey, Avery, what are you doing here?" His question has me flinching as if he slapped me. I mean, he texted me this morning about this date saying how excited he was. His words are a knife in my chest. What does he mean, *what am I doing here*? Hurt slams into my stomach, knocking the wind out of me. All of my earlier anxieties come rushing back. Clearly, he's changed his mind, and instead of telling me, he stands me up. Despite my anger and confusion, there is a small part of my brain warning me to be gentle. That there's more to the story. I must have been standing there parsing through my own thoughts for a while because he was staring at me like he was waiting for an answer.

"Huh?" I ask.

"I asked you what you're doing here and why you look all dressed up?" Is he serious right now? Tears begin to sting behind my eyes. I won't let him see how much this hurts, so I become angry, instead. My hands clench into fists, no doubt leaving half-moon crescents in my skin from my nails. My eyes blaze with irritation that he dares to stand there, looking dumbfounded. I should walk away and calm down before saying something I'll regret, but I really don't care right now.

"*What am I doing here*? You have got to be fucking kidding me." My voice comes out in a humorless laugh. His continuous, blank expression only adds fuel to my fire.

"Well, Cas do you remember our conversation where you asked me out? A date you claimed to have been waiting forever for?" Things start to click for him, but I'm not finished.

"I—" he starts, but I hold my hand up and continue my rant.

I let out a frustrated sigh, swatting away that voice telling me to let him explain like a pesky fly. "Cas. I'm tired, and angry, and to be honest, a tad disappointed. I was so excited to go out tonight with you and even got all dressed up. Clearly the excitement is only one-sided because you would have shown up, instead of looking at me like I have three heads." I start to walk away despite his attempts to get me to stay. I make it off the porch before turning around, needing to get this off my chest.

"You know, I get it if you thought I was what you wanted but ended up changing your mind. I know you're still in the early stages of recovery and I would understand if you need more time. If you had communicated *any* of that to me, I would have been hurt, of course, but I would have given you time." I give him a forced smile before turning around and walking away.

"Avery!" he shouts, but I pick up my pace, yearning for the safety of my bed so I can let it all out.

The second I close my front door, I collapse and completely lose it. So much for crying in my bed. My body is a blender and my feelings are the ingredients. As the emotions swirl together, I become so overwhelmed that hot and salty tears fall from my eyes.

I don't know how long I've been sitting on the floor, but a soft knock followed by a soft voice has my head snapping up. My heart wants to be petty and ignore him, but my body has a mind of its own. Despite my hurt, the way he says my name has shivers of electricity rippling down and heat pooling between my legs.

"Avery, please open the door. I can explain everything, but I need to see your face," he pleads. I am so close to giving in. My hand is braced on the doorknob, my forehead resting on the door. When he says my name again, his voice cracks and I swing the door open before I realize what I'm doing.

"Cas. I don't think we should be having a conversation right now. Maybe us taking this next step isn't in the cards for us. I—"

"No, baby. Just no. Avery, I need you, especially now. I—just please hear me out?" he pleads.

All my previous thoughts and questions fly out the window when I notice how puffy and red his eyes are. "Cas," I whisper. And that's all it takes for his body to succumb to uncontrollable shaking due to his sobs. He looks like he's on the verge of collapsing, so I pull him inside and manage to bring him to the couch before he collapses into a ball in my lap.

Just like that, it's as if Cas' pain pulled the plug, letting all my anger swirl down the drain. All I'm left with is feeling helpless. Cas, who keeps his feelings under lock and key, is an absolute mess. I said some hurtful things to him earlier, but I didn't expect him to react this way. Guilt is a heavy boulder in my body and the urge to apologize sits on the tip of my tongue.

"Babe, it's okay. Shh, you're safe. I'm sorry if I—"

"Avery, no, please don't. You're not to blame here."

"But I—" He places his hand atop mine, stopping me mid-sentence.

"Avery, listen, please. You are not to blame for any of this. I..." He pauses as if he was thinking about what to say next. As much as I want to have my say, my gut tells me to remain silent.

"I started seeing a therapist a little while ago. It was recommended to me during treatment." It doesn't matter how many times we talk about being hospitalized from his overdose. I still wince a little every time.

"Wow, Cas, that's great. I'm really proud of you. I know that can't be easy," I say, a little stunned by his confession. My fingers tremble as they play with the soft, wavy tendrils of his hair. I hope that he doesn't pick up on what I'm feeling. This is about wanting him to feel better and not about me and my fears. His eyes are closed as he lets out a sigh of contentment, but when his eyes finally open, all I see is pain. My heart flips in my chest, but not in a good way. In the *I know what he's about to tell me is going to rip my heart out of my chest and break it in a million pieces,* kind of way. I settle on running my fingers gently through his hair, hoping that this simple touch conveys what my words cannot.

"It was difficult to go in the beginning. I was only planning to go once and then be done. I thought therapy wasn't going to work for me. That I was broken beyond repair—"

I interrupt him before he can continue. "Cas, it breaks my heart when you say things like that." I look down and see he's no longer looking at me. I stop playing with his hair and bring my hands up to cup both sides of his face. I wait for his eyes to meet mine before I continue, knowing how important it is for him to understand what I'm telling him.

"Cas, listen to me. *You* are not broken. You grew up with shitty circumstances that had nothing to do with you. *You* did not ask to have the father you have. *You* are beautifully whole. I know you can't see it. I know you don't believe me. My hope is that one day, instead of seeing a shattered mirror beyond repair, you see stained glass. A beautiful masterpiece of different shapes and colors that are wonderful alone, but together tell the most beautifully unique story."

"Avery, you're too good for me." He sees me shaking my head, ready to argue, so he continues. "No, you are. I wonder every single day what I did to deserve someone like you in my life. You're selfless, although lately you've learned to put yourself first. You see and accept people for who they are without judgment. You were my first friend when I came here. I was in awe, seeing this eight-year-old strut her way over with such confidence. She didn't give me any choice but to be her friend, and I knew then that you did me the biggest favor ever." He pauses, needing a moment to collect himself.

"How I treated you back in high school, I—"

"Cas, you don't have to go there. It's okay." But he shakes his head.

"No, I need to. You deserve this. I look back at those moments with shame and disgust. Here was this beautifully kind woman who didn't ask for anything in return, and I took advantage of that." He pauses a moment, almost as if he is unsure what to say next. He removes himself from my lap and turns to face me with his whole body.

"There are things about me you don't know. Things I didn't remember until this morning. Before getting into all of that, you have to know and understand something first." His eyes were so intense I couldn't look away even if I wanted to.

"I didn't change my mind about you today. I want you just as much, if not more, than when we were growing up. It physically hurts knowing you think your feelings are one-sided. I'm going to promise, no, I will *show* you how much I feel for you every day. You're so much more to me than my best friend. You're my home, my lifesaver, my rock, and my..." He pauses, causing my heart to race. The look in his eyes goes soft and the gray in his eyes pierce deep into my soul. "Avery, you are my first and only love. I always knew how special you would be to me, but by the time I could put into words how I felt, I just couldn't." He lets out a laugh that doesn't reach his eyes. No, his eyes simultaneously ask a question and search for an answer. Cas quickly continues as if his vulnerability has a time limit, so I don't get the chance to say those three words.

He loves me. That confession sends a wave of butterflies to my stomach. He loves me. I repeat to myself, feeling warm and fuzzy as if my body is wrapped up in my favorite Christmas onesie.

"Avery? What's with your face? You have this goofy grin," he says.

I bring my hand to my cheek and realize that I do, in fact, have a big grin on my face. "You told me you love me. I guess I'm just wondering why you never told me?"

"I never told you because I wasn't what you deserved. You know who my father is, but you never knew the extent of how bad it was. Not telling you was my own fault. It wasn't as if I didn't trust you. I thought that if

I let you all the way in, I would lose you. My therapist has been helping me work through my feelings. She's helping me understand that what happened to me wasn't my fault. It's hard to accept, especially with this new information I learned about myself."

The hesitation radiates off him in waves, so I grab both of his hands in mine and bring them to my chest. "Cas, I love you, too. I love everything about you, the good and the bad. You are stronger than you know. I can tell this is difficult for you to talk about, so you can tell me whenever you want. Nothing you say will change how I feel. Whether you tell me today, tomorrow, a month, or a year from now, I will listen and still love you." He looks at me with teary eyes and leans his forehead against mine.

"I was sexually abused as a child." His confession causes me to snap my head back to see his face still bowed with shame. I can't help but just stare. My brain is a computer stuck on the loading screen. So many questions enter my mind, but he continues before I can ask any of them.

"I've been having these weird recurring dreams that were always so vivid. I would awake in a cold sweat and fear in my eyes. They involved this little boy and a dark room. I pushed them away because I didn't know what they meant at the time, dismissing them as silly little dreams. It wasn't until my therapist saw me having a flashback, that's what those dreams are called, that she diagnosed me with PTSD. I started to share these dreams with her during our sessions.

"This morning, I felt off. I was too numb to feel excited for our date. My therapy session was earlier today when I told her that the flashbacks and nightmares were getting worse. She asked me to do a writing exercise, which unlocked something in me, causing another flashback."

Then Cas proceeds to shatter my heart. I have to choke back the bile that's threatening to rise out of my throat. How his dad let various men use and abuse Cas just so he could avoid paying for his addiction. I'm not sure how I could hear all of this with the loud ringing in my ears from my anger. Who the fuck does that to a child? I always disliked his father, but now I despise him. He doesn't deserve to live. May he always catch red lights or, even better, break every bone in his body. May he get his dick chopped off and shoved down his throat. May he—*Avery, reel it back, girl.* Your brain is getting chaotically dark. I hope to God I never see that bastard around Cas again, because I won't be able to resist the urge to kick him in the balls.

I must have said this out loud because Cas stares at me. "I knew you had a temper, but I didn't know you had murderous tendencies." He chuckles.

"I don't *normally* have them, but for your father, anything is possible. How can someone do something like that to their own fucking child?" No longer able to sit down, I start pacing back and forth frantically.

When Cas touches my shoulder, it alerts my body's natural startle response. So, I guess I was lost in Avery land, because I didn't even notice him come up behind me.

"Avery, baby, listen. My dad is a sick fuck who only cares about his next high. I learned a long time ago that there's nothing I can do for him and I stopped trying to change everything. I didn't tell you any of this to piss you off. I wanted you to know me, all of me. You have been so open and vulnerable with me that I wanted to be able to do that for you. I didn't forget our date on purpose, I—"

"Cas, no, you don't have to explain anything anymore. You had a long and emotional day. Thank you for letting me in. I will still hold you to that date you promised, but it can wait. Right now, you're exhausted, so let's call it a night so you can get some rest. We can try again tomorrow, the next day, or whenever you want that make-up date." I try to walk towards the door, but his hand on my arm stops me.

"Avery, I-I don't want to be alone right now. Can I stay here with you?" he asks.

"Cas, I don't think that's a good idea. As much as I want to, you need to take care of yourself right now. We have time for that later." My jaw drops at his sudden laughter. "Oh, so sleeping with me is laughable now, huh?"

"No, no, no, no. Avery, I agree. Sleep is needed, but I don't want to sleep alone. I was going to ask if it's okay to stay here and actually sleep with you. I need the comfort of your arms right now...I'm scared to fall asleep."

That confession has me walking towards Cas and into his familiar, strong arms. He has already given so much of himself today that I find myself wanting to give a little back. "Of course, let me get changed into some pajamas and we can go to bed."

I blink back the rainstorm that's building behind my eyes as I get ready for bed. The weight of today hits like a ton of bricks, but I need to put my feelings aside for now. Cas' comfort is my main priority. I'm dressed in my favorite pair of pajamas and make my way over to my bed to find an already passed-out Cas looking peaceful and beautiful. I crawl under the covers and bring my body against his, hoping to provide him the comfort of being the big spoon.

"I love you, my little Casanova," I whisper into his ear.

"I love you, too, freckles."

I lay next to him, listening to the even rhythm of his breathing, and my heart hurts. Inside this beautiful man is a wounded boy who's healing. Cas may think he's broken beyond repair, but all I see is a warrior.

Our conversation about him being broken beyond repair repeats on an incessant loop in my brain. Cas needs to know just how beautiful I think he is. Cas' breathing is a soothing melody in the background, but I'm buzzing with excess energy.

My mind drifts toward the journal that sits in a box in my childhood bedroom closet. I glance at Cas to make sure he's fast asleep before sliding off the bed. He's out cold, but I still tiptoe out of the room and head toward my former bedroom. Inspiration to write music again strikes me like a bolt of lightning. I carefully pick the box off the closet floor before sitting cross-legged on the bed.

My fingers dance across the smooth cover, and if I listen closely, I can hear it whispering lyrics into my soul. It's the same journal Cas gave me all those years ago. A journal that I haven't written in for years. I take a steadying breath before I close my eyes. I feel the fuzzy comforter beneath my bare thighs as I hone in on the thoughts and feelings swirling around in my mind.

When I open my eyes, I glance down at the paper and see two words: *Stained Glass*. The pen drops out of my hand, landing on the floor with a soft thud. I have no recollection of how they got there, but they're the words that I used with Cas earlier. I pick up the pen and pour out everything I'm feeling onto the page, faster than I ever have before.

I have been writing for so long my fingers are starting to cramp. Tiny droplets decorate the silky page of the journal. I delicately press the pads of my fingers to my cheeks, noticing their dampness for the first time. Everything I wasn't able to communicate earlier lies before me. I notice a melody buzzing in my brain. I quietly rush down stairs toward my music room so I can put everything in my head down on paper. I lift the fall board of the piano that my parents gifted me for my golden birthday, and I swear I hear it sing with excitement. My fingers glide across the cool keys. When my ass hits the bench, I flinch at how cool it feels against my skin. *Damn, I've really missed playing.*

I let my heart do the playing for me, and soon enough, my thoughts and feelings become a song. The tears I held back earlier now fall fast and hard. After quietly finding and writing all the necessary notes, I close my journal and hug it to my chest, allowing myself to sit in the heaviness that is my emotions.

It's sometime later before I feel composed enough to go back upstairs. I place my journal in the same spot as before crawling into bed next to Cas, sadness and love plaguing my heart. I want to share this with him, but something tells me that now isn't the proper time. Right now, he needs to know that he's worthy and deserving of my love.

Chapter 26

Cassidy

Who doesn't love a good hand necklace

MY EYES FLUTTER OPEN and my head is in the middle of a construction zone with all the pounding. It's as if I drank an entire bottle of tequila, but I haven't been able to touch that shit since my junior year of high school. Panic is my new factory setting since remembering my childhood trauma. My eyes frantically search my surroundings and my heart rate feels like a child going at it on a new drum set. I'm not in my room, but I'm also not in my nightmare. Something shifts next to me and I'm frozen.

Don't make a sound. Don't let them know you're here. If you just remain still, maybe they won't hurt you.

Okay, think, Cas. What would your therapist have you do? Fuck, it's hard to think when my brain and body are on alert. A soft, sleepy moan sounds next to me and my eyes snap toward the direction of the noise. Tension melts out of my body like a quickly deflating balloon. My eyes scan the now familiar room and it all clicks into place. I'm not in the middle of a flashback. I'm at Avery's. I vaguely remember last night, and even though I'm happy in her arms, how did I get here? I shift out of her hold and I'm gifted with a sleepy smile that sends fire throughout my body.

Avery is an absolute goddess in the morning. Her wavy hair is tangled and splayed across the pillow like rose petals. The early morning sun peeks its way through the window, bathing Avery's ivory skin in its warmth. It doesn't matter if Avery is underneath the moon's glow or the sun's glare, she is astonishing.

"Good morning." Her voice is coated with sleep and an emotion I can't place.

"What's wrong?" I blurt out.

I take a moment to scan her face, searching for clues as to what she might be feeling, but she interrupts me before I can ask.

"N-nothing's wrong. Nothing you said last night upset me and nothing happened after you fell asleep," she says, but it seems like she is trying to convince me and herself.

"Something happened. It's in your eyes." I brush a thumb against her cheekbone while searching her face for clues. She brings her hands to mine, laying them there in a reassuring gesture.

"Cas, I'm okay, I promise," she says. Her words don't convince me, but her voice tells me it's not time to push it yet.

I think back to the last time we fell asleep together. It doesn't even compare to waking up in the same bed as her. Spending the night with Avery provides the same comfort as my favorite pair of gray sweatpants. I want a lifetime of mornings with her, tangled hair and all. I want a lifetime of everything with her.

Avery breaks the silence by laughing hysterically. This isn't her normal, musical laugh that fills me with warmth. No, this version is husky, making me overcome with a desire so intense I'm surprised I don't combust.

"Cas, what's with your face? It keeps changing and I can't keep up. One minute you have this goofy look on your face, and then you look like this. All like serious and just different."

I'm at a complete loss for how to describe what I'm feeling. We've been circling each other like vultures, both wanting to take the next step in our relationship. My personal insecurities and demons always have me pulling back. Hurting Avery again makes me feel physically sick, even worse than when I went through withdrawal. I've been staring at her mouth for far too long with desire. Desire to finally do something I've been dreaming about for a little over a decade.

I force myself to look into her eyes to see patience and love staring back at me.

"Cas, come on. Talk to me. Your silence is freaking me out."

My mind is a tornado of want. I want to bathe in her strength and bask in her radiance. I want to finally break this tug-of-war game we've been playing. I know talking through things is the best option, but it's like my body told my brain to take a seat.

My hands cup her face before my insecurities have a second to catch up. Eyes that were once wide open with concern flutter closed. I keep my hands pressed against her cheek and allow myself to sit with the sensation. Her skin is so soft and silky, and it takes every part of my self-control not to lean in and lick it. Instead, I brush her cheekbone with my thumb, sending tiny shocks of electrical currents through my arm with each stroke. Her soft hum vibrates against my hand, sending a jolt that starts at my fingertips before making its way down south.

I remove my hands and collect myself before I pounce on her. Avery needs to know just how special she is to me, that she's my only. My brain knows that, but the rest of my body is telling me to take the chance and go all in. Avery needs to know this isn't just sex for me, that everything needs to be special for her. She deserves to be cherished, and the only way I know how to show her I'm serious, is through my actions. Her eyes open, and there's a mixture of desire and confusion behind those intensely green eyes.

"What are y—" she says as I tuck a piece of her hair behind her ear.

"Doing something I've wanted since I was fourteen," I say. Before I can lose my nerve, I lean in and kiss her. Her surprise comes out in a quick intake of breath that has me pulling back for a second. Shit, I already messed this up. I wanted to kiss her and thought she wanted it, too, but maybe I misread all those signals. She doesn't give me much time to ask if this is okay before grabbing my face and bringing my mouth back to hers. The kiss starts off sweet and soft, testing the waters. The second she hears me groan, the direction of the kiss goes from gentle, to greedy and demanding. Our teeth and tongues come together so quickly you would think it would be painful, but it's the complete opposite.

I've often daydreamed what kissing Avery would be like, but none of those fantasies measure up to what's currently happening. She tugs on my lower lip bringing me out of my head and back into the current moment. I initiated the kiss, but Avery took over and it's incredibly sexy.

I always took Avery for the slow and gentle type of woman. Avery, who always rolls her eyes and scolds me every time I make a sexual joke or innuendo. This Avery is a firecracker who's completely ravaging my mouth. I wouldn't be surprised if they're permanently swollen. I place my hands on either side of her face, meaning for us to slow down, but she takes it in a completely different direction. My hands roam from her face down to her hips, giving Avery the courage to swing one of her legs over mine to straddle me.

I'm drowning in my own desire, and if I keep this up, it'll become more difficult to stop. I feel my taking-it-slow plan begin to crash and burn. She breaks the kiss, and this is my moment to stop things before they continue, but then she starts to take her shirt off. I place my hands over hers, gently shake my head, and say the words that might literally kill me.

"Avery, let's not go there right now," I say softly, looking into her eyes. Eyes that hold so many different emotions. I'm not entirely sure what she's feeling, but she gets off me quickly before I can ask her.

"Oh my God, I'm so sorry. I'm so embarrassed." Avery acts as if I burned her with how quickly she leaps off of me. She turns away from me, but I can feel the humiliation and hurt radiating off her body. She's hunched over as if she's trying to make herself small. Did she not feel how much I needed her when she was straddling me? Honestly, it was borderline pathetic how much my body was screaming at me to be with her. I touch her shoulder, but she shimmies out of my reach and heads toward the bathroom. I start to go to her, but she closes the bathroom door and the sound of a click stops me in my tracks.

"Avery, please open the door. We need to talk about what happened. It's not what you think," I say. The silence that answers me is haunting. "Avery, please?"

"Ugh, what's there to talk about? I made a complete ass of myself assuming you wanted to take things further. Gosh, Avery, how could you be so stupid? You aren't his usual type. Blonde bombshells with big boobs. I can't even compare to them," Avery mutters to herself, but I hear her loud and clear.

"How could you *ever* think you are comparable to those girls? You're unique and in your own league and not like any of those other girls." Shit, that came out all wrong. I clear my throat and try again, but the door swings open and there stands Avery, looking like a pissed-off cat.

"Like I don't know that already. Way to rub it in my face, Cas." Despite how much Avery's confidence has grown, there's still a part of her that doesn't feel worthy. I have no one but myself to blame for that.

I have to think quickly, because if I know Avery, she's about to walk away. As she begins to storm past me, I reach out, pull her back, and shove her against the wall beside the bathroom. I grab her face and stare at her with such intensity that I'm surprised neither of us explodes.

"Avery, does this face look like someone who doesn't want you?" Anger slowly begins to drain from her body. One of my hands travels slowly down the side of her body and goosebumps form on her skin. My hand finally lands on the side of her hip as her hands fly up to grip my shoulders. I take one of her hands in mine and glide it down my own body. All the way down to where my dick is still throbbing and hard. "Does my *dick* fucking feel like it doesn't want you?"

Her sharp intake of breath gives me my answer. Her eyes slowly travel upward towards mine where she finds desire burning behind them. She opens her mouth to speak, but I take her mouth with my own. It's my turn to be fast and greedy, and that's just what I do. My tongue tangles with hers with such speed and intensity as if this were the last time. I close the remaining distance between us, trapping her hand between our bodies. She moves her hand up and down my dick, the friction causes an explosion of lust and need in me. My fingers grab onto her hair, wrapping it around my fist and tugging with just enough force without causing too much pain. Avery lets out a whimper and the angle allows me to deepen the kiss. Taking my hand out of her hair, I move it to rest on the base of her throat and begin to squeeze.

Avery's response is to increase the pace of rubbing, even squeezing my cock a few times. My other hand moves to cup her ass. I nudge my leg between hers and she opens a little wider. My hand that's gripping her ass moves towards her inner thigh, close enough to feel the heat radiating there. I squeeze a few times before breaking from the kiss. With my hand still there, my voice comes out raspy. "Does it still *feel* like I don't want you?"

Unable to speak, she rapidly shakes her head. "Avery, you have *no idea* how much I want you. All those other girls never held a candle to your radiance. I was so fucked up in high school and knew you would never want to be with someone like me." I pause for a moment, then continue.

"I did everything I could to date the opposite of who *I wanted*. You were someone who had the power to see me. As much as I wanted that, I was too scared to go out and get it. Instead of dating someone who was kind, loving, tender, and funny, I went for fake, manipulative, and distant. So when you said all those girls aren't you, you're right—but not in the way you think. You're my lighthouse when I'm lost, and no one else has ever been that for me. You're so much more to me than any of those other girls and will continue to be that for me as long as you let me. I only stopped us earlier because when we finally have sex, I want to make sure you are cherished in the way you should be. I need to let you know it *is* different with you and will *always* be different with you. I want to give you everything and never want you to feel like you are just another number to me."

Avery stares at me for a moment, contemplating what to say. "Cas, I..." she says, sounding flustered. I rarely see this side of Avery and it does something to my heart. "Cas, you don't need to be gentle and soft with me. I—"

My look stops her cold. Before she can finish that sentence, I'm pulling her close to me. Our bodies are pressed so close together you would think we were one. My hand shoots back to her neck, but this time I don't squeeze. My lips make their way slowly towards her mouth, and just as her lips part, my mouth moves towards her ear instead and whispers, "Baby, I *never* said anything about being gentle or soft with you." I take my hand off her neck and bring my face close to hers. "Be ready at six. Oh, and Avery?"

"Hmm?" Is her only response.

"This time, I *will* show up, and we *will* finish what we started. That's a promise I *intend* to keep." Avery stares at me completely shell-shocked and I can't help but shoot her a playful smirk in return.

I make my way toward her bedroom door before turning around. "Avery, don't you ever forget how fucking sexy you are. Your smile, your laugh, your body. I could spend hours worshiping every inch of you and it'll never feel like enough. When I leave, I want you to look at yourself in the mirror and own every single part of you. Because every part of me likes every inch of you." With that statement, I walk out of her room with a wicked smile and a sense of excitement that I haven't felt in a while. I look down at my still-hard dick and groan in frustration. If I'm to make it through the evening, I may need to jerk off first so that all the attention is on her and her needs.

Chapter 27

Avery

He'll want to stay in an eat something else for dinner

WHAT THE FUCK JUST happened? Never in my wildest dreams did I think our first kiss would happen like that. In my fantasies, it was always sweet and slow with a tenderness to make a girl's heart swoon. What happened was a toe-curling, fire-burning, passionate kiss that rocked my world. And I'm *still* fucking turned on.

The craziest part about it all was that *I* was the one to go there. Cas was giving me the kiss of my dreams. The second he pulled back, the thin string of restraint snapped in half before turning feral. My mouth attacked his and my body devoured every second of it. I do as I'm told and stand in front of my mirror and own every single part of me. My face is flushed and my body hums with so much excess energy I could power an entire village.

"Girl, are you okay?" Bri's sudden presence has me jolting back from the mirror as if I got caught doing something naughty. I nod my head as words have failed me. Brianna smirks at me and gives me her bullshit face. I try to turn away from her, but she stops me.

"Holy shit. Oh my God! You fucking did it, didn't you?" she screams at me.

"Don't know what you're talking about." My hands are suddenly buzzing with energy, so I focus on making myself busy. Brianna's gaze shifts towards the rumpled mess that used to be my bed and points at it.

"Bullshit, I know for a *fact* that once your head hits the pillow, you're out like a light. Don't even get me started on your face, girl, because, well, have you seen yourself?" I walk over to my floor-length mirror and gasp at the reflection staring back at me. My eyes are black with desire, with the slightest ring of green around the edges. My face is flushed and I can see redness where Cas squeezed my neck earlier.

Most importantly, I look blissfully happy. Even though we didn't do anything, I looked like I just had sex. Bri wasn't done talking because she grabbed my shoulders so I could face her again.

"See what I mean? Also, I saw Cas leave your house right as I was pulling in, and he had this wicked expression on his face. So start talking." She sits on the bed, which forces me to stop and sigh.

"I hate you, Bri. Ugh, fine! Okay, something *did* happen, but not what you *assume* happened. We just kissed. That's all."

"Okay, first of all, you love me, and you know it. Second, I call bullshit."

"Brianna, I *promise you* that was all we did," I reassure her. I contemplate telling her everything that happened this morning. I can still feel the heat where Cas' hand squeezed my neck, sending a throbbing pulse between my legs. Damn, I never thought I'd like that kind of thing. The sound of Bri clearing her throat snaps me out of reliving that moment and potentially embarrassing myself.

"Earth to Avery. Where did you go and why are you doing that thing to your neck?" She looks at me as if a toddler decided to do my makeup.

"My neck?" My face scrunches in confusion.

"Yeah you're squeezing it and your face went all dreamy-eyed." I finally cave and tell her everything. Brianna is never one to be stunned speechless, but right now, she is making a solid impression of a fish. I have to wave my hand in front of her face a few times while calling her name before she comes back to me.

"I'm sorry. I think I just stroked out. You *attacked* Cas this morning by straddling him and going for his mouth like your life depended on it. *Then* he slammed you against the door, gave you a hand necklace, and you rubbed his dick. Who are you and what have you done to my Avery?"

"I-wait. A hand necklace?" I chuckle.

"Yeah. It's when the MMC puts your hand on your neck and squeezes you in a sexual way. A hand necklace," she repeats.

"*MMC?* Girl, what the fuck are you talking about?"

"MMC. The main male character. Girl you need to read my smutty books," Bri says while rolling her eyes.

"Oh right, MMC. Of course, how could I forget," I say sarcastically.

"Whatever, now stop changing the subject. What happened?"

"Girl, I don't know what came over me. One second it was all sweet and tender, then I just attacked him. The craziest part of that experience was that I *liked it,* especially that hand necklace thing. Everything escalated so quickly and it was exhilarating. I've never been so turned on. Want to know what he said to me before he left?" Her nod gives me the courage to continue.

"I told him that I didn't ask for him to be soft. He said, and I quote, 'Baby, I never said anything about being gentle or soft with you.' Then told me to be ready by six and left."

"Holy shit, Ave, that is some kinky ass shit, man. I am feeling a little revved myself. I may have to...wait, are you going out again tonight? You just went on a date yesterday, and you are going out again so soon? Damn, he must want you badly."

As much as I want to tell Bri that we never went out yesterday, it's not my story to tell, so I just nod my head. "Yeah, I guess so. I mean, I *am* pretty damn irresistible."

"Hell yeah, you are. Now, let's figure out what you're going to wear tonight and make sure you look sexy as hell. I assume Cas didn't give us much to work off of again?" With my nod, she continues.

"*Men*. I swear, they never give us enough information." She makes her way over to my closet and my thoughts travel to the conversation with Cas last night. I will not let his father ruin this moment, so I shove those thoughts into a drawer and lock it up. I readjust my focus on Bri tearing through my closet. Even with her back towards me, I know she found something. I can sense her *Bri is a genius* face before she turns around.

"Bow down to the clothing goddess," Bri says while showing me what she picked. In her hand is a sexy, black, floor-length, one-shoulder dress with a slit that stops mid-thigh. Her other hand holds another pair of death trap heels in bright red.

"I think you do the same hair as last time, but this time do like a daring red lip and shimmery gold eyeshadow with a cat eye and some lashes. You will look stunning. So stunning that he will—"

"Want to stay in and eat something *else* for dinner," I finish for her with another roll of my eyes. Just imagining him do those things to me freaked me out, but now it doesn't sound as crazy as it did the first time.

"See? You're learning. Now, to get you in the mood, I think you need to ask for a dick pic. It's always helpful to have a visual aid when you want to get your engine revved for later," she says, wiggling her eyebrows.

"Brianna Mae, I am *not* asking for a dick pic. Besides, you only want me to ask for one so you can see it yourself." I laugh.

"Guilty. I mean, Ave, Cas is hot, like *really* fucking hot. Can you blame a girl for trying? I just need to see what you're working with to make sure you are getting your needs met. But whatever, be a selfish bitch then," she says as she hands me my outfit.

"I love you, too, Bri," I say while hugging her.

"Yeah, yeah, yeah, love you, too, I guess. I'm leaving now. Try not to get too in your head. I will call you later because I'll need details on how it all went," she says, walking towards the door.

"I wrote him a song!" I blurt out. Her hand remains on my bedroom door knob for a minute before she turns around and stares at me.

"Can you repeat that? I must have hallucinated because it sounded like you said you wrote a song," she says, looking shocked.

"You heard correctly." My heart flutters in my throat and my skin feels hot. Bri continues to stare at me with a shocked expression.

"Bri say something, please, because this frozen expression is making me antsy."

"I—wow that's amazing. I mean, shit, Ave, I know that writing is a tricky subject for you. When was the last time you wrote anything?" Her question shouldn't surprise me. It's a valid question and yet it still shocks me.

"Remember when the three of us hung out during our sophomore year?" I ask.

"Yeah—and remind me to let Cas know that threat still applies. But what does..." She pauses when recognition finally hits her face. "Wait, you mean to tell me that you haven't written anything since then?" I nod and swallow the emotion down, not wanting to cry. That time in my life was difficult for me. Finally having my friend back only to have him taken away by his own demons sucked. I'm grateful that with years of therapy I've learned to accept that the past happened and it doesn't have to impact the present.

"I mean wow, Ave, that's a long time to go without writing. But I am so proud of you for writing again. From everything you've told me, it sounds like Cas was your muse or something." She chuckles. I snap my eyes to hers so intensely that her laughter stops abruptly. "Holy shit, you're serious?" she asks.

"I-uh, I think so?" I shrug.

"Wow, that's just. Wow. And now that Cas is back—"

"I'm writing again. It just makes sense, you know? Him being my muse." My voice comes out shaky.

"Well, regardless of the reason, I'm glad you are writing again. Can I—can I read it?" she asks hopefully. I want nothing more for her to read it, but a part of me hesitates because it's raw and emotional. Yes, it's based on the conversation Cas and I had, but the lyrics don't give anything away. I'm still silently contemplating whether or not to share or not when she interrupts my thoughts.

"You don't have to share if you don't want to, Ave. I'll understand if you want to keep it to yourself, but if you do want to, I would love to listen," she gently says.

"It's not that I don't want you to listen. I do. It's just if you do listen, you have to promise me not to ask what it's about. You just have to read it and be okay with not asking any questions," I say, slightly scared of her reaction.

"Okay," she says matter-of-factly. I hesitate momentarily before walking past her to grab the journal. I pause outside of my bedroom and take a deep breath before entering and handing it over to her. She begins to read and my leg shakes with anxiety. Bri huffs out a sigh and stops reading to look at me.

"Avery, I'm going to need you to sit on the floor. I can't read this with your legs causing an earthquake," she says, returning her attention to the journal. I sit on the floor in front of my bed, feeling like I'm at the far end of the line waiting to get inside my favorite amusement park. She puts her hand on my shoulder, indicating that she wants to talk. When my eyes meet hers, I find tears there. My face pales like a character in a suspense movie, waiting for something terrible to happen.

"This is incredibly beautiful, Avery. You feel every single emotion with your words, and it's just, it's breathtaking and heartbreaking. Thank you for sharing it with me. Please tell me you shared this with him or that you will. And please, please, *please* tell me you are entering this song into the contest?"

"I haven't shared it with him yet. I was just waiting for the right moment. And I'm nervous he won't like it. As for the contest, I'm, uh...well, I'm considering it. You think I could win with this song?" I ask.

"Avery, that man *adores* you. Of course, he's going to love it," she replies. "As for winning, Avery, this is Grammy-level shit. I think you need to enter it." Bri and I made casual conversation before she stood from the bed and said, "Anyways, enough emotional talk. You have a date to get ready for. I'll be by my phone eagerly awaiting a play-by-play." She gives me a playful wink before walking towards the door.

My eyes flicker over to the bed where the dress and shoes lay. This is it, my first date with Cas. I mean, you think that after everything that happened this morning, I wouldn't be nervous. My body is trapped in barbed wire and the spikes are my anxious feelings, poking into me. I look at the clock on the end table closest to my bedroom door and it reads 11:00 a.m.—seven more hours until he comes to get me. I have no idea how to pass the time, so I reach for my phone and text him.

Me: Hey

Cas: Hi, yourself. I can't wait for tonight.

Me: Me too. Is it weird that I'm nervous? I mean, after this morning, I feel like I shouldn't be, but I am.

Cas: I'm just as nervous, maybe even more so now.

Me: Now?

Cas: Yeah. This morning was, well, hot as fuck. I just feel like I built up this expectation in your head of what it will be like and I won't measure up.

Me: I feel the same way. But after how we connected this morning, I don't think that will happen. Let's promise each other now that we'll be honest if things get weird or either of us doesn't feel it.

Cas: Deal. But Avery?

Me: Yeah?

Cas: Now that I have tasted your lips, I need to taste every part of you.

Woah, this conversation escalated quickly. This seems to be the theme of our friendship. Relationship? Situationship? His words play on repeat in my brain, causing the heat to pool between my legs. Those words continue to float around in my brain, so I reach for my vibrator, hoping to release some of this tension.

Chapter 28

Cassidy

She's my home

IT'S FINALLY HAPPENING—MY FIRST official date with Avery. Anxiety and excitement are two boxers circling each other, waiting to see who throws the first punch. I find myself checking the clock frequently.

This morning was fucking hot. It took all of my willpower not to devour her completely. The way she pressed against my body felt like two magnets finally coming together. Just thinking about it gets me hard. My hand moves towards my dick to release the growing pressure when the sound of my phone pings with an incoming text. I open the text excitedly, thinking it's from Avery, only to have my heart stop beating. No matter how many times this fucker texts me, my anxiety spikes every time. This time though, I'm ballsy enough to text back.

> **Unknown: *image* You know you wanna get fucked up. You think you're done with this shit? Once a junkie always a junkie.**

> **Me: What the fuck do you want from me?**

> **Unknown: Guess you'll find out soon enough.**

What the fuck? I'm pissed that this fucker keeps texting me. I'm even more pissed at myself for my mouth involuntarily salivating when I saw the needle in the picture. I've done so much work on myself, yet the sight of a fucking needle has me fighting a craving I hoped I'd never have again. Whoever this is seems to know this and finds new ways to contact me, no matter how many times I block the previous number. My gut feeling is that I know who this is, but I just can't put my finger on it. The sound of an alarm blaring startles me into the current moment.

Shit, I have thirty minutes to get ready. How did the time fly by so quickly and why can't I remember anything in the last half hour or so? I make my way to the closet in search of the perfect outfit for tonight. While sifting through every option, I notice my hands are shaky with nerves. I've been on many first dates in my lifetime, but never while sober and never with Avery. Everything has to be absolute perfection tonight, as she deserves nothing but the best. My hand brushes a silky, emerald button-down shirt and plain, black dress pants. The shirt matches the color of her eyes, making my decision on what to wear easy. I take the quickest shower of my life and race against the clock to finish getting ready.

I'm ready to go and realize only fifteen minutes have passed. I sit down and focus on some breathing techniques my therapist taught me to help reduce my anxiety levels. After a few minutes, my heart rate has slowed and my breathing is more regulated. Before heading downstairs, I give myself a once-over in the mirror to ensure everything is in place. I am halfway out the door when I realize the flowers I picked for Avery earlier today are still sitting on the table. I run back inside, grab them, then bolt out the door.

When we were kids, Avery always gravitated toward the wild lavender lilies that grew in between our houses. I knew I needed to pick some for her. As I approach her door, my heart is beating so fast I'm surprised it hasn't jumped out of my chest. I take a calming breath to steady my nerves. Flowers in hand, I knock on her door.

"Come in. The door's open," Avery says.

I open the door, not sure what I expect to see. "Avery, you really should lock this door. What if I was—" The rest of my words fall away and I stare. In front of me stands this goddess of a woman in a stunning black dress. Her wavy hair brushes over one shoulder in the most beautiful and sexy way. My gaze roams her face, noticing her eyes have this gold dust stuff across her eyelids that brings out her green eyes with such intensity I lose my balance. Her full, pouty lips are painted blood-red. My throat goes dry as my eyes travel down her body. The flowers fall to the floor with a soft thud. My eyes land on her thigh, exposed by the slit in her dress that travels so high that one wrong move and I will see everything underneath. My eyes continue their journey down her body, and on her feet are these extremely high heels that as red as her lips.

The second my eyes land back on her face, my feet move swiftly on their own accord. I slam her up against the wall. Her wild eyes are the invitation I need to lean in, but her words stop me.

"Can I ask you for a favor?" Avery's hesitation piques my interest.

"Anything," I reply, hoping she'll allow me to continue.

"Can you do that thing you did earlier today with your hand?" My throat goes dry and my face grows hot.

"What thing?" I ask, feigning innocence. "You mean this?" I take my hand in hers, dragging it down my body towards my dick and pressing her hand against it. She grips it in her hand, but shakes her head.

"Was it when I touched you here?" My hands travel to her hips, gripping with gentle pressure. She bites her lower lip and shakes her head again.

"Then what do you want me to do with my hand, Avery?" My voice comes out rough and raspy.

"I think you *know* what I want, Cas," she whines, tone laced with desperation.

"I want to hear you say it. I need to hear you beg for it," I whisper.

"Put your hand on my neck and choke me like you did this morning. Please?" Avery begs, catching me off guard and stealing my breath. Who knew that underneath the innocent girl exterior is someone with a freaky side. As much as I want to do all these things to her, I remind myself to slow down.

"I will gladly do it, but baby?" I ask.

"Hmmm?" She peers up at me from under her long, dark lashes.

I slowly lean in to whisper in her ear. "Take my hand and place it there yourself," I demand.

Avery's eyes widen. I start to think that maybe I pushed it too far, but then her hand moves up and covers mine. There's a brief hesitation, but what she does next has me wanting to screw the date. Just throw her over my shoulder and have my way with her. Avery places my hand on her exposed thigh and slowly glides it up her body. Her skin is silky smooth, I just want to sink my teeth into her thigh. Her black dress is as smooth as her skin as I feel it bunch underneath our hands. Avery is fully in charge here, making me want to get on my knees and worship her. My hand beneath hers moves painstakingly slow. She wants me to feel every inch of her and she knows it's killing me. My hand finds her breast and I pause to squeeze it, noticing her head falling back, exposing her sexy as-sin throat. She only allows me to linger at her breast for a few seconds before my hand finally comes in contact with her throat.

"Cas, please," she begs me a second time. That's all the invitation I need. My mouth comes down hard on hers, our teeth and tongues colliding and crashing into each other. Avery's salted caramel taste mixes with my coffee aftertaste, the perfect combination of bitter and sweet. A perfect metaphor for who we are individually and how well we complement one another.

We stay locked in that moment, my hand sitting still on her neck as we kiss. She pulls my bottom lip into her mouth, biting and tugging with enough force that the hand that's placed on her neck squeezes in response. It sends her reeling. Her hand moves down my body too quickly for me to stop her, not that I wanted her to. She slips her hand inside my pants, an amazing feat considering the tension and hardness from my arousal has made my pants extremely tight. I assumed she would do what she did last time, sliding her hand up and down me.

The second Avery's hand dips into my underwear and squeezes my painfully hard dick, my hips involuntarily thrust into her hand. The sensation of her warm hand stroking and squeezing feels so good that I almost don't notice the pressure of my hand on her neck increasing. That sends her flying even higher, increasing her pace and causing enough friction to start a fire. I totally lose sight of where I am and what our plans are, but the feeling of me being close to coming snaps me back to reality. I pull my lips back from hers and loosen my grip on her neck. Her hand is still gripping me, but her stroking has stopped.

Both of us stare at each other, gasping for air. I can only imagine her heart beating as fast as my own. I look at Avery, my sweet, innocent goofball with a wild side and a take-charge attitude. Her hand still cups me. I place my hand on her wrist to try to remove it, but her squeeze only tightens, causing me to close my eyes.

I let out a slow and steady breath, hoping to cool my body down. "Avery, sweetheart, you are *killing me* right now."

"I know," she answers so confidently, it borders on cocky.

"You have *no idea* how much I want to take you right here, but I promised you a date and I'm following through," I say.

She sighs and playfully rolls her eyes. "Fine, we can go on this date, but when we get home, you better be prepared to continue where we left off," she says, finally backing away and taking the warmth with her. I miss it already.

She bites her lip, her smile sinister. She seems very satisfied knowing I'm still hard as a rock. I, on the other hand, am far from satisfied. I quickly adjust myself, hoping to avoid public humiliation.

"Let's go before—"

"Are those for me?" she asks.

"Hmm? Are what for you?" I ask, slightly confused. Then look down to where she is pointing. Oh shit, the flowers! I completely forgot about those.

"Shit, yeah, sorry! Meant to give those to you, but uh, I got distracted." I lean down to pick them up and notice that many of the petals are either smashed or broken. "Well, they *were* supposed to be for you, but they seem squished and ripped now. I'm sorry, I can get you new ones and promise not to drop them." I attempt to move past her to throw them away, but her hand on my wrist stops me. I look up to see her eyes shimmer with unshed tears.

"Cas, I—no one has ever brought me flowers before," she says before looking at me, blinking rapidly. Way to go, Cas. You made her cry. I reach my hand out to comfort her, but she stops me.

"Damn it, Cas, are you *trying* to make me look like a raccoon? I need a minute to blink away the tears so my make up stays put," she says. What does she mean, no one's ever bought her flowers? Have they *seen* how Avery looks?

"I don't understand how no one has ever bought you flowers?" I say, dumbfounded.

"Well, I, uh—I've never really been with long enough for them to get me flowers before," she says, looking away with sudden shyness. Her first confession shocked me, but this one floors me.

"Avery, how is that even possible? I mean, *look* at you. Not only are you breathtakingly beautiful, but you have a heart of gold that any man would be lucky to have. I find it hard to believe that anyone lucky enough to date you wouldn't want to do so seriously," I say with slight irritation.

"They didn't have a problem getting serious. It was me," she says, looking up at me with vulnerability filling her eyes. Time stands still at her statement and my body feels like a statue.

What could she possibly mean by *it was her*? There's nothing wrong with her. Why on Earth would she think that she's the problem? A sharp pain radiates from my hands and that's when I notice my hands are balled into fists. *Breathe, Cas.* The warmth of her hands over mine brings me back to her. My mouth opens, ready to tell her how special she is, but she shakes her head.

"There was only one person I wanted to get serious with," she says, and if I wasn't already head over heels in love with this woman, this would have done it for me. I blow out a slow breath to calm my racing heart before bringing my hands to her shoulders and pressing a quick kiss against her forehead.

"There is only one person I want to get serious with, too," I tell her before pulling her into a hug, desperately needing comfort. Her cheek rests on my chest while mine rests atop her head. Being in her arms feels safe.

"As much as I want to stay here with you like this, we should probably get going." I reluctantly pull out of Avery's arms, grab her coat off the rack, and place it on her shoulders. Her fingers interlace with mine as we make our way toward my car. Something she said earlier hits me. *When we get home.* That single statement sends comfort throughout my body and pleasant warmth in my chest. Avery is my home, and I will do everything in my power to prove to her that I can be hers, too.

Chapter 29

Avery

Date 2.0

MY STOMACH IS FILLED with Pop Rocks, crackling with excited energy as we walk towards his car with our hands linked. My chest feels like it's about to explode just thinking about the flowers in my kitchen. They aren't just any flowers, though. He brought me lavender lilies, my absolute favorite. The fact that he paid close attention to me causes heat to radiate between my legs. No one has ever paid that much attention to me, and if I let myself, I could get used to it.

As we approach the car door, courage overtakes me, and I spin around before he can open it and drag his lips to mine. My hands tangle in his hair as his hands grip my hips. The kiss deepens as our tongues come together in the most seductive dance. I tug on his bottom lip and my grip on his hair tightens. His fingers dig deeper into my hips, causing my dress to wrinkle. He pushes my back against the car door as I pull on his lower lip one more time, before my tongue travels along his jaw to his ear.

I lick, then bite his earlobe and whisper, "That was for the flowers." I lower my mouth to his jawline, alternating quick licks and bites before pulling away. "And that was for always kissing me first. I figured it was my turn to play a little." I give him a playful push before opening the car door. I slip inside and track his movement toward the driver's seat, a seductive smile on my face.

He turns towards me the second he's in the driver's seat. "Avery, if you hadn't stopped that, we would have *never* made it to the restaurant." I stare at him for a minute before laughing, remembering what Bri said earlier. He looks at me with a perplexed expression, making me snort-laugh. *Very attractive, Avery.*

"What's so funny?" he asks.

"When I was getting ready for the first date, well, the one that didn't happen, Bri told me to look good. Good enough that instead of going out to dinner, you would want to stay home and have something *else* for dinner." I clasp my hands over my mouth in horror. Holy shit. I just said that out loud. I hold a breath waiting for his reaction, unsure what it will be, but then I hear him laugh.

"That sounds like something she'd say," he says with a smirk and a wink.

Cas has one hand on the wheel, the other is gripping my thigh. His thumb strokes the sliver of bare skin, back and forth, and my body hums with pleasure. The silence is nice. I love how we don't always have to fill the space with mindless chatter; we can just enjoy each other's company. Still, there has been a question on my mind as of late.

"Hey, Cas?" I whisper.

"Yeah, baby?"

"Do you ever wonder what would have happened if we dated all those years ago? Like, if we actually said how we were feeling?"

Cas purses his lips, pondering the question I asked. I almost want to take it back, but I remain silent.

"I don't think it would have worked out." Cas' answer, while expected, is still disappointing.

"Oh..." I respond.

"I was a mess back then. I wouldn't have been the guy you needed and deserved. You and I are like a semi-colon. Back then, we put a necessary pause in our friendship. We didn't know where we were headed or who we would be. If we got together back then, our story would have ended with a period. But because of you letting me go when you did, you added the little comma under that period. Because of you, our story was allowed to continue when it was the right time."

Words don't seem sufficient enough, so instead I lean over and give him a peck on the cheek. Cas really does say the sweetest things to me sometimes. When I pull back, Cas has an introspective look on his face that wasn't there before.

"Cas, is everything okay?"

"Yeah, I'm just thinking of things." Well, that was vague. Vagueness and my anxious thoughts have a toxic relationship, so I need to clarify things before I overanalyze.

"Bad things?" My voice rises with a note of panic. He must have heard it because he reaches for one of my hands, interlocking our fingers. He brings our joined hands up to his mouth for a quick kiss to reassure me.

"I promise, baby , they're good things." He pauses to look at me. "Very good things." His eyes fall back to the road, but our fingers stay interlocked and rest on his thigh.

"So, you gonna tell me where we're going *now*? Or will you keep it a secret until we get there?" I whine playfully.

"You'll have to wait. We're almost there, though, so you won't have to wait much longer." With those words, I sigh and look out the window while the world softly blurs around me. It's oddly warm this late in the evening, so our windows are rolled down just enough to allow in the natural breeze.

Cas begins to slow down and that's when I see a beach unfold before me, my body humming with tranquility. Being near the water always puts me at ease and erases all of my worries. I wish we could go hang out at the beach and just be, but I don't think that's what Cas has in mind. I think we're about to pass the beach, but instead we are heading toward it. Are we going where I think we're going? My head snaps in his direction and I see Cas with a goofy ass smirk on his face.

"Oh my God! Cas, you didn't! How? What? How?" All these questions come flying out of my mouth in rapid fire. But he keeps driving, ignoring them all.

"I can't *believe* you are taking me to The Lagoon. This place has been booked solid for months! How did you manage this?" I turn to look at him with questioning eyes.

He shrugs. "I know a guy," he says matter-of-factly.

"Who the hell do you know who has a connection like this?"

"My buddy is friends with the owner. I made a call and he hooked me up," he responds.

"Well, look at you, Mr. Fancy Man. Who knew you had all of these connections? I've been dying to come here, so thank you." I lean over to kiss his cheek. I can't help but dance in my seat with anticipation and excitement as we reach our destination.

"I'm so glad that my first time here is with you and that we finally get our chance at a date." Our gazes lock. I can feel the love and yearning igniting between us. We must have stayed there too long because the sound of the valet knocking on the window jolts us back to reality. Cas gets out and walks around the car to open the door for me before handing the keys and a ten-dollar tip to the man in a purple, suede jacket.

His hand finds mine and he starts leading me toward the restaurant entrance, but stops me before we enter. "It's the same for me, too," he expresses.

"What's the same for you?" My voice comes out in a whisper.

"That I get to share this experience with you." He says, leaning down to press a quick kiss to my lips before we make our way inside the restaurant.

I've heard about how beautiful this place was, but being here with Cas is a fairytale. The Lagoon is next to the beach, so you can listen to the crashing waves as you eat. In the middle of the restaurant lies a large wooden dance floor with couples already moving together as a jazz band plays on a slightly elevated platform. Above the dancing couples are hundreds of fairy lights hanging from four large wooden columns on each corner of the dance floor. My attention shifts towards the seating area where I notice the tables all gleam chestnut brown and are in various sizes to fit small or larger parties.

We make our way to one of the more intimate tables with a trio of white, pre-lit candles sitting in the middle of the space. Cas pulls the chair out for me, then walks over to the other side of the table.

"Cas, this place is amazing. And isn't this view just breathtaking?" My voice comes out breathless, and my eyes are filled with wonder and amazement.

"Truly stunning," Cas says. When I look at him, his eyes are glued to my face.

"I meant the beach view, Cas."

"I know what you meant, but the view I'm looking at is better than any beach." He takes my hand in his and gives it a light squeeze. The waiter makes his way over to us, and I can't help but stare at Cas while the waiter speaks. Cas looks at me with amusement on his face, and that's when I realize the waiter is staring at me with a question in his eyes. A blush creeps up from my neck, making my face feel hot as I murmur an apology. Cas struggles to hold in his laugh while I ask the waiter to repeat the drink specials to me.

I take my hand back so we can take a moment to study the menu. Everything looks so delicious that I'm slightly overwhelmed. We both end up ordering the same dish: chicken parmesan and a side salad. While the silence in the car was comfortable, I was glad that conversation picked up at the table. We talk about our days and laugh at our inside jokes and childhood memories. I'm really hoping that he won't bring up the song writing competition. I'm still waiting for the perfect moment to share the song I wrote for him and I don't want to ruin the moment. I really love seeing him like this, carefree and open.

"So you know how I told you in the car that I was thinking good things?" he blurts out. When I nod my head, he continues. "I've been stuck on something you said earlier today." I try to wrack my brain of all the things I said, trying to figure out what he's referring to.

"You said, 'when we get home,' and it has me thinking. Being with you feels good, and every time I touch you, it feels like I'm home. I just want you to consider me your home, too," he says with the raw vulnerability of a child. This side of Cas is an arrow straight to my heart. Cas being so open and raw is still all new to me. It's something that I could get used to.

"Cas, you have to believe you deserve it. You feel like home to me too. I love how I can be myself around you. I can't make you believe anything I tell you. That's something you have to learn to work through. I can only hope my words will be enough for you." It still breaks my heart to see him struggle with his self-confidence. In high school, he always came off as self-assured and cocky. Now, I wonder if that was genuine or if it was all an act to hide what he felt underneath.

"Speaking of working through things. I've actually been meaning to talk to you about something." Cas' gaze refuses to meet mine, an anxious tell of his I've picked up on. I know his toxic view on anxiety and how it's this taboo thing. I've tried to talk to him about how it makes me feel. I've always known Cas struggled with anxiety. Ever since I was diagnosed, it opened my eyes to others who suffer—Cas being one of them. Before our friendship went to shit in high school, I tried to talk to him about his anxiety. It never went well. Besides our epic fight in the hallway, that was the only other time we got into it. No matter how many ways I spun it, Cas never could see how his view on anxiety affected me.

"What did you want to talk about?" A million and one scenarios play out in my head and I bring my focus to my breath, forcing myself to regulate my breathing before it becomes too erratic.

"I'm sorry." Well, that's not what I expected him to say.

"Sorry? What are you apologizing for?"

"For how I made you feel about anxiety. I've been working on accepting my own issues with mental health. The more I thought about how I viewed mental health, the more I realized I was kind of a dick to you about yours. I–I'm sorry that I ever made you feel like there was something wrong with you or that anxiety was this abnormal thing only crazy people have." Cas clears his throat and when his gaze finally locks with mine, I can see genuine remorse and empathy shine back at me.

"Cas," I whisper as I move to cover his hand with mine. When I open my mouth again, he shakes his head.

"No, please let me finish. You are a goddamn warrior. Your anxiety makes you special. It makes you beautiful, kind, and an overall badass. You tried to get me to understand that in high school and even though I wasn't ready, I should have never said that I wasn't crazy. The fact that I made you feel anything other than amazing doesn't sit well with me. You embracing your anxiety has actually helped me accept mine, so I guess a thank you is necessary as well. So, thank you."

The wind has been officially knocked out of me. That's the only way to describe the sensation in my stomach as I catch my breath. An invisible weight I hadn't realized I'd been carrying melted off my shoulders. I hadn't realized I was still holding onto that pain until this moment. With his words, he took a pin to a recurring anxious thought and popped it.

"I, well, thank you, that means a lot. I didn't know I needed to hear that until now. I'm glad you're coming to terms with having mental health issues. It's never made you a broken man, Cas, because you never were. I adore every part of you, and now I have another piece of you to hold, cherish, and protect. Thank you for finally understanding that anxiety isn't such a bad thing. So many of us struggle with it and it's normal." A mix of relief and happiness prick behind my eyes, but I blink them back.

"You are everything I could have ever asked for, Avery. I have a long way to go in regard to working on myself. But you make me feel like I can do anything. Your bravery is inspiring and I strive to be strong like you."

"You already are. This conversation? The vulnerability you shared? That is beyond brave, it's inspiring. Cas, a year ago, you wouldn't have shared any of this. You've grown so much and it's been beautiful to witness."

"Thank you, Avery. From you that means everything."

The arrival of our food interrupts our conversation, but I'm content where it ended. Plus, there will be endless conversations like this in the future. For the first time in ages, Cas and I seem to be on the same page and I couldn't be more giddy.

We sit in comfortable silence as we eat and my gaze keeps flickering toward the couples dancing in front of the band. I must have been zoned out because I suddenly noticed that Cas extended his hand towards mine in a silent question. I place my hand in his without hesitation as he leads me to the dance floor.

He twirls me once before gathering me close. He puts one hand on my lower back while his other hand nestles between our bodies as we sway to the music. My cheek rests against his chest. Bliss is dancing with the man you've loved since you were fourteen. It feels like walking into Disneyland for the first time. We continue our slow, rhythmic swaying, and our gazes lock onto each other.

"Remember the first time we danced?" Cas asks.

"Yes, of course, I do," I reply.

"I wanted to kiss you then, but chickened out. I didn't want to make things awkward if you didn't want to kiss me."

"I wanted you to kiss me. When you ran off, I thought I did something wrong."

"I think we've definitely made up for it," Cas whispers in my ear before nipping my earlobe with his teeth. My spine shivers and goosebumps covers my skin.

The sun is beginning to set, the sky various shades of pink and orange, perfectly complimenting the restaurant's fairytale vibe. My hand moves from his shoulder to his neck, squeezing gently and communicating my needs without words. He leans down just as I'm leaning in and our mouths meet in a slow, dreamy kiss that has my toes curling and my head spinning. The kiss is soft and tender, and we don't feel the need to rush, savoring the moment. Eventually, he pulls back and just looks at me.

He brushes his thumb against my cheek and my body hums with pleasure. I close my eyes, wanting to soak in the movement of his thumb against my skin. I don't want this moment to end.

"Avery," he says in such a gentle, loving way that my eyes snap open.

"You're so damn beautiful. Every time I see you, you take my breath away. You stole my heart at fourteen, and I hope to God you never ask for it back." I'm at a loss for words and my throat tightens as my eyes sting with the threat of tears. My hand rests on his cheek. Cas presses a kiss to my palm while still looking at me with lust in his eyes.

"Say something, please?" he pleads.

"You had my heart at fourteen, too. It's yours for as long as you want it, as long as you'll have me," I tell him.

"Avery, no one else is it for me. You are my endgame." The seriousness in his tone should scare me, but instead, I find it reassuring.

"Avery?" he asks.

"Hmmm?" I respond as he leans down to whisper in my ear, sending shivers up and down my spine.

"I think it's time for dessert." His words make my knees weak, and if his grip on my back wasn't so tight, I would collapse. I bite my tongue and a metallic taste fills my mouth. He's waiting for my response, but no words come out of my mouth. The only thing I seem capable of doing is nodding my head.

We settle our bill and rush out of the restaurant so fast you'd think it was on fire. We all but jump into the car and speed off. Although the restaurant isn't far from our houses, the drive feels like it's ten times longer. He takes one hand off the wheel to squeeze my knee, causing my body temperature to spike. He doesn't stop there, though, as his hand slowly makes its way up my thigh, squeezing with each pause.

When his hand grips my inner thigh, my eyes roll back in my head and a moan escapes my mouth. He seems content keeping his hand there, but my body is way too hot. He needs to see how much he's affecting me right now. I take his hand in mine, slowly guiding it underneath my dress, letting him feel how wet I am.

"Fuck, Avery, that's all for me?" he asks. His voice is raspy, heavy with lust. Instead of answering him, I guide his hand back and forth, rubbing against my lacy, black underwear. The friction causes my breathing to come out in pants. He tries to pull his hand back, probably to gain some control, but my grasp is firm and I quicken my pace. It feels damn good to be in control. His name leaves my mouth in quick staccato pants, increasing in volume and intensity. I'm so close it's almost painful, but his words stop me.

"Avery, damn, that feels good. But if we keep going, we're going to end up crashing this car." His fingers cup my pussy and he rubs me a few more times before he's able to release his hand from my grip. I'm left sexually frustrated and unsatisfied. Like when one of my favorite shows ends on a cliffhanger and I have to wait to find out what happens. I look over and nearly come at the sight of him bringing his fingers into his mouth. The same fingers that were almost inside me. My sexual frustration intensifies like a boiling pot of water that's about to spill over with each passing second. My hand reaches in between my thighs to give myself some relief, but the quick look he gives me stops me dead in my tracks.

"Don't you even *think* about doing that right now. We have danced around this long enough. I will be the one to make you come. I will be the one who makes you come so many times you forget your own fucking name, and that is a promise I *intend* to keep." That declaration shuts me up and I shift around in my seat, trying to get comfortable, but my desire is making it damn near impossible.

Chapter 30

Cassidy

I'm going to treat you like the goddess you are

THE DRIVE FROM THE restaurant is a lust-filled blur. I barely resist the urge to pull the car over and fuck her in the backseat, but I don't want our first time to be on the side of the road where anyone can see her. A naked Avery is for my eyes only and I would happily go to jail for murdering anyone who dared look at her.

I pull into my driveway and I can feel Avery's confused expression burning a hole into the side of my face. The sound of her talking fades like a song that's coming to an end. It's not until I feel her hand on my arm that I realize I am lost in my thoughts.

"Huh?" I ask, hoping to come off cool and collected, but my voice sounds rough and gravelly.

"I asked you why we're parked here. I thought we were going to go to my place. What about your grandparents?" she asks.

"They're out of town for the next few days. We have the entire place to ourselves." Her breath hitches and her body shivers with anticipation. My hand slides down her leg towards the inside of her thigh. Her thighs clench together, trapping my hand in place, and I can't help but laugh.

"Avery, I have *very* specific plans for you tonight, but it requires us to get out of the car and into the house. I promise my grandparents aren't here. Want to know why?" I ask.

"Why?" Her question comes out as a soft moan.

I slowly lean in, hoping to build some suspense, and whisper in her ear, "I was the one who told them they needed a trip out of town."

She's quiet, her eyes are unfocused staring into the distance. *What if she changed her mind? What if this isn't what she wants?* I swallow my anxious thoughts down and try to be direct.

"Freckles?" She gives me no response so I try again. "Hey, tell me what you're thinking. If you want to back out and wait a little longer, we can. You need to be in this as much as I am." My nerves threaten to steal the ounce of confidence I have. *What if I imagined all of the signs? What if she changed her mind? What if she thinks I'm not good enough? What if*—but she interrupts my thoughts.

"I'm just thinking about how to run as quickly as I can inside your house and up the stairs without breaking both my ankles." She turns to look at me, desire sparkling behind her eyes. With those words, I'm out of the car and over to her side with lightning speed. Before she can move any further, I scoop her up and throw her over my shoulder. Her initial surprised gasp turns into a fit of giggles, but stops immediately when my hand grabs her ass.

"Cas, put me down. Our neighbors will think we're crazy!" she shouts. I ignore her and continue walking into the house with her tossed over my shoulder like a rag doll.

I don't give two shits what the neighbors might think as we make our way to my front door. My mind is strictly on what I'm about to do to the woman in my arms. My hands tremble so much with anticipation that

I fumble, trying to unlock the door. It takes a few tries, but eventually, we're inside. I start to make my way up the stairs, but she stops me.

"Wait!" she shouts." I want to try something." Her tone has me both on edge and curious.

"What do you want to try?" I ask, my curiosity growing. Instead of answering, she somehow shifts around in my arms. Her hands are now gripping my shoulders and mine are circling her hips, forcing me to tilt my head back slightly to look at her. We stay in this position for a moment, and I desperately want to know what she's thinking right now.

I don't have to wait much longer because her body starts to slowly, torturously, glide down my front. My grip on her tightens, pressing her further into me. As she continues her journey down, my eyes roll back in pleasure and I feel myself harden even more. Her feet barely have time to touch the ground before I pin her against the wall.

"I have *always* wanted to try that move," she says.

"Oh yeah? And did it measure up to what you imagined?" I whisper in her left ear. She tilts to allow me more access.

"Mmmmmmm," is all she manages to say. My mouth trails up and down her neck, alternating between light kisses and bites. Avery squirms beneath me as her hands wildly explore my body. Before she can continue, I take both of her wrists in one hand and raise them above her head.

I lean in closer to her and say, "Not yet. I told you I had plans, and I intend on following through." My mouth closes the remaining distance between us. The taste of desperation and promise is the perfect mix as my tongue tangles with hers. She angles her head, changing the direction of the kiss, and every nerve in me ignites. My body is a switchboard and Avery is the operator. Her gasps and moans send me into overdrive. I push my erection into her and she starts to grind against me. *Shit, this is going too fast. I need to slow down.* I try to inch away and gain some of the control back, but that excites her even more as her pace increases. *Fuck, I'm not going to last. But it feels too damn good. Focus, Cas, focus!* I break the kiss to collect myself and stare at her. Her once green eyes are almost black with want.

"Avery, if you keep doing that, I'm going to come too soon." Avery's hands fall softly on my shoulders with the gentle beauty of leaves brushing against the grass in the fall breeze. I kiss her lips quickly before taking one of her hands and leading her up the stairs toward my room. I make it all the way up before the panic hits. Avery's been in my room many times, but never like this. There isn't anything crazy hidden inside my room, but having her inside with the intent of having sex with her scares me.

She senses my hesitation and squeezes my hand in reassurance. Her voice, thick with lust, comes out in a purr. "Cas, we don't have to if you don't want to. I'll understand."

That snaps me back to the moment and wipes away any hesitation. "What? No. Of course, I want to do this. It's just—this is our first time and I don't want to disappoint you."

"Cas, look at me," Avery demands. I feel her hand cup my chin, redirecting my gaze to her face. "Remember everything that happened this morning?" When I nod, she continues. "I was telling Brianna about what happened between us. I was so turned on by the memory that as soon as Bri left, I grabbed my vibrator and came twice while thinking of you. I don't think I'll be disappointed, at least not unless we *only* sleep."

I sighed in relief, but then her words hit me. I turn around, pressing my back to the door, resting one hand on the doorknob. "So, the thought of me made you come twice, huh?" That's all the courage I need before opening the door and pulling us both inside. I lead her towards my king-size bed, laying her down gently before bringing my mouth to her ear. "Let's see if the real version can make you come three times." Her eyes widen briefly before a playful smirk takes over. Her hands grab my shirt and drag my lips to hers. I let her take over for a minute, enjoying the sensation of her tongue wrestling with mine. I'm thankful for the cinnamon candy the waiter gave us with the check. The sweet yet spicy taste of the candy only amplifies the experience. Avery's head is caged between my arms, locking her in place. She pulls on my lower lip with her teeth, and my body's automatic response is to grind up against hers.

I pull myself back before she can deepen the kiss. "So I learned this trick in therapy to help when I'm feeling high levels of anxiety or struggling with a flashback."

"Are you...is everything okay? "

"I'm good, baby. More than good knowing you're about to be in my bed at my complete mercy." To drive the point home, I glide my hand up her body, gripping her neck in the way I know is guaranteed to make her needy and wet.

"I learned this thing called grounding in therapy. I'm supposed to name five things I can see, four things I can touch, three things I can hear, two things I can smell, and one thing I can taste. It's helped me out a lot. But I want to use it in a different way."

"Different how, exactly?" she asks with a skeptical look on her face.

"I want to worship every inch of your body. I want you squirming beneath me, begging me to fuck you. I want every single one of your senses to come alive beneath my hands. I want you teetering the precipice of delirium before pounding into your pretty pussy. I'm about to treat you like the goddamn goddess you are."

Avery gasps, her eyes become hooded, and I can see her pulse thrumming erratically in her neck. It's safe to say she's no longer skeptical about our little exercise.

"Y-yeah, I think, um, we can try that," she stammers.

"Good girl. Listen, I love this dress on you it's hot as fuck. But it'll look even better on my floor." I spin her around and attempt to search for the zipper.

"It's on the side," she whispers. My dick is screaming at me to rip off the dress, but my mind tells it to chill the fuck out and take it slow. My fingers trace the zipper. I feel her shiver beneath my touch. Slowly, I unzip the dress. The moment it drops to the floor, I am stunned speechless. I felt her underwear in the car but I wasn't prepared for all of this. I take a step back to admire her in a see-through lace bra and matching panties. Avery is curvy in all the right places, causing a groan to escape my mouth. My gaze travels down her body to her red heels and I almost lose my focus.

I grip the back of her thighs, forcing her to grip my shoulders so she doesn't fall. I feel the wicked grin stretch across my face before gently tossing her on the bed. Her tits bounce and all I can think about is having her perky nipples in my mouth, sucking, nipping, and licking them until she's screaming for my cock.

"Wait, the shoes. Should I take them off?" she asks.

My fingertips trail over her body leaving goosebumps in their wake. My hands grip her hips before leaning down to whisper, "Leave them on."

I shrug out of my suit jacket, tossing it toward the dresser, my focus solely on the radiant woman before me. I scan her body from head to toe, drinking in everything that is Avery like a man dying of thirst. She's here, sprawled atop my bed like she was meant to be here. Like she belongs here. Her ivory skin is the perfect contrast to my dark sheets. Her skin sparkles beneath the moonlight, causing her freckles to stand out in contrast to her pale skin. As much as I want to continue staring at her, I'm eager to see more of her. I reach out and pull her up so that we're nose to nose.

Our mouths meet desperately, exploring and tasting as if this was our only chance. Our lips dance seductively with each other while my hands explore her body. My fingertips glide across her silky skin, leaving a trail of goosebumps in their wake. I pull back to look at her, scanning her from head to toe. Her auburn hair cascades in waves on my pillowcase, and my fingers tingle with the urge to reach down and caress it. Her body is a damn masterpiece painted with luscious curves and I just know we are going to fit perfectly together.

Chapter 31

Cassidy

5 4 3 2 1...But make it sexy

"LET'S START WITH FIVE things I can see. You have the most beautiful green eyes I've ever seen. They're truly captivating. When I touch you here," I say, touching Avery's inner thigh and watching her eyes become cloudy, "your eyes get hazy and it drives me insane." I tighten my grip and watch her eyes roll into the back of her head, her body arching slightly.

"Then there's your skin. You have the softest skin I've ever touched. All the freckles on your cheeks and nose make me want to kiss each one individually." I spend my time kissing them all over her face, from her forehead to her chin.

"When I do this," I exhale a warm breath in her ear, causing her body to shiver, "you get these goosebumps, and it lets me know you're feeling what I'm feeling. Then there's your throat, silky and perfect. And when I do this," my hand moves up her thigh and onto her throat as I gently squeeze, "your eyes roll back into your head and you bite your lip, making me want to keep my hand there forever."

"Then there's your mouth, full and pouty. It's so fucking sexy. When I do this," I say, pulling her bottom lip between my teeth and tugging just hard enough, "you arch your back like that, pushing your body into mine."

"Finally, but most importantly, are these things right here," I trace my fingers over the lace of her bra before undoing the clasp with a slight pinch of my fingers, reveling in the gasp that escapes past her lips. She quickly shimmies out of the garment before tossing it to the floor. I take her breasts in each of my hands and squeeze. "Your breasts have been in every single one of my fantasies. I have jerked off to the thought of them more nights than I can count." I squeeze them again, harder this time, as I rub my thumbs against her nipples in a circular motion. They harden and a slow, seductive moan escapes her lips. "When I do that, you make the most delicious sound I've *ever* heard. It makes me absolutely crazy."

I look back at her eyes which are glazed and hooded. "Cas..." My name comes out in a throaty whisper. "Please, I can't take it anymore. I need you inside me," she demands, trying to pull me on top of her, but I resist.

My hand falls back onto her neck and her eyes snap open, her focus zeroing in on mine. I stare at her and say, "Oh, Avery, after I'm done exploring your body, I am going to fuck you so hard that you won't be able to say anything other than my name." My grip tightens on her neck and her body goes wild beneath me. Her responses are slowly driving me insane. I want to say screw it and give her what she wants, but I need to finish what I started.

"Now, why don't we focus on touch," I say, scanning her body, figuring out where to begin, knowing where I want to end. "You have the most incredible hair I have ever seen. I swear I could come right now from just seeing it wild and loose over my sheets." My hand grazes across her cheeks before bringing both hands into her hair. I allow my fingers to play with a few strands, barely resisting the urge to bury my face and inhale her scent. "So silky and soft," I say as I drag Avery up into a sitting position and grab a fistful of her hair. I pull it so her head is tilted back, leaving her neck exposed. Her hands shoot to my biceps. The more I pull her hair, the harder she squeezes.

"Caaaaaaaas, please. I am dying here—oh," she moans as I tug a little harder and my mouth crashes down on hers. Giving her just a fraction of what she's demanding.

"I want to drive you crazy. To make you as fucking crazy as you make me feel," I tell her. I release my hold on her hair and bring my hands down towards her ribcage. "You know, I never thought I would find a ribcage sexy, but yours haunts me in my dreams every damn night." I rub my thumbs slowly along the sides of her stomach, watching her breathing turn into pants. "Fuck, Avery, that sound is driving me crazy." I find myself completely lost in the soundtrack of her passion. I bend down and replace my fingertips with my lips, kissing my way up to right under her breasts. My tongue darts out, swirling around her erect nipple before pulling it between my teeth, tugging it gently. I let it go with a soft pop before turning my attention to her other breast and repeat the same steps. Her hands shoot from my shoulders to my head, locking me there for a minute as she screams my name.

I wiggle myself out of her death grip to refocus on my goal. My hands move down to cup her ass. "Now, *this* is truly incredible. I've always been more of a boob man, but Avery, your ass has changed my mind." I begin to massage it and her body arches just the tiniest bit, her hands moving to cup her breasts. "Ahh, someone likes that, huh?" I add more pressure and her legs wrap around me, pulling me closer. "I have imagined you bent over my bed as I take you from behind so many times." I spank her hard enough to leave a mark before moving on.

"Now, I think it's time to feel inside you, don't you think? Do you want that, baby?" I ask. My desire is threatening to beat right out of my chest. This is actually happening. Finally, something I have only thought about for years. Avery beneath me, stunningly beautiful, and she's letting me in, all the way in. Sex is one thing, but I want her heart. I want everything with her. I want the laughter, the smiles, the heartbreaks, and the fights. She's the most special person, and now that she's here and ready to make that next step. Let's just hope I don't fuck this up. I can't fuck this up. *Okay, focus, Cas.*

"Y-yes-yes I d-do," she stammers out, and she unwraps her legs from around my waist. My hands slowly trail down her body, feeling every inch of her delicate skin. This drives her crazy, causing her to become more antsy below me. I stop my hands at her hips, firmly pressing my fingertips into the slight dip in her curves.

"You're so cruel, Cas. Straight up fucking cruel," she says, and I can't help but chuckle.

"Didn't anyone ever tell you to be patient?" Her glare only makes me laugh harder. My hands slide down further to grasp the inside of her thigh with one hand and cup her pussy with the other. She's already so wet for me. "Damn, Avery," I say with clenched teeth as I try to maintain my composure. I rub my hand back and forth across her panties, feeling the wetness transfer onto my hands. She starts to moan when I slip my fingers into her pussy. Her body begins to thrust her hips against my hand when my pace increases.

"Cas, oh my G—" Her sentence dies on her lips as I move my fingers in and out of her, teasing her slit. Avery gives me an evil look beneath her lashes and I let out a chuckle. I know exactly where she wants my fingers, but why not have fun with her? I find her clit and rub in slow circles, not wanting to ramp up the pace yet. Something about teasing Avery turns me on, so I brush the pad of my thumb once or twice over her sensitive bud before slowly sliding my finger out. But my attempt is hindered when Avery's hand claps my wrist, caging me inside her. *Well, well, well.*

"Is this where you want me, Avery?" She hums her response, but that isn't enough for me.

"What was that? Words, baby." I lean down so that our noses are touching. "Tell me where you want my fingers, Avery," I demand.

"Inside me. I want your fingers inside me now!" A wicked smile spreads across my face while my fingers stroke her clit. I start nice and slow, torturing her before increasing pace and pressure. Avery chants my name repeatedly, getting louder with each stroke.

"Cas. Cas, *Casss*—" she moans. I insert another finger, hoping that she'll let herself give in to her orgasm soon enough.

"Avery, fuck. You're so warm and wet. Your pussy takes me so well I can't handle it." I increase the pace and pressure even more. As her thighs tighten around my hand, her moans come faster and louder. "Does this feel good?"

"YES! Fuck Cas. Keep going! I am so clo-ose." The last part of her moan comes out in quick staccato sounds. I feel her start to contract around my fingers and can tell she's almost there.

"Come on, Avery. You're close, I can feel it. Let go for me, sweetheart. Just let yourself go." I increase the pressure incrementally, and then she lets go, coming on my fingers while screaming my name. "Good girl, that's it. Let go." She lets out a final moan as she finishes. I slide my fingers out and bring my other hand to her neck to bring her focus to me.

"Goddamn, Avery. Just hearing you moan and scream is enough to make me come." Her eyes are glued to mine as she watches me bring my fingers inside my mouth. "Fuck, the way you taste? I could live off your taste for the rest of my life."

Leaning closer toward her trembling body, I whisper, "Avery, baby, my patience has officially run out, but you've been such a good girl, so I'm going to take off the rest of your clothes and then mine. I'm going to taste you with my tongue first, then give you what you asked for earlier. I want to feel you come on my tongue and my dick. Are you okay with that?" I growl.

She arches towards me and nods her head. Shit, this is about to get even more real. I feel like a teenage boy who's about to see a woman naked for the first time. Even though I've been with multiple women in my lifetime, this feels like the first time for me. Her tight heat pulsing around my finger felt incredible. I could get lost inside her and I wouldn't complain. This is Avery and me, and I'm ready to get to the finish line with her.

I undress quickly before fully undressing her, leaving nothing but her shoes on. I place myself in between her, throwing her legs onto my shoulders. She crosses them at the ankle and I give her a wicked look before my tongue finds its way inside her. As soon as I'm in, her body rocks against my face and she arches her back again while moaning. My tongue makes slow, circular movements around her clit repeatedly, making her breathing come out in short pants. I flick, and lick, and suck, over and over again.

"Cas, fuck, how are you so good at this? Like if you want to go pro at oral, you could. I'd support this career decision. Wait, no, that tongue belongs to me and only—" I bite down gently on her clit and then soothe it by bringing it in between my lips. Her loud scream does what I was hoping it would, to stop the conversation and allow her to just enjoy.

I peek up to find her kneading her breasts and pinching her nipples. A smile crosses my lips before I bring myself back between her legs. When I add nipping into the mix, she lets out a loud, ear-piercing scream. I continue this pattern, alternating between slow and fast, and it isn't long before she's contracting around me.

Her legs grip me tighter and all my patience is gone. I pick up the pace. She finally lets go and the taste of her explodes on my tongue. So sweet and uniquely Avery, a taste I want to experience for the rest of my life. I force myself to slow my pace, gently easing myself out of her. I bring my mouth to hers, mixing our tastes together. She seems to like it because she takes my tongue in her mouth and sucks, sending a whole new set of sensations toward my dick. If I don't take care of that soon, I might go insane.

I reach into the drawer of the nightstand next to me and pull out a condom. I try to rip open the package, but my hands are so shaky with anticipation that Avery ends up taking it from me.

"Allow me," she purrs while ripping open the package. She rises to a kneeling position and looks at me from under her lashes while slowly rolling it on. I groan, and my head rolls backward. Once the condom is on completely, she squeezes my dick and gives it a few pumps.

"Avery, we'll have time for that later, but right now, I need to be inside of you or I'm going to explode," I say, my voice hoarse. I lay her back down and inch her closer to the edge of the bed. I push one of her legs to the side as far as it will go and bring the other to wrap around my upper back. She adjusts herself into this position. I stare down at her with a question in my eyes.

She nods her head enthusiastically while guiding me toward her entrance. I slowly inch my way inside of her and hear her gasp. I stay there for a second, not yet fully inside of her. I circle my hips to get her used to my length. She doesn't seem to think it's enough because she demands, "I *know* that's not all you got. I want you all the way in, and then I want you to fuck me as hard and fast as possible. Just when you think it's hard and fast enough, I'm going to demand more."

Something inside me snaps. I push myself all the way in, giving her what she asked for. I drill myself into her over and over while increasing my pace. "Is this what you want or do you want me to fuck you harder?" I pant. Sweat glistens on our bodies and we become so slippery that she tightens her leg on my back.

"Harder, Cas! Harder!" she demands. I change our position, lifting her hips off the bed, bringing her other leg around my back, and pumping even harder and faster. Her moans are becoming more frequent, driving me to go as deep as I can. But I know I'm not going to last much longer with each pump pushing me closer to my climax. Her hips reach up to match my thrusts as we move together like we've been doing this all our lives. I change the angle again and it causes her to let out soft cry.

"Cas, I'm so close. Don't stop, please! Don't sto—*oooh*," she gasps as I change the angle again, causing her to pulse around my dick. We are racing toward the finish line, and I feel myself growing closer and closer.

"You have never had anyone fuck you this good, have you? No one will ever be able to again. This is mine. You are mine. Say your mine," I demand.

"No one has fucked me like you. I am yours. I am oh-so yours," she screams as she comes. Seconds later, I grunt my release. I slow down our movements, eventually pulling out, only to collapse on top of her. Our breathing is rapid and our heartbeats are slamming against our chests. I roll myself off of Avery to take care of the condom. I climb in bed behind her and she snuggles up against me, causing my dick to twitch. Avery turns around, slinging her leg across mine and resting her head on my chest. I run my fingers up and down her back and let out a sigh.

"Cas?" she asks.

"Hmmm?" I ask, my eyes closed and my hand still moving up and down her back.

"I love you," she says, then presses a kiss to my chest and nuzzles her head into the crook of my neck.

"I love you, too, freckles." And with that, she falls asleep as I sit there, listening to her slow breaths. She looks peaceful in her sleep, and I am overwhelmed with love for this remarkable woman. I kiss her temple and whisper, "I love you with all of my heart, Avery, and I will love and protect you for the rest of my life." I close my eyes and drift into a peaceful sleep.

Chapter 32

Avery

They made a what?

Early Fall of 2023

THIS MORNING I WOKE with a satisfied smile, blissfully happy. Yesterday was a whole new type of sexual experience. No one has ever paid that much attention to my body before. After getting a taste of Cas, I want more. Who knew that rough sex was my kink? Or maybe it's just rough sex with Cas that does it for me. I smile and reach across the bed, hoping for another round, but Cas isn't there. I shoot up into a sitting position, looking around the room, but he's nowhere to be seen.

The most delicious smell has my stomach rumbling with the same intensity as a monster truck revving its engine. The thought of Cas cooking me breakfast brings a smile to my face. I turn to check my phone for the time and squint at the brightness. I put my phone back down but not before noticing I had unanswered text messages. It's seven in the morning, and I *know* we didn't get much sleep last night. Cas loves his sleep and gets grouchy when he doesn't get enough, so why is he up early making breakfast?

I shrug my shoulders and head towards his closet for something to wear before heading downstairs. Even though his grandparents aren't home, I still don't want to walk around their house completely naked. My fingers come across one of Cas' favorite hoodies. I hurriedly put it on, noticing that it comes to my mid-thigh. I search everywhere for my underwear, finally noticing it hanging off a lampshade. I shake my head and can't help the smile that spreads across my face.

I make my way downstairs, fully intending to give him shit. "Cas, why was my underwear hanging on the lampshade? You must have been desperate to fuck m—" My words fall out of my mouth when instead of Cas in the kitchen, I see his grandparents. My eyes widen, and my cheeks are hot and flush.

Oh my God.

"Well, good morning to you, too, Avery. Boy am I glad our plans were cut short due to the birth of a great-grandbaby. Michael, remind me to send them a card," Evelyn says with a smirk while sitting at the kitchen table, drinking her coffee. "How did you sleep last night?" she asks.

"I, um, fine. Thank you." I look behind me as my brain calculates the best way to escape this situation without being rude.

"Sit down, hon. I'm making pancakes and bacon," Michael says. His back is to me, but I sense him holding back his laughter.

"Oh no, that's okay. I'm not that hungry. I, uh, I'm just going to head upstairs and take a shower." I turn around and run up the stairs, but Evelyn stops me.

"Please, sit down, dear. I'd love the company. Coffee?" My mind is flashing a giant error message, preventing me from formulating coherent thoughts. I answer her with a quick nod. She goes up to the counter and pours another cup. I sit there, silently cursing Cas and his audacity. She returns to me with coffee and a plate of food. "Eat up. It looks like you need the calories this morning." She winks at me.

"*Oh my God.*" I place my face in my hands to hide the embarrassment. I can only imagine how red it is.

"Oh, sweetie, don't be silly. You and Cas are both adults. And, honestly, it's about damn time y'all got together. Isn't that right, Michael?"

"Sure is, Evelyn. And I believe I owe you twenty dollars, too," he says, then pulls out his wallet and hands her the money.

"Wait, why do you owe her twenty dollars?" My brows furrow, and a small frown breaks out across my face.

"Oh, we had a bet, you see. Michael thought y'all would never figure your shit out while *I* thought y'all would be getting it on as adults. And even without the outfit you're wearing, the look on your face says it all. All I have to say is *finally*." We sit in silence for a while as I scarf down my food and coffee as quickly as possible and then get the fuck out of there. The coffee scalds my tongue, but that's the least of my worries right now.

I quickly finish my last bite and start to rise out of my chair when she places her hand on my arm. "I am happy for you, darlin', but I want to make sure that this is something you want. Don't want to have any broken hearts to mend if it implodes." I knew this was a conversation that was likely to happen, but I wasn't expecting it this soon.

I swallow my mouthful of food and take a breath before responding. "I've wanted this since I was fourteen. I don't plan on breaking his heart," I say.

"Honey I said, broken hearts. Plural. You both can break each other's hearts, and I don't want to kick his ass if he breaks yours. You're family, Avery, and no matter what happens, we'll always love you like our own."

My throat feels tight with emotion. Standing up, I pull Evelyn into a hug and plant a kiss atop her head. "I love you guys, too." My voice comes out thick and shaky. I walk over to Michael to hug and kiss him before going upstairs to shower. I stop midway on the stairs and look down to see them dancing together in the kitchen, breakfast temporarily forgotten. The love they have for each other is something I've wanted my whole life. Something I've wanted with Cas. And now, it might just be a possibility. I let out a soft sigh and continued walking up the stairs.

I step out of my clothes and into the shower, hoping to wash away the embarrassment of that entire conversation. The sound of a door creaking open and closing causes me to freeze.

"What the fuck? I'm in here. A little privacy, please?" My demand doesn't deter the intruder, but I hear a familiar voice.

"Oh baby, I know. But your request for privacy has been denied," Cas says. He steps into the shower with me, backing me into the tile before I can tell him to fuck off.

"Hi, freckles." And then his mouth crashes into mine, my protest dying on my lips. His tongue tangles with mine and a moan escapes me before I can stop it. My hands move from his chest into his hair to drag him closer to me.

I push him away as I remember who's downstairs. He looks at me with lust and confusion, then tries to bring his mouth back to mine. I place both hands on his chest, stopping him.

"Absolutely not, Cas. Your grandparents are downstairs. And while we're at it, a little heads-up would have been nice. I walked downstairs in nothing but your hoodie and my underwear, thinking it was you cooking me breakfast. I talked about my underwear being on the lampshade and admitted to us having sex to your grandparents. Your *grandparents,* Cas!" He looks at me for a second, then starts laughing. What a jackass.

"It's not funny, you asshole. I was mortified." I slap at his chest repeatedly before he finally takes my hands and pushes them over my head as he presses me against the wall.

"I texted you this morning saying I was going out for a run and that they were back early, but you didn't check your messages, did you?" he asks.

Damn it. I *knew* I should have checked my texts "Fuck. No, no, I didn't." I sigh.

"So then *technically,* what happened downstairs isn't my fault." He can sense me getting ready to argue, so he continues quickly. "Still, I'm sorry you were embarrassed, and next time, I will try to warn you ahead of time." His lips crash into mine, causing my head to spin.

I pull back again, thinking of my conversation with Evelyn. "Thank you, that's all I ask. Oh, did you know your grandparents placed a fucking bet on if and when we would have sex?" His stunned expression tells me he is just as shocked as I am. Still, in disbelief, I recount what happened downstairs, but leave out the part about potentially breaking each other's hearts.

He thinks about what I said for a minute before I see a wicked grin cross his face. "So, want to make it so Gram really earned her twenty dollars?" he asks, wagging his eyebrows at me.

"Absolutely not! They are *downstairs,* and them knowing we had sex is already embarrassing enough. They don't need to hear us having sex," I say a bit desperately.

Bringing his mouth to my ear, he whispers, "What if I *promise* to be quiet?" My body responds without my permission, arching closer to him. My head rolls back, giving Cas access to my throat.

"That's great, but what about *me*? How are you going to keep both of us quiet? You're good, but not tha—" His hand shoots to my neck, squeezing in quick pulses. A moan threatens to leave my lips, but his mouth comes down on mine, muffling the sound. My hand instinctively reaches for his dick, wrapping my fingers around it and tugging it towards my entrance, telling him exactly what I want.

"Avery, we can't. No condom," he says, frustrated. My only reply is to continue stroking him slowly at first, then faster. When the pressure on my neck increases, I pause mid-stroke, a plan forming in my mind.

"You know, you took *such* good care of me yesterday. It's only fair to return the favor." Slowly, I make my way down his body, touching and teasing until I'm on my knees—one hand on his thigh, the other gripping him.

"Avery, you don—" is all he can get out before my mouth slides around his tip, sucking and licking the little bead of pre-cum. His hands are on the tile wall of the shower, holding him upright.

With my hand still wrapped around him, I take my mouth off him and look up at him under my lashes. "Let's see how quiet you can be." A wicked smile breaks across my face before taking him all the way into my mouth. My hand tightens around his length as it moves in rhythm with my mouth. I alternate between slow and quick strokes, wanting to tease him like he did to me yesterday. The hand that rests on his thigh moves to cup and play with his balls, causing his hips to thrust deeper into my mouth involuntarily. With a soft pop, I take him out of my mouth and grin up at him underneath my eyelashes. His fingers fist in my hair and pushes his dick back inside, fucking my mouth with force. My eyes widen with shock, but I adjust quickly. I claw at Cas' thighs, reminding him who's in charge. His face is all contorted with trying to remain as quiet as possible.

"Avery, I am so close. Let me take over." He tries to take himself out of me, but my grip tightens.

Cas looks down, but I shake my head and pause to say, "Nope, you tasted me in your mouth yesterday. It's my turn." I return to what I was doing, quickening my pace, knowing he's just seconds away from coming. I squeeze his dick a few times in between strokes, and that's all it takes to have him explode all hot and sticky in my mouth.

He drags me up by my neck, slamming me into the bathroom wall, sending a delicious wave of lust through my body. I lick my lips, removing the remaining traces of him around my mouth, and watch his eyes darken to almost black.

"Please tell me you're on the pill," he demands. His hands grip my waist when I nod and he hauls me up against the wall. My legs wrap around him and my head falls against the tile. He seats himself inside me as we adjust to this new sensation of having nothing between us. He pumps and thrusts as hard as possible, always hitting the right spot.

"Avery, that was the hottest fucking thing I've *ever* experienced." His words come out in quick, short grunts that match each of his thrusts. He adds a finger into the mix to rub my clit so fast and hard that I find myself coming in seconds. My legs begin to shake and my toes curl so hard, it borders on painful. My head falls back against the cool tile and he bites my neck while still thrusting inside me. I can feel myself contracting around him and have to bite my lip hard to prevent a scream from erupting out of me. Moments later I feel his rhythm falter before he comes inside of me, his pace slowing to a stop. He's still inside of me, bracing me against the wall, my legs wrapped around his waist. Our breathing is rapid, our hearts pound in our chests.

"Now, that's one way to say good morning, isn't it?" I ask.

"It's my new favorite way," he says, pulling himself out of me and lowering me down. The water is now frigidly cold, so we hurry up, washing ourselves and taking turns under the spray.

Chapter 33

Avery

Cas' song

THESE LAST COUPLE OF weeks with Cas have been pure bliss. It's not just mind-blowing sex. Okay, the sex is fantastic. What I cherish the most, though, is our genuine emotional connection. Cas has given me the best gift: a lover and best friend wrapped up together, and now that I have it, I don't ever want to let it go.

My mind, however, has been occupied by two things: Cas and the song I wrote about him. Every time I think about sharing it with him, terror runs through my body. I haven't sung in front of anyone in a long time. Each morning, I wake determined to share it with him, but every day I find a reason not to. It doesn't help that Bri constantly asks me about his reaction to the song, and my excuses are becoming increasingly pathetic. Instead of facing her head-on and being honest, I avoid her texts and calls.

As I lie in bed, I obsess about the box in my old bedroom. Maybe it'll give me the confidence to share my song with Cas. A frustrated grunt leaves my mouth and I aggressively push off my blankets before walking to the room to grab it. Soon enough, I'm clutching the box in my hands like it's my only lifeline. My heart gallops inside my chest as I stare at the notebook for what feels like an eternity. This isn't your average journal, though. It's not something you'd use to bitch about your day or swoon about your current crush. This book was given to me for the sole purpose of composing my music.

Communicating my feelings usually comes naturally to me, but sometimes the words become lodged in my throat, making it impossible to speak. My mom gave me my first journal at the age of ten. It first started as random scribblings about my day. Then those scribblings turned into poetry, which eventually led to songs. Whenever I couldn't make sense of my feelings, I grabbed my notebook and began to write as everything began to click together in my mind.

Music was my form of therapy. This notebook has me walking down memory lane to the day Cas gave me this notebook.

Summer before high school

It was a warm, sunny, August day and school was set to start next week. The sun's warmth felt like the Goldilocks story, not too hot, but not too cold. I tilted my head toward the sky as my hair swirled in the wind. Cas and I were sitting out on his grandparents' dock, feet dangling, skimming across the top of the water. I was in my yellow sundress and Cas in his black jeans with holes in the knees and a gray tank top. It never mattered how hot it was. He was always in jeans. There was something soothing about sitting next to my best friend and staring out at the calm water. We would start high school the following week and I grew increasingly nervous.

"Can't believe we're going to be freshmen next week," Cas said, reading my mind.

"I know. I can't believe it. I'm excited, but nervous. It's such a change from what we're used to. I just don't know what will happen," I said.

"You have nothing to be nervous about. People are going to love you. I mean, who wouldn't?" Cas asked, looking at me with an intensity I hadn't seen before. Before I could process what that look meant, he continued, "I, uh, I have something for you, but I have to go and get it. I'll be right back."

After a few minutes, he ran back towards me, carrying a black shoebox. I looked at the box, and when my gaze landed on his face, I burst out laughing. "You got me shoes? Awww, you shouldn't have." I chuckled.

"Don't be such a smartass, Avery. Just open the box," he said. My hands reached for the box, but he hesitated, slightly pulling back. "I saw this in the store and thought of you, and, uh, you can tell me if you don't like it. I hope you do, but it's okay if you don't. You can tell me you like it and then never use it again. I uh—" I placed my hands on the box and looked into his eyes. His voice was shaky, and he talked so fast that it was hard to keep up.

"Cas, please just give me the box. I'm sure I'll like whatever it is because it came from you." After a few deep breaths, he finally let go of the box. I stared at it for a moment before opening it. I wasn't entirely sure what to expect, but it wasn't this. Staring me in the face was a velvety, forest-green journal with two silky black ribbons securing it closed. I stroked the journal, feeling its softness glide across my fingertips. I removed it from the box, untying the ribbon to discover the most beautiful golden pages. So many emotions fluttered beneath my chest. At first, I was confused about why he got me this, but also touched that he went through all the trouble to get me this beautiful notebook.

I didn't even hear the sound of the camera going off because I was too stunned. I must have made a face, though, because his next few words took me by surprise.

"You don't like it." Cas' body oozed disappointment.

"What? No! Cas, I love it. I'm just confused by why you would gift me this journal."

"You deserved to have a special journal just for your music. Something to put all of your beautiful songs into," he said quietly, not quite looking at my face.

Tears welled behind my eyes and I was grateful he wasn't looking at me. I needed a moment to collect myself. This was one of the nicest things anyone had ever done for me, which meant even more coming from him. I caressed the notebook gently as if it were fragile and might break apart any second. My vision clouded and hot tears rushed down my face.

"Damn it, Avery, I didn't mean to upset you. I know you love writing, and you're so talented. I shit, I'm sorry. Here, give it to me and I'll take it back. Don't worry, I'll fix it." I returned the journal to the box and threw my arms around him.

"Cas, you will do no such thing. This is one of the nicest things you could have done for me. I will cherish this journal forever and can't wait to start writing in it. If you take it back or apologize for getting me this, I will throw your ass into this lake." He hugged me back, and this hug felt different somehow. I put that thought away to process later. I pulled back and reached for the journal, touching it again to make sure it was real.

I had been slowly stumbling since the beginning of summer break. But with this one moment, this one act of kindness, I knew. I gazed up at his beautiful face through tear-soaked eyes. I realized I had fallen head over heels in love with my best friend.

Present day, Fall of 2023

When I place the box on the end of my bed, it tumbles to the ground with a soft thud, scattering its contents across my bedroom floor. Setting my journal aside, I reach for the box and that's when I see the photo from that summer. Cas was always taking photos. With his grandfather being so talented at photography, it made sense that Cas would take to the hobby, as well. And he's stupidly good at it. Cas being Cas, would shrug and make some self-deprecated joke anytime I told him so.

My fingers caress the photo and I can feel the emotions of that day as if they were happening in the present. Any doubts I had about sharing my song with him now flew out the window. The thought of him walking around feeling like he's broken is the encouragement I need to follow through. I place the photo in the box and place it on the bed. Reaching for my phone, I text Cas before I lose my bravery.

Me: Hey, are you busy?

Cas: Not really. What's up?

Me: Can you come over? I have something I want to show you.

I am waiting for his response. Those three little dots dance for a few seconds. My heart feels like it's in my throat with how fast and hard it's beating.

Cas: Be there in five.

I let out a long, unsteady breath and call the person who always comforts me.

"She's alive. I've been texting you," Bri answers.

"I know I've been avoiding you. I'm sorry. I was just calling to let you know I'm doing it today. I texted Cas and he's on his way over." I don't need to clarify what I am doing because Bri knows. She always knows.

"Fucking finally. How are you feeling?" she asks. My thoughts and feelings pour out of me too quickly. I should be worried that Bri won't understand what I'm saying, but she's known me too long.

"Girl, that man worships the ground you walk on. He's going to love it. Trust yourself. Trust your talent, but more importantly, trust his feelings for you. I read the song and it is good, Avery. Like professional-level, good. Just let go and sing your beautiful heart out."

"I knew you would be the person to call to help calm me down. Thanks, Bri. I honestly don't know what I would do without you." My heart rate slows and relief wraps around me like a warm hug.

"Duh. You don't need luck or good vibes because he'll love it. Trust that gut of yours, and make sure you let me know how it goes. I love you," she says.

"I love you, too, bye."

Cas enters my music room at the exact moment I hang up the phone. "Oh, so you say, 'I love you' to everyone?" I know he isn't serious by the teasing nature of his tone.

"You know I love you. That was Bri on the phone, giving me some last-minute courage and advice."

"Why do you need courage?" he asks. His eyes follow mine as I reach for the journal. "Is that..." he asks. I nod my head while hyper-fixating on his facial expressions.

"Wow, I haven't seen that thing in ages. I can't believe you still have it." Cas moves past me toward the box before looking up at me. He walks toward me and gently picks up the photo as if he's afraid he'll damage it. Cas clears his throat before continuing. "You, uh, you kept this?" he asks.

"Of course, I kept it. It's a beautiful photo, Cas. Despite how I felt for you during high school, I still cared about you. The photo and notebook came from you so that makes them important to me. I do have a confession, though. When we stopped being friends when you were, well, you know." I still can't say the words. My eyes cast downward.

"Using heroin? It's okay. You can say it."

"Right. Anyway, do you remember when you told me about your child-hood a few weeks ago?" He stares at me in confusion, so I keep going. "You questioned me about my feelings and asked if I was okay, and I kept saying yes." I search his face, watching his confusion turn to recognition.

I continued. "Well, I kind of lied. I wasn't sad, but that night after you fell asleep, I felt inspired to write. It's something I haven't been able to do since you relapsed." A mix of sadness and guilt coats my voice. Clearing my throat, I continue. "I was so angry and hurt you chose drugs over me and every time I tried to put pen to paper, nothing would come out. I thought maybe I could write in the old notebooks, but still nothing came. So yeah, I haven't been able to write again until recently, until you."

Finally gathering my courage, I look up at his face and see it flutter with emotions.

"I-I'm so sorry. Damn it I just...while I was using, I was only concerned with my next high. No one else mattered. The fact that you stopped writ-ing because of me makes me feel like a huge asshole. All the apologies in the world will never fix that. I can't believe I took that away from you," Cas says while putting his face in his hands.

"Cas, look at me." I wait for his eyes to lock with mine before continuing. "I didn't say any of this to make you feel bad. I said them because you deserve to know how big of a deal it is that you're here with me now. You've awoken so much in me and I'm forever grateful. I asked you to come here because I wrote something for you and wanted to share it. Is that okay?"

"Yes, of course, I want to hear it. I would be honored." When they say the eyes are the window to the soul, they weren't kidding. A mix of love and awe swirls behind Cas' eyes.

"Okay. It's called *Stained Glass*." I hear his intake of breath. And before he can speak, I close my eyes, take a deep breath, and begin to sing.

Chapter 34

Cassidy

What will I find if I keep unbuttoning?

AVERY GETS LOST INSIDE herself whenever she sings. My mind is a crowded mall and my thoughts are the people trying to make their way to the exit. But I push them aside to listen to her angelic voice. Avery has always been super talented when it comes to her writing. Her raw vulnerability does something to me, making me feel all fuzzy in my chest. I remember hearing her sing for the first time when we were teens and I was in awe of her then. It's been way too long since I've listened to her, though. I push my shame away and let admiration wash over my body from the top of my head to the tips of my toes.

When she told me the song's title, it sounded familiar, but I couldn't quite explain why. As the song progresses, it's obvious who she's singing about. Avery has always allowed her music to speak for her. She has the perfect song for every emotion she's feeling. To hear her sing about me is a whole new experience. I didn't think I could love this woman anymore, but here we are. I feel the cracks and bruises from years of emotional trauma begin to heal. I'm so lost in what she's doing to me, that I didn't even realize she stopped singing.

"Cas?" she asks hesitantly. Something in my gaze must have alarmed her because her arms were suddenly around me.

"Cas, I'm sorry. I didn't mean to upset you. I just wanted you to see what I see when I look at you. I didn't even thi—" I stop her by covering her mouth with mine. I can't convey my thoughts and feelings into words yet, so I pour them into the kiss instead. She has to know that what she just did for me is far from upsetting.

I reluctantly pull away from her lips only to bring my hands up to either side of her face, taking a moment to stare into her eyes. She reaches up and brushes a thumb across my cheek, and when I look down, I realize it's wet. I brush my fingers across my cheek, surprised to find them damp. No wonder she thought I was upset. I begin to clarify that they're tears of joy, but her mouth crashes into mine, stopping me. Avery's kiss is hungrier than mine, and it takes all my restraint to pull away. "Avery, I want this moment just as much as you, but I want—no, I *need*—to go slow."

I chuckle as Avery lets out a frustrated whimper. She's insatiable, but I don't want to fuck her right here on the piano. I can feel my willpower slipping, so I stand up grab Avery by the waist and throw her over my shoulder. Avery's laughter turns into a moan when I smack her ass. She returns the favor by grabbing my ass and the small ounce of willpower I had moments ago is almost completely gone. I bolt up the stairs and by the time I reach Avery's bedroom, I'm simultaneously out of breath and turned on.

I gently toss Avery on her bed, watching her bounce a few times before she settles in. Fuck. This woman is breathtaking and she's all mine. I lean down to tuck a few strands of hair behind her ear and just admire her beauty. She tries pulling me down on top of her, but I shake my head and stare at her.

"Avery, you're so damn beautiful. You're my safety net, and I feel seen when I stare into your sparkling green eyes. You see through all the walls I put up and through all my bullshit. You see *me*. You make me feel like I deserve to be loved and, more importantly, to be loved by you."

"Cas—" she starts to speak, but I shake my head, leaning down to press soft kisses across her face. I start at her forehead, then make my way to each eye, kissing them closed. I move my mouth to her right temple, then her left, my lips never leaving her skin. I kiss the tip of her nose, then both corners of her mouth, before capturing her in a gentle kiss. I coax her mouth open, allowing our tongues to tangle together.

Our tongues dance together in smooth, graceful strokes before impatience takes over and it turns to frantic and desperate. Her hands move quickly towards the bottom of my shirt, trying to take it off, but I bring her arms back down to her sides, cuffing her wrists with my hands. I pull my mouth from hers, only to trace her lips with my tongue, stopping in the middle of her mouth to tug her lip gently with my teeth.

The whimper that escapes her sends my body pulsing with heat. I remind myself to take it slow, no matter how badly I want to devour her. One of my hands goes to her neck, her eyes rolling back in response as she remembers the last time. She looks up at me, pure desire sparkling in her eyes. Instead of squeezing, I caress her neck, moving my hand to one side of her throat while my mouth finds the other side.

I gently tug at her ear with my teeth before moving down to the sensitive spot underneath. I know this spot gets to her because her back arches toward me and she groans. I whisper, "I *love* it when you make that sound. It makes me want to fuck you fast and hard."

Avery looks at me with a wicked gleam, she says, "That's how I like it."

I groan in agony. She's killing me right now. "I promised to be gentle, and that's what you'll get." I press a lingering kiss to her mouth while slowly unbuttoning her dress. "You have to know what you do to me when you wear dresses like this. So soft, free, and beautiful—just like you," I murmur. I continue undressing her, but freeze when I get to her chest and see nothing underneath the fabric. I growl and look back up at her face. "You're trying to kill me, aren't you? If I keep unbuttoning, will I continue to find you naked underneath?" My mouth goes bone dry and my face starts to flush.

Licking her lips, she brings my head to hers, and when I think she's going to take my mouth, she moves to the side and tugs on my ear with her teeth, whispering, "Keep going and you'll find out soon enough." She's going to be the death of me, but at least I'll die a happy man. I soon find the answer to my question as I take in her creamy skin dusted with freckles. The curve of her breasts makes me feel like a man dying of thirst, and she's the only one who can quench it.

I slide the dress off her shoulders, pressing short, open-mouthed kisses along her neck, shoulders, and collarbone. I make my way down to her breasts, playing with one while I take the other in my mouth. She instinctively wriggles beneath me, placing her hands on my head and securing me there. Her moans increase as I flick my tongue against her nipple while thumbing the other with my hand. I tug gently with my teeth and her breathing increases.

"Cas, you're driving me crazy. I need you now," she huffs while her hand starts to journey towards my cock. I stop her before she gets there.

"Baby, if you do that right now, this won't last much longer. Patience, " I say, chuckling at her as she lets out a frustrated sigh. My hands move down to her stomach and I kiss every inch of her before I find myself at her inner thighs. My teeth graze against her soft flesh, causing her to tremble uncontrollably. I place my fingers in between her legs, teasing her inner folds. Her nails dig into my skin.

My eyes lock with hers and a smirk forms on my face before I push one finger inside her. The feeling of how wet and slick she is makes my head spin as fast as a cotton candy machine, and a groan escapes my lips. Her hand moves in an attempt to keep me inside of her, but I'm too quick. When I pull my finger out, Avery fixes me with a murderous glare. It's adorable. I can't help the laugh that comes out.

"Oh, is this what you want?" I ask, wiggling the finger that was just inside of her. I bring that finger to my mouth and slip it inside. "Mmmm. Damn, Avery, do you know what you taste like?"

"Hmmm?" she asks.

I glide down her body to whisper in her ear, "You taste like mine." My whisper comes out as more of a growl before I place myself between my personal altar. My finger begins to rub her clit in a slow, circular motion. My pace alternates between quick and slow strokes—just enough to drive her to the edge, then bring her back down again, keeping her orgasm at bay.

"Fuck, aaah faster, please. I can't take it anymore. Yes, right there, don't—oh *God,*" she screams. So I give her what she wants, but this time I push a second finger inside of her, and she goes wild beneath me. She screams my name repeatedly and I feel her on the verge of an orgasm. I pull my fingers out before striping the rest of my clothes off.

"I need you now, and don't give me any more of this slow bullshit. I need it fast and hard because I feel like I am about to—" That's all she manages to say before I slam my dick into her, giving her exactly what she's asking. I change the angle by bringing one of her legs over my shoulder so I can go deeper, causing her screams to intensify.

"This is what you get for writing that damn song. For always seeing me. For being mine. Is this what you want? Me to fuck you this hard? You like it dirty, don't you, baby?"

"Y-yes. Please, just keep going." She shifts just slightly, allowing me to hit that sweet spot.

"That's it, Avery. Take this dick like a good girl." She begins to scratch and claw at my back, which makes me pound into her even harder. "That's right, claw at me. Make me yours. Brand me with your marks. Just like I'm branding this pretty pussy of yours. Be a good girl and come for me. Come on this dick, freckles," I grunt.

Her hips move to match my thrusts. I know she's close, so I bring one of my fingers back to her clit to help her get there quicker. It doesn't take long before she starts contracting around me and she finally lets herself come. I keep up the quick, rapid pumps, knowing that I am close to coming, too. I spread her other leg wider so I have more room. I feel myself on the brink of an orgasm when another one pulses through her more intensely than the last. "Fuck, Cas!" she yells, and then I come on that final scream of my name.

"That's right, baby. Scream my name. I want everyone to know who owns this pussy. Who owns this pussy?"

"Ca—oh my God!" she screams. I slap her pussy which causes her to scream out and arch her back.

"Wrong answer. Who owns this pussy? Say it," I growl.

"*You do, Cas.* You own my pussy. You own all of me. Now shut up and fuck me," she snarls.

"Your wish is my command," I whisper. I continue to pound into her, giving her exactly what she asked for. She swirls her hips and her pussy keeps contracting around me. And when my orgasm hits, I come so hard I see stars. I slow my pace down significantly as both of us start to come down. I collapse on top of her, still fully seated inside of her as we steady our rapid breathing. I grudgingly pull myself out before going to grab a towel to clean her up. After tossing the freshly used towel in the laundry basket, I crawl under the covers and pull her into my arms. Her head rests on my chest as my fingers run up and down her back. I feel content lying in silence with her next to me. My eyes start to close when her words break through the silence.

"You know, Cas, you never *did* tell me your thoughts on my song. You had tears in your eyes. I hope I didn't upset you," she says, looking at me with concern clouding her eyes.

How could she think this would upset me? Her words moved something in me, making me feel a different kind of nakedness. I gently kiss her forehead and look down at her beautiful face. "Avery, honey, I'm not sad. Your song made me feel seen, loved. You made me feel like I wasn't the drug addict, the burnout, or the loser. Your words made me feel like you saw Cas, the man."

She reaches up to cup my cheek and I see tears start to form in her eyes. "Cas, I have *always* seen you. Even when you were struggling, I *always* knew that the Cas I grew up with was in there. You're not your addiction, your trauma, or your mental health. You are a man who struggles with those things. You have so much kindness, passion, and drive. But most importantly, you're healing and that's beautiful. I see you putting in that work, and I am so fucking proud of you for doing it. Healing is not for the faint of heart, and you have one of the strongest, purest hearts I know." She pulls me down for a slow, lingering kiss before letting me go.

"Remember that summer before our freshman year when I walked in on you singing one of your songs?" I ask. Recognition takes over her face as she nods, but looks away.

"Avery," I say, pulling her face back to mine.

"Hmmm?" she asks.

"After I left your house that day, I turned back to look at your bedroom window and something shifted. That was the moment I knew I was in love with you." I hear the sharp intake of her breath and see her eyes widen. I preemptively open my mouth to fix what needs fixing, but she touches my lips and shakes her head.

"Y-you did?" she asks. When I nod my head, she continues. "You remember when you gave me that journal?"

"Of course, I remember," I say.

"That was the moment that I fell in love with you." No matter how many times she says that it still surprises me. *She* loves *me*.

"High school must have been rough, seeing me become so self-destructive. If it makes it any better, I was just as miserable back then. I was so in love with you, but I knew you probably didn't return my feelings because of who I came from and what I was doing to myself."

"Yeah, it wasn't easy. I remember going to bed every night, hoping you would snap out of it. I know now that it's more difficult than that, and you had demons you didn't realize you were fighting. I'm not angry or upset with you anymore about any of that, and you *are* deserving of me," she says while pushing some of my hair out of my face. "*Of course,* we spent all this time secretly in love with the other...*jackass,*" she says while laughing.

"Oh, I'm a jackass, huh? Let's see how much of a jackass I am when I do this," I say and bring my hands to her hips, swinging her legs over my shoulders. I give her one of my wicked grins before I wink and slip my tongue inside her.

Chapter 35

Avery

You have your murder face on

Mid Fall, 2023

WAKING UP IN CAS' arms is something I'm not sure I'll get used to. I shift my body to face his, hoping to catch a glimpse of him before he wakes. He's so beautiful when he sleeps. I barely resist the urge to tuck a strand of wavy hair out of his face.

Last night was incredible. I poured my heart and soul out to Cas through my song so that he would stop seeing himself as broken. Part of me hopes that he sees himself for all that he is, while another part of me can't shake the feeling he isn't fully there yet. His father did a number on him, and the thought of him going through that alone makes my blood boil as my rage comes full force.

The sound of rustling sheets beside me pulls my focus back into the present moment. "Good morning, freckles," he says before leaning over to give me a quick kiss. As he pulls back, a look of confusion crosses his face. "Hey, are you okay? You've got your murder face on right now."

"My what?" I ask.

"Your murder face. It looks like you want to execute whoever you're thinking about right now. You have these deep creases on your forehead and your eyes? They become this darker shade of green when you're irritated. The lethal look on your face right now shouldn't be sexy as hell, but it is. It makes me want to do all sorts of things to you. Who's on your mind that has you thinking murderous thoughts?" he asks with a goofy-looking grin on his face.

"Your dad," I say matter-of-factly. His face falls.

"Avery. He doesn't deserve your hate or anger. You can't go back and change it or rescue me from it all. That hate and anger is wasted on him," he says, tense with a hint of frustration.

Is he seriously telling me I can't be angry right now? I pull myself out of his arms, fully intending to give him a piece of my mind, but he quickly tries to right himself.

"Avery, I know what you're thinking. I know you. I'm not telling you that you can't be angry. I'm just saying he doesn't give a shit, and neither should you," he says. I know he sees the look on my face because now Cas is frantically babbling.

"No, you, I—*fuck*, this is all coming out wrong. I'm trying to say you can be angry, but my dad doesn't even give two shits about anyone other than himself and his habit. He's a selfish bastard, and I...I just don't want to see you upset over him."

I abruptly shoot myself off the bed and walk towards the dresser, needing space. The angel and devil are arguing on my shoulder. One saying I can and should be angry with Cas for telling me how to feel. The other is saying Cas is right and he doesn't want me wasting my energy on that man. I try to work through my tangled thoughts, but nothing seems to work. I feel Cas' arms wrap around my waist and my body instinctively melts into his.

"Hey, tell me what's going on in that head of yours?"

"I-I..." I can't finish my sentence as images of his abuse play in my mind. He didn't tell me the details, but my brain is being hella creative right now. Each scene makes my stomach bubble with nausea and I start to squirm in his embrace.

I bolt out of his arms, running out of the bedroom and into the bathroom, shutting the door behind me. I find myself hunched over the toilet dry heaving. I can't—I just can't believe that this happened to him. A child should never have to go through something traumatic, yet Cas went through it all. I think about that eight-year-old boy with this fresh lens and my heart breaks for him.

A soft knock on the door startles me and I'm mentally beating myself up for not locking the door.

"Avery, baby, are you okay?" he asks, but all I can let out is a choking sob. "I'm coming in." My eyes are closed, willing the dizziness and nausea to vacate my body. I focus on the coldness of the toilet seat and the soft creak of the door opening and closing. Cas' warm body sits down beside me. I flinch, surprised by his close proximity to me. He's holding my hair in one hand and rubbing soothing circles on my back.

"Baby, listen. My dad, he's a sick fuck. I wish I didn't tell you any of this. Then maybe you wouldn't be disgusted by me," he chokes out.

Despite the spinning in my head, I snap my head in his direction and look at him. How can he think I'm disgusted by him? I'm racking my brain, trying to find an answer, when I remember squirming underneath his touch only moments ago.

"Cas, I'm not disgusted by you. That's not it at all. I flinched because I was making your trauma about me and how I feel. I should be comforting you, not the other way around," I croak out.

Cas remains silent for a moment. I'm frantically searching through the maze that is my mind trying to find the exit. Each roadblock I come across is another self-doubt my mind throws at me. I'm about to apologize for whatever I said or did, but he's pulling me into his lap. His rough palm is the perfect contrast to my smooth hair, bringing me a sense of comfort and ease.

"Avery, listen to me. Yes, this is my trauma to process, but you've been a part of my life for so long that it affects you, too. I'm still trying to work on not feeling disgusted with myself, so I automatically assumed you felt that way about me." His voice comes out shaky and soft, and when I look into his eyes, it seems like he's fighting back tears.

"Cas, I could never be disgusted by you. You were a fucking child. You were supposed to be protected, and he failed you. If I'm disgusted, it's with the bastard who took advantage of you. It's at your shitty ass father for putting his needs above his child's. I'm disgusted with myself for not knowing what you went through. That I wrote that damn letter—" I burst into tears, my entire body shaking. I have been hanging onto everything for too long that the dam has officially broken.

Cas doesn't respond to anything. He just cradles me in his arms and holds me. I should feel self-conscious about soaking his chest with my tears, but I have no room for that feeling. We never really talked about the letter, except when we fought. I still feel guilty for writing the letter, even more so now that I understand him better. If only I had done more in high school or tried harder to get him the help he needed. If only I didn't give up on him too quickly. If only...

"Maybe if my childhood were normal, I wouldn't have had any of this happen to me," he says.

I wince. "I said that all out loud, didn't I?"

"You did. Yes, you wrote that letter to me, and it did break me a little, but I never did thank you for it."

I look up at him, confusion written all over my face. Wait, what? Why would he want to thank me?

"Thank me?" My mouth is set in a frown while my brows are scrunched together.

"Yes. You had to do it. Not just for you, but for both of us. I would have kept going down that path where I cared about nothing other than getting high. Well, that and you. But of course, back then, I was cocky and thought you would always be with me. I took advantage of your kindness and forgiving nature. So the letter you wrote was my wake-up call. I knew I needed to change because a life without you is not worth living."

"Cas, I was so hopelessly and painfully in love with you. It's on me to think that my love for you would get you to see reason. Eventually, I got tired of you playing puppet master with my heart, so I wrote the letter.

That day you overdosed, it tore me up. I almost didn't give you the letter. I almost caved that day, letting you back in," I say.

"I'm glad you didn't. If you did, I don't think I'd have remained sober. And I know we would not be where we are now. And I *really* like where we are right now." He nuzzles my neck and I sigh softly. He's right. If we kept continuing that cycle, it would have exploded into tiny shards, unable to be put back together again.

"You're right. I also really like where we are. Especially where we were last night. I just still can't help but feel like I failed both the eight-year-old and adult Cas." My voice comes out so softly that I almost wonder if he heard me.

"Avery, it's not—" he starts to say, but I shake my head and he stops.

"I know it's not my fault and I didn't fail you. I love you so much, and want you to be safe and happy. I just can't wrap my head around having no control over what happened, and I *hate* it." I feel his chest shake beneath my head. I look up at him, thinking I said something to upset him, only to see him laughing.

"Are you seriously laughing at me right now?" My eyebrows are raised so high they practically touch my hairline, my words coming out louder than intended.

His humor turns to shock before he speaks. "What? No. You just reminded me of something my therapist said. She's been helping me sort through my feelings and letting go of the blame I carry."

"Smart woman."

"Oh she is, Actually, you would love her. She's helped me out a lot. Maybe one day, you can come to a session with me?"

Going to one of his therapy sessions would be helpful, but I don't want to make it about me. "I would be honored to go, but this is your healing journey. I'm happy supporting you from the sidelines. It would be counterproductive if you have to constantly calm me down from the rage I feel at what happened to you." I respond.

"Avery, when you truly love someone, you learn to compromise a little. I've," he shifts our positions so that we're face to face. His hands cup either side of my face, his thumb brushing across my cheeks in a soothing pattern.

"Freckles. I have spent many years being selfish and only caring for myself. Let me learn to be a little selfless and take care of you. A big part of my healing process includes you."

I stare into my favorite gray eyes and tears threaten to spill over. Cas' eyes widen, but I'm shaking my head, attempting to stop the rabbit hole of his anxious thoughts. "These are happy tears, Cas. I have everything I want and need in my life. I have friends, family, and you. I have a job I love and a cat—" I stop abruptly. I don't actually have a cat, just a rescue that I've fallen in love with.

"Did you just say a cat? You finally got one of your own? But wait, how come I haven't seen it around here? Are you in the process of getting it?" His questions are like stabs to my heart. I don't know how to answer his questions without sounding stupid. It's been years since my parents' death. I have no legitimate reason why I can't get a damn cat myself. But for some reason, every time I say fuck it and make the move to get one, either guilt eats me up or the damn cat I've grown attached to at the shelter has already been adopted. It feels like the universe is shouting at me that a cat just isn't in the cards for me.

"Avery, where did you go?" Cas places his hand underneath my chin, forcing me to look at him.

"So I used to volunteer at the animal shelter which turned into me working there. You know how badly I've wanted a cat, and I still do. My parents left me the house, but I still think of it as their home. And bringing in a cat feels wrong somehow which sounds dumb—" The grip on my chin tightened.

"Aves. I never want to hear those damn words out of your mouth ever again, you understand?" My eyes widen with shock and maybe fear. He rarely raises his voice at me; having him do so now is no different.

"Y-yes, I promise," I stutter.

"Good girl, now continue." He presses a quick kiss to my forehead, all anger leaving his body.

"I still feel like it's betraying their wishes somehow. I can't explain it. Yet, I've grown attached to different cats over the years. Every time I say fuck it, I'm getting a cat it's already been adopted. I'm close again this time, but I know she'll be adopted when I'm finally ready."

"What's her name?" My eyes squint in confusion. Why does he need to know her name?

"I—um, I've named her Binx, but her name currently is Mauve. Wanna see a pic of her?" I ask, and he nods his head. I pull myself out of his arms and walk into my bedroom for my phone as he follows behind me. I scroll through the thousands of pictures of her, looking for the perfect one to show him.

"Here she is." My eyes soften and I can't help the cheesy grin that breaks across my face.

"She looks like yours, baby. One day you'll have a cat of your own." His face has this look that I've never really seen before. It looks as if an idea or something has formed inside his mind. I don't care to overanalyze it right now, so instead, I pull his mouth down to mine. The meeting of teeth and tongue is slow and sweet as I pour all the feelings from today into this kiss. With this kiss, I make my own promise to protect him and his heart at all costs.

Chapter 36

Cassidy

If Avery wants it, she'll get it

Winter of 2023

AVERY AND I HAVE been taking turns between each other's houses over the past few months. So when I wake up alone for the first time, it feels like a loss. We aren't living together, and everything is new, but I could get used to waking up beside her every morning. I roll over to her designated side of my bed, where the delicious scent of her floral shampoo still lingers.

Avery has given me so much in the time I've known her. She wrote me a fucking song, for Christ's sake. I both need and want to do something to show Avery how much that song means to me. I rack my brain, trying to find the perfect thing when I get an incoming text from Avery. She's wearing the world's largest smile while holding a tiny gray ball of fur. Both Avery and the kitten are completely infatuated with each other and that's when I remember the promise I had made to myself all those years ago. After a bad argument with her parents, Avery ran into my arms with tears streaming down her face. I don't remember every detail of the fight, just that she asked for a cat and they yelled at her. Seeing her tears gutted me and I vowed to myself to make her cat dreams come true.

I look at the photo she sent me again with a newfound excitement buzzing through my body. Fear quickly replaces my excitement when a text from a random number interrupts my search for the shelter's number.

> **Unknown: Surprise, surprise. It's your dad. Did you guess it was me? Of course you didn't, you ain't as smart as you think you are. Listen, I've gotten into some hot water lately and you need to come bail me out of trouble with the guys. Be a good son and help your old man out.**

My phone slips out of my hand and onto my bed with a soft thud. I feel like I've been locked in a small room and someone pressed a button, causing the walls to close around me. I collapse onto the floor and can't seem to catch my breath. Why does he always do this to me? My life is finally going well, I'm finally making all this progress, and one text threatens to take it all away. My vision begins to blur as all of the previous texts begin to make sense. It's been my dad all along, waiting for the right moment to announce himself. I'm not going down this road again, so I send my reply.

> Me: I'm not fucking help you out. Lose my number and go ask one of your "buddies" for help.

Instead of obsessing over my negative thoughts, I block the new number again and head towards the shower, hoping the hot water will calm my racing heart. The shower helps slow my heart rate, but does nothing for my foul mood. I still intend on moving forward with my mission of getting Avery her dream cat. I find the number I need in no time and my heart beats aggressively in my throat with each ring that sounds on the other end of the phone.

"Thank you for calling The Furry Hearts Sanctuary. This is Tanya speaking, how can I help you?"

"Hi, my, um, girlfriend works there. She told me about a cat named Mauve that's in the shelter. I was wondering if she was adopted yet?" My heart beats in rhythm to the rapid keystrokes of a computer. My patience is like an outdoor ice rink in the spring, one step and you're falling through it.

"Oh yes, that cat is still here. I can put you through to our adoption counselor, Avery—"

"No. Please don't. This is a surprise for her. Can I go through this adoption another way?" My voice cracks at the last word. Tanya holds my hope in her hands. She remains silent, most likely thinking of a polite way to say no. What she says next surprises me.

"I mean, normally we don't do something like this, but for Avery, we will. We just love her and she's been torturing herself for far too long." I pump my fist into the air, thankful she can't see me on the other end. We start to go through the paperwork over the phone and I take out the credit card my grandparents let me use while I'm not working to focus on my sobriety.

"Okay, great. I have everything. The only concern I have is if this is a surprise, how will you keep it from Avery?" she asks.

"Shit. *Sorry*, I mean, I didn't think about that. I uh—" Damn it, why didn't I think of that? How am I supposed to get this cat for her without her knowing? My brain hurts with all this plotting and planning. That's when Tanya interrupts my thinking.

"I can send her home early today. I mean, we aren't all that busy. If you can have someone come get the cat and take her home, then surprise her somehow? Would that work?"

I immediately think of Asher. He's been one of the best surprises that has come out of my reconnection with Avery. Well, him and Max. Those two are a package deal. "Tanya, you are a genius. I can send my friend Asher to pick up the cat once Avery gets home. Thank you so much. I appreciate it." I share my plans of taking her out and then going with her to the shelter under the guise of wanting to see the cat in person, knowing full well it won't be there.

"You're welcome, that sounds like a fantastic plan. I'm so thankful to be a part of it. I know she's going to a great home. I will talk to Avery as soon as I get off the phone with you. Cas?" she asks.

"Yeah?"

"You're one of the good ones. Avery's lucky to have found you."

"It's more like she saved me. Thank you so much, Tanya. I appreciate your help."

As soon as we hang up, I'm opening my text threat with Asher to ask for his help. That's when I notice my camera sitting on my nightstand. I grab it and as soon as I turn it on, it fills with photos of Avery. During my friendship bootcamp idea, I wanted to document every moment. I had no idea what I was planning to do with it. I still don't. The aforementioned list is in the top drawer and I know that whatever I decide to create it has to include this list.

I look up creative photo ideas on Google and the results are overwhelming. I scroll for what feels like five minutes when I finally stumble upon the perfect gift. It's a photo album covered in music notes. I quickly hit purchase on Amazon and select same day delivery. This is perfect. I can put the list in the front slot and the rest of the photos will go in the remaining slots. The photo album will have plenty of extra spots to put our future moments into, preferably one with her in a floor-length, white gown. I've never really thought about Avery and I making it to the aisle, but that's because I never thought I'd stand a chance with her. Now that things are different, of course I want to marry her. She's it for me, always has been.

I return to my text app and send Asher a quick message, letting him know of my plan and asking for his help. His confirmation comes not even five minutes later.

Everything is all set, so I grab my camera and head downstairs. I have my keys in hand, and the second I'm out the front door, I feel eyes on me. But when I look around, no one is there. I instantly think of the text I got moments ago and wonder if the two relate to each other. It can't be a coincidence, right? I close out of that tab in my brain before heading to Avery's, where I wait for her to come home.

Chapter 37

Cassidy

Who doesn't love cats and tacos?

AFTER ABOUT THIRTY MINUTES of waiting, her car pulls into her driveway and her eyes lock onto mine. Avery's out of her car within seconds and is running full force at me. I go to meet her halfway and brace myself for the impact, but I fail miserably. We both go tumbling into her yard and her lips crash into mine before I can say hello.

"Cas? What are you doing here?"

"Well, hello to you, too, freckles." I chuckle.

"Oh, sorry, hi. Now, what are you doing here?" she asks again.

"Taking my girl out. I'm thinking we go to your favorite taco place, and then you can show me the cat you love so much. You in?" I keep my voice as steady as possible, knowing Avery can tell when I'm up to something. She just knows me that well.

"Really? Ahh okay! Let me just change out of my work clothes and we can go." She's off of me as quickly as she crashed into me. It takes her ten minutes to get ready and out the door before we head out.

We park outside of Uncle Tito's Taco Joint, a well-known taco joint that Avery and I used to frequent in middle school. We both order three carne asada tacos with everything on them plus chips and guac to share.

Avery digs in the second our butts hit the bench. This girl loves her tacos and always has. We eat silently while my mind races, hoping the plan is working. That feeling from earlier of someone watching me comes back. I attempt to block it out, but Avery catches on.

"Cas? Hey, what's wrong?" Her voice is full of concern as she touches my arm.

"Nothing, baby. Everything is perfect." My smile is extra bright. I feel like scum lying to her, but I can't tell her what's going on when I don't understand what's happening myself. I look at her and see her studying me intensely. I put my taco down and turned toward her. "Seriously, Aves. I promise everything's okay." I'm not doing a very good job of convincing her, so I change the subject instead. "There is something that's been on my mind lately."

"Oh? What's that?"

"I uh, well, you know I've been going to therapy. And, well, you know about my addiction issues. So, I thought maybe I can do something to help people?" I shrug, not wanting to make a big deal out of it. She just stares at me, mouth agape. "It's probably a stupid idea. Forget I said it." Externally, I'm cool, calm, and collected. Internally, snakes are slithering around in my stomach and threatening to squeeze around my lungs.

"Cas, no, it's not. It's—I think that's a wonderful idea. Are you thinking like a counselor or something?"

I don't respond to her questions. Instead, I lean down to kiss her like no one else is around. She resists at first, but eventually melts into the kiss, moaning when our tongues meet. I feel myself growing hard, so I pull back, not wanting to embarrass myself.

"Um, why-what-what was that for?" she asks. A blush spreads from her cheeks to her chest.

"For always believing in me. For seeing me the way I want to see myself. For just being you, Avery."

"You're welcome." Her confident grin is contagious as I feel the corners of my mouth pull into a matching grin. How did I get so damn lucky?

"Yeah. I was thinking like a counselor or something. I want to make a difference in someone else's life."

"I know you can. You can do anything, and it makes me so damn proud to see you finally realizing your potential. I can't wait for you to find your passion. For you it'll be helping people. And for me it's helping animals. Does this make us some sort of power couple?"

I can't help but laugh. She's just so goddamn incredible.

"I guess so. How did you know you wanted to help animals?" I may be finding my passion later in life, but hearing her talk about hers inspires me to be better. To do better.

"I have my parents to thank for that. Despite their cat allergies, they loved animals. I mean, you remember when my dad and I would bird-watch. An activity you invited yourself to, by the way. Becoming a veterinarian wasn't in the cards for me, I was still able to put my passion into a job. And soon enough, you'll be doing the same thing and I am so fucking proud of you." Her voice cracks on the last word and I know she's fighting tears. I'm fighting back some of my own. We spend the rest of our time eating in silence.

"Thank you, baby, that means a lot. As for hijacking your birdwatching activities with your dad, it wasn't about the birds. I didn't give a damn about that. All I wanted was to spend time with you. I clung to you because being around you, I liked myself a little more. Being within your orbit made me feel worthy as opposed to worthless." Avery's face flushes and I lean over and kiss her cheek.

We clean up our spot, and as we throw away our trash, my anxiety comes knocking on my door like an unwanted visitor. This plan needs to go perfectly. I got a text while we ate that Asher had picked up the cat and was driving her to Avery's. *It's now or never, Cas.*

"Now, how about you show me that cat you love so much?" Her eyes light up and her smile is a mile wide. I school my face because I know when we get there, the cat won't be there. She'll be sad and heartbroken, but it'll be worth it in the end, right?

She all but runs to the car, and we are off. The entire car ride is spent with Avery's endless chatter about how amazing this cat is that I almost don't hear the pinging of my phone. I assume it's Asher saying everything is set, but when we pull into the place, there's also a missed text from an unknown number. Why can't he just leave me alone? Whatever, I'll deal with that shit later. This moment is all about Avery, who's already out of the car and bouncing on the balls of her feet in the parking lot.

I barely get out of the car before she grabs my hand and drags me into the shelter. We are greeted by a middle-aged woman with salt and pepper hair and turquoise glasses that have a matching chain attached. She greets Avery with a warm hug before turning to me.

"Hello, you must be Cas? Avery cannot stop gushing about you. I'm Tanya." She sticks out her hand as if we don't know each other. Technically, we don't, as I've only talked to her on the phone. Bless this woman for pretending she's never spoken to me before.

"It's nice to meet you. We are here to see a kitten named Mauve. Avery showed me her picture, and I just needed to see her in person." I grin at Avery, holding in my worry about what will happen.

"Oh, I'm so sorry, but that cat was adopted today. She's going to a real nice couple." I give this woman props. She looks genuinely heartbroken. Tanya deserves an Oscar for this performance.

"Wait, what? S-she wa-was ad-adopted?" Avery's words come out choppy and full of sadness. I feel like an ass for making her feel this way, but that moment passes knowing what's waiting for her at home. Still, nothing can prepare you for when the love of your life clutches your shirt in her hands while sobbing uncontrollably.

"Baby I'm so sorry. I didn't think she'd be adopted. Why don't we go home, get in our comfy pajamas, and watch *Hocus Pocus?* That'll make you feel better." She's still crying pretty hard, so she just nods her head.

On the way home, I hold Avery's hand, listening to her soft sobs. I remind myself over and over that everything will be fine when she gets home. I pull into her driveway, but Avery is passed out from emotional exhaustion. I scoop her into my arms and enter her home bridal style while my camera bag hangs over my shoulder, heading up the stairs toward her room. She begins to stir in my arms, and that's when the cat decides to let out the loudest meow I've ever heard.

Avery's head snaps up, and she's blinking rapidly, momentarily disoriented. The cat lets out another meow and Avery all but leaps out of my arms when she sees what's sitting on her bed. I get my camera ready to snap the perfect photo as Avery stares at the tiny ball of fur on the bed. I can't wait to add this final photo to her album. I checked earlier today and it said the package has been delivered and I'm grateful I spent the extra ten or so dollars to get same-day shipping.

"Cas! What. Is. That?" she all but shouts.

"That, Avery, is what we call a cat." Avery's response is to roll her eyes at me before cocking a hip, looking at me with an are you serious expression.

"No shit, Cas. What is it doing here?"

"It's your new cat. I believe you know her? She currently goes by the name Mauve. Although, I'm sure you'll change it to something else, Binx. perhaps?"

"Y-y-you got me a cat?" she whispers. I nod my head and she flings herself into my arms. "But why? I didn't do anything to deserve you doing this for me."

"Because I wanted to and because I love you. You believe in me. You see me. Avery, you wrote a fucking song for me. I know you wanted a cat, but couldn't do it for yourself. So, I went out and did it for you."

"I—" she chokes out.

"I didn't mess up, did I?" I ask, suddenly feeling insecure.

"No, you did not mess up. Cas, this is incredible. The best thing anyone has ever done for me in a long time. A thank you seems too insignificant, but thank you."

She walks over to the cat, picks her up, and cradles her in her arms. Avery is nuzzling the kitten, making her purr. I hurry up and snap a photo before speaking. "You don't have to thank me. I'd do anything for you. Now, what do you say to watching that movie and cuddling your new cat?" I ask.

"You mean *our* new cat," she corrects me. That word *our* does something to me. It's a simple, yet powerful word that pushes straight into my heart. The sound of my phone buzzing in my back pocket bursts the happiness bubble I was just in. Avery is in the kitchen making popcorn, so I can check who the messages are from.

> **Unknown: You think you can threaten me, Cassidy? Think again. I think it's time to up the stakes here, hmm?**

> **Unknown: If you don't help me out of this mess, I'll have to pay sweet Avery a little visit. The guys would really like her. She always had such a sexy little figure. Are you fucking her yet? *images attached***

I stare at the messages, my body frozen like an animal that's been spotted by a predator, my good mood completely gone. All these texts so far have only been about me. It's one thing to go after me, but he crossed a line. My blood turns to ice when I stare at the photos attached.

They are all of Avery.

My body feels like it's been thrown into one of those electric fences. Suddenly everything falls into place, the constant fight or flight, the feeling of someone watching me, no, *us* for months. I take a deep breath. I *cannot* have a panic attack in front of Avery. She'll want to talk about it and I can't get her involved, it's not safe, so I put on my biggest smile before turning towards her. Of course, she sees right past my fake smile.

"Cas, hey, what's wrong?" she asks.

I bring my hands to her face, doing my best to persuade her that everything's okay when it's not. "Freckles, I *promise* you I'm okay. Just going to get some rest. I'll come over after so we can play with the cat, and then maybe *we* can play a little." I know she isn't convinced, but I'm relieved when she lets me go.

I make my way back to my house almost tripping over the Amazon package on my doorstep. I quickly grab the package and run upstairs, needing to be alone when I respond to him. As much as I want to ignore him, he's changed the game. This time he's added Avery into the mix and I can't have him anywhere near her. Now that I understand what happened to me, I know what those men are willing to do. My dad doesn't give a flying fuck about anything other than getting high. I either bail him out, putting myself in harm's way, or avoid him entirely and put Avery in danger. The decision is easy, giving me the courage to reply to him.

Me: Don't you dare lay a finger on her. Touch Avery, and you will live to regret it. Tell me when and where to meet you and how much to bring. After all of this is done, don't ever fucking contact me again or I will go to the cops and tell them everything. Including what you let those men do to me. You think I don't remember, but I do. I remember everything now. I'm no longer going to keep protecting you. You don't deserve it.

Chapter 38

Avery

Mini boudoir session

SOMETHING'S GOING ON WITH Cas. And from the look on his face yesterday, it's something terrible. He acted weird at Uncle Tito's Taco Joint and again when I returned with popcorn ready for our movie night. I just have to trust that in time, he'll tell me what's going on when he's ready.

It's the face he made before he noticed me coming from my kitchen that is burned in my brain. I can't shake the feeling that something terrible is about to happen, but I push the thought down. Clearly, I'm overreacting.

The sound of meowing startles me and all those anxious feelings melt away. Cas went out of his way and adopted a cat for me. *A cat.* The little creature saunters toward me and cuddles on my stomach, headbutting my hand for pets. When he took me to the shelter yesterday, I was devastated that she was adopted. Of all the cats I've grown attached to over the years, she's been my fave. Then, Cas carries me upstairs, and what's waiting for me? A freaking cat!

I scratch underneath her chin, her purrs vibrating against my finger, and my love for Cas flows through me. How is it that one person can provide both stability and spontaneity all at once? I wanted to show him my thanks that same day, but he had other things on his mind.

I have no *idea* what to do to thank him, but I know of the perfect person to ask. I place Binx next to me so I can reach for my phone and dial Bri's number.

"Hello?" she answers, her voice coated with sleep. I glance at the time. Shit. It's 6:00 a.m.

"Damn it, Bri, I didn't realize it was so early. I can call back later," I say, feeling slightly guilty.

"Bitch don't you dare apologize. What I want to know is why are *you* up so early? Did someone get some last night? Say hi to Cas for me," she teases.

"He's not here, Bri. I, um, it's easier if you come over," I plead.

"On my way," she says, hanging up the phone before I can mutter my thanks. I make my way downstairs with a hungry cat meowing in my hand. I reach for the wet food, and the second it's in her bowl, she races over and scarfs it down as fast as she can. A few minutes later, the door opens and Bri's voice comes barreling through.

"I have arrived to help. Now, what do you have to tell me that can't be over the—" Bri stops mid-sentence staring at Binx. "What is *that*?"

"This, Bri, is what we call a cat. You know, those pets some people have?" I say humorously.

"Fuck off. I know what it is, but *why* is it here, and *how* did it get here?" she asks. I recall everything that happened yesterday.

"So the boy got you a damn cat, huh? And you need my help with what exactly?" She smirks.

"I need your help figuring out the perfect way to thank him for this." I sigh, looking at the ceiling and trying not to meet her smug expression.

"Oh, I know the *perfect* way for you to thank him. Here's what we're going to do. We're going to get you a whole new outfit, come back, and take some sexy pictures to send to him. Then I'm getting the hell out of here, and *you*, my dear friend, will ride him like a cowgirl."

Usually, I would roll my eyes and let her know the flaws of her plan, but honestly, it's kinda genius. In fact, I'm actually excited and a whole lot turned on. I look up at her smiling. "Let's go!" I say, momentarily surprising her.

"Damn right! Let's fucking do it," she says while dragging me out the door.

Hours later, we returned home with two bags filled with everything I need and then some. Bri went a little crazy at the sex shop, throwing this and that at me, and I was a tad bit overwhelmed. I excuse myself to put on the outfit we agreed would make Cas the craziest. Inside the bag is a dark green corset with black lace detailing throughout and a zipper down the back. To top off the outfit, I pull out my favorite pair of black, suede, thigh-high boots.

I put everything on and take a deep breath before exiting the bathroom to get Bri's opinion. She looks at me and her mouth drops open. "Damn, girl. From now on, you should only wear lingerie because you look hot as fuck," she exclaims. I head over to my full-length floor mirror and stare at myself. She's right. I do look good. The corset hugs my curves in all the right places and pushes my boobs up so high they're practically spilling over. I slowly turn to the side to find that the material in the back barely covers my ass.

"Okay!" Bri states and rubs her hands together. "Now, let me do your hair and makeup, and then we can take pictures that will have Cas running over here panting and ready," she says and then gets to work.

Once she is all done, she brings me back to the mirror and I'm stunned. My hair is in voluminous, beachy waves. My eye makeup is smoky and my lips are a deep red. I place a hand to my face, then my hair, and turn towards Brianna. "Thank you, you're a genius."

"I know. Now let's take some sexy photos," Bri says while shimmying her shoulders. I lay on my new black, silk sheets, Bri insisted I needed for the photoshoot. She directs me to pose in what feels like a million different ways. We sit next to each other on the bed, scrolling through them all and finding the ones we like best.

"This one," we both say at once. It's of me laying down, head placed at the end of the bed, arching my back with my hand between my legs. My eyes are open, looking playful yet seductive at the camera while biting my lower lip.

"Yes, this is the one you'll send him. He'll be over here within a matter of seconds. Now I'm getting out of here before he arrives. I expect a detailed report on what happens." Bri's about halfway out the door when I shout at her.

"I'm submitting the song I wrote for Cas to that songwriting competition." She whips her head around, staring at me in shock.

"You are? Oh, Ave, that's incredible. Have you told Cas yet?" she asks.

"No, but I plan to soon. Maybe tonight? I'm not sure. I'll know when the moment feels right."

"Just do it soon. And don't you *dare* back out. Send it now and think about it later. Okay, I love you, but I don't want to be around when Cas gets here," she says without glancing at me before bolting out of the room.

I grab my phone and pull up the application. Everything is filled out. I just have to be brave and hit send. I let oxygen fill my lungs in hopes of it giving me some courage before pressing send. There, I did it. No going back now.

Now, for the photo. I stare down at my phone, feeling self-conscious. I have never sent a sexy photo before. Before I can chicken out, I pull up our text conversation to type out my message.

Me: Hey, can I get your opinion on an outfit I bought?

Cas: Sure, but don't you have Bri? She might be better at this than I am.

Me: I want your opinion, though.

Cas: Okay, go ahead and send it.

Me: * image*

My heart pounds as I wait for his reply forever. Five minutes pass and I panic, thinking he doesn't like it. Before I can send another message, my phone pings, and three seconds later, my front door opens. Bri must have left something. I take a steadying deep breath and open my text.

Cas: Fuck.

The door to my bedroom slams open, but Bri isn't walking towards me. It's Cas.

"Goddamn it, Avery, you're trying to kill me, aren't you? Come over here and let me take care of you," he says, voice husky.

A sudden burst of confidence flows through me and I throw my phone down on the dresser before turning around with lust in my eyes and a seductive smile. "Oh no, my dear Cas, it's time *I* take care of *you*," I purr. I walk over towards him, grab his hand, and shove him down onto the bed, causing his head to bounce a few times. I stand over him, looking down at this man for a minute, before straddling his lap.

Chapter 39

Avery

Avery, the dominatrix?

I HAVEN'T ADMITTED THIS out loud, but taking charge in the bedroom has been an item on my sexual fantasy bucket list ever since I've started having sex. In the past, I've never felt the courage to follow through with it. Not until now. Not until Cas, who has unknowingly crossed off many items off of this list. Sex in the shower? Check. Going down on me? Check. Yeah, that one is kind of sad, but in my past relationships, no one has ever done it. Rough Sex? Check. So, yeah, it's obvious this man is checking all the boxes.

Now as I look down at him, I'm hesitant. So far, he's taken charge—except for in the shower. My confidence is replaced with fear as I internally freak out. Will he enjoy this? Yeah, I took over in the shower, but I never went as far as going full on dominatrix mode. Cas blinks up at me, concern etched across his face.

"Avery? Hey, what's going on? You okay?" he asks.

"Well, I've had this, uh, bucket list. Things I've wanted to try sexually. I've had it for a while and well, I haven't been able to cross things off. Not until recently. But, I'm having a hard time with the last item."

"A list, huh? What's on it, and more importantly, what is the last item you need to check off?" Cas smirks.

"Well there's shower sex, rough sex, and having someone go down on me. All things you exceeded expectations on, might I add." I bite my lip in hesitation, worried what he'll think about the final item.

"Hey, talk to me, baby," Cas says while his thumbs stroke my cheek.

"I, well I wanted to be what they call a dominatrix? But now I'm nervous. You did such an incredible thing for me yesterday and I wanted to find a way to say thank you. It's stupid. I look stupid. I'll change." I start to get up, but his hands go back to my waist in a tight grip, keeping me in place.

"Don't. You. Dare. That picture you sent me was fucking hot. If you weren't home when you sent it, I'd have gone out to find you and dragged you right back here to fuck you senseless. You are not stupid, and you sure as hell do *not* look stupid. I'm here, baby. Use my body, Avery. I'm all yours."

Use my body, Avery. I'm all yours. That's the encouragement I need to follow through with my plan. I take his hands off my hips to stand up. Before he can say anything, I lean down and make my first demand, "I'm in charge now, and you'll do as I say." He groans before his hands finally let go of my hips. Being in charge feels liberating.

"I am now in charge. If you break my rules, you'll suffer the consequences. Now, take off *all* your clothes and do it quickly. I don't have all day," I say, hand on my hip with a quirked brow.

He licks his lips and moves into a sitting position, but he slowly removes his shirt instead of following the directions to take the clothes off quickly. When his eyes meet mine, they have a hint of challenge, almost as if he doesn't believe me. I smile wickedly and force his legs apart so I can stand in the middle. "That's how you wanna play, huh? Fine, I warned you." Then in one quick movement, I take one of my feet and press the heel into his chest so that he's lying flat on his back. I climb on top of him in a straddle position, grinding up, down, and then circling my hips over his dick. He grunts and groans, so I speed up my pace, and when his hands start to fly to my hips, I jump off of him.

"Avery," he groans out my name and you can hear the sexual frustration in his tone.

I look at him with fake pity. "Poor baby, you aren't satisfied, are you? Maybe you'll listen to me when I make my demands. You'll take off all your clothes quicker if you want to be rewarded," I say. The words are only halfway out of my mouth before he starts stripping at lightning speed.

I'm staring at a fully nude Cas and my eyes travel down his body, landing on his fully hard cock. "Good boy," I say while pushing him back down on the bed. I almost miss the hitch in Cas' breath at the praise. I, again, spread his legs wide enough so I could stand between them before getting into a kneeling position. His face says he knows what's about to happen, and I smile wickedly at him before placing my mouth around him. I work him hard with my mouth stroking, sucking, and licking as fast and deep as I can.

Not wanting him to come apart on me yet, I take my mouth off him and slither my way up his body to kiss him senselessly. His hands try to move towards my hips, but I use my hands to handcuff his wrists at his side. "Remember it's me who's in control now, so you better be good and listen."

"You know, I'm getting tired of wearing this corset," I say while turning around, glancing back over my shoulder with a gleam in my eye, making my next demand. "I need you to unzip me, but do it slowly. I don't want anything to rip." He all but jumps off of the bed, ready to unzip me. He starts fast, so I turn out of his grip just as quickly.

"You have a hard time listening, don't you? It's a shame that you have to be punished," I say, reaching for my zipper, slowly bringing it down and watching his eyes roll back in his head. He always likes to undress me, so I know this moment is torture. Fully unzipped, I shimmy slowly out of the corset and let it drop to the floor. I'm completely naked except for the thigh-high boots. "You really should have listened," I tsk playfully.

"Avery, *please*," he begs.

"Back on the bed you go and get there quickly." Cas clumsily scrambles onto the bed and I can't help but grin.

"Here's what's going to happen. I'm going to climb on top of you and ride you so fucking hard that you won't know what hit you. You can touch me only in the places I say and when I say it. Break any rules, and well, you know what'll happen by now." I smirk.

"Yes, mistress," is all he can manage, pupils dilated and breathe erratic. *Mistress?* Oh, I like that. Cas smirks up at me as I sashay over to him, making sure I put a little extra swing in my hips. The bed feels soft beneath my touch as I crawl over his body so I can straddle his hips. I guide him towards my entrance and take him completely inside of me. I grind my hips in a circle, hitting all my glorious spots, and moan out his name in a low husky sound.

"Give me your hands." I place his hands on my breasts before he can respond. "Touch me here," I say. As soon as he does, my back arches and I slowly move up and down on him. He starts kneading and squeezing. But when he uses his thumbs to caress and pinch my nipples, my body involuntarily picks up speed. I lean over to change the angle, allowing his dick to hit my g-spot, causing flashes of light to dance behind my eyelids.

I continued to give him access to one breast, but then took his other hand in mine, bringing it to my neck. "Now choke me and choke me just hard enough." My demand comes out hoarse with lust. He starts with a light touch, but I guide my hand back up to his and show him how much pressure I want. "Keep doing that. Keep squeezing me there until I stop. I won't stop until I finish. Then we'll worry about you." That demand sent the both of us into a frenzy.

His quick squeezes match my own movements, and the faster he squeezes, the faster I ride, coming completely undone. "Do-don't stop. Cas, don't you dare fucking stop!" I shout out the last part, my orgasm so intense it catches me by surprise. I feel myself pulsing around him, riding out my pleasure, still in complete control. Before he could come, I hopped off him. "Stand up, now!" He stands up so quickly I'm surprised he didn't fall over from a head rush. I get on my knees to finish what I started earlier by taking him back into my mouth, moving at an even faster pace than before. His hands grip my head as he starts thrusting into me with quick rapid pumps, and he's close. Like last time, he tries to pull out, but my grip tightens, and once again, I let him come in my mouth. And when he pulls out, I look at him under my lashes with a wicked gleam as I swallow.

Both of us are trying to catch our breath and come down from that high, but I'm still reeling. Taking charge felt powerful, and I wondered why I'd never done this before. Actually, I know why I haven't done it before. Cas brings out the wild side in me. He brings me over to the bed, and we cuddle while we wait for our breathing to become normal. Laying there content and satisfied, I snuggle deeper into the crook of his neck and he is the first to speak.

"Avery, that was, wow. Like, just *wow*. Who knew being a sub would be something I'd be into. New kink unlocked thanks to you." He leans down and kisses my forehead.

"I felt powerful and sexy. I've never done that before, and I am glad my first experience was with you." I look up at him with a hopeful look in my eyes and I see that his head is cocked to the side and he's wearing a cocky smirk.

"Why are you looking at me like that?" I ask.

"You. You did that, you took charge." He flips us so that he's on top of me before continuing. "That was hot as fuck, baby. I need to let you take charge more often." He briefly presses his lips to my forehead before getting up to put his clothes on.

"I did do that, didn't I? It was exhilarating and I'm fucking proud of myself." My smile stretches across my face to the point of it being painful. I watch Cas get partially dressed with a confused look. "Wait, why are you getting dressed ?"

"You should be proud of yourself, baby. It was incredible. I have something for you but it's at home. I'm just gonna run home and grab it before I let you ravish me again for round two." He bolts out of my room like The Flash, shooting me a wink over his shoulder. Too stunned to move from my bed, I stay tucked under the covers, waiting for him to return. After about five minutes, he's back and carrying a giant ass package the size of his torso.

Cas' breathing is rapid, probably from running like a maniac, and is wearing the cheesiest grin I've ever seen. He allows himself a minute or so to catch his breath before walking back to the bed, practically throwing the gift into my lap. I push myself up into a sitting position as my eyes ping pong between Cas and the gift.

"What's this?" I ask, knowing he's about to give me some sarcastic remark. What he says though surprises me.

"Oh something I've been working on. Go on, open it." His smile is infectious and I can't help but grin back at him before tearing into the paper.

I don't know what I was expecting, but it wasn't this. In my hands is a stunning photo album full of memories from the last couple of months. The first page has a list and each item has been checked off. Tears prick behind my eyes as I look up at him.

"Cas..." My voice is breathless and soft.

"Well, see, when you told me I needed to show you that this time was different, I knew I needed to take it seriously. So with help from Asher and Max, we developed the best friend boot-camp plan. The plan was to remind you of some of our favorite childhood memories by recreating them in the present. I knew I had one chance to show you this time was different, so I wanted to make it perfect. Then I figured it would be a good idea to have it all laid out in a photo album so that you can look at it and maybe smile. That piece of paper on the cover is the original list I wrote and knew I needed to include it."

"I, wow, I don't know what to say. You did this all for me?"

"Avery. I would do anything for you. You've brought me back to life. You've shown me what it is to be a friend. You've given me everything by simply existing. It's you. It's always been you." I put the photo album on the floor gracefully before jumping into his lap. My arms are wrapped around his neck, our noses touching. My eyes continue to leak tears and my heart is so full I'm surprised it doesn't burst.

"I, thank you. I love this so much. I can't wait to fill the rest of these empty spaces with future memories. This is one of the most thoughtful gifts anyone has ever gotten me. I love it, Cas."

I grab his face in my hands and kiss him. "And I love you." Time and life cease to exist out of this moment. It's just me and the boy I fell in love with all those years ago.

Chapter 40

Cassidy

Please come home to me

IF I COULD DO one thing for the rest of my life, it would be to kiss Avery. Okay, yeah, the sex is great—really fucking great, but something about kissing her gets to me. The softness of her lips and the faint cherry taste of her favorite Chapstick. I think denying myself the pleasure of being with her plays a big part of that.

I really need to talk to her about the threats from my dad. If I had it my way, I wouldn't tell her at all. I don't want to taint her sunshine with hurricane Frank. But because it involves her directly, I need to tell her. I pull back from her kiss looking into her desire filled eyes and internally curse my father.

"Cas? Why did we stop?" Avery's face sports the most adorable pout that makes me want to say fuck it all and just continue kissing her.

"I, um. I have something I need to tell you and I'm not sure how you're going to take it."

Her eyes widen with fear and I can all but hear the wheels turning in her head. "What? Is it me? Do you not want—" I plant a quick kiss to her mouth to stop her anxious thoughts.

"Baby, no I want this. I want you but, um...well something has been happening to me these last few months. Something that I tried to avoid and pretend didn't exist."

Avery's fear is replaced by concern as she sits and waits for me to continue. The question is how to actually have this conversation. *Fuck it. Rip the Band-Aid off, Cas Just do it.*

"For months now, I've had the sneaking suspicion someone's been following me. I shrugged it off as me just being on edge. Then the texts from an unknown number started coming in. At first, they were all directed at me. Calling me a junkie, tempting me with pictures of needles. Most of the time, I ignored it, hoping they would just leave me alone. Well, it turns out it was my dad the whole time. He's back on his bullshit. I was planning to continue to ignore him, but he upped the ante." *Rip the Band-Aid off, Cas. She needs to know.* But, I can't seem to find the words.

I wait for Avery's brain to catch up to the bomb I just dropped. After a few moments, recognition hits her face and I can see her physically holding back her anger.

"What? What does he want?" Avery seethes with anger. I can practically feel the heat radiating from her.

"He found himself in hot water again and he wants me to bail him out. I wasn't planning on doing it, but this time he's involved you. And now I can no longer ignore him."

"Involved me how?" she asks.

"He sent me multiple pictures of you, threatening your safety. So in order to keep you safe, I have to meet with him, meet his demands. I have to save his ass yet again and pray I make it back safely."

"Cas, I don't want you to go. I don't trust him at all. You're newly sober and I—" she stops herself with a sharp intake of breath.

"You don't want history to repeat itself," I finish for her.

She hangs her head in shame. "I'm sorry, Cas, what an awful thing to think."

"Avery, look at me." I pause and wait for her eyes to connect with mine before continuing. "It's a valid fear, Avery. I get why you would think that. It's happened more than once. You don't need to apologize for your fears, baby. I get it and I don't fault you for it. I wish I didn't need to leave you baby, but that's no longer an option. I need you to stay here and not involve yourself any further. You're already involved in this way more than is comfortable for me, but I told you I'd let you in on what's happening. I need to stop this. Can you do that for me?" I hold my breath, waiting for her answer.

"While I don't like this one bit, I can do that. But I need you to come back to me, Cas. I've done life without you and I barely survived. I can't do it again."

"Oh, baby." I chuckle while shaking my head. "You're my person. I know what it's like to live without you and I don't plan on repeating it. I want to see you laugh and hold you when you cry. I want to watch that little dance you do whenever you're happy or excited. I want to take you out, show you off, and dance with you in the rain. I want every moment of forever with you."

"You're my person, too. I love the way you hold me when I cry. The way you laugh at my silly jokes or the way you go out of your way to make me smile. I love how you let me in. You inspire me to be the best version of myself and push me out of my comfort zone. You are my first, only, and last love."

I crush my mouth to hers and shift my body so that I'm on top of her. She never got dressed after our last time having sex. Thank fuck for that. I pull out of the kiss and move to the end of the bed while simultaneously throwing off the covers. Grabbing onto her feet, I pull her to the end of the bed causing her to let out a shriek.

"Cas, what are you doing?" Avery's breathing has picked up its pace and her eyes are filled with need.

I position myself between her legs. My hands move from her feet up her thighs parting her legs as wide as they'll allow. My head moves closer to my holy grail and blow a puff of air over her pussy, eliciting the most delicious moan out of her.

"I'm about to eat my favorite meal." I smirk before diving into her pussy with my tongue. She screams and wriggles so much, causing me to place a palm on her stomach to keep her from moving. Then I feast like a king, softly nipping at her clit before massaging it with the ridges of my flat tongue. I open her wider with two fingers from my other hand, giving me deeper access.

Remember when I said if I could do one thing for the rest of my life, it would be to kiss Avery? I could do this, too. I could eat her out for every meal if it provided the nutrients I needed to survive. She tastes so fucking good that it makes my head spin. I pump my fingers in and out of her while sucking on her clit with increasing pressure.

"Cas, fuck. Don't stop. Harder...damn it, harder!" she shouts. What my baby wants, she gets. So I suck her as hard as I can and I feel the impending orgasm begin to shake through her body. I apply more pressure to her clit and curl my finger in the right spot, which makes her scream my name. Avery keeps coming and I lap it up like a dehydrated dog before slowly decreasing my pressure and easing out of her.

Avery is satiated with her eyes closed and a sleepy smile playing across her face. I want to stay and cuddle with her, but my time is ticking and I need to deal with my dad. I kiss her forehead and tuck her in as her eyes flutter open. She looks so vulnerable, lying there with a worried look on her face. Avery's face breaks out into a worried expression as she reaches out to cup my face. I can't help but lean into her touch.

"Come home to me, Cas. I need you and I don't want to do life without you." Avery offers a strained smile. This is eating her up inside. but she is trying to be brave for me.

"I will come home to you, baby. I don't want to do life without you, either. Go to sleep. I'll be home before you know it." I lean down and kiss her forehead before making my way to the door.

I sent a quick text to Bri asking her to come keep Avery company. I don't want her to be alone. If I trust anyone to protect my girl, it's her best friend. She responded with an okay and a threat to chop off my balls and force feed them to me if I hurt her best friend again. Yeah, I think having Bri take care of her is the best option.

Chapter 41

Avery

He needs to be okay

I WAKE UP FEELING satisfied. I reach out to pull Cas closer to me, only to find it empty. Sadness threatens to take hold of me, but then I remember our conversation. I sit up abruptly, running my fingers through my hair, trying to calm down my frantic heart. He promised things would be okay and he asked me to trust him. That's what I have to do. I head toward my closet to put clothes on and noticed one of his shirts mixed in with mine. I mean, with how often we spend at each other's houses, it makes sense to keep some articles of clothing in each other's closets. Now more than ever, I'm grateful for it. I need something of his to cling to and on the plus side, it still smells like him.

The sound of the door opening and closing has my heart in my throat. *Cas?* He's back already? That was quick. I grab a pair of panties and put them on before heading downstairs. Only it isn't Cas standing in the doorway, but Bri.

She waves her phone in the air and I know without words why she's here. Cas must have called her because he didn't want me to be alone. Which means that whatever he's dealing with is more dangerous than he let on. I run down the stairs, taking them two at a time before launching myself into her arms, not giving two shits about me being pantless. The second her arms wrap around me, the floodgates I held back from Cas bust open. Loud, ugly, and uncontrollable sobbing takes over my body. Bri just holds me, calming me with her presence.

I don't remember making it to the couch, but here I am with my head in Bri's lap as she plays with my hair. The crying hasn't stopped and I can already feel the headache forming behind my eyes. My best friend just continues comforting me in silence and I couldn't be more grateful. Eventually, my eyes become heavy with exhaustion and I fall asleep still curled in Bri's lap.

I wake up to the smell of freshly brewed coffee, waffles, and my stomach making the most obnoxious sound. On the coffee table in front of me are two Advil and a glass of water. I pop the pills and guzzle the water before walking over to find Bri at the table with two plates full of food and two cups of coffee. God, I love my best friend.

We eat in silence, which is perfect, because I'm still trying to work out the mess that is my mind. I'm finishing my final bite of food when I hear Bri clear her throat.

"How are you feeling?"

I swallow the remaining coffee in my cup before answering her. "I'm a mess, Bri. So much has happened in the last twenty-four hours. And since you're here, I'm guessing Cas called you?"

She nods her head. "Yup. Well, he texted me, but same diff. Oh, and don't worry—I plan to make good on my promise to force feed him his balls if he hurts you. You're welcome." I can't help but laugh at her. Fuck, it feels good to laugh right now. The next thing I know, words are pouring out of me like a busted pipe. I share my fears and concerns about him going back to see his dad. I told her of our most recent experience of mind blowing sex, as well as the gift he got me.

"It was seriously amazing, Bri. He's so thoughtful and sentimental." I pause, looking down at my now empty plate. "He needs to come home, Bri. I can't be without him again. It was too painful."

"He'll come home, Ave. He's too stubborn not to. Plus, I have to live vicariously through you in regards to your sex life. My vagina is as dry as the Sahara Desert."

"Well, I'm sure *Asher* would love to help you with that." I waggle my eyebrows, doing anything and everything to distract from the darkness of my thoughts.

"Yeah....no. Not happening. He's not getting anywhere near this pussy. He can beg all he wants, but it's not happening. Now, I'm going to clean up our food while you go upstairs and take a shower. You need to clear your head. Plus, you smell like sex. After you're done, we can watch a movie and binge on popcorn and ice cream." I throw my napkin at her before circling around the table to kiss her cheek.

"Thank you for coming, Bri. I love you so much and I appreciate you being here for me." I squeeze her shoulders.

"I love you, too, Ave. I'd do anything for you."

I head upstairs and take the longest shower of my life. I cannot fully ease the anxious thoughts and fears from my brain, but there's something about showering to cleanse your mind and body from stress and tension.

As I'm toweling off, I grab my phone and send a quick text to Cas, letting him know I love him and that I'm waiting for him to come home to me. Seconds after I put my phone down, it dings with a new notification and my heart flips. I grin and grab my phone with relief, thinking it's Cas. When I open my phone, it's not a text notification, but an email alert from the songwriting competition.

I'm already stressed and worried about Cas that I hesitate to open the email, expecting to get a rejection. It's now or never. What's the worst thing that can happen? When I open the email, my eyes can't process what they see. I did a double-take to see if I was seeing things correctly. I rush downstairs, anxious to tell Bri the news, and I want that damn popcorn.

"I don't smell any popcorn, Bri, and you'll never guess what happened. But, you better have a good explanation—" I stop abruptly at the sight of her face. Panic instantly fills my body, my heart beating in my throat. "What? Why do you look like that right now?" I ask.

"Avery," she says with so much emotion behind her words.

"What? What happened?" I demand.

"There's been an accident. Cas, he—something happened, and he's being rushed to the hospital. We don't know—" but the rest of her words fade to black as I collapse to the floor. My heart feels like it's about to burst out of my chest.

"I n-need-to g-go s-see h-him," I stammer out, my voice coated with panic.

"I'm not sure if he's allowed visitors yet," she says.

"I don't give a fuck, Bri. Take me to him. Now." She nods her head and we head out to the hospital. The drive over is a complete blur. He needs to be okay. He just needs to.

Chapter 42

Cassidy

Frank

SOMETHING TERRIBLE IS GOING to happen. This thought isn't entirely off base when it comes to my dad, as trouble always seems to follow Frank everywhere he goes. I shouldn't be going to see him, but Avery's safety is more important than my own. Just thinking her name makes my heart pound erratically in my chest.

I grab my keys and phone and head out to my car, a mixture of anger and nerves dancing around my stomach and chest. Every time I see my dad, all hell breaks loose. The check, well, my grandparents' check, weighs heavy in my back pocket. I want to hand it over to him as quickly as possible and then book it, not wanting to be involved in his drama. I just hope my grandparents don't ask any questions. Yes, they have given me access to their account, but I don't want them to know that my father is back in contact with me. I've come too far to fall back now.

I type in the address and wince. The last time I was there was when I overdosed. The closer I get to my destination, the more memories come flooding back. My grip on the steering wheel becomes so tight that my knuckles turn white. I try to focus on calming my frantic pulse, but it doesn't work. And if I don't pull over soon, I'll end up crashing the car. So I pulled over and worked on techniques my therapist taught me to help calm me down.

The sound of my phone buzzing has my pulse racing again, but something tells me I need to look at it. The second I turn my phone over, my heart sings a happy tune. She texted me. My eyes fill with tears of relief, knowing that I have her waiting for me at home. That helps steady my breathing enough to continue driving.

Thirty minutes later, I'm back where everything went up in flames. I look out of the windshield to the dark alley and see my dad talking to three men with their backs toward me. I get out of the car and stand there waiting. It takes him a moment to find me, but when he does, he points in my direction. When the three men turn around, my heart drops to the floor.

I know these men.

They are the same assholes who hurt me when I was a boy. The same men who also gave me the fix that caused my overdose. My body is stuck in one of those cryotherapy chambers. Each breath is a knife to my lungs.

"I knew you'd come. See? I told you he'd come."

"I have your money." My voice is coming out far more controlled than I feel. *Thank God.*

"Hold on, son. I think it's time we had some father and son bonding time, don't you?" he asks while smiling. His teeth are yellow and chipped with quite a few gaps in his mouth. His once full, wavy, black hair is thinned with a giant bald spot on top of his head. He's sickly skinny and his skin has a yellowish tint to it. He looks like a villain straight out of a movie.

"No. I want you to take the damn money and leave me alone. Leave Avery alone."

"Ahhh, she's a real beauty, isn't she? She would be a good time. It's smart of you to send someone over to make sure she's safe."

His words are like a gunshot to my heart. "What do you know about me sending anyone over there?" I ask.

"Didn't until just now. Damn, were you always this gullible?" He chuckles while taking out two needles. I have no idea what's in them, but I know it's nothing good. "Do you want in? For old times' sake? Once a junkie, always a junkie. We can get high together like we used to. You were always good with making payments on time for me. Since you decided to be a pussy and overdose, then get clean, it's been hard."

I glance down at the beat-up, rickety table with what I assume are used needles full of heroin in the middle of the alleyway. For a second, a split second, I think about caving. My mouth waters again with the temptation to fill my body with that false sense of happiness. I lick my lips and I notice my father tracking the motion with a smirk on his face. That smirk washes away any inclination to use. Honestly, I'm kind of disappointed in myself for even thinking about it.

"No!" I yell.

"You think that because you're sober and shit now, you're better than us? You'll never be better than us. You're still a worthless piece of shit that will never amount to anything. A girl like Avery can do better than the likes of you. Oh, I've been watching you. I was biding my time, waiting for the right moment to contact you. I watched you and I watched her. I thought you caught me a few times, but you're too stupid to notice. Avery looks real good, son. Real fucking good." He winks.

He confirmed what I already suspected. I wasn't crazy. And it wasn't just anyone stalking me. It was my fucking father. I take the check out of my pocket and thrust it into his hands. He takes one look at the check and laughs. "See, I was planning on taking that check from you and never looking back. But then you had to show up acting all better than me and shit. We don't trust you. Who's to say you won't snitch on us to the cops?" he asks, gesturing to the men behind him. "I think it's time to teach you a lesson, one you won't likely forget. What do you say, boys?" he asks the men and their matching slick grins make my stomach turn.

I know they want me to respond, but these fuckers don't deserve any part of me. I stare at them, nostrils flaring and glaring at them.

"Hmm, not speaking, huh? Well, we think that maybe we need to add a lot more numbers to that check of yours. It's the least you could do with all the bullshit you caused," he says.

"How many numbers are we talking about?" I ask. When he says the number, I laugh. "Absolutely fucking not. You don't deserve any more money. Hell, you don't even deserve the amount of money on this check. You're either going to take it or leave it. Maybe *I will* call the cops. I'm so sick of you and your shit. I'm not going to join you on any more of your adventures and sure as hell won't bail you out of your shit anymore. So take the damn check or leave it," I say, holding the check back out to him.

He just continues to stare at it, still not taking it. I get a glimpse at his face and see pure evil before I turn to walk away. I barely make it three steps before I'm slammed against the brick wall. My head hits the brick with so much force that I start seeing stars.

"You're going to regret that boy," says one of the men. He has his elbow on my throat, applying enough pressure that my vision begins to fade, gasping for breath. Visions of Avery play in my head. Her curled into the crook of my arm or lying beside me. Her dancing with me in the rain, our first kiss, her underneath me during our first time. Our first exchange of I love you's. She floods my mind, becoming increasingly clear while I struggle for air. I try to wriggle free, but I have no such luck. *This is it. They're going to touch me again. I'm going to be payment again.* I brace myself for the feelings, knowing that my only option would be to sit there and take it. Before I can brace for the impact, the man holding me in place is pulled off me by none other than my dad. I cough aggressively while trying to fill my lungs with air. My dad pulling his groupie off of me wasn't to help me in any way. Frank is the devil incarnate. He gets off on my pain and suffering if his smirk is anything to go by.

"Now, now, boys, let's not get ahead of ourselves. He can still serve some purpose for us."

I start to back away from the wall and towards my car. I make it about halfway before my dad presses a gun to my back. "I wouldn't go anywhere if I were you, son. We aren't finished yet. You need to be punished."

I slowly turn around, the gun now pointing at my stomach. "Please don't do this. Please! You don't want to kill me, do you?" I plead.

"You're right. I don't," he says, then takes a few steps back before pivoting. "Fuck it! I don't care," he says before he pulls the trigger, causing a radiating pain in my stomach. The last thing I remember is looking down at the hand that was once on my stomach to see it covered in blood. I look into my father's eyes, completely dumbfounded.

"Hey. What's going on over there?" I don't have the energy to search where the voice is coming from, but I'm grateful for that deep, baritone breaking through the tension of the moment. My battle with consciousness is a losing one, but I hear a mix of cursing and feet slapping against the pavement. My body collapses, but instead of my head meeting the pavement, I'm cradled in a pair of strong arms.

"Hang in there, man. I called 911 and they're on their way." My eyes become unbearably heavy and I'm not sure how long I've been laying in this stranger's arms. The last thing I hear before I lose the battle with consciousness is the faint sound of a siren.

Everything around me slowly fades to black before I completely lose consciousness.

What the fuck? Where am I? I frantically search for a way out, but all I see is endless white. It's fucking blinding. I can faintly hear the sound of sirens and it reminds me of my dream with Avery all those months ago. This can't be happening again. I promised her I would come home to her. I've let Avery down again. I've broken yet another promise to her. I failed at protecting her, now my father has complete access to her.

Is this what death feels like? How did everything turn south so quickly? I had everything my father requested and it still wasn't enough. Frank. Fuck. I can't believe I was shot. My own fucking father shot me. And now I'm dead, never to touch a human again. I'll never be able to touch Avery again. The pain I feel is a bulldozer with my body being the thing that's demolished. Despite me dying, I'm still somehow able to move my body. My head is in my hands as tears stream down my face. I'll never get to hear her laugh, or cry, or sing ever again. I completely failed at the one thing I promised her: to come home to her.

The sounds of people shouting around me are so faint, like cicadas buzzing in the distance. Before I can process what's going on, I feel this shock jolt me back into the present moment and I stare up at four pairs of eyes.

Chapter 43

Avery

The worst case scenario Olympics

MY MIND HASN'T TURNED off since Brianna told me about an accident.

Accident.

Cas.

Hospital.

Deep breaths, Avery, deep breaths. It's been a year since I was last in this hospital, sitting in the same rigid, maroon chairs. I never imagined being here again. The slight flickering of the fluorescent lights reminds me of a nightclub. The scent of lemon and bleach is so pungent it burns the hairs in my nose. Unable to sit still much longer, I pace back and forth on the

ICU's hard, linoleum floor, wearing out the soles of my shoes. They say no news is good news, right? So why do those words increase the rapid beating of my heart? Dizziness slams into me with the same ferocity as one of those spinning tunnel rides at the carnival.

I force myself to sit down and bring my attention to my surroundings. Bri is to my right with Evelyn and Michael to my left. Their love and support are my cocoon. The warmth of their comfort is a giant bear hug, yet I still can't help but feel alone. My heart and soul are in that operating room. All I can do is wait, feeling completely and utterly helpless. There's a bomb inside my chest, ready to detonate.

I try to breathe through the panic, but it only amplifies. I thought I was hiding my feelings pretty well, but Bri noticed. "All your pacing makes me nauseous, and your face is so white it's practically translucent," she says. Before I can respond, she's dragging me into a chair, forcing me to sit down. I open my mouth, wanting to argue, but the fierce look in her eyes shuts me up before I even get a word out.

"You sit down and try to relax. Listen, we don't know what's happening. I get it you're scared, but remember that no news is good news." She means well, and her attempt to get me to take care of myself doesn't go unnoticed. I should be relaxing and not jumping to the worst-case scenario, but I'm at war with my mind and it's a losing battle.

"I understand you're worried about me, and I love you for it. It's just that after everything that Cas and I have been through, I—" I choke on my words, so I take a half-assed attempt at a deep breath before continuing. "I can't get it out of my head that it's goodbye. It doesn't seem fair that Cas is about to be taken from me before we had a chance to grow." My voice is so raw and soft that it barely comes out, and I'm surprised that Bri even heard what I said. She brings her hands up to frame my face. I can feel the warmth of her smooth palms trying to break through the chill I feel.

"Oh, honey, sorry doesn't feel like a big enough word, but I am sorry. I hate seeing you like this." She pulls me into the biggest hug. "Just tell me what to do and I'll do it. Want me to harass every nurse and doctor within a five-mile radius? Done. Want me to go get every comfort food out of the vending machine and bring it to you? Done. Just please let me help you." Her voice croaks with desperation.

I pull back from her hug to look her in the eye. "Bri, you simply being here is already so much more than I could ever ask for. I love and appreciate you so much. Just don't leave me alone." With shaky hands, I bring them to rest atop hers and squeeze, hoping it shows that I mean what I say.

"Then that's what—" Her voice abruptly cuts off and my eyes collide with the doctor who has my heart in her hands. My heart beats faster with each step the doctor takes toward us. Her expression is unreadable, doing nothing to soothe the fluttering in my stomach. She starts speaking, but the ringing in my ears makes it impossible to hear. *He's dead. She's coming to tell me they couldn't save him.*

If thinking of the worst-case scenario was an Olympic sport, I'd take the gold. You know, anxiety at its finest. I'm forced to watch this scene play out, wishing for a remote to change the channel. But there's no remote for real life, and I can't rewind or pause this moment.

He's dead, I repeat back to myself. I can no longer feel my body. Time is at a standstill. The anxious part of me decides that now is the perfect time to share all the things we will miss out on. I'll never get to see a sunset with him again. He won't ever get to hang with his grandparents, playing board games and pretending to be bad at them so that they can win. I won't ever get to kiss him, see his smile, or hear his laugh. He'll never get to chase after his dreams or become a father. We won't ever have the life we planned for ourselves. That last thought breaks my heart the most.

Brianna's embrace brings me back to the present. I shake my head, clearing the mental fog and searching for the doctor, but she's nowhere to be found. I blink a few times trying to rid my brain of the mental cobwebs. When I open them again, Max and Asher are sitting next to Cas' grandparents, providing them comfort. When did they get there? How did they get here? I go to open my mouth to speak, but Bri's arms are squeezing the life out of me.

Seeing Bri's tear-soaked face is all it takes for me to lose my shit. My body collapses to the floor and I begin hyperventilating. She joins me on the floor, wrapping her arms around me. I'm aware she's talking, but it takes me a few seconds to focus on her words. When I'm finally able to comprehend what she's saying, my brows furrow in confusion and I feel anger bubbling in my throat.

"I honestly thought it was all over and just felt completely helpless that I couldn't do anything to help you. You know me, always needing to know what to do. Before that miracle worker delivered the best news, I was unprepared for how to help you." She says all this so quickly, that it took me a minute to process.

"What do you mean, good news? He's fucking dead. How could you say something like that to me?" I ask. Out of the corner of my eye, I notice Asher stand up and make his way toward us. When Bri shoots him a look over her shoulder, his steps falter. Bri lifts my lifeless body off the floor and grips my arm with enough strength to keep me from falling. We make our way to a more secluded part of the hospital so that I won't make even more of a scene.

"Honey, what are you talking about? You heard what the doctor said didn't you?" She's looking at me with a perplexed expression.

"I, um, yeah?" Wait, did I? I was so wrapped up in my head, that I questioned if I heard what the doctor said. Then seeing Max and Asher at the hospital, my mind has been a clusterfuck of chaos.

"Uh, I, um," I stutter out, unable to form a coherent sentence.

"Damn. I should have noticed when you said nothing to the doctor. You were looking right at her, so I assumed you heard what she said. It all makes sense now. When I hugged you, it felt like you were a million miles away."

Sitting me down, Brianna relays everything the doctor said. Cas suffered from a gunshot wound to the stomach, but he pulled through surgery very well and is set to recover fully. If everything keeps progressing at the current rate, he can move out of the ICU within a day or two.

The adrenaline begins to wear off and I find myself no longer able to keep my eyes open. Brianna offers to take me home as I am in no condition to drive. Even though I'm about to lose my battle with consciousness, I need to talk to his grandparents before we leave.

I try to make my way over to them, but my body is too tired to carry itself. Bri has her arm around my waist, dragging me over to them. Evelyn's glassy, bloodshot eyes snap up to meet mine. We don't say anything, we don't need to. Instead, we let our bodies do the talking. The moment she stands up, I am transferred from Bri's arms to hers. We just hold each other, allowing the embrace to say everything our words can't convey. Soon enough, I feel Michael's arms wrap around me. We hold each other, relief leaving our bodies like steam does from a boiled kettle.

I step out of their arms and smile, allowing my face to show how grateful I am for them. They nod their heads and squeeze my shoulders before walking down the hall. My eyes sting with exhaustion, but I have two more important people to talk to before I go.

Asher and Max are sitting next to each other, eyes trained on the floor, giving me and Cas' grandparents our privacy. They must sense my eyes on them because they bring their gazes to meet mine. They almost look as tired as I feel. Cas hasn't had the best support group, but these two men have given him so much. They have been so great and supportive, taking him under their wing and showing him that he deserves friendship.

Asher gets up first and goes to hug me, but I shake my head. "I need to get this out before I pass out. Asher. Max. I wanted to thank you for showing him a true, healthy friendship. I can't thank you enough for all the support you have given him. He's used to people lying and manipulating him to get what they want, but you two never did that. You know about his struggles, yet you chose to see the person underneath. Even with him buried beneath so much rubble, you took the time and helped him through it. You saw Cas, the one I always knew was in there. So for all of that, thank you." My last few words come out wobbly as I'm holding back fresh tears. They look at me, both of their eyes glassy and before I know it, I'm being squished between them in a hug.

"You don't have to thank us, Avery. We're here for him and will always be there for him. But we're here for you, too. Yes, we're his friends, but we're yours, too. We would do anything for either of you." Asher is the first to speak.

"Yeah, what Ash said. We're here for both of you. Now, go home and sleep, Ave. You're dead on your feet, and we don't need to get questioned for dragging a body out of the hospital today," Max says while placing a kiss on the side of my head.

I'm always grateful for Brianna, especially today. She knew that I was going to everything in my control to get to Cas–even though I wouldn't be able to see him.

My body is completely lifeless, my energy depleted. I'm not sure how Brianna managed to get me in the car, but she did.

I glance over to Bri, my heart full of love and appreciation. "Thank you for today. I couldn't have survived without you," I mumble.

"I got you, always, Ave," Bri whispers back to me. Exhaustion greets me like an old friend and the second her hands wrap around my body, I'm out.

Chapter 44

Avery

Hi, freckles, fancy meeting you here

THE SOUND OF MUFFLED voices from downstairs brings a smile to my face. My body cracks and pops when I stretch due to hours of inactivity. When I head downstairs, Bri, Evelyn, and Michael are gathered around the kitchen table with mugs of coffee in hand. My eyes shine with affection for these people. I bite my lower lip in a failed attempt to stop the tears from free falling down my cheeks.

"Hi, honey, how are you doing? Did you sleep well? Are you hungry?" Evelyn asks. Evelyn's comforting words have me closing the remaining distance and wrapping everyone in a bear hug.

My stomach growls, answering her last question, so I decide to answer the first two. "I'm doing okay, all things considered. As for sleep, well, I slept like a baby. How long was I out for?" I croak. My hand flies to my throat and my eyes widen in surprise at how rough my voice sounds.

Before either Evelyn or Michael can respond, Bri speaks up. "Girl, you slept for fourteen hours. I had to check on you a few times to check if you were alive."

"I guess that's why I sound like I smoked a pack of cigarettes. I um, well, I wanted to thank you all again for dealing with me at the hospital. I know y'all were going through a lot, too. It means a lot to me that you were there for me, too."

"My little squish, we'll always be here for you. You're an extraordinary woman, and like Cas, I knew it from when I first met you. You always took care of everyone else and put yourself last. You've grown into a woman who has found the balance between selfishness and selflessness. We love you just as much," Michael choked out, making me hug him a little tighter.

"I mean, of course, you love me because, who wouldn't? I am fucking amazing." Brianna expresses a confidence that makes me laugh.

"Yeah, yeah, yeah, whatever, Bri," I say, affectionately rolling my eyes. I turn toward Evelyn and say, "Do you know when we'll get to see him?"

"He's supposed to make the move from the ICU tomorrow. I gave the doctor your number so that you're among the first to know when he's moved." Those tears that were threatening to release earlier now come pouring out of me.

It wasn't until three days later that I was able to visit him. I'm a walking bundle of nerves as I walk up to the front desk. "Hi, my name is Avery Douglas and I'm here to see Cassidy Andrews."

"ID, please?" she asks dispassionately, without making eye contact.

"Um, yes, of course, here you are."

She clicks the keys on her keyboard for a minute before handing me a piece of paper. "Here's your visitors pass, room 313. Elevators are down the hall to the right." I barely glance in her direction, muttering my thanks before following the directions she gave me. My heart races as the elevator ascends to the third floor. As the second the doors open, desperation to see him amplifies.

Seeing his name scrawled in dry erase marker on Room 313 has me releasing a breath I wasn't aware I was holding. Somehow, I find the strength to knock on the door, and the second it opens, my body crumbles to the floor. Way to go, Avery. You couldn't even make it five steps without collapsing. My vision becomes so cloudy, causing the room to blur around me. The second he speaks, I crumble even further.

"Hey, freckles, fancy meeting you here," he croaks out with exhaustion. Words fail me, and he seems to understand he'll have to do most of the talking.

"Come here, baby, let me hold you." The desperation in his voice gives my legs the strength to walk over to him. One second I'm walking, and the next, I'm cuddled in his arms and feeling safe. I'm home. His embrace is my favorite cozy sweater, providing softness and warmth. I never want to live outside of his arms ever again.

I know looking at his face while saying these next words will break me, so I keep my eyes closed. "Cas. Oh my God. I didn't...I didn't—"

He cuts me off with a quick kiss. "Avery, baby, I'm okay. Breathe," he says to me. My breaths are shaky, and as much as I try, I can't get a full deep breath for the life of me.

"Bri...hospital...accident...not coming home..." Most people would have a hard time understanding this gibberish, but not Cas. He knows.

"Avery, I'm okay. I'm safe and I'm here. I'm here holding you and you are here being held by me. Focus on that." His voice is hoarse from the trauma, but it's that vulnerability in his tone that is providing me comfort. "I told you I would make it back to you. Even though it's not in the comfort of either of our homes, I kept my promise. Focus on that, Avery. Nothing else matters but you and your safety."

"You ended up here because of me. I can't—" My voice comes out high-pitched and panicky.

"No, baby. I ended up here because of *him,* not you. I couldn't take the chance of him following through on his plans. I will always do what I can to keep you safe. My dad already took so much from me, I couldn't let him take away one of my reasons for living." His words sound so convincing, but I'm still struggling to come to terms with that.

"I was so scared I lost you."

"I'm sorry I scared you. I'd never forgive myself if anything happened to you. I love you and will continue loving you for as long as you'll have me." Cas choked back his tears.

"I love you, too. I want you for a lifetime, even though it doesn't feel like enough."

"We've wasted too much time talking." Then I grab hold of his face and kiss the living daylights out of him. I don't remember who deepened the kiss or who tightened their grip first, but his groan had me pulling back.

"Oh my gosh, I'm sorry. Did I hurt you?" I ask him, looking frantically around for any signs that he's in pain.

"Um, no, I'm fine. I, uh—" Cas clears his throat. "Um, that was not an *I'm in pain* grunt, Avery," he says with a coy smile.

"Well, if you aren't in pain, then wha—" I toss the blankets back and look down. I can't help the laugh that escapes my mouth. "Oh, oops." I shrug.

"Yeah, had you not stopped that kiss, I'm sure the nurses would have yelled at me. I don't think I'm allowed to do anything physical for a while. Plus, I don't want to lose special food privileges." I playfully smack him and continue laughing because he's right.

"Yeah, this is probably not the place to do that. Wait, how long is *a while?*" I frown at him. My attempt at getting him to smile fails as he stares back at me so intently, it wipes the smile off my face within a matter of seconds.

"At least six to eight weeks. I want to tell you what happened with my dad, but I want to make sure you're okay before saying anything." He looks at me with a serious expression that makes my anxiety skyrocket. I nod my head, not knowing what to say.

"I gave him the check he was demanding, but of course, he wanted more. As I turned around to leave, one of his buddies slammed me against the brick, choking me. I felt like my life was about to end. At that moment, all I saw was you. Every moment we created together flashed through my mind. Thankfully, he let me go but as I tried to escape, my dad had other plans. H-he pointed a gun at me and smiled before shooting me."

"What? Your fucking father *shot you?*" I screamed.

"Shhh. I don't want you to get kicked out. I just got to hold you again and don't want you banned. But yes, my fucking father shot me right in the stomach. I vaguely remember someone telling me help was on the way but I don't remember anything after that. I'm just glad they got me here in time. My dad...he thought he found a good hiding place, but he was too fucked up and hid outside of the crime scene. Cops found him within seconds, gun still in hand. Avery, they arrested my father."

"That's a lot to take in. You've had a rough couple of days. No one expects you to put on a brave face and keep going. You were betrayed and shot, for crying out loud. It's okay to feel what you're feeling."

"I honestly don't know what I did to deserve someone like you—my kind, smart, and sexy as hell, Avery. My Avery, who, for some reason, has chosen to love me back," he says with such raw emotion.

I grab either side of his face so that he has no choice but to look at me. "Cas, you deserve me because you are *you*. You are my best friend, my rock, a part of my soul. You're loving, and kind, and you make me a better person every day. You accept me for me, and loving you is one of the best things I have done," I say and stay in his arms, feeling safe and warm.

"I love you, Cas," I say. Our conversation must have worn him out because he was sound asleep. I kiss him on his forehead before walking toward the pullout couch next to him. As I lie down, I stare at the beautiful man sleeping. The puzzle piece that's been missing from my heart slides effortlessly into place.

Chapter 45

Cassidy

I want to be your somebody

Early Winter (January), 2024

AFTER BEING IN THE hospital for about a week, I'm finally getting released. I look over at the pullout couch and Avery who's curled up in a ball. She hasn't left my side in the last four days. After everything that's happened, she's still here and wants to be with me.

I can live a sober life and still feel fulfilled. I know that Avery chooses me because she wants to, not because she feels pity. I deserve to be loved. My feelings of not being good enough come up occasionally, but I'm getting better at managing it.

Avery, though, she's it for me. I see her begin to stir and my heart just melts. "Good morning, sleepyhead," I say.

Her eyes rapidly blink, adjusting to the light before focusing on me. "Good morning," she mumbles.

"Come here, baby," I say. She makes her way over to me and curls herself into my embrace. She feels right here. I promise never to take her for granted again. I place a kiss atop her head and she nuzzles herself into the crook of my neck.

"You get to come home today," she says, still groggy from sleep.

"I get to come home today," I repeat, rubbing my hands up and down her arm. She lets out a sleepy hum while her hands lazily trace the outline of the tattoo on my hand. I wonder if she'll notice.

"Cas...what is this?"

She noticed.

"It's a date," I casually say.

"I *know* it's a date, but what date is it?"

At the time, I was confident she would love it, but now that she's looking at it, I can't help but overthink that it wasn't a good idea.

"Cas?" she asks again.

"It's, um. Well, it's the date when you finally became mine. I just got it recently. It felt like a good idea at the time, but if you don't lik—" Avery gently squeezes my hand, causing me to look into her face.

"How have I not noticed until now? Whatever, Cas, that's one of the sweetest things you've done for me. And that's saying a lot, because you've already done so much. I love it, and I love you." She places a quick kiss on my lips. She pulls back with a contemplative expression on her face.

"Are you..." She pauses.

"Am I what?" I prompt her.

"When you go home today, are you going back to your grandparents' house?" she asks, all flustered. Fuck, she's beautiful when she's flustered.

"Well, I didn't think about it. I just assumed I'd go back to their house to recover. Why?" I ask behind a hint of a smile.

"Oh, good. That's good," she says halfheartedly.

"Avery, out with it," I respond.

"I was just hoping that maybe you could come home with me, and I could help you," she says while looking down.

I take her chin in my hand so that she has no choice but to look in my eyes. "I thought you'd never ask. Yes, my answer is yes. I'd love to come home with you," I say, kissing her lips.

"Then maybe you can stay with me even after you heal?" she asks.

"Why, Miss Avery, are you asking me to move in with you?" I ask.

She looks up at me under her lashes, her eyes shining with vulnerability. "Only if you want to. I mean, I want you to. I like having you there, but if it makes you uncomfortable or you need space on your own to heal, I—"

"Avery," I say, waiting for her to turn in my direction. When she does, I continue, "I don't want space. I want to wake up next to you every morning and be the first person I see. I said it before, and I'll say it again. I want to be your somebody, just like you're mine. So yes, I'd love to move in with you. Honestly, I was planning to slowly move my things in there, anyways, and hope that when you noticed, you wouldn't do anything about it."

She chuckles while playfully punching my shoulder. "You're such a jackass," she says, then rests her hands on my cheeks. "But you're my jackass," she says, trying to kiss me, but I stop her.

"Hey, I want to t—" I say, but she interrupts me.

"I have something to tell you!" she shouts, her face radiating excitement. Whatever I have to say can wait.

"Okay, what is it, freckles?"

"Remember that songwriting competition I told you about?" I nod my head in response, and she continues. "Well, I uh, um, I entered that song I wrote for you, and it sort of, kind of. Won." Bashful Avery is a personal favorite of mine. The way she scrunches her nose and her face gets flushed.

"Avery, I'm so damn proud of you and honored you chose that song. I knew you would kick ass in that competition." I grab hold of her face, peppering soft, quick kisses all over her while she giggles.

She playfully pushes me away so she can continue speaking. "Cas, wait, there's more. Not only am I being signed to a record label, but I won $100,000 in prize money. I've been figuring out what to do with the money and then I found the perfect idea. I want to create a program through my shelter to help trauma victims afford emotional support animals. I was hoping maybe it could be something we do together. I know you have a lot on your plate with healing and all, but—" My lips are on hers, silencing any doubt she might have had. Sometimes, you don't need words to convey how you feel.

I break our kiss, but keep my thumbs where they are. "Yes. I think that's a fantastic idea. It actually kind of goes hand in hand with what my plans are for my life. Remember when I talked to you about possibly wanting to help people with addictions?"

She nods her head, and so I continue. "Well, I want to be an addictions counselor specializing in trauma. My therapist has been wonderful and has helped me process this mess. I know I can help others as well. Eventually, we can work on your idea together."

She looks at me with tears in her eyes, but she shakes her head as if she knew what I would say. "Cas, I think it's a fantastic idea. I'm so proud of you for finding what you want to do with your life. You are going to make a difference in this world, and I can't wait to see it happen."

"Thank you for always believing in me, especially when I didn't believe in myself. You have given me so much of myself back. If it wasn't for your endless love and support, I'm not sure where I'd be."

She touches my face. "Cas, you did this on your own. It's because of *you* that you are the man you are today," she says before bringing my mouth down to hers and kissing me. We would have continued to explore each other's mouths if my doctor hadn't interrupted us.

"I see someone is feeling good today," the doctor says. "Even though you get discharged today, Cas, remember you can't do anything physical for a couple of weeks while you heal," she says while looking at me with a smug expression.

Before I can speak, my grandparents enter the room. "Cas can't keep his hands to himself, huh?" my gram says while wiggling her eyebrows. The doctor nods her head, making my gram let out a short, but loud cackle.

"Typical! It's a good thing you came in when you did, Doc, because who knows what would have happened," my grandma says while sending a wink my way.

"We certainly can control ourselves. Don't need to give the doctor more reasons to keep me here," I say, shaking my head while Avery's face turns bright red before burying it in my chest.

"Well, everything's looking good. You're healing up nicely, but recovery will be painful and slow, so don't overdo it. I provided your grandparents with resources for physical and mental health therapists. The physical therapist is a must, but the mental health therapist is optional. If I were you, I'd reach out to them because you might need help processing everything," she says as she walks towards the door. She stops in the doorway and turns back around. "Your discharge paperwork is on its way, and Cas? I am glad you pulled through. It looks like you have a lot of people who love you. Take care of yourself," she says before walking out.

The next hour or so is spent signing paperwork and finalizing testing to confirm I am ready. I told my grandparents of my plan to go to Avery's to heal and couldn't help but laugh at their response.

"It's about damn time," they said in unison.

"We can start moving your stuff over today and the rest of this week-end. I'm so glad you're still with us, Cas. We don't know what we would have done if we lost you," my grandpa said while choking back tears. He rarely cries, so when he does, I can't help but cry alongside him.

"I love you both so much," I say before they both envelop me in a group hug.

"Well, we'll let you two be and start moving everything over. Avery, is your spare key still where it normally is?" my grandma asks her, and she nods. "Perfect, we'll see you both later."

"So, ready to get out of here and go home?" Avery asks.

"I've never been more ready than anything! I finally got a wish I've always wanted."

"Oh yeah? What wish is that?" she asks.

"That I finally get to call you my home." I lean down, conveying all my feelings with my kiss.

"I love you, Avery," I say the second we part.

"I love you, too, Cas. Now let's go home."

Epilogue

Cassidy

Speech in one hand and a heavy weight in the other

Early Winter, 2026

I'VE COME A LONG way since my overdose three and a half years ago. I'm still fighting my demons and working to maintain sobriety daily. A big part of my success is because of the person sitting in the auditorium's front row. Her continuous support and encouragement are the reasons I'm on this stage today, preparing to give this speech that will hopefully change our lives. Avery sits in between my grandparents, all three of them holding back tears. Next to them are Bri and Asher. Despite everything Bri has been through recently, she still's here to show her support. Her face is completely blank, and I don't think she's fully present, because she has allowed Asher to hold her hand. Bri's face may be void of all emotion, but Asher is looking at her like she hung the moon.

I'm focusing a little too hard on Avery's face that I miss my name being called the first time. It isn't until I see Avery laughing at me that I bring my focus back to the present moment. I make my way to the podium, speech in one hand and this weight in my pocket.

I begin my speech with the usual thank you for coming before sharing my struggles with addiction. I mention how my therapist helped me work through my sobriety and the trauma I've tried to bury. I talked about how she inspired me to get my certificate in addiction studies with hopes to get my degree when I've had a few more years of sobriety under my belt. With all that I went through, and how alone I felt, I want to provide that support to someone else. That maybe someday I might be the only person who believes in their power to change.

I take a moment to collect myself before switching my focus to the stunning woman dressed in a long, emerald green, evening gown. I glance at my gram thankful for her help planning all this. I mean, she didn't give me much choice since she caught me ring shopping on my laptop. Avery's creamy skin is the perfect contrast against the dark, emerald silk of her dress. I take a slow, deep breath and continue.

"I want to take a moment and mention one person specifically. I knew when I was eight that she would be one of the most important people in my life. She's been my rock and encourages me to be the best version of myself. She's in the audience right now, and even though she doesn't like the spotlight, I'm hoping she'll come up anyway. Avery, can you come up here for a second?" I ask, trying to look as calm as possible when a million butterflies fly around in my stomach.

Hundreds of eyes scan the crowd looking at her as she moves towards me. She is so beautiful, and each step steals another breath leaving me gasping for air. Her arms wrap around me and I instinctively melt into her.

"Avery, my Avery, I have loved you for as long as I can remember. I love your strength and your willingness to try new things with me. I love you even when you yell at me for being a dumbass, which, spoiler alert, is often. I love that with every smile and laugh, you take my breath away. I love how you challenge me when I'm wrong and support me when I need it most. I love everything about you, and I think this is long overdue, but—" I say as I barely pull out the ring before she screams at me.

"Yes! Yes, yes, yes, yes, of course, I'll marry you, Cas!" she exclaims.

"How do you know there is a ring in this box and not a pair of earrings or a bracelet?" I ask behind a smile so wide my cheeks will hurt for years.

"I swear to God, if it is one of those things, I will throw you off this—"

I cut her off with a kiss so deep, so passionate, that I forget where we are. That is until the university's president makes a throat-clearing noise that brings me back.

"Oops! I would apologize for that, but I've been waiting forever to ask this question." I shrug while chuckling.

I bring my attention back to Avery and get down to one knee. "So, I would like to finish this proposal since I was interrupted. Avery. They say if you love something, set it free. And if it was truly yours, to begin with, it'll come back. You had to let me go once and it honestly saved my life. My promise to you, from this day on is to prove to you that I deserve your love. To continue being a better man, lover, and friend. If you say yes, I'll be the best husband and hopefully, someday, father I can be. Will you marry me?"

"Yes, one thousand times, yes!" she says right before she launches herself at me.

In that exact moment, I know that everything will be okay. Whatever life throws my way, I'll be able to handle it because I have her by my side. I get to spend the rest of my life alongside my best friend. Now, I finally get to be her somebody.

THE END.

Bonus Chapter

Avery

A girl has needs

Early Winter, 2024

I'VE BEEN A BALL of anxious energy since Cas left for his eight week check up. *Everything will be fine. He'll come back in one piece, Avery. Chill the fuck out.* No matter how hard I attempt to hammer the mental nail straight, it always seems to come out wonky. Cas, hospitals, and my anxiety are a deadly combination. It gives oil and water vibes—they never mix well. Cas left the house at 12:00 p.m., and for the last two hours, I've been oscillating between pacing the floor of the music room and sitting on the piano bench, trying to transform this anxious energy into song.

My eyes glaze over while the incessant sound of the middle C key fills the room. Anxious thoughts buzz around in my brain. Every time a positive thought manages to slip through the iron gates, it becomes lost in a puff of smoke, leaving ashes in its wake. I glance down at my new Apple watch—a because I love you gift from Cas—and notice it's been two hours, thirty minutes, and fifteen seconds since he kissed me goodbye and walked out the door.

Speaking of countdowns, it's been weeks since we've had sex and I've become quite familiar with my trusty vibrator—also a gift from Cas. I believe his exact words were, *I'm sorry we can't fuck right now, but I want to make sure that pretty pussy of yours gets taken care of.* Goddamn. Thinking about it now makes my pulse race and my body twitch with need. Vibrators got nothing on Cas' dick, but a girl has needs. I told him I'd be more than happy to wait, but he quickly called me on my bluff when he walked in on me pleasuring myself. The next morning, during breakfast, I might add, he slid over a familiar purple box with the familiar shimmery, black, delicate cursive scrawled across it. Allure Desires. A place Cas and I stumbled upon while coming home from a date night. He did a u-turn so fast, I felt my food from dinner slosh around in my stomach. We spent over an hour in that store and may or may not have bought most, if not all, of their stock for couples.

My eyes flicker to the stairs, envisioning where my device is currently resting: in my top drawer of my bedside table. A faint pulse begins to form between my legs and my heart rate spikes with anticipation. I mean, it's not guaranteed that Cas will get the all clear for sex today. About a million and one things could pop up to prevent us from being intimate. It won't hurt to play with myself a little. Cas did request I only play when he's around. My little masochist loves to torture himself apparently, but what he doesn't know won't hurt him, right?

With my decision made, I leap up from the bench so fast my knee hits the bottom of the piano. I let out a silent curse, but push the pain aside as desire overrides my throbbing knee. I make it two steps when I hear the sound of the door opening and slamming shut. Cas' heavy footsteps are quick and desperate. Within seconds, Cas is standing in front of me, blocking the path between me and my orgasm.

"Cas, hi." My greeting comes out breathy and my horniness practically oozes from my tone. His beautiful gray eyes are now black with want as he stalks toward me. I instinctively take a step back. Cas cocks his head to the side, his mouth tilts into that panty-dropping smirk. He knows *exactly* what he's doing to me right now. If he tells me that the doctor gave him the all clear, it's RIP to my pussy because he's about to utterly destroy me.

"C-Cas w-what's happening?" I internally cringe at how desperate I sound. But can you really blame a girl? I haven't had his dick inside me for eight weeks. That's fifty-six days, one thousand and forty-four minutes of fucking myself. DIY orgasms aren't the same as a good old fashioned dicking.

"I think you know, baby. But I'm gonna need you to say it." Goddamn Cas and his cocky attitude. It's like my own form of lubricant and I feel my panties dampen even further.

"I, um. Did you get the all clear?" I'm surprised Cas even heard me at all with how soft my words were. But he did, because he's suddenly in my space. The clean, fresh oxygen I was once gulping down is replaced with leather and fresh pine. Cas wraps his hand around my throat and forces me to look into his eyes. I try to push back what I was about to do to the back of my mind. Cas has this innate ability to see right through me. Sometimes I swear he was a bloodhound in another life, because this man can sniff out when I'm not being truthful. My pulse flutters rapidly inside my neck and when Cas moves his face there, slowly inhaling, my head falls back. It isn't until his grip on my neck tightens and he moves his face to look at me that I realize I'm in trouble.

"Yes, Avery, I did, but I'm curious about something." Uh oh. He *knows*.

"Hmm?"

"What were you about to do when I walked in earlier?" Cas growls.

"I—well I was about to, um. Look, I know you told me you wanted to watch me get off. But you weren't here and I was worried and ho—"

Cas cuts me off by crushing his lips against mine. The kiss is brutal, but in the best way. He's in complete control and I willingly surrender to him. The once silent room is now filled with grunts and panting. We kiss each other as if it was our last time. To be fair, it's been weeks of slow, sensual kisses. Don't get me wrong, I love the slow moments between us. But fiery, take charge Cas is a personal fave of mine. Cas' teeth sink into my bottom lip and he swallows my whimper by thrusting his tongue back into my mouth. I don't realize we've been walking backward until my back hits a hard surface and the sound of random notes clashing together has us jolting apart. *Oh, fuck that's right. We're in the music room and we just stumbled over my piano.*

We're both breathing heavy, but the time apart does nothing to extinguish the hunger in Cas' eyes. He pulls me flush against his chest before closing the piano, his gaze never straying from mine.

A wicked grin breaks out across Cas' face and the pulse between my legs intensifies. "Avery, you dirty girl. You were gonna fuck yourself, weren't you?"

This entire interaction has robbed me of words, so I simply nod my head.

"What am I gonna do with you, hmm?" Cas rubs his thumb along my neck, applying pressure to the pulse point. It shouldn't feel this damn good, but it does.

"Anything." That single word comes out as a moan.

"Not good enough. Let me try again. What do you *want* me to do with you?"

I take a deep breath, jut my chin out, and say with as much confidence as I can muster in my current state, "I want you to fuck me, Cas."

"Good girl. You wanna be fucked right here? In your music room?" Cas' head tilts to the side while caressing my neck with the tips of his fingers.

"Y-yes. I do," I stammer out.

"Good girl. Turn around and put your hands on the piano. I want your legs spread nice and wide for me. You want me to bend you over this piano and fuck that pretty pussy of yours from behind?"

"Please," I beg, knowing he loves when those words leave my lips.

"So pretty when you beg for me, baby. Now bend over, I wanna see how wet you are for me."

I do as he says and when my cheek meets the cool, smooth texture of the piano, it sends a shiver down my spine. Well that, and the sound of my panties ripping in half has me shaking at the knees. Cas wastes no time as he inserts a finger inside me. It should be pathetic at how easy he glides inside of me, but I don't care. Eight weeks is too long, and if I'm being honest, I feel like I've been wet the entire time we've been abstaining.

I move my head, glancing over my shoulder just in time to see Cas bring the finger that was once inside me into his mouth. His eyes slam shut and he lets an animalistic grunt.

"Fuck. I've missed how you taste. I've been living off my memory for weeks, but it doesn't do justice to tasting you." Cas kicks my legs wider before getting on his knees, and without warning, his tongue is inside me. My head spins as his tongue swirls inside me. He licks me from front to back and then starts over. Cas licks me like I'm his favorite popsicle. My hands don't have much to grip onto, so whenever Cas hits the spot I love most, I find my arms slipping. My legs are trembling and all I want him to do is take my clit in between his lips and suck. I grind myself on his face, searching for the friction I desire.

Cas' breathy chuckle hits my clit and I'm momentarily blinded by the pleasure it brings. "My girl is greedy for me. Where do you want my tongue, baby? Use your words."

"Lips. Clit. Suck." My words come out in incoherent pants. I shake my head and try again. "I want you to put my clit in between your lips and suck on it."

"That's my girl." I can barely process those three words before his tongue flicks my clit once. Twice. Three times before taking it between his teeth and sucking as if his life depended on it. I lose control of my hips as I begin to aggressively grind against his face. Shame and embarrassment have no room in my brain. I don't care. I just want to come apart on Cas' tongue.

"That's right, baby. Ride my face. I want to feel you come apart on my tongue," Cas says before sucking my clit again. Cas alternates between sucking and flicking his tongue. I feel heat pool in my lower abdomen and at the base of my spine. My toes curl so hard they begin to cramp, but I don't care. I've waited so long to feel his mouth wrapped around me. The orgasm is a storm brewing inside me and when Cas nips at my clit, the rainclouds break and I'm coming harder than I have in months. Cas drinks me in like a man desperate for water. It isn't enough though. I want him inside me. Fucking me so hard the piano shakes.

Cas must hear my thoughts because as soon as I come down, I hear the sound of his zipper. "Baby, that was so fucking hot, but I need to be inside of you."

"Yes. Fuck, yes I want th—"

My words fall off when Cas slams into me from behind with enough force that the bench groans against the floor as it moves closer to the piano. I feel so full, and not just because his dick is inside me. I've missed this connection with him. During Cas' recovery, we focused on our emotional connection. Going on dates, cuddles on the couch. We even revisited some of Cas' best friend boot camp. While I loved doing all of those things, I missed the connection I got whenever he was inside of me. It's more than just physical. It's the sense of safety and care that I feel when he fucks me. With him, I'm never afraid to try anything because I know he's always open to doing different things. It's the overwhelming feeling of love and trust between us. When we have sex, it's a testament to how far we've grown both individually and as a couple.

Tears begin to blur my vision, and Cas being Cas, picks up on it. "Shit. Aves, did I hurt you? We can wa—"

"No, you didn't hurt me. I just missed this is all. I guess I'm feeling a little sentimental," I interrupt him. "Please don't stop, I was promised sex against the piano. And if you stop, I'll just go upstairs and use the toy you gave me." I'm intentionally poking the bear. Especially knowing Cas loves being challenged.

"Like hell you will," Cas growls before slamming back into me. This position is a personal favorite of mine because this angle allows him to get even deeper. Cas fucks me hard and fast. Our grunts and moans are music notes that surround us. A beautiful love song that only we could create. Cas fucks me so hard that we can hear the piano begin to make noise. And while it's too heavy to truly move, it groans beneath our combined weight. A weight that feels heavenly against my back.

"Baby, you're gonna give me another orgasm. I want to feel your pussy squeezing the ever loving shit out of my cock." Cas' fingers move to my clit, rubbing in a slow, circular motion.

"Cas, fuck. Yes, don't stop," I scream out. His fingers pick up speed and I focus on the sound of his balls slapping against my ass. The pressure begins to build inside me and then Cas goes and pinches my clit, which has me seeing stars.

"Fuck Cas. I'm—"

"I know, baby. Keep coming for me, freckles. I'm right behind you." My orgasm seems endless, and moments later, I hear Cas let out a loud curse before I feel liquid heat spill inside of me. I'm dizzy with the sensation, and like myself, Cas' orgasm seems never ending.

Cas pumps his cock inside me a few more times before reluctantly slipping out of me. He picks me up in his arms and brings me over to the denim blue, velvet chair in the corner. The only sound is our rapid breathing and when I curl against him, I can hear the frantic beating of his heart.

I take one of his hands, placing it in the valley between my breasts, allowing him to feel my heartbeat. They beat in rhythm. Two separate souls singing the same tune. The tears I've managed to keep at bay earlier fall freely. Cas doesn't comment on them, nor does he try to stop them. He knows they're happy tears. He just cuddles me closer.

"I love you, Cas," I whisper.

"I love you too, baby. I can't wait to do that again in about five minutes."

"Five minutes? Are you insane, Cas?"

"Not insane. I've gone eight weeks without being inside you. You bet your ass we're about to have a goddamn sex marathon, freckles." Despite everything we just did, his words turn me on. But for now, I'll cuddle up inside his arms and bask in this very moment.

Playlist

New religion (feat. Teddy Swims)—All Time Low

Kiss me— Sixpence None the Richer

4 EVER 4 ME—Demi Lovato

Lights down low—MAX

Something special—joan

Friends Don't—Maddie & Tae

2002— Anne-Marie

Paralyzed—Big Time Rush

Boyfriend—Big Time Rush

Slow Hands—Niall Horan

Can't Help Falling in Love—Haley Reinhart

Stupid in Love (feat. HUH YUNJIN of LE SSERAFIM)—MAX

Unconditionally—Katy Perry

Beautiful Soul—Jesse McCartney

Nonsense- Sabrina Carpenter

Acknowledgements

After about a hundred menty-b's later, this book is officially out in the world. This experience has been a journey, with many tears, laughs, and wtf moments. I stomped through the trenches of imposter syndrome only to come out on the other side stronger than when I started. If I, a person with major anxiety and self-doubt, can do this than you can too. There are many people who helped me believe in myself—even when I couldn't. And for that, I am eternally grateful.

To my crew of editors Jessica Booth (@jesssicaboothauthor), Julia-Diaz Young (@chicklitistheshit) and Hannah G. Scheffer-Wentz (@english-propereditingservices) for working endlessly to make my baby the best it can be. Thank you for your endless encouragement and pushing me when I needed it. You guys are the real MVP's. While I may not know how to spell forest, I never felt judged by any of you for my many *many* mistakes. My book wouldn't be what it is right now without your magic hands.

To my cover designer, Sam Palencia (@inkandlaurel), your talent astounds me. Stumbling across your page and watching my vision come to life is something I will always cherish. You took what I presented to you and knocked it out of the park. It's everything I could have ever wanted and then some.

To my beta and alpha readers. Thank you from the bottom of my heart. Y'all have helped the many—yes many—cracks in the foundation. Without you, my release date would still be up in the air.

I wanted to thank my best friends, Destiny, Bambi, and Doobs for embracing my weirdness and never giving up on me. You guys are a huge part of this book and I'm forever grateful for your endless love and support. Y'all are stuck with me—you know too much. But seriously, your presence in my life has molded me into the woman I am today. There are not enough 'I love you's' and 'thank you's' in the world to express my gratitude. To kaybee for always being such a fierce protector and encouraging me to pursue my dreams.

Thank you to everyone who has been with me on this long awaited journey with me. I want to thank my @saltedcaramelmadams and smutty bitches for always believing in me, especially when I wanted to give up. From trauma bonding from an internet scam to showing up at an author event late, our friendship was written in the stars. You all are my guiding light and I will always cherish our friendship. Thank you to Days (@the.diazdiaries) for our late night conversation one day that resulted in me dreaming of this book. Talking about emotional books with you is always incredible.

To my family, thank you for always having my back. Thank you for encouraging my creativity and to always pursue my dreams. When I shared the news I was writing this book, your excitement was contagious, and it pushed me even harder to make this dream a reality.

Finally to my survivors. You are powerful. You are strong. You are resilient. I want you to know that I see you. I hear you. And I believe you.

About the author

Natalie Knolls has a degree in clinical psychology and works closely with trauma survivors. She has a passion for advocating for believing in survivors' stories as well as giving them a voice when they cannot speak for themselves. In Natalie's debut adult romance novel, Be Your Somebody, she tackles childhood trauma and mental health in a heartbreakingly beautiful way. Besides attempting to reduce her ever-growing to-be-read list, Natalie can be found snuggling with her two cats Kringle and Chestnut, or singing karaoke at her local bar. She also enjoys performing on stage through various musical theater productions.

You can find Natalie on Instagram and TikTok @authornatalieknolls.